# An Ogham Wood

Published by Avalonia
BM Avalonia, London, WC1N 3XX, England, UK

www.avaloniabooks.co.uk

An Ogham Wood
© Cliff Seruntine, 2010

First Published by Avalonia 2011

ISBN 978-1-905297-45-0

Typeset and design by Satori

Cover Art "An Ogham Wood" by Marc Potts © 2010

British Library Cataloguing in Publication Data. A catalogue record for this book
is available from the British Library.

# AN OGHAM WOOD

## Cliff Seruntine

Published by Avalonia

WWW.AVALONIABOOKS.CO.UK

# Foreword

*An Ogham Wood* was a labor of love invested in things I am very passionate about: the marvels of nature, the wonder of enchantment, the faérie faith, the enduring power of love. When I wrote *An Ogham Wood* I determined to pour all these things into the tale and not hold back. But I wanted to create something new, as well—a tale that was at once a fantasy and a history, a contemporary adventure and a legend of magic. I wanted to break rules—get away from the tired notions of prophecies and kings and invading hordes that are the perennial grist of so much fantasy fiction. And as the world is rarely ever so clear cut as to offer truly villainous villains or entirely virtuous heroes, I wanted my tale to reflect that, too. The project seemed to take on a life of its own, and what I believe emerged was a new myth—a bittersweet thing of haunting magic, perilous beauty and elusive truth.

The reader will notice shifting styles in the narrative. The story takes place in the contemporary era and by and large the narrative reflects that. But a good portion of the tale is based on Celtic folklore as conceived by the people of its setting, the Island of Manannan, and when the story shifts to the folkloric perspective, the narrative shifts to a more colorful language as might have been used by an old Irish or Scots storyteller—what was once referred to as a *seanachie*. And yet the roots of the tale go far deeper, into the primal myths of the Celtic peoples. When this happens the narrative shifts yet again, reflecting a higher language style, as myths are often related. I had been concerned that the narrative shifts might have been somewhat disconcerting, but those who have read *An Ogham Wood* have universally commented that they liked the stylistic changes— that it helps place the tale in each of its various eras.

Also in relation to language, I should remark on my choices in spelling. Though there is a strong British Isles flavor to the tale, and the main character is American, the story is set in Canada, so in general spelling reflects Canadian English. Canadian English has always been a hodgepodge of American and British spelling styles though in recent times it is trending more and more toward the shorter, more phonetic American. In keeping with the setting, I have chosen to go with the contemporary Canadian style, though I have incorporated the odd British or American usage.

The story was conceived and almost entirely written during a three week vacation when I sailed on waters off the wild coast of Alaska not too far north of where *An Ogham Wood* takes place. But books aren't written, they are rewritten, and for many months afterward I refined the story with the help of my beloved wife and the encouragement of many friends. I would like to thank my wife, Daphne, for her helpful commentary and all the quiet time she made possible. I would like to thank the owner of a very special little tea shop on the Kenai Peninsula for all the evenings she let me stay after closing when I forgot the time while revising the manuscript. I would like to thank Sean and Jen Bascom for their enduring friendship and encouragement, and the Scadians of Oertha for the endless late night bardic rounds where they brought myth to life with many a cup of ale and mead and medieval song under a ceaseless boreal twilight.

Finally, a very special thank you to Marc Potts for his visionary artwork that became the cover of this book. And another very heartfelt thank you to Sorita d'Este and David Rankine of Avalonia Books, who believed in this tale so much as to say it was a story that had to be told, and then for making it happen. Thank you for your countless hours of hard work and dedication, and the many long conversations we have enjoyed along the journey.

Last, but certainly not least, thank you to my two great daughters, Arielle and Natalia, who were as excited as I about every step of the process. I have sought all my life to give you knights and magic and enchanted forests. Hold it dear, my girls!

Cliff Seruntine
Nova Scotia (Canada), February 2011

*"In the popular creed there is some strange connexion between the Elves and the trees.  They not only frequent them, but they make an interchange of form with them."*

*The Fairy Mythology,* **Thomas Keightley**

# Chapter One

*Such cries the fair Asrai weep,*
*when Wisps no more the fens will keep,*
*O who will guard the Westering Land,*
*with shadows dashed,*
*enchantment banned?*

*The Lament of Hawthorn*
*Seoridean, Bard of the Westernmost Tuath*

The most beautiful thing about the sea was how it made him forget. Sweyn had always held to that. After his mother died of cancer when he was a child, Sweyn used to paddle a sea kayak with his father to numb the pain. When he and his father bitterly parted ways many years later, sailing helped heal the wound. When he lost his wife, he simply floated away like so much flotsam upon an ocean whose greatest gift was forgetfulness. It was so easy to get lost in the rhythms of his small ship, the routine of checking position, keeping watch, mending sails, washing lines, polishing and varnishing endlessly. There was always activity to do in the small space of the vessel, and the creaking and the groaning of the timbers, the timeless play of waves, the liquid music of water rolling across the hull, all of it conspired to wipe out the thoughts, the memories.

Sometimes Sweyn awoke and did not know for certain how long it had been since the last date he remembered. Sometimes he was not even certain of the year. Best of all was when he could barely wrap his mind around the things he needed so desperately, so desperately most of all, to forget. When the gales blew. On approach to one nameless port or another, at night, when the phosphorescent waves washed over sea walls and broke over submersed rocks, unseen but deadly, well capable of ripping away keel and bilge should he wander back to a memory and forget to watch his compass and stay his course. At such times all his concentration was focused. There was only his body working hard to make his vessel do what needed to be done. Reef a sail. Shorten a sheet. Dare a jib. The vessel required seamless attention. He knew the vessel and worked her automatically. His muscles were wiry but strong, flowing like fluid over bone, wrought of long days' exhausting work, all to make a vessel of many tons do the will of the single man who piloted her.

And all to forget.

The sea was a balm. It could wipe away memories. It could do away with the pain of the past, with the pain of loss. And so he called the sea his abode. He had for many years. Once it was the salt air, the sound of rolling surf, the lucid skies that called to him. Once it was the thrill of seeing far-flung shores, the promise of peoples and places unseen. But now it no longer mattered. The sea was an amnesic. Better than alcohol. Better than a vat of the hardest liquor. It was a place to lose the self and the soul. And so he drifted, from bay to cove and port, and sometimes merely hove-to upon vast aquamarine expanses, always moving, going nowhere, not in long years. He drifted, detached, looking only for the oblivion of the waves.

And there were times when Sweyn could almost forget. The dreaded memories could almost be shoved totally aside, or pushed most deep into the dark recesses within the human soul where they might be buried and forgotten and never resurface again. Several times he had come close. But when he approached the precipice of such oblivion he felt he teetered on the edge of some sacred space, perhaps akin to the Nirvanna of nothingness sought by so many monks of the exotic East. If he could just tip across the threshold of mind and spirit into that tranquil emptiness, and let go once and for all, perhaps the past would release its death grip and he could be the one thing he had always longed to be, a man not haunted. But his ghosts were cagier than he, for at those very moments when he stood at the frontier of his long-sought bliss, a black cold formed in the core of his breast. And foolish questions provoked his mind to unwanted thoughts.

Do you want to forget, truly? Who will remember her if not you? What would be left if you let her go so completely that you could not recall her at all, not even her name? His father and all the hell of his traumatic youth, sure, he could let that go. Gone, like the waking after images of nightmare, that side of him could slip away and he would feel none but the better for it.

But when he stood on the brink of forgetfulness and the relentless beauty and indifference and vastness of the sea promised to swallow up his mind and thoughts once and for all, he could never let go. The bitter truth was, the memories which pained him the most were also the dearest. They haunted him with their warmth and tormented him with their loss. He could bear neither to look back upon them, nor to release them.

At times he had thought about letting the sea go a step further, and make his oblivion complete. So easy it would be to go to sleep in his berth in storm-tossed waters, and leave his vessel to its own devices, to its doom. Easier still to simply step off the transom on a good beam reach somewhere far from shores. He had thought it out, how that might be. He would do it near sundown. He would just fall in, tread tropical waters and watch the beautiful form of Starry Sea reduce in the distance, till at last she was a spot upon a dimming horizon, following her course by the guidance of the autopilot. And when at last she had gone far out of sight, perhaps to be found and claimed by some lucky soul and change his life for the better, Sweyn could just stop treading, close his eyes, and let himself float down to where forgetfulness is assured, into the dark place beneath the rolling ink of the nighttime sea.

But he never could do that. It wasn't that he was afraid to die. It would be more true to say Sweyn was afraid to live. But it would be the same as coming to that mindless point when he let the abandon of the sea swallow up his memories once and for all. All the goodness ensconced in those painful recollections would vanish with him, and he could not bear to let what those memories contained vanish entirely from the world.

And so his memories drove him to persist. And something else, perhaps, but for the life of him he could not understand what. Whatever it was, it kept him from simply drowning in a bottle, or in the waves. It kept him merely drifting, bobbing, atop and over one endless wave after another.

In that moment his vessel was cascading down a rolling wave, heaped up high and steep by a rapidly building wind. He was an adept seaman, but he hardly noticed. Nor had he plotted a course. He only went, sailing swiftly, mindlessly, keeping a beam reach to the wind, following it wherever it led, for what else was there in life for him but to follow the wind, a storm-tossed spirit condemned to relentless journeys.

He ignored the world around his vessel and looked only inward. There, a side of him, cold and analytical and professional, and more dead than the rest of him, told him he did not have to be this way. He could get help. He was suffering an illness, a deep bitterness of mind. Depression. He needed to mourn, and to say goodbye. But he could not. It hurt too much to mourn, for mourning required thinking on that which had been lost. And that which had been lost had been too wonderful to lose. He could not bear to go there. And so his heart was torn. He could not hurt and heal. He dared not mourn and forget. He could only drift, and drift, and wander, carrying his pain and his memories at as much distance as the sea allowed.

A girl came up the companion way. A woman really, but the way of her was girlish, somewhere between that shy age of discovery and the full blossom of womanhood. Her hair was ruby, so lustrous it possessed an inner fire like the fine garnets cherished by gemologists. She was pale skinned, in the way of most true red heads, but her eyes possessed that unusual red-gold hue sometimes found in very fair folk. They were like the eyes of a cat, clever and astute, burning with an intelligence that seemed to hint at an awareness of hidden things. She moved with the grace of a cat too. Her slender form ghosted up the steep steps of the companionway and into the cantered cockpit as though she walked on a level surface. She moved across the short space of deck, up over the bench, to rest in the seat beside him with the fluidity of a ballerina. Often he had thought she must have taken lessons and been quite good somewhere back in her teen-aged years, but when he had brought it up to her, she had laughed and shrugged it off, saying she had never danced that way. "They say some of us have the grace of the little people," she had told him once, her reedy voice spiced with a thick brogue that told of links to the British Isles. But she never spoke of her past. For her, it was a closed book. And given his own tumultuous childhood, he could understand her desire not to go there. Her past was past, just like his.

She held a mug of steaming tea in her hands. Though they were en route to Hawaii from Washington and had already traveled five hundred miles south and west away from the mainland, they had had the misfortune of encountering a late season northwesterly, moving south. In its death throws it brought increasingly bitter air, to the point where Sweyn was beginning to see his breath in wispy streamers that vanished behind him in the building wind.

"Do ye think it'll be a gale, then?" Eilwen asked of him.

He scanned the slate sky. Amorphous clouds formed a lowering ceiling. It seemed as if all the sky were swathed in a sheet of mist, and the air itself was getting heavier. He nodded to her, took the mug gratefully in one hand, and gulped down several swallows of the warming liquid.

The mixture was fragrant, the scent of it lingered on the tongue as well. It tasted of blossoms he could not recognize, and spices and herbs not to be found in a common market. The warmth of the steaming liquor spread through him like gentle fingers massaging the blood back into his chilled skin. It was her own concoction, an old family recipe handed down "from the old country." It was naturally sweet and, along with its warming properties, invigorated him as well as if he had had a catnap.

They bantered back and forth as he finished the cup, then set it aside in an enclave normally reserved for the sailing winch. Till she brought the tea, he had been thinking of putting on the autopilot and letting the device man the helm for him a bit while he went below for a quick warm up. But now he felt a hundred percent better. Smiling despite the chill, and the building cold wind, he rested a hand gently on her knee and said, "I don't think it'll get too bad. It's too late in the season, and the weatherfax hasn't given any cause to think something big is in the works."

Eilwen, for all her strong heart, was new to the sea. She shared it gladly with Sweyn, and she took to every aspect of it well, but there was a lot of adjustment in it for her as well. It was all new to her, this cruising life, everything from the glory of setting sails in the air of a crisp, new day to the grimy work of cleaning bilges before buildup of muck got a chance to foul the electric bilge pump. She was a novice with a natural love for his maritime world. And though she was taking to it as her own, she had never before ridden through a real, true blow.

He shrugged in way of reassurance. "If it blows, it's no big deal. Starry Sea is a sailboat, love. She's made for the wind. We'll heave-to, put a pot of tea in a thermos, and ride the rollers like kids on a roller coaster."

The idea of waves big enough to compare to roller coasters may not have been the best analogy, for Eilwen's pale skin became a shade whiter. He understood her feelings. The sea is an intoxicating place to be, until one faces the prospect of encountering one's first true gale. The only way to develop the confidence to see one through was to undergo the experience for oneself. Sweyn had been a novice too, once, some twenty years before. He remembered how it was. Now Eilwen must herself undergo that baptism.

But she was too nervous, and there was no call for that. She would see. A boat like Starry Sea was made to ride the winds and a gale was just a big blow. To change the subject and ease her mind, he leaned his head toward the now empty mug and brought up a topic he had suggested many a time before. "You should sell that stuff. People would come from far and wide to drink your teas."

While his goal had mainly been to divert her, it was no empty compliment he paid. They had talked about the prospect before. She was good with herbs, apparently having picked up some unique lore on the matter in the course of her unusual, half old world upbringing. And she loved working with them. At their home in Glacier Falls, on the west coast of Washington, she kept a splendid herb garden. Everything grew there, all the herbs he could name on a gourmet grocer's shelf, and many, many plants he had neither heard of nor could pronounce the name of. She made medicine from some of them, simple but effective home remedies. He had once seen her give a dose of some syrupy decoction to a neighbor's coughing child and the cough immediately quit. Later that week the neighbor had come by with a thank you card and words of heartfelt appreciation, for nothing the doctor had given her child had eased the chronic cough.

And Eilwen also spiced food with her herbs. The dishes were to die for, strange things he had not had in all his life of traveling to foreign ports. He had enjoyed at her table—when they first started dating—a strange stew which seemed to contain some edible kind of grit. Later he learned it was some unique blend of haggis, a dish he would have thought revolting, made of sheep innards and unrolled oats stuffed into a sheep's stomach. He had tried confections of valerian and other herbs which soothed more potently than would have a glass of rum. She made a slightly sweet, astonishingly good wort from oat malt and some herbs she would not name. In her cupboards were jar after jar of varieties of dried chamomile, wormwood, bluebell, rose and rosehip, catnip, comfrey, marshmallow, and a cacophony of other herbs, stored, dried, decocted, infused, powdered, crushed, and folded. The house smelled of earth and green things, and the scent permeated her as well.

But most special of all were her teas. Some could send a confirmed insomniac to his dreams, while others could beckon a confirmed narcoleptic to the waking world (and he should know, he had once given them to a couple of his own most difficult patients). Some could drive away the most persistent body aches and others could halt and turn a fever in an hour. But the most spectacular of all her magical infusions were those she blended for the pure enjoyment of sipping a fragrant cup of tea. They were delightful mixtures, full of flavor and fragrance and liquid gold warmth that flowed through the veins with a soothing, yet invigorating effect that Sweyn had once clinically described as "far more complex and satisfying than simple caffeine."

But Eilwen had always been reserved about her gift with herbs, shrugged off Sweyn's compliments as the mere—but not unappreciated—sweet nothings of a man in love. But today, with a storm imminent as the winds built and the barometer steadily dropped, the sea becoming noisier around him, she broke his concentration from the demanding act of steering at a smooth forty degree angle over the waves with the surprise statement, "I have indeed decided to start a tea shop."

He looked at her, sure at first she was teasing. But there was a twinkle in her eye, the kind that harbingers plans in the works, and happy business. Sweyn could read those kinds of cues well. He was a certified expert at it.

She continued. "And I am going to call it Enchanted Herbs, because ye're always telling me how magical my teas are."

Sweyn raised his eyebrows, happily surprised by the news. He raised a hand, balled loosely, to give her a playful tap on the chin, when suddenly her eyes grew wide and she sat up straight, looking to port of Starry Sea.

"Would ye watch the waves, now, or we've all had the last of my splendid teas!"

He jerked his head left and saw that he had let his attention falter from the rudder too long. Starry Sea was coming to take the natural course of any sailing vessel, abeam of the wind. Calmly but immediately he veered the helm hard to port till her bow was angled forty degrees off the rollers once more. He chuckled. She had good sea sense about her, but these waves presented no risk, not yet. Hitting their rounded tops would make for a bumpy ride, but not roll his hefty cutter.

He patted her knee again and thanked her for the timely directive. She rose to go back below, muttering something about men drivers and no wonder their insurance is higher.

********

11

A large wave rolled under the boat and shook her heavily, startling Sweyn back to the present moment. He let out a long gasp, coughed, sputtered, as if he had been drowning. It was always like that when he came out of a flashback, though they had come and gone so often he was learning to transition between them and the real world better after all these years. At least this time the flashback had been a happy one, with her alive and sparkling beside him. Coming out of the bad ones was worse, much worse. But even the happy ones bit, for they forced him to face all over again what he had lost. Eilwen was gone, three years now, and all that was left to him were memories hard to bear that came and went at their whim, like ghosts.

But there was no time to think of it. Wind and waves were building around him, demanding his full attention. The wind was going pretty good now, twenty-five knots. To a lesser seaman it might have been time to heave-to. For Sweyn, who had spent so much of his life upon the waters, it was no more than a challenge, something to keep his thoughts from turning inward, where the real storm raged. In there, he was always on the brink of tears like rain and rage like a tempest.

There had been times when he had broken down like that, for months after that tragic spring night three years ago. He had railed against the acrimony of life, the callous cruelty of whatever sublime beings allowed him a brief sense of love and closeness, then ripped it all away and tore it to shreds as though it all had been the practical joke of bored gods who toyed with men's hearts for sport. He had railed until he nearly lost his sanity and vomited his hurt, and the rest of his heart too, out into the world. In the end only a numb husk of himself had remained, and that part took to the sea once and for all, seeking oblivion.

A thousand days ago that had been, to the mark. "But who's counting?" he asked himself silently. And, of course, he knew he was. He was counting the days as if waiting, but for what he did not know. Perhaps the next flashback. He lived in terror of them, for every time they came they made all the grief new again, and they stole a little piece of himself in their passing. But he also longed for them, for in those brief instances of insanity he was with her again, with Eilwen, when life was worth living.

But there were times when the dark memories came. Then there were only horrible recollections of screams in the night, fire on dark water, and the silhouette of a man watching beneath the wan orange illumination of sodium vapor streetlights. When those flashbacks came, he did terrible things. He stabbed at the air with knives. He smashed heavy tools into fittings. He became crazed and dangerous, in a desperate, mad attempt to get at that dark figure.

Perhaps it was those dark flashbacks as much as anything that kept him drifting upon the sea. When they came, who knew what terrible things he might do. It was certain that he had done terrible things in the past.

He had shed blood.

But no time to think on that now. Cold spray blew off a wave, and he realized his mind had wandered again. He forced himself by sheer will into the moment. The wind had picked up to thirty knots, and without attention to the helm the sailboat was broaching, turning beam to the wind where a building wave might roll her.

And suddenly a bizarre thought hit him. He could not be certain, memories of the past days were a strange, timeless blur, but he could not recall the last time he had taken a position fix with his sextant, or simply glanced at his chartplotter.

And with that thought he realized the local water was cold, but that could not be right. He should be somewhere just south of the equator, in the middle of the Pacific. He blinked, looked around, and exclaimed, "Where the hell am I?"

A coast was coming into view. Lots of mountains. Blue sky over the mountains, presenting a calmness that belied the storm force winds that drove Starry Sea relentlessly toward them. His seaman's instincts began to take over as he pondered questions which must now be answered. What kind of coast lay out there? Were there riptides? Rocky outcroppings? Unexpected shallows where submerged mountains nearly surfaced from the sea, but not quite? On some coasts there was the small chance a whirlpool could be encountered, though they were exceedingly rare. Of greater concern was passing ship traffic. Though the sky was yet clear, the weather would likely bring clouds and poor visibility. Or the building wind could curl the rollers into whitecaps and rip foam from them, creating a white haze. He might encounter some great nearsighted freighter in that soup that would plow him under, or worse, some other vessel his own size whom he might accidentally harm. Sweyn had little care for himself, but he was not yet so bitter that he would callously bring hurt to others. So he let himself shift mental gears, focusing on the concerns of piloting a sailing yacht. It was his special oblivion, a way to drown out the pain of all the memories, the fair and the foul.

He began by considering the prospect of a forced landfall. The wind was blowing him hard toward the exposed shore, and he didn't see much chance of avoiding it. But to land safely, he needed to know the lay of the coast, and he was forced to face again the startling fact that he had no idea where he was. He could have been somewhere off Siberia, or ten thousand miles away near New Zealand for that matter.

He shook his head briskly. It felt as if he were shrugging off intoxication, yet he had drunk nothing.

The land before him was rugged. There was no sign of civilization: no smog, no lights, no roads to be seen through binoculars. Certainly he had drifted somewhere remote and wild.

"How long has it been since I got a fix on my position?" he thought again and tried to recall. But the more he pondered it, the more it came to him that his last days or weeks had passed as a blur. "Am I dissociating?" he wondered aloud. Was he really losing it that bad?

Since the loss of Eilwen he had never really been concerned for where he was going, and sometimes would pass several days without glancing at charts. But for all that, he was too much the seaman not to at least take an occasional position fix. He felt responsible for his vessel if not for himself. But now his mind held only hazy recollections of sitting by the wheel, steering straight and true on some unknown course to a perfect beam reach wind for untold days and nights. He had not even glanced at his compass in all that time. Not once!

"What's wrong with me?" he whispered quickly.

But land was approaching fast and the wind still built. The anemometer now read thirty-five knots. He could try to beat into it and get away from that strange coast, but that would put the boat through a terrible pounding. Starry Sea was a heavy cruising vessel, not some lithe racer, not so nimble as to turn into such a wind as this and slice easily through the mounting rollers. He might be better off to try to find some small cove in that rugged coast.

Maybe.

He was now running seven knots before the wind with perhaps twenty miles to land. Less than three hours to find a safe haven; in sailors' terms, the blink of an eye. He had to know where he was. He rounded Starry Sea, and the brief moment the vessel turned broadside to the waves she took a mighty pounding, nearly laid flat to her mast by the onslaught of wind and water. But the faithful old cutter completed the turn and he rolled up her genoa, set the mainsail to heave her to. Fixing the helm just to windward, he plunged down the companionway ladder and used a bit of his precious electricity to operate the chartplotter. It took only a minute for it find and indicate the vessel's position, though the minute seemed much longer with Sweyn's growing awareness of the looming coast. Yet despite being pressed for time, the need to assess his position and act quickly, what he saw on the glowing color liquid crystal screen of the chartplotter froze him. It could not possibly be.

Certain there must be an equipment flaw, he turned off the chartplotter, then turned it on again a minute later. Another timeless minute followed as it reacquired its position. West coast, it read, British Columbia, not too far south of the Alaska panhandle.

He shook his head, utterly in disbelief. The last time he had taken a position, he had been drifting becalmed in warm waters south of Hawaii, in the doldrums where wind rarely blew. Since that time he had no clear recollection. Just sitting and sailing, riding the wind on his beam.

"So how much distance have I covered?" he asked himself silently. Several thousand miles, at least. But that would have taken weeks. No wind would blow steady and true on his beam for weeks. He could not possibly have done nothing but sit at the helm and steer all that time. Could he? He recalled the hypnotic effect of driving. Some people can get in their car and drive to a place and when they reach it, they have almost no recollection of the act of getting there. This was like that. He only vaguely remembered the act of sailing, but he had no idea of what exactly had occurred between when he started and when he got here, nor how long he had been at it. And he damned sure knew he hadn't plotted a course to bring him this way. Could he have come here by accident? What were the odds? Could he have piloted his vessel for weeks in driver's hypnosis? He might be messed up, but he knew he wasn't that messed up.

"Am I?"

He reached right and grabbed his log, opened it swiftly to his last entry. He had always been a rigorous log keeper, keeping track of every hour of engine time used, every bit of maintenance performed, every course plotted and run. Opening it, he saw his last entry was on April 14. He checked the date on a digital stopwatch hanging from the porthole near the tiny navigation station. It confirmed the date as yesterday. But there was something wrong with the entry. The handwriting didn't look like his. And all it reported was: Still sailing northwest—to the Island.

The Island?

A coldness ran through his gut. He looked suddenly right, into his stateroom, then left, into the aft stateroom, then the galley. It felt as if he were searching for someone, someone who might have written that entry, but surely there could be no stowaway aboard. "You can't sneak onboard this little sailboat," he told himself aloud, as if for reassurance.

Then a more horrible thought occurred to him. He began saying symptoms out loud. "Loss of time. Dissociation. Stress. Paranoia." He was—or more

14

accurately, had been — a psychologist, though it seemed now like it had been in another life altogether. He already knew he suffered depression and posttraumatic stress disorder. Knew it, but didn't care, didn't feel there was anything to be done about it except hope to heal or asphyxiate in it. Either way, he didn't care. But it could get worse. Under the right distress one could experience fugue, a strange sort of delirium that set one wandering and senseless.

A wave smashed into Starry Sea's hull, rolled over the deck of the boat. Sweyn was lurched violently forward, banging his head against the stainless steel frame of the porthole over the navigation station, then fell back onto the settee, where he flopped over like a rag doll and slid off the starboard settee, down between the table leg and the settee where he lay unconscious and immobile, firmly braced against the violent rolling motion of the storm-tossed little cutter.

*********

The sun continued to climb the chill sky, and approaching clouds made it grey over the sea, though a band of clear blue was tucked behind the ridge of serrated mountains towering in the northeast. Their height and ancient, massive strength held back the onslaught of the weather. Pale light shone through the smooth slate of cloud, leaching out the color from the world beneath. The sea became the color of the sky, the color of ash from fire pits which had once burned hot but had long since gone cold. The unusually colored hull of Starry Sea, sky blue on deck, azure down the hull all the way to the waterline, faded into two muted tones. The rigging had been color coded to help Eilwen find her way around the sails long ago, when she had been a novice aboard Starry Sea. White for the mainsail, red for the staysail, and blue for the huge genoa whose massive stay was mounted into the bowsprit. Now all these vivid colors seemed to blend like vegetables whose essence has been sapped away in boiling stock. Even the bright orange reflective streamers flying from two of the vessel's six shrouds — which Sweyn had set up to add visibility to his boat — lost their vividness, fading to a wan yellow as if drowned in smog.

But there was no smog. The air in this part of the world was pure, as pure as can still be found. It was sweet with the smell of forestland growing dangerously, rapidly closer, and tangy with the salt spice of the roaring sea. It bit with the nip of a clean cold squall descending on Starry Sea from the southwest. The growing murk was due to nothing other than weather conditions growing dreadful, misty rain and the wind ripping foam from waves. Had Sweyn been conscious, he could no longer have seen the land.

But Sweyn was not conscious. He lay below upon the sole of the salon, wedged tightly between the leg of the table and the starboard-side settee. Had he been awake, he would have been in pain, for his ribs were bent to near breaking. But luck had not entirely failed the leathery mariner, for this was also the safest place for him to be, for the sea rocked the boat wildly, and twice knocked her down. But while he was held steady, the last knockdown had torn the clew of the mainsail from the boom. Still attached to the mast at two points, the sail flapped wildly, crepitating like the smack of little thunder claps and the cracking of small fireworks. It shook the mast so furiously that the whole vessel shuddered.

With no sail to hold her hove-to, Starry Sea turned abeam to the frothing sea. She rocked violently as her keel was grabbed by each passing wave. Within the vessel, pantries flew open and unsecured dry goods spilled out, creating a wet mess of flour and sugar in the galley and on the sole. A large handheld spotlight flew from a cabinet over the navigation station and smashed into the starboard settee, falling harmlessly onto the cushions over Sweyn's left shoulder. Had he been standing there, the impact of the blow might have been lethal. At the least, he would have had broken bones to remember it by.

But Starry Sea was a sound little ship. Built seventy-five years earlier of solid oak and purpleheart, her spine and ribs were thick and curved to hold the sea. Her keel was built right into the lines of the ribs and spine so that it almost formed one solid piece with the hull, giving the vessel incredible strength. Half her ten tons she carried as lead ballast, and it was this weight that held the boat keel-side down into the waters, despite the mad waves. So luck was with Sweyn in this moment: luck that he owned a sound, if old, vessel; luck that he had kept her up so well, loving her as his own kin, nursing her to the best of health. Starry Sea had stamina to hold her own. At least for a while. But no vessel can stand up to the pounding of the sea forever, and without a skipper to implement good tactics, a sea storm will eventually win out. But in this moment Starry Sea had no skipper. Her skipper had found a moment of perfect oblivion at last, a moment where he was not haunted by any memories whatsoever.

In honor of those memories, Sweyn would never have taken his own life, though if the sea was going to take him, he had no qualms. If he had been awake, he might have considered this a fitting way to wink out of the world.

But luck was not through with Sweyn. It had not been luck that gave him a coldly professional, detached father who drove him away in the end. Nor had it been luck that stole away his beloved Eilwen. But as fate would have it, it was luck that brought the storm, and something like it that brought him north, beginning so many weeks ago, with hardly a conscious reckoning, sailing mindlessly with a strange beam wind that never failed, never wavered. And though a storm raged around him that might easily have swamped the unmanned vessel, luck saw that the small bit of line holding the anchor to the bowsprit was stripped away as the bow plunged into a wave and was momentarily awash in its incomprehensible force.

Starry Sea rose on the back of that wave, her bow flying clear of the sea, then plunged down the face of another, her keel biting deep into the water so that she seemed to surf. The natural aquadynamic tendency of her lines moved the bow ahead as she shot down the waves and this time the anchor, a hefty fifty pound bruce, was ripped from the bowsprit, training chain, and then rode, behind it.

The little cutter was thrust ahead by the wind while the weighty anchor and its heavy chain and rode were pulled out by the cartwheeling action of the rolling waves, dragging the anchor rapidly out and deeper into the sea. Suddenly, the rode reached its end. But it had been fastened in two places by the meticulous seaman, one inside the anchor locker at the forward most part of the bow, and another at the starboard bow cleat. The anchor line stretched taught as the bruce anchor caught the water, digging into the brine almost as if it dug into the loose sand of a tropical anchorage. The pressure on the line was tremendous, but the hardware on the bowsprit was beefy and solidly joined to the ship. Starry Sea shuddered half way up the next mighty white-crested wave, then she pitched around on the rode as if it were a bridle, now facing directly into the onslaught of the sea. Now the waves came at her from straight on, were cut by her bow, and foamed and hissed harmlessly by.

Several black faces appeared just for an instant in the foam. They could have been sea otters, but it was far from land for sea otters. More likely they were the stormed tossed roots of sea onions, knots of kelp. But they did not look like it.

The wind shifted, backing so that it ran somewhat parallel to the looming coast. It dragged Starry Sea with it. But the wind still worked the cutter landward, and the craggy roots of mighty mountains waited, now only a few miles away.

Time passed. And as it went the wind began to relent, but it did the little cutter no good, for the seafloor was rising to meet the land, causing the angry sea to throw up wild waves. The angle of the hull shifted a bit, or perhaps the bruce anchor did through some quirk of imbalance in how it was fastened to the boat, so that the little cutter came to rest at an angle slightly off the wind. In this luck was also with Sweyn, for now Starry Sea sidled a bit more eastward as she was blown north, as surely as if unseen hands of brine and flesh of fishy things urged her that way. And Starry Sea made her way in a direction Sweyn would never, ever in his life have willingly chosen to go, not even if failing to go that way would have cost him his life and sunk his precious cutter, the last thing he still loved, the last thing he still believed in.

For the sea was pushing him home. Not his birth home, where his imminent father still practiced his hoodoo and called it psychotherapy. Nor did it push him toward Glacier Falls on the Olympic Peninsula of Washington, where he and Eilwen had once lived happily in a rainforest chalet, where she grew her herbs and he ran his charter business. No, what the sea did was far crueler. It pushed him toward the island of Eilwen's birth, a place she had hated and was so bitter against she refused ever to speak of it. And because she had hated it, Sweyn also hated it.

Though sometimes, late at night when he slept alone in the double birth of his stateroom, he could almost make out a familiar feminine voice whispering over the lull of the waves on the hull, telling him: "Go home, Sweyn."

But he had no home. Everyplace that was dear to him bore memories of her, and he could not bear to be reminded of so much loss. This hated island was especially rife with her memories, even though he had never been to it. But she had grown up there; it was part of her. She would be everywhere in it, and for that reason, if nothing else, he would never have chosen to go there.

But the sea gave him no choice. It blew him relentlessly, inexorably to the Island of Manannan.

His thoughts took shape; consciousness sparked. He opened his eyes and wished he hadn't. There was a pain like a spike in his skull. Reaching up, he felt tenderly at his forehead. It was bruised and sore, but the skin had not broken. There was a mighty lump, though. But to make his head hurt worse, something was creating a grand cacophony, rattling and banging around up above at tremendous volume. The steady snapping, whipping noise was punctuated every couple seconds by a huge, violent clatter, the sound of metal clashing with metal. His foggy mind found it hard to isolate the source of the ruckus, though had he been more clearheaded, he'd have known in an instant and averted the next disaster. But perhaps this too was a strange twist of luck.

He tried to move and found it impossible. It felt as if another spike had been driven into his chest. He looked down and saw how he had been wedged tight between the single leg of the table and the settee. He raised his arm and pushed up on the table. It lifted on hinges that were attached on one side to a spice-shelf-slash-wine-wrack, bringing up the attached leg with it, freeing him. The relief was immediate and for the first time in he did not know how long he could breathe normally. But his chest was stiff and sore and the act of breathing hurt, especially where his ribs had been bent cruelly by the table leg. Carefully, he moved out of the way and set the table back down, making sure the peg in the foot of the leg found its way into a small hole in the sole drilled especially to hold the table leg square and sound.

Slowly, not yet quite certain of his balance, he took to his feet, hands instinctively grasping overhead for the teak rail that served as a handhold. He was not woozy, nor nauseous, and he was immediately relieved, for it meant he had probably not been concussed. The sea still heaved under him, though, Starry Sea rising and falling on mountainous swells, and he had to watch his footing. Then he noticed the terrible mess in the salon and cursed under his breath. It would take days to clean up properly.

Suddenly, the peril his boat faced returned to him. He glanced out a porthole and saw white foam crests curling past, hissing like freshly opened soda cans as they went. It took him a moment to realize his bow had turned into the waves. Dimly he wondered how that could be. The last he recalled, he left the helm with the vessel hove-to. She should have been pointing about forty-five degrees off the wind and waves. But in another instant the source of the tumult above was realized as his mind cleared and his well-honed seaman's instincts found place again, and the mystery of his bow-on angle to the sea was forgotten.

The mainsail! It was flying loose! He turned to dash up the companionway, but no sooner did he set his foot upon the first step than there came a tremendous tearing noise, as if an Atlas had just ripped a phonebook in half all at once.

He burst up the steps, spun on his heel, grabbing the railing of the dodger and looking up over it. The main, which had been reefed, had broken free of the binding ropes and had been flapping around wildly against the shrouds, secured to the mast only at the peak and base. And just now it had ripped, tearing neatly from the bottom to the top, from halfway along the foot of the sail to the luff. The torn half could still be seen blowing away in the wind, fluttering over the breaking waves like some drunken seabird, till, a quarter mile off the stern, it dropped from the sky, hit the water, and vanished from sight.

He cursed then as only a seaman can curse. He had, in that moment, effectively lost his primary engine. He still had his diesel below, but a diesel is an ungainly source of propulsion for a sailboat, and his sailboat in particular was designed to sail, not motor. Without his mainsail his craft would find no steadiness over the waves. She would sway precariously in any mild wind. Travel without his main was dangerous, at best.

Instinct took over again, though. The first order of business—minimize the damage. He had been wearing a harness and he secured himself to a jackline to keep himself from going overboard should he lose his balance. Then he climbed up around the dodger, intending to take down the flailing remnant of the mainsail and put an end to the clatter of its shackles smacking into the aluminum mast.

Watching the wet, rolling deck before him, gripping handholds with white-knuckled fierceness as he worked his way forward, he made his way to the mast. He loosened a line from a mast winch and began to ease the sail down, furling the torn remnant quickly as he worked so the wind could not grab it. It was soaked and sprayed cold droplets into his face and eyes. The cold quickly penetrated his hands, burning his fingers, but he continued his task, heedless of the pain, lowering the ripped sail to the deck, pressing the folds under a foot to hold them against the wind, hanging onto the hoisting sheet and the torn sail for his life, freezing till his teeth chattered. Then, suddenly, the wind died. It took only seconds, and then, like the cessation of a whisper, it went away. The rain also broke in that moment, and streams of sunlight shafted down from breaks opening in the clouds.

He looked up from his work and found that Starry Sea had just rounded a point and been blown into a bay. He had rounded points and found shelter from winds before, but never so abruptly. He looked to his left. Steep, wooded mountains rose against the wind, now coming mostly out of the west. The mountains ended in abrupt cliffs at land's edge, forming an immediate wall against the weather, cutting the outside world off from this sheltered bay. Still, he should have had to drift further back into the bay for the mountains' shielding effect to really take hold. It was odd the wind should break so abruptly, with the wide open sea only twenty yards behind him. And even if the bay provided a particularly effective wind block, that should not have arrested the rain, nor broken the clouds.

But he was well aware that strange things happened at sea. Still, knowing that could not have prepared him for what would happen next.

He looked ahead and was frozen by what he saw.

Some dark thing, almost as large as a man, was crouched on two legs in the bowsprit, just in front of the windlass. It was matted in dark, wet, wiry hair. Pointed teeth gleamed from a pink mouth, as though it were grinning. It stared silent and still at him. It could only be some odd marine animal he had never before seen, and was no doubt as surprised by his presence as he was by its. But the face, half hidden beneath that snarl of wiry hair, looked queerly human. Long fingered handlike paws clutched at something sinuous and creamy white. A strip of sailcloth, it seemed to be. And then, with a grace surprising from the gangly, crouching wild thing, it slipped off the bow into the brine, even now calming to easy five foot rollers with the passing of the storm-force wind.

He stood frozen there, clinging to rope and torn sail, close beside the mast. Starry Sea settled out under him, riding the gentling surf easier now. He paid the change no mind. His jaw was half open, full of wonder, like when he had been a boy in a sea-kayak and had seen his first grey whale broach the surface from no more than two arm lengths away. The experience of marine life was one of the best salves of the sea, one of the wonders that could temporarily drive away the pain, but never in all his years afloat had he seen such a beast as what he had just witnessed. With the wind gentling to under ten knots, and the clouds breaking up into compact fluffs of white cumulus with streamers of afternoon sun bursting through, he let go the ragged main and stepped forward, eyes glued to the spot where the creature had been.

What in the world had it been? Something he did not know? Maybe even something heretofore unknown and unseen by man. Could he have inadvertently discovered a new species?

He stepped up to the bowsprit and knelt where the thing had been. Watery paw prints were visible on the wooden deck. At least he had not imagined it. Gingerly, he touched a print, traced his finger through it. The print was disturbingly human, bulbous where a heal might have been, elongated toward the balls of the feet, wide before the toes. And there were little circles where toes might have been. If he did not know better, he would have sworn these were the prints of something very like a man.

Movement caught his eye to starboard and port of the bow. Dolphins swam beneath the surface, gliding alongside Starry Sea, slipping playfully beneath her keel. On a calmer day he might have been able to see them better, but in the recently stirred up water, still hazy with bubbles and remnants of foam, they were dark shadows beneath a green surface. They moved as fluid elementals, casting about playfully as they chased each other and dared dives under the keel. Occasionally, a shadow's tail seemed to fork, as though it were legs, as though it were the phantom of a man, or a woman, gallivanting about down there. He stood up, holding onto the liferail with his right hand, the left wrapped around the furled genoa for support.

A sea otter poked its head out of the water, stared intently at him, at Starry Sea. These creatures were notoriously curious, fascinated by vessels and especially music. Their precocious habits endeared them to him. Sometimes he would drift in a cove and play music loudly on the boat's stereo to entice them. Then they would gather round about the cutter, floating on their backs as they listened to the music and watched the boat with a queer-bright curiosity. But this otter regarded him with something more. Its dark gaze seemed to bore into him, and there was an unsettling sense of intelligence burning in its night-black eyes. Sweyn gazed back. Time ceased to pass as man and sea animal studied one another. The dolphins continued to slip fore and aft, and sometimes traded sides. When at last the otter rolled over and slipped beneath the waves, and the spell was broken, Sweyn did not know how much time had passed. A long time, surely.

It was then he realized why the boat's bow had mysteriously turned into the waves. The bruce anchor was out all the way, somehow having come loose of its tie-down while he was unconscious, and acted as a sea anchor. "The first time that's ever happened," he thought, and rose to go back to the cockpit where he would engage the windlass and pull the anchor back in.

But turning that way, he suddenly faced the stern of Starry Sea, the direction in which she was drifting. The great clouds were now half gone. A high sun spilled warm gold, illuminating steep mountains, dark woods of deciduous trees, and a break in the mountains where flat land spilled out toward the sea. There lay a small, green valley, and a silver band of river ran through the midst of it, emptying into the bay. At the mouth of the tiny river was a small village. He was perhaps two miles away now, but he could make out the forms of whitewashed plastered cottages and larger wooden structures, all trimmed with vivid blues, greens and reds. The sunshine spilled down upon the village as if marking it for landfall.

And he knew the place, too. He could not believe he was here, had never, ever intended to come here. Would never have dared it, not in the blackest pit of his nightmares, for if unsought memories were anywhere to be found aside from Glacier Falls, they were here, in this village he had never been to before in his life. But by the profile of the village against the verdant valley backdrop, and its unusual Old World architecture, which he had seen before in photographs and an oil painting Eilwen had kept over the fireplace in their chalet at Glacier Falls, he could tell this was Man-by-the-Sea, Eilwen's birthplace. Memories of her would be thick there, and being in the midst of them would cost him dear in sorrow. But also in this place was the inheritance Eilwen had left him, a legacy he never considered claiming.

Yet Starry Sea continued to drift landward, and he leaned against her forestay, weak-kneed. For all he was worth, he'd have turned and run back for the sea right now if he could. But Starry Sea was crippled, her mainsail gone, and no telling what other damage she had sustained while he had been insensible below. The wind carried him toward the village's peer while the strength seemed to flow out of him like water. He had things to do, preparations to make for landfall, an anchor to bring in, a sail to secure, fenders to put out, and a hundred other things to attend to. But it was all he could do to stand and hold his balance and keep his sanity against the memories which threatened to overwhelm him now, bright and dark memories goaded into consciousness by the sudden, unexpected presence of this village, and this Island, where Eilwen had grown up.

"How did I come here?" he begged of the air, but no answer was returned.

He was lost, he knew. Half mad, he knew. And now he felt powerless, a thing he had never before felt, not upon the sea, his element. Yet it was the sea which carried him relentlessly home.

# Chapter Two

*Some spin wool for homespun cloth,*
*some spin silk for finer stuff,*
*some spin gold and fair the treasure*
*some spin mist and hard the measure,*
*I spin the geas and lives I weave,*
*with twines of luck to bind the sheaves.*

*Elidurydd*
*The Lady of the Brooks*

The sea drove him a mile closer to shore. From his vantage on the bow, where he stood confused and frozen, he could make out the lay of the place. Beaches of grey sand stretched out in a wide crescent south of Man-by-the-Sea. Just east of the village lay shallows — he could tell as he watched the diminishing rollers, now only four feet high, break into white foamers where the waves climbed up the rising sea bottom and toppled over themselves. The water there also had a murky look, the way it gets around thickets of kelp. That area was a navigation hazard to be avoided at all costs.

Beyond the shallows were moors that stretched back to an unbroken forest of hardwood which wrapped around both village and bay in the manner of a protective cloak. The hardwoods were a bizarre sight here in the Pacific Northwest where coniferous rainforests predominated. But Eilwen — the mere recollection of her name made him wince — had told him long ago that the original settlers of the Island had planted the forest some two centuries back. According to legend, the settlers had gone all over the Island sowing seeds that replaced the autochthonous cedars and spruces, tamaracks and firs. The seeds came from European hardwood forests, and the trees that sprang from those seeds had taken well to the sweet, rich loam of the Island. At least, that was the story according to the old rememberers. (What was it she had called them? The seanachies?) The hardwood forest soon came to cover the whole Island, from the beaches back to the heights of the mountains on the north side where the land was rugged and inhospitable. It had displaced the old forest entirely, and grown with such amazing fecundity it looked as if it had existed on the Island since long days before the coming of the colonists.

Man-by-the-Sea itself was a tiny hamlet, spanning only a couple hundred yards of beach. It appeared to go back no deeper, ending abruptly at the forest's edge, and to the north at the river. Whorls of smoke rose from many of the brightly painted shops and cottages. The storm had brought cool temperatures and some of the occupants had lit hearths. Eilwen had told him the villagers disdained many modern amenities, including the use of liquid fuels, and the white tufts of smoke he spotted had their origins in wood and peat. Even from out here, he could smell the pungent fragrance of the smoke.

He could see no power line poles from this distance, and though there were paved roads along the waterfront, only a few cars and trucks used them, meandering patiently up and down the village's byways. They appeared as crawling painted dots, gleaming metallic in the brightening sun. The cars weaved around slower things in the road, pedestrians and, he realized after a moment, horses drawing carts.

He breathed shakily and worked his way back to the cockpit, reached under the dodger for his Steiner binoculars, faithful old rubber-armored 7x50s, and glassed out the scene. It was a sight out of time and reminded him of someplace else he had seen once.

Many hundreds of miles further north on the southern coast of Alaska was a small, old Russian village. The villagers lived in high-gabled cottages and log cabins. The men worked in drab canvas pants and flannel shirts. The women wore bright layers of thin skirts handmade from pastel colored cotton and simple white blouses cut in nineteenth century Russian peasant style. Capped in white bonnets and wrapped in brightly dyed shawls, the women appeared as blossoms against the endless dark evergreens of the north. The villagers harvested fish from weirs, grew gardens for their produce, and hunted for their meat. They were secluded and introverted, and among themselves spoke a dated Russian. They had cars and electricity, but otherwise were very traditional. Their community appeared to have leapt into the modern era straight out of the nineteen century.

Sweyn had seen their village on a cruise many years ago before he had met Eilwen, when he had sailed to Alaska to see the unbroken reaches of forest, the crystal rivers, and fish the abundant wild salmon. Man-by-the-Sea reminded him of that secluded Russian-Alaskan village. But where the Russians could only be described as traditional, these folk were nothing less than backward. They shunned and distrusted technology, using it no more than was absolutely necessary. They had few cars, no village power plant, and when they needed electricity, they made it themselves with home generators or small windmills mounted on polls. Man-by-the-Sea was locked in the past, and Eilwen had described it as "doggedly stagnant." For that reason alone he could understand why bright, adventurous Eilwen had abandoned the Island almost nineteen years ago.

He dreaded going there. It would be inbred and he would be out of place. Worst of all, it would be haunted with her memories. But there was simply no choice. He could not take Starry Sea back out to sea without a mainsail, nor without an inspection of her hull. But he could make the excursion as brief as possible. As soon as he made land he would order a sail and have the vessel hulled. He could sleep on the boat and avoid the village. With any luck he could return to sea in a week. He took another shaky breath, gathered his wits and his courage, and made ready to make landfall.

He went to the binnacle and flipped the switch that activated the windlass. The powerful electric motor turned the cam that drew in the anchor rode. He paused the hoisting every fifty feet to go below and forward to the anchor locker and make sure the rode coiled neatly so it would not tangle. Eventually, a loud thump and growl of metal announced he was now raising the chain secured to the end of the rode. Fifty feet more and the chain was in, the anchor firmly seated on the pulpit. He went forward and tied off the anchor, this time doubly securing it with two short lengths of quarter inch braided line so it could not possibly come undone of its own again. Then he returned stern, started the engine and was pleased to hear it rumble smoothly to life. He steered toward the seawall just east and south of Man-by-the-Sea. When the boat was lined up with the entrance to the tiny fishing harbor he activated the autopilot and went forward to the mast and gathered in the remains of the ruined sail, inspecting it as the hank came down.

He shook his head. Never in his life had he seen such a tear work through a sail. It was sundered vertically, a neat rip from leach to foot, halfway along the sail's width. The tear was remarkably clean, almost as if it had been cut with a knife. He frowned. Freakish this was, yes, but he had seen strange things upon the lonely reaches of the sea. Yet he could not help but recall the uncanny creature on the bow, holding what looked to be a strip of sailcloth in a handlike paw. He could almost believe the creature had sabotaged his sail, but that was ridiculous.

He went about readying the boat for landfall. There were seacocks to close, fenders to tie off, spring lines to position, and more.

*********

He had tied off to a slip on the north side of the docks, a place occupied only by a stray fishing boat and a single other sailing yacht, passing through. Starry Sea bobbed at her spring lines which he had snuggly secured to hefty cleats on the wooden pier. It did not take him long to find the harbormaster, explain how he had taken damage in the storm, and arrange an indefinite stay. The harbormaster was a leathery man in his early seventies, still spry, who wore a white cap emblazoned with an anchor snagged in rode sewn of gold and red thread. He looked every bit the old seadog and even smelled of brine and rum. Sweyn found himself surprised the old fellow did not smoke a curved pipe and speak with a plethora of guttural "ayes" and "mateys." As it was, the harbormaster was possessed of a thick brogue, like Scottish or Irish, with a touch of something else, maybe Welsh. It bothered Sweyn, for it was one more thing to remind him of Eilwen, who had had just the same odd music in her tongue. Years ago she had told him that all of Man-by-the-Sea's inhabitants had been something like Tinkers, having their origins in the Celtic countries of the British Isles. They had originally settled in Scots dominated Nova Scotia, but were not content to remain in a land with so many "Outsiders," which seemed to mean anyone not of their number. They wandered the New World over several decades, making their way slowly west, till they came to this uninhabited island and settled in. Having seldom had contact with the outside world, they still retained their accents and cultural distinction. The harbormaster was frank and friendly, and offered to provide Sweyn whatever help he could. Despite himself, Sweyn liked the rough-edged seaman. He paid the harbormaster for a week worth of slip fees in advance and inquired where he could find a chandlery and phones. The harbormaster directed him across the street for phones, and south for the chandler.

He made his way across the street to a hardware store that also doubled as a bait shop and called an old and trusted supplier in Seattle who already had the sail specifications of Starry Sea on record. From that company he ordered a new mainsail, thread, needles and other bobs and bits he would need to tend to the mending and maintenance of his sails. Then he headed south along a paved street in the direction of the chandler.

The business was not big. Man-by-the-Sea had only a small fishing fleet, a dozen or so aging wooden trawlers that could be seen bobbing at the piers behind the diminutive seawall. This one business provided a variety of services for them, everything from installing and maintaining their plumbing and hardware, to mending nets and painting hulls. The building seemed deserted when Sweyn entered it. There was no one in sight, and the inventory, a collection of zincs, cans of epoxy and marine grade paint, and various fittings for plumbing and boat propane systems, was covered with a layer of thick grey dust. And only half the shelves even held inventory. The other half merely stood empty. Perhaps a little later in the year when the fishing season opened these shelves would be covered with net, line and buoys. Sweyn called for someone and received no answer. He stepped past the aisles, looking down each one, but no one was to be found. As he worked his way toward the back of the shop, movement caught his eye. It turned out to be a hefty tiger striped tabby, thickly furred and well rounded from too many meals and not enough mousing, lounging on a pillow on the counter beside the cash register. One paw rested possessively on the till, as if the feline were guarding it. It eyed him with the semi-interested suspicion typical of its species. A cigar smoked in an ashtray beside the cat, and for a moment Sweyn was confronted with the Alice in Wonderland image of the cat sitting at the till, counting colorful Canadian money and smoking the smelly stogy. Sweyn pushed the image away and chalked it up to too many sleepless nights at sea.

He stepped up to the counter. A large, blank notepad was there and a pen lay beside it. Taped to the counter beside the notepad was a sheet of paper that announced the proprietor was out on business and would be "back later." The note also left instructions for the reader to write down what he needed and leave the request. Several such messages were already taped helter-skelter to the counter, requests for marine paints, tackle, blocks, and other miscellany of mariners.

"Well that's just great," Sweyn grumbled. "Back later" might mean minutes or days in a backwater wash like this, and he did not want to spend a minute more in Man-by-the-Sea than he had to. But there was little choice, so he took the notepad and wrote on it the pier where Starry Sea was tied, and a request to dry hull the boat ASAP. He was just tearing off a bit of Scotch tape to affix the note to the counter when an obvious thought occurred to him: the proprietor must be nearby if he left a cigar smoking in the ashtray. No sooner did he think it than bells hung from the front door chimed at the entryway. He turned and saw a middle-aged woman enter the shop carrying a large, heavy box awkwardly in her arms. Sweyn hurried over to help her with the package, but she shooed him away and staggered to the counter where she set it down with such a solid thump the cat actually deigned her a glance before returning to the more serious business of looking down its stubby nose at Sweyn.

"What can I do for ye?" the woman asked Sweyn as she took the stogy from the ashtray and inserted it into her wide mouth. She was rotund, with a serious face, and wore a skirt of some drab yellow material, hefty workman's boots, all topped off with a dainty blouse over which she wore a dark blue, thick slicker. She was a study in contrasts, blue-collar grandma. Sweyn could picture her sitting in a rocker, embroidering and sipping tea, while bellowing commands and curses at a crew of rough fisherman from the bridge of a storm-tossed trawler.

Sweyn glanced outside. The sun was fully out now and her garb must have been hot. He decided to make no comment on the coat and said instead, "I didn't expect anyone. The note said you were out for a while."

She snickered. "Oh, that. Well, I had to grab a shipment," she patted the box, "but now I'm back. Local folk know what to do if I'm no' here. But yer no' from these parts, are ye?"

Sweyn shook his head. "I've got a boat I need hulled. I've been through a storm and I have to look her over."

"Take some damage, did ye?" she said. Like everyone else here, she possessed the odd brogue, a mixture of British Isle accents and a bit of Canada.

"I don't know. Maybe," he replied. "I'd like to get her out of the water and look her over soon as possible. Patch her up if she needs it. How soon can you do it?"

"Ho, like we have lots to do around here," she chuffed as she began to remove items from the box, more pipe fittings, and set them haphazardly at the counter's edge. "I'll send my boy to tend to it tomorrow. He's out painting old Kilcutty's boat this moment."

"Thanks," said Sweyn. "I appreciate it. How much do I owe you?"

"Well, let's see what ye needs to make her whole first, eh? Could be nothing more than a paint job. Could be a lot more. If it's more, we can help with that, then we'll talk money." Sweyn agreed the job could get more complicated. He had no idea how Starry Sea had fared while he lay unconscious down below. But all the same, he would like to have fixed a price for at least some of the services to be rendered. This smile and a handshake small town business made him uncomfortable. But the old lady refused to set a price till she knew what would have to be done for his cutter, save to assure him "Ye'll be please with the quality of the work and the size of the bill."

Finally, he agreed to her terms. What choice was there, really? At least the cutter could begin receiving service immediately, unlike in busier ports where he might have had to wait days or even weeks. The only problem was that, with the boat up on blocks as of tomorrow, he would have to find someplace else to sleep a bit sooner than he had planned. He asked where he could find a hotel.

"Ho!" she guffawed, "Like we be a big town with lights and tourists and all, down there like Prince George! Laddy, ye and that other yacht down in the peer, which sailed in here last fall to pass the winter, represent the sum of our annual tourist industry. There's no hotel here. No' even a cottage with a room to let. Our Island's out of the way and we like it that way."

"Then what's a visitor to do?" he barked, nonplussed.

"A question we dinna' have to tend to, much. If ye needs, there're lots o' woods round about. If ye camp near to the village, but no' too near anyone's land, I dinna' think folk will be put out. No' saying as ye have to bide me, but I would no' go too deep in the woods. This is wild country, if ye take my meaning."

He grunted affirmation. Eilwen had told him about the woods. The locals believed them haunted. Despite that nonsense, it was certain that this far north wolves, bear, and moose ran in them, making camping a hazard. In any case, he did not keep camping gear aboard Starry Sea, save what was contained in a small "abandon ship" bag beside the life raft. And he couldn't see himself living in the forest like a wild man for the next several days, coming into town grubby as a hobo to tend the boat. And, for the love of god, who ever heard of a town without so much as a single bed and breakfast. Could this place actually be that cutoff from the rest of the world? All these years he had thought Eilwen must have exaggerated that part, but it appeared she had not.

He thanked the shopkeeper for her help and said he would return the next morning to oversee the hulling of Starry Sea. When he stepped out of the musty shop, the clouds had almost entirely gone and sunlight spilled abundantly from a lucid sky, but it did nothing to improve his spirits. In fact, it seemed the increasingly cheery weather mocked him, his predicament.

In the back of his head he had been afraid things would turn out like this. Man-by-the-Sea was as isolated and unaccustomed to visitors as Eilwen had said. Not in the habit of receiving travelers, it offered no accommodations. And once he started tearing into his boat things would get messy. Wires and pipe, electronics panels and bilge covers, and every cushion and tool on the boat would soon be scattered all over the sole and deck. And while he had at first fooled himself into thinking he could get the repairs done and be out of here in a week, the truth was — when he faced it — that it would take his sailmaker at least a couple of weeks to fabricate and ship a new mainsail. And it would take at least that long to service his vessel. Just surveying her for damage would take the better part of several days. He could not possibly live on Starry Sea during the repairs, and camping was out of question.

But he was not without options. He looked up the road going north, the only road leading out of Man-by-the-Sea. According to the stories Eilwen had told him, the Cottage where she grew up lay that way, "at the very end of the northern path," she had said. But just the thought of it gave him shivers. Could he bear to get that close to something that had been so close to Eilwen? She had been part of that place. There, memories would flit like wayward phantoms. They would haunt every hollow shadow. In the midst of so much of what had been her world, the presence of memory would overwhelm him. The flashbacks would come. The pleasant ones were hard enough to bear, but the dark ones would come too, forcing him to relive the scent of sea-borne fire, the terror of cloth shrouds. Fists pounding in humid darkness.

But his father would have demanded he face his fears. Look them in the eye and talk about them till they are meaningless. Vivisect what haunts you till it's powerless, that's what he would have told Sweyn. Except that Sweyn did not buy his father's psychobabble anymore. Once he had. He had admired his father so much he had followed in his footsteps and become a psychologist himself. But now Sweyn had no respect at all for the profession. It didn't make grief any less real. It didn't drive regret away. Psychotherapy was witchdoctor medicine! And Sweyn did not believe in superstitions.

But the real dilemma lay in the fact that Sweyn could not accept Eilwen's death. How could he accept the loss of someone he loved more than life? How could anyone? Better to rail against it and suffer the consequences of denying reality than to dim her memory. However painful, he would never let Eilwen go.

So he was torn. To accept her passing was to diminish her. Yet the memory of her was tearing his soul apart. And the north road epitomized his inner struggle. To walk that path, he must face the memories he struggled to keep, yet keep at a distance. And so he hesitated upon the path, fearing to go, fearing to stay.

Yet for all his trepidation, deep within he knew he must go. There had been so much of his sad, wondrous wife he had not understood. Three years is such a short time to get to know someone so remarkable and complex. If he went to the Cottage, he might learn something more of her.

He took a step toward the north road. The world cantered horribly, sweat rose to his brow. He suddenly seemed to be floating, detaching from himself, an inner observer of a terrified man.

"Breathe," he told himself shakily. "Breathe." He managed several deep and tremulous gulps of air. Slowly, as he regained his runaway feelings, the almost-fit of panic passed.

His father had been right in one thing: he must face his fears. Only doing so could he survive two weeks on the Island. Only then could he take the north road. And the truth was, he wanted to. He would never have come to this place willingly. Never! But now that he was here, he did want to go that way, if only for a little while. Just long enough to take in where she had lived, and keep her a little bit more alive within.

Just to see if he could overcome his phobia, he took another step in that direction. It was like pressing into the cold north wind. Like forcing a path through a thicket of thorns and brambles. His haunted mind held him back as much as his hungry heart pressed him on. An eternity later he forced another step. Moving his feet felt like lifting ingots of lead. But he managed it, and soon after he managed another step, then another, and another. Each step was daunting, but he moved north nonetheless, and so doing proved to himself he could make himself go that way. It was a terrible and wonderful power, for he knew that passing that way might allow him to reflesh the desiccated bones of her memory. The possibility was alluring, yet dangerous, for the heartbreak of such memory had already driven him to the brink of complete breakdown. If he were to bring that much of Eilwen back into his head, how much of himself would be left. Perhaps his sanity would retreat once for all to a waking vision of times gone by, a permanent flashback of when Eilwen was alive and well with him, riding the waves upon Cerulean.

And why not, really? Alone and happy with his delusions. He could live with that, he decided.

Enough for now. With the few practice steps he had just taken he had proven to himself he could face going that way. His course was now set, and once Sweyn decided upon a course he was not one to sway. Later tomorrow, after Starry Sea had been hulled and partially pulled apart, he would walk the north road and discover whatever there was to discover, and see how much of himself remained afterward.

He turned around and started back toward the heart of the village. The sense of relief was immediate. The coldness went. The staccato thudding of his heart calmed. He could breathe easier. By the time he returned to his vessel, he had laid another plan. Tonight, after he had looked over Starry Sea, he was going to find a pub and drink himself stupid.

One little bit at a time, he thought to himself. Just go slow. You can handle it.

*********

He returned to Starry Sea to find a young man waiting for him. The young man introduced himself as the chandler's boy. He had heard about Sweyn's mishap on the ocean and felt he should help him get his boat out of the water as soon as possible. "I would no' feel right leaving an injured boat overnight to her luck," he told Sweyn in the Island's singsong brogue. So he had cut from his other job early to give this priority.

The boy's name was Finn, a youth in his very early twenties. He was stout and fair-haired and had the look of a person whose business was the sea: wiry muscles, taught-skin, tanned and already crinkles of crows' feet around the eyes. He wore the homemade canvas trousers Sweyn was coming to learn were common among Man-by-the-Sea males. Similar to jeans, they buttoned up front and were stitched with thick twine. Usually brown or tan in color, they appeared to be a bit tougher than the jeans so common among folk on the continent east. The youth seemed competent as he used a small launch to tow Starry Sea into the narrow birth where a massive harness was immersed in the water and the lift, resembling a great cage on enormous tires, idled, waiting. Expertly, Finn brought Starry Sea to a complete stop over the submerged harness and secured the cutter in place. Then he climbed out and engaged the lift. It took fifteen minutes to raise the ten ton vessel out of the water. Sweyn, who had been hovering on the deck like a mother hen, climbed off as the deck came level with the walkway around the birth and turned to regard the operation. Despite the boy's youth, he was masterful, a real tradesman. Soon Starry Sea was up high and dry and Finn was backing the lift away from the birth. They proceeded down a dirt road to the dry docks, and Sweyn walked out in front to direct passersby around. The lift moved at only a mile an hour and often Sweyn had to slow his pace so as not to get too far ahead of it. When Finn finally got Starry Sea over a waiting cradle of joists and blocks, Sweyn made sure everything was correctly aligned and in order, then watched as Finn lowered her gently down. He went round quickly, snugging up the braces which kept Starry Sea from tipping over on her keel, for though she might have been a fine, well-balanced craft out on the water, here on land she was out of place and crippled.

Once the sailboat was securely set, the boy unfastened the harness, bid farewell to Sweyn with a crisp two-fingered wave, and drove the lift back toward the chandler. Sweyn watched him leave for a minute. He respected that kid, he decided. He knew his stuff.

When the lift turned a corner, Sweyn turned and faced his vessel. Her bottom paint was dirty and in places stained with algae or crusted with a few barnacles, but the hull appeared sound. There were no obvious signs that she had been breached. He breathed a sigh of relief. Hull damage could have taken the better part of the summer to repair, and while he might manage to make himself face a couple weeks in Man-by-the-Sea, he could not bear a full season here, he knew.

He climbed aboard and began a more thorough survey of the boat from topside. It was then that he spotted two problems, one major, and one not so major but still requiring attention before he took to the water again. The anchor hardware on the bowsprit had suffered when the anchor went overboard during the storm. When the anchor had hit the water and pulled Starry Sea around—a stroke of luck which undoubtedly saved his life—tremendous pressure had been exerted on the rode. It had pulled so hard that a portion of the stainless steel fairlead had warped, and the metal plate bracing it had buckled so badly that the metal was partially torn; a jagged edge now exposed which could chew through the rode. But that could be easily repaired.

The more serious problem involved the mast. Without a scatter of sailcloth to obstruct his trained eye, he quickly discerned the mast boot, where the mast met the deck, was cracked. Without a fully functional mast boot, the mast would not sit firmly in place. If he were to raise sails under such a condition vibrations would result that could crack the mast, or even the deck itself. The mast boot would require repair or replacement. Unless that could happen fast, it would mean even more time on this rock.

But vessels like Starry Sea were no longer built. He could not simply order the part from a manufacturer. It would have to be custom fabricated, and that would be both time-consuming and expensive. He closed his eyes and clenched his fists till his knuckles were white and the crescents of his nails bit crimson into his palm. The mast was the driveshaft of a sailboat. With mast and mainsail busted, he was doubly crippled. The seaman felt as if his leg were broken.

He reigned in his thoughts and stuffed down his feelings, though it was like shoving hot lead into a pot of water. Within he sizzled and crackled till it seemed he must burst. But he went on with his inspection of Starry Sea, keeping notes on other little things he needed to do to get the vessel seaworthy again. Several hours later he had a list eighty-seven items long, adding to it such things as rebedding a seacock and changing the zincs. Most of it was relatively minor things which could have waited. But he was a meticulous seaman, and men like him were why a seventy-five year old wooden vessel like Starry Sea remained sound and beautiful after all these years. But then, for him, Starry Sea was more than just a boat or a bit of maritime tradition. She was a part of him, his key to the only oblivion that ever brought a semblance of peace to his soul, out among the wind and waves and stretching horizons.

Besides, if he could get the custom work done soon, he need not remain in Man-by-the-Sea all that long. The other items could be tended to at the next port. Perhaps he would reach for Alaska, or Victoria, and put in there to finish the projects. It was as good a plan as any.

He pushed his hands into his pockets and pondered quitting for the day. Battling the storm on the sea and another storm in his heart had given him a beating, inside and out. It was time to rest, sort through his thoughts and try to figure out, once again, how in hell he had come to be here at all. How could he simply have misplaced himself for the weeks it would have taken to sail thousands of miles? That question ate relentlessly at him, and the answers presented by his psychological training frightened him. Fugue. Amnesia. Dissociative identity disorder. Could he be coming to such depths of madness at last? Perhaps it had really been only a matter of time, pre-ordained since the burning of Cerulean.

Terrible thoughts. Terrible thoughts requiring he give them consideration. Even so, if it had been a bit earlier in the day he would have gone instead back to the chandler and sought out a metalworker to start on the mast boot project. But the sun was already westering and the shadows were growing long. Man-by-the-Sea was a sleepy village and the folk called their nights early. Businesses were closing.

He might as well call it quits now. Take that thinking time. Perhaps he would go below and get some dinner going. Or, instead, he could go find that pub, eat something that wasn't dried and didn't come from a can, and slosh down a few cold ones. He had not yet made too much of a mess inside Starry Sea. Later he could stumble back and topple into his bunk in the forward stateroom.

Or you could go there now, he thought. Don't procrastinate, it'll eat at you. You'll wake up in the dark wondering where she is and nightmares flashing in your eyes, nightmares that won't go away.

*Go there now.*

He stood on the deck for a long time, considering, while the sun moved lower in the west. It was true, he knew. If he put it off, it would eat at him as at a raw wound all through the night. He'd be lucky to sleep at all, and he would need to be rested if he was to get the vessel taken care of tomorrow. Practicality forced his hand. He made his choice. He went below, packed a small duffle with a few things, got a set of keys he never thought he would need, and climbed off the grounded little ship. Taking a deep breath, he began the trek up the north road.

It took only minutes to leave the tiny village behind. Beyond it, spread out in the little valley, sleepy farms were scattered over gentle hills, each meadow divided from the next by wooden fences painted bright white or red. The spring snows had only recently melted and the grass was still golden, but sheep and the occasional pony grazed contentedly in the herbage. At the back of the meadows, near the line of the hardwood forest, gaily painted yet practical cottages of trimmed, squared logs sat in the shadows of the trees. They were steeply gabled with wood shingled roofs, and tufts of grey smoke curled contentedly from chimneys of brook stone and mortar. It was an idyllic setting, and it disturbed Sweyn deeply. Aside from the occasional cry of a raven or magpie, or the bleating of sheep, it was entirely quiet. There was no music of water on the hull, no howling of wind in the shrouds, no rustle of sails. The silent peace of the land was eerie to him. Dangerous. It did not shield him from unwanted memories, and he found himself wishing he had visited that pub before leaving Man-by-the-Sea.

* * * * * * * * *

The villagers were nothing if not friendly folk, though curious might have been a better word for them. He had not walked two hundred paces when a wagon—a horse drawn wagon, if you please—carrying a married couple in their mid-thirties and several kids, stopped and the driver offered him a ride. He accepted and the couple brought him up the road a little over a mile till they reached a small dirt path that led left to their farm.

Along the way they admitted that seeing a stranger was a novelty for them. Very politely they asked if Sweyn would tell them a little about himself. He had not felt like talking as the difficult minutes took him slowly north, but politeness demanded a reply. He told them he was a cruiser, a sea gypsy, and that he had quite literally been blown into their island by a storm. "Were you on your way to Alaska before that?" they wanted to know. He shrugged and nodded, for what else could he say? *Er, one moment I was sailing south of the equator, heading for the trade winds below Hawaii, the next thing I know, a storm is forcing me into your wretched coast.* No, better to keep his madness and sullenness to himself if he were to be stuck on this rock a while. But he was relieved when, after twenty minutes, they said they had reached their farm. Sweyn bid them farewell and they asked where he was headed.

"Dundubh Cottage," he shrugged.

The couple looked at each other then, their expressions metamorphosing from open friendliness to something queer and unreadable. Even their pack of young sons, horseplaying in back, ceased their puppy dog tumbling on sacks of seed and gaped at him, faces coated in sweat and dust, blond locks burnished bronze by the low ruby sun. The moment was frozen in time, or at least etched into Sweyn's memory, but the spell was finally broken when the man turned to face him again and said, his brogue thicker even than that of the villagers, "Ye'll find no one at the Laird's Cottage. No one but old Coppin's been in the place since the Lady left all these years ago."

"Aye, eighteen now and more," added the farmwife, whose hair was long and black and drizzled curls over her pale cheeks and half screened her dark eyes. "She was little more than a girl then."

Her husband turned back to her, nodding. "Aye, Fawn, that's the truth of it. Eighteen and a half years now, it's been. And sorry years at that, with no Lady and no Laird to tend the Island or the Cottage."

The couple seemed to share some unspoken memory, and for just a single moment there was a sparkle in their eyes. But then their expressions grew wistful, and the lady said, as if to herself, "A sad story, that."

The man nodded. Sweyn wondered if somehow they had heard of Eilwen's death. But the man turned again to face Sweyn and said, "Coppin's a shrewd one, if a bit odd. But he's kept the place well enough, best as any one man can, I suppose. Though he never goes out off the grounds, ye know. Never to town or the pub, or even to ceilidhs, which I've always thought was passing queer. Terrible lonely way to live."

Long ago, while telling Sweyn tales of the strange Cottage where she had grown up, Eilwen had mentioned Coppin. Apparently he was some kind of caretaker. A bit of a butler, a bit of a groundskeeper. Sweyn was surprised to learn he continued to dwell at the old house, it being deserted so many years. But then, Eilwen had said he was very old and had been there as long as she could remember. Probably the place was as much home to him as it had been to her.

The woman, whose name may have been Fawn, or it may only have been a term of endearment, said to Sweyn, "Ye'll be visiting Coppin then? Never heard tell him having kin. Any at all."

"No, not quite visiting," Sweyn told her. "The place is mine."

This brought a different and completely unexpected reaction from the couple and the boys in back. The color blanched from the adults' faces. The youths, who had been quietly jostling for a better vantage of the stranger, became still as stone.

"Do ye tell me that now?" said the husband then. His voice had gone low and soft. "Ye'll be the new Laird then?"

"Just visiting," said Sweyn. "That's all. Just passing through."

He could see countless questions brimming in their eyes, but the last thing he wanted to do was talk, least of all about the circumstances of his inheritance, so he waved, turned briskly, and started up the north road again. After a minute he heard the clopping of the horse's hooves, the creak of wagon wheels turning. Glancing back, he saw the wagon rolling down the long path through the meadow toward the farmhouse and breathed a sigh of relief.

Shortly, the paving gave way to gravel, and another mile later gravel gave way to dirt still tacky from the recent thaw of winter snow. He trudged ahead, ignoring the mud clinging to his boots, slowly passing other gaily painted farmhouses, but he never gave them a glance. He was lost in thought, for something they had said ate at him as he went. They had referred to the last resident of the Cottage as "the Lady," which could only have been Eilwen, for her mother had died when she was a child, and her younger sister only a few years after, leaving Eilwen as the last O'Shee to dwell there. But "Lady" was an awfully grand term. He knew the O'Shees had held some wealth, but had they been so prominent on the Island? If so, Eilwen had never mentioned it.

He puckered his lips and blew out a perplexed sigh as he tried to make sense of it. Wealth usually indicated influence. His best guess was that maybe, long ago, the O'Shees had been influential, maybe even something like petty nobles. The people of the Island were very traditional. Perhaps they still referred to the O'Shees with titles out of habit.

The shadows lengthened as he walked on, and the sky grew magenta, then amethyst as it deepened into twilight. Around him songbirds crooned the evening chorus. Ravens and magpies picked the remnant seed of last year's harvest from fields recently freed of snow. Abruptly, he passed the last farm and then there were only a few compact cottages scattered along the last mile of road in thickening woods, each with a curling tuft of smoke drifting over a chimney of uncut brook stone. Some of the cottages were built of cut lumber whitewashed with colorful trim of green and gold. Steep gables were a ubiquitous quality of the local architecture. But as he moved deeper into the forest, the construction of the cottages changed. Instead of painted lumber, the walls were plastered and the steeply pitched roofs were thatched, though tarps hung from them in places. The tarps had been used to protect the thatch through the winter, keeping it from becoming waterlogged beneath British Columbia's sticky, damp snow.

But Sweyn kept his eyes on his feet as he walked, his hands stuffed deeply in his pockets, paying no heed at all to the charming cottages or natural beauty. The statements of the farm family continued to nag at him. He knew there were things about Eilwen she had avoided speaking of. It had never bothered him till now. When people lose loved ones, the image they keep in their hearts of the deceased becomes an ideal, precious and irreproachable, but not quite real. But confronting the possibility that his wife had kept secrets from him gave him cause to wonder what might be left of that image after he fleshed out her memory?

Turn back, an inner voice warned. That was fear. It emerged quiet but strong from a dark, unwholesome place deep within. But he determined that nothing could make him love Eilwen any less. Her past was past, and he would cherish the three short years he had had with her regardless of whatever he might discover. So in answer to the inner voice, he pressed on. This was a healing step for Sweyn, a decision of courage he had not possessed the resources to make only yesterday.

As he neared the farther end of the little valley, the dirt path began to wind this way and that, weaving through thick stands of towering hardwoods that looked as if they had stood for century upon century. In the forest, evening shadows engulfed him. Animal sounds and movement of unknown shapes ghosted through the darkness gathering beneath massive boughs. But as Sweyn went, he only looked at the earth just before his feet, unmoved by the beauty or the mystery of the night wood.

**********

*One can dodge the future, but only for so long. One can walk the lonely path through the deep wildwood where no other folk are found, but eventually the future will be found. And it does not matter if the path forks left or right, or one turns round and goes back again. The future is such a beast as cannot be evaded. It is always the destination, no matter where you turn.*

Eilwen had written that not long before she died. Sweyn had come across it as he packed away her journals after the funeral. It was tucked into an entry made only a couple months before the end. More and more, in those days, he had found her looking out their chalet north and west, over the sea, in the direction, he knew, of her Island. She never spoke of it, he never asked her—talk of home was hard for both of them—but he could tell something was growing on her mind. Some waxing darkness, some pull toward the place of her origin. No ferries from the mainland passed that way. No planes flew to the Island. But if she wanted to return to Man-by-the-Sea for any reason, all she had to do was ask. He would take her there himself. He was confident she would speak the wish to him if the time came.

The memory of that was on his mind when he reached a point where the path ended abruptly at a wooden gate, once whitewashed but now the old paint was faded, in places flaking and crumbling away, the wood underneath dark and half-rotted from neglect and the frequent rains along the coast. His eyes were drawn up the lines of the cantered planks of the gate to the hill beyond. The hill suffered a scattering of shrubbery which had once been ornamental but now had gone wild and spread chaotically, so that now the foliage seemed to be frozen in the act of exploding over the ground. Tendrils drooping from bushy branches and shoots from woody runners; the once-elegant shrubs now devoured the yard. Here and there were a smattering of oaks and blackthorns and rowans, dark arboreal silhouettes against the twilight, absolutely still in the calm air. Their boughs spread out over the places not occupied by the aggressive shrubs, and even the smaller blackthorns seemed to guard the grounds protectively, brooding and watchful. In the spaces between shrub and tree, sweet calf-high grass grew, jade in the wan light. The path beyond the gate was demarcated by uncut stepping stones laid down long ago with such skill that each seemed to fit a groove prepared for it by the other stones. So precise was their situation that no weeds grew up between them, and the path they marked wound and twisted its way to the summit of the broad hill, where it crashed into the great hulking dark truth of Dundubh Cottage.

He stood quietly, awed and frozen by the sight of it. And he thought, "Eilwen, why did you never tell me?" But there was no answer, not even the ghostly voice of distant memory. Yet if a ghost should dwell anywhere but a dilapidated graveyard, then this surely must be such a place. It was a fey place, a lonely place, and it reminded him of ancient dreams too misty and cobwebbed to fully recall, of childhood tales meant to send frissons up and down the spine. Perhaps, had he been another man, one not so direly numbed by life, he might have felt wonder at the sight of Dundubh Cottage. But now, as he looked upon the great, dark vastness of it, he felt only bewilderment. For no cottage was Dundubh Cottage. Keep would be more apt. Lair, even. It was massive. In size it could only be compared to an English manor, and a great one at that. A main structure that appeared to be a hundred paces across and three stories high was the central feature. On the first floor of the main structure tall windows with rounded arches and deep overhangs predominated. But the windows were irregularly spaced, as if a blind architect had thrown darts at the wall and said, "Cut here!" One window might be ten feet from its neighbor, but the one after it only a yard, and then nothing but stone wall for twenty paces. The windows were plate glass and all were dark, with heavy curtains behind them guaranteeing concealment of whatever lurked within. The second floor's windows were bizarre round affairs, perhaps three feet in diameter. The third floor appeared to have no windows at all, but narrow arrow slits like those found in medieval castles for archers fighting a siege. A parapet surmounted the flat roof of the main structure, and battlements were set along it. The walls were built of an odd mix of timbers and great dark uncut stones which, like the stones of the path, were fitted together expertly amidst the timber.

Dundubh Cottage had been expanded north and south. On the south side was an addition built of massive square-cut rough timbers laid horizontally. Rectangular windows of traditional design were spaced regularly along the walls. But the windows were the limit of the structure's normalcy. The addition was a full three stories tall. The wood was pale, as if it had not been painted. Perhaps it was stained, or only treated against rot. A great door, at least twenty feet high and rounded above, was set into the middle of the first floor of the addition. A balcony wrapped around the entire second story, providing shelter for a porch that surrounded the entire first story. Antiquated furniture was scattered up and down porch and balcony, showing that once, in happier days, residents of the house had spent much time out of doors, taking their ease in the fresh air at the garden's edge. The balcony was protected by elegantly carved wooden rails, though the wood had darkened and suffered for lack of attention over the years. The roof over the third story was steeply arched and extended far out, providing cover over the balcony. Flying buttresses leaned against the walls of the structure and tree-shaped stone pillars supported the overhang of the roof. Several uncut stone chimneys rose from this addition, emerging from the roof like stalagmites. Set around the outer edge of the roof were statues of strange creatures carved of pale stone. Some were hideous willowy beings with cunning faces. Some were magnificent horses with flowing manes. Some were tall slender nude maidens with mischievous but not unkind eyes. Other creatures there were too, such as could hardly be described, like clouds with faces, and toadstools with eyes, and even images of ordinary seals.

But the extension on the north side of Dundubh Cottage was the most bizarre of all, a great round tower made of stone. The first story met the base of the main structure, fully as wide in diameter as the main house was long. This story was built of carved, local stone, the blocks immense and strong. A dark mortar, the color of elder berries, was worked in between those places where the masonry was slightly less than perfect. But those places were few. In most places the stones had been joined so expertly it seemed nothing more than their weight was needed to fit them together. No windows were visible in this part of the tower.

The second story was similar to the first in construction, though not quite half its diameter, so that it was not physically attached to the main house. It was set off center of the first story, and deep, wide windows were placed around its circumference, curtained with heavy crimson. In the fading light the windows looked out over the grounds like searching eyes, and seemed to contain eldritch secrets behind their ruby irises.

The third story was again a third smaller than the second level, perhaps thirty paces wide. Shuttered windows, slender and high like arrow slits, marked it.

The fourth story of the tower marked the highest part of the house, and it was also the most bizarre, for it was nothing like any structure that should by rights be attached to a house. Great carved blocks of stone stood on end around the circumference of it, nine in all. The stones were dark shadows against the deepening sky. Each stone stood a dozen feet tall, perhaps three broad. Each must have weighed many tons. Wide gaps were open between the standing stones. Over some, but not all, horizontal slabs had been laid. There were five such slabs, two touching each other, the rest scattered around the odd structure as if haphazardly, forming a broken roof. Years before Sweyn had seen the famous Stone Henge while sailing up and down Great Britain, and this structure was clearly reminiscent of it. But this henge was certainly no replica, for not only was it built at the top of a tower, but a great standing stone was erected at the center of it. The central stone was rounded, perhaps a yard in diameter. Black it was, like the spaces between the stars, and it seemed to possess a luminous fire at its heart. It was as if ruby flame had been frozen within obsidian.

He stood motionless at the gate, breath stolen, eyes riveted. A chill not derived of cold possessed him. His skin prickled. Things whispered to him in the darkness of the path, ghosts of memories flittering, bearing warnings in faded voices. And the warnings all brought to bear the same chilling message: his memories of Eilwen were but bones. In their three years together he thought he had known her so completely, but he had been wrong. She had held tight to secrets unspoken, unfathomed, and when the wind blew out of the northwest, bearing the fragrance of the sea, she grew quiet and dark, and her secrets brought her sorrow. He had thought perhaps she had escaped an abusive upbringing, or simply could not let go the place where she had buried her mother and sister. But whatever the real truth was, it was far stranger, and she had kept it to herself, except for one time and one time only, when she had almost opened . . .

Only one time . . .

Don't go there! a side of himself warned.

But it was too late. It was much too late. The great obscene presence of Dundubh Cottage stood like a well of shadow against the brink of night, and its very existence demanded he look beyond the mirage he had thought was Eilwen. Whatever she was, wherever she had come from, her story was far deeper than he ever suspected. And if he should turn his back upon the questions raised by the sight of her monstrous home, he must face a lifelong knowledge that he had never known the woman he loved and lost and spent his days pining for. A sad fate to waste away for only a shadow.

Whatever the consequence, fate had brought him to reckon with the truth of Eilwen.

The dam was breached, and memory overflowed. He seized a gate post, squeezed till splinters pierced his hand, a last desperate ploy to ground himself to the moment.

It failed. His mind tumbled back five years to a night in Glacier Falls when Eilwen was with him and the mere act of living didn't hurt . . .

**********

The chalet was quiet, and only the chirruping of crickets and the lonely call of an owl were born upon the night air. A warm evening breeze soughed through boughs of fir and cedar. It came from over the sea and bore the tang of brine through the open windows, past gently rustling cream-hued curtains. It also picked up the scent of Eilwen's herb garden, dozens upon dozens of varieties of flowers and weeds and ferns gathered from the forest, some of which she used for medicine, some to spice food, and some for blending her extraordinary teas.

They sat in the dim light of a single candle, side my side, bodies touching in the easy way of companions who are long close and comfortable. They had been quiet, sipping infusions of rowan berry and chamomile blossom, birch twig tips and bluebells. The tea was naturally sweet and tasted of flowers and brought a sensation of calm. It made him think of soft feather beds and the steady rhythm of grandfather clocks. Sweyn eased his large hand over Eilwen's small, delicate fingers and she leaned her head on his shoulder. Her hair was red flame, shoulder length and curly, and the silken touch of it on the skin of his neck was like the brush of butterfly wings.

They had been talking, making lovers' plans. Long, peaceful lives. Children. Work. Dreams and desires. They spun their hopes together like a net, and meant to catch only a bit of happiness for themselves. Sweyn wanted to make a new start of his life, doing something he loved. He wanted to take to the sea for a living, buy a sailboat for pleasure charters and to teach others how to harness the wind and ride the waves. He could see no better way to spend his days than upon turquoise waters beneath a warm sun, coming home to his lady by night, and sharing all the moments in between. For her part, Eilwen wanted to do something with the herbs she loved so much, and Sweyn had encouraged her to pursue her passion and start a tea shop. Her infusions were nothing short of magical. They could freshen one in the morning without caffeine, and relax one at the end of day without tranquilizers. He had no doubt that anyone who tried her tea blends would become a regular customer.

Sitting next to her, he recalled when he had first met her in a used bookstore in the San Juan Islands a year before. She had seemed fragile and shy, and more than a bit out of place. Between her brogue and her fey manner, she had the air of a damsel of old thrust into a much jaded era. But as he had come to know her he had learned she was neither fragile nor shy. She possessed an inner fire. Her delicateness was like that of a woodland doe, full of vigor and a gentle strength. He was powerfully drawn to her from the very first. She possessed a sense of wonder and centeredness that he desperately needed, and she was willing to share.

But he could never really understand what she saw in him. When she encountered him he was only a wandering seaman living on Starry Sea. Once he had been a doctor of psychology, but he had become disillusioned with that career. He no longer believed in it at all. Now he was a man in his mid-thirties in a sort of identity crisis, unable to determine his goals or his center. He had asked her, once, after they had been seeing each other for two weeks, what on earth did she see in him. She had laughed and said she liked men who smelled of the sea. That was good enough for him; he would not test fortune by asking for anymore reason than that.

So now they sat on the couch by the light of a single candle, fragrances of herbs and sea mingling in the dark, weaving their dreams round one another till even the owl slept. The deep quiet of the wee hours stole through the forest, and the candle flame flickered in a pool of molten wax. They too fell silent with the night, and for a long time the only language that passed between them was through the touch they shared. But she looked often to the window from which the breeze blew in out of the northwest, and at last he asked softly if she would tell him of her home.

She was quiet so long after the question, her breathing smooth and deep and rhythmic, that he thought she had drifted off. Gently, he put his arm around her shoulders and kissed her fiery hair, pondering whether to get her a sheet and leave her to sleep on the couch or carry her to bed.

Her voice came then like the tremulous sigh of a faltering breeze, breathy like the half-blown note of a flute. "It's a part of me best forgotten." She spoke it like a wish.

Sweyn kissed her brow. His voice was deep and fluid as the ocean. "If you can't go there, I understand. I would like to know you, is all. It's so much a part of you, and I don't understand it at all."

She looked slowly up into his eyes. They were jade and grey, like the sea before the coming of a storm, when clouds scuttle low over it. Eilwen was always drawn by Sweyn's eyes, for they, like everything else about him, spoke of the sea. He was a man, sure enough, but the spirit of the sea was within him. It might be more correct to say he was an elemental, and belonged to water more than he belonged upon it.

He regarded her patiently. If she remained silent, she knew he would say nothing. But, in truth, all he wanted was to know her better. And so she bit back her good sense and told him a little, just a little. He could never understand her world, but this man, who had thrown his whole life and lot in with her, he deserved something. So she began: "When I was young I grew up in a very big house, though we weren't exactly well to do. It was called Dundubh Cottage. The name means the black keep, and the reason for it is unknown to me. Lost in history perhaps, or maybe its kept in the journals of my ancestors. It was an unusual place, but I was happy there.

"I had a mother and a father and a sister, six years younger. Everything was perfect. But then I lost my da. And then my mum. Nothing was right again after that."

"Your parents died?" he asked. "Eilwen, I'm so sorry. I didn't know."

She shook her head. Her slight form seemed to grow smaller. She shivered. "My da left us. My mother died of a broken heart. I thought it would be just my sister and myself then. I was old enough to take care of us by then. But then" (she hesitated) "then I lost my sister too . . . to the forest. There was nothing left except bitter memories, so I left soon after. But I dinna' go peacefully. I despised Dundubh Cottage and the wood all round. It had taken everyone I loved. I hated it so much I might have burned it to the ground. I went to live in Man-by-the-Sea for a time. But it was too full of ancient traditions that tugged at me, for all our folk are drawn in our hearts to the old ways. But I dinna' want the old ways any longer. So I left the Island altogether. I came here. The years passed. I found ye."

She fell silent. Her eyes were round and sad and full of unspoken things. It was only a little, what she had said, and he was hungry to know more. But talking even this much about it had been hard for her. He did not have the heart to press for more. There was time. He would go gently, till she was ready to talk of it in her own good time. For Eilwen, he could wait a lifetime.

But he did not know then just how little time they had. Horror has a way of sweeping upon one so fast, out of nowhere, in the least expected moment.

*********

And then, in the beat of a heart, the flashback was over. It wasn't an unpleasant flashback this time, but nonetheless it left him short of breath, heart thudding, feeling like he had been drowning. He gasped for air and clung to the gate till the world ceased to wobble, his knees steadied.

Oh, how he wished for the waves, for a sail full of wind and his craft beating against it at a heady heal beneath the stars. But such balm was beyond his grasp. Starry Sea was grounded and he was landbound, with none of the things he cherished to soothe his soul.

Around him the still air smelled of hardwood forest and the giddy life of new spring. But the salt sea was in it too. It was a small island, and he could faintly detect the sea at the fringes of his senses. It was one small, precious thing he still could cling to, and slowly he calmed, centered himself. He breathed deep, let the air free in a quivering sigh. At least the memories had not taken him to worse places, to a night of fire and screams and white shrouds.

He regarded the gate as if it were dangerous, then pushed it. Tired, rusted hinges wailed a pitiful protest. And then he stepped onto the grounds of Dundubh Cottage, the legacy left him by Eilwen. It was an inheritance he would as soon have never seen, would have sold long ago but for a promise.

It seemed, when he stepped across the threshold, the night held its breath. The crickets ceased their chorus, the night birds their symphony. For an instant, only a single instant, the leaves did not even rustle with the new breeze just beginning to build in the south. The only sound there was in that moment came low from the north, where a grove of aged apple trees descended from the Cottage right down to the crumbling wooden fence that demarcated the boundary between grounds and woods. It was the sound of steps lightly taken. He turned slowly, expecting perhaps a deer mincing beneath the boughs. What met his eyes was a pale figure wearing a gown of white. Half concealed in shadow, the form was unmistakably feminine even though it was illuminated only by the light of spring stars. The woman passed beneath aged apple trees budding tender new leaves. She ghosted from trunk to trunk, flowing as she went in the liquid way of a dancer. And then she began to sing as she went, the notes sounding as if they spilled from a flute of crystal. His ears caught the lyrics:

*In green glens where flower*
*herbs of bluebell and shrubs of rose,*
*the Lady in her summer bower*
*suffers ne'er when the cold wind blows.*

*The Lady in her summer bower,*
*where a wildwood of black oak grows,*
*conducts from her vasty tower*
*the land no chill zephyr knows.*

*So luminous is her estival dower*
*many a courting laird comes from afar,*
*but Elidurydd in her summer bower*
*bides but summer breath and summer star.*

Her voice was delicate and breathy, like the plaint of the wooden flutes of Ireland. The tune she sang wove up and down, spanning two octaves, and the key was such as he had never heard before. The notes fit no scale of Western music, some seeming to land just beneath where C should be, and some well beyond A, yet others fell precisely into place, familiar Bs and Gs and bittersweet Fs. The melody was the most beautiful he had ever heard, and it made his heart ache to hear it, though the girl was distant, the strains of her song coming to him like pollen drifting on a summer's breath. But the music called to him and he took a single step off the path, only to hear her better. All he could see of her in the starlight was a gauzy gown of white contrasting hair black as the night itself, spilling over a willowy frame.

And then she too seemed to become aware of his presence, for she froze like a doe caught in a spill of light. And he swore he saw her eyes glow, just as a doe's might have. Then she turned and fled into the darkness of the trees, gliding over the ground as smoothly as a boat slips over glassy water, with no other sound but the brief rustle of fabric over leaf fall.

And then she was gone.

And it was dark.

And the crickets fiddled and the night birds composed, and he stood alone and lonely, a shattered man in the many shades of twilight, with the moment of perfect stillness ended. The tune echoed in his mind, bits of pieces, scintillating like dust of shattered diamond, but with the damsel's passing he could not wrap his mind around the whole of it. Only fragments of the lyrics remained, emblazoned in his memory, a small salve for bittersweet recollections.

He stared into the darkness where she had vanished, wondering who she had been? A servant girl from the Cottage? He knew only of the old keeper, Coppin. A neighbor girl, strolling in the night. Maybe. But another thought flitted, unwanted, into his mind. Eilwen had once described her deceased sister to him. "Small and fair. Hair like a raven's wing." But it could not be. Eilwen had said her sister was dead. And when Eilwen had passed away, the deed to the Cottage had gone to him unchallenged. There were no other heirs. He considered pursuing the damsel to learn her identity, but the thought of chasing the girl through darkness repelled him. It would frighten her, and he could not bear that. It was a small Island. He would see her again, surely.

He turned toward Dundubh Cottage, his unwanted house, shattered echoes of the girl's song flitting through his thoughts. And he feared, for deep down inside grew the certainty that his own dear Eilwen had not been the person he had believed, and there was more happening here than he could know.

Don't go there, the ghosts of memory warned.

He did not want to. But the eastern sky was whitening with the dawn, and reality fell apart.

# Chapter Three

*A Manx,*
*A Scot,*
*for sea-god plots*
*Down 'neath the greeny brine-O.*

*Lostling,*
*foundling,*
*paths confounding,*
*And o'er the salty winds blow.*

*A nursery rhyme of the*
*children of Man-by-the-Sea.*

He sat in a comfortable if aged leather recliner in the south wing, the smaller wing of the great "Cottage," and the one which had the closest resemblance to an ordinary abode. The south wing turned out to be the only portion of the house still in use, the only inhabitant of its labyrinthine halls being the old caretaker, Coppin. The spring morning was chill and the little old caretaker bustled about a broad round stone hearth that occupied the middle of a massive den. Walls, floor and ceiling of the den were constructed of pale polished oak, ornamented with sculpted moldings portraying images of acorns and hazel nuts, apples and salmon. The hearth itself was large, fit for a king's hall. Constructed of clay and naturally polished brook stone, it was a full six feet in diameter, but the fire Coppin had built to a side of the great bowl of it was diminutive, little more than a collection of twigs and fist-wide gnarled logs of fast-growing birch. The fire was so small compared to the vastness of the den that it seemed it should have no chance of warming the great room, yet it quickly took the edge off the morning chill.

The old caretaker was hunched and frail, and as he worked he muttered around a long, slender pipe tucked between wiry lips. When he puffed on the pipe the room filled with the fragrance of mint and forest. The old eccentric was smoking sprigs of mint and herbs in a pipe as long as Sweyn's forearm.

Coppin fussed with a kettle suspended over the fire by a cast iron hook set into the mortar of the chimney. While he waited for the kettle to sing, he carved cavities into scones and laid them upon a silver tray. Then he used a tablespoon to stuff a tan sweet cream and jam of local raspberries, bright and red, into the hollows of the scones. When the breakfast was all prepared and the kettle whistling cheerily, he poured water into a teapot and dropped in a mesh ball packed with herbs harvested fresh from a small, stone-enclosed garden behind the house. Sweyn was afraid to ask but he was sure it was the garden where Eilwen used to play when she had been a little girl, and later learned the herblore she had applied to create her healing potions and teas. Indeed, the aroma coaxed from the steeping herbs was strongly reminiscent of one of her special blends. The fragrance was pleasant, but summoned memory so powerfully it almost made him gag.

Coppin brought the tray over to Sweyn and set it on a stool. The tea was amber, the scones golden vessels of jam and cream. He dabbled at a scone, the first food to cross his lips since the day before yesterday. But his hands were shaky and he could scarcely hold the scone. No matter, his appetite had fled and he could find no interest in the fine but simple fare. Too many things had happened all at once, and now that he had a moment to sit back and take stock, he found a whirlwind of impossibilities stalking his thoughts.

Foremost was the nagging problem of how he had come to be here at all. His last clear and coherent reckoning was of floating just south of the equator, drifting idly in the doldrums. Then a wind, strange and cool, hailing out of the east and bearing the fragrance of a northern forest, had come up. He had raised his sails and veered north, toward the equator, no other goal in mind than riding a crisp beam reach for a while. That had been weeks ago. And then came a blur of days and nights during which he continued to sail that same beam wind on a starboard tack. But somehow he had turned slightly east and kept his tack, needing do little else but sit at the helm for thousands of miles while he crossed weather zones where the wind should have blown from the opposite direction, forcing course changes and shifting sails. But the weather had never varied, the wind had held steadily off starboard at fifteen knots all those weeks, so that even by night, when he must have fallen asleep at the helm—something he had never done before in his life—the wind continued to propel him north, ever north, with a slight declination east, until he had been driven to the shores of this time-forgotten island by too much ill luck to believe only luck had been involved.

As if that were not freakish enough, there were other things to eat at him. Along the entire way he had not thought to check his chartplotter or so much as take a bearing from the noonday sun. Without even a glance at sextant and charts, it had been the equivalent of sailing with a blindfold on. Never in his life had he neglected proper navigation, yet in all those weeks it had never even occurred to him. The truth was that until yesterday he had had no awareness of what he was doing, or where he was going, and he had not even given it a thought till the moment he was almost aground on the Island.

Given that, the odds that he should have accidentally made landfall at the birthplace of his wife were laughable. The Island of Manannan was a tiny out-of-the-way crescent in the north Pacific, a needle in a sea of haystacks. Far more likely it was that he had unconsciously desired to come here and steered a course for the Island. But even if he had acted unconsciously, what chance could he have had of reaching the Island without actively navigating? You needed more than just a bearing to plot a boat's course. Ocean currents, wave action, and magnetic deviation would have led him hundreds of miles off course without frequent position fixes and course adjustments. But he knew he had done none of that. There had been no navigation marks on his charts. No calculations in his log. The chartplotter had even been off when he came back to himself. The more he thought about it, the more he realized how implausible it was that he should be here. It was like a nightmare he could not wake up from.

He laid his head in his palms, rubbed his tired eyes, and tried to sort through his memories. He could recall bits and pieces, but it was all broken up and foggy, as if he had gone on a drunk the whole time, but not a drop had crossed his lips. There had been no liquor aboard Starry Sea in months. Even in depression, he had never been much of a drinker.

But at the moment he wished he were a drinker. It would be easier to add alcoholism to his list of problems than deal with the implications of his predicament, for only an insidious mental illness remained to explain it. It was conceivable that he had acted in fugue, set a course here, plotted it, and then threw his notes overboard in a fit of paranoia. He was mad in so many other ways already—depression, flashbacks, violent mood swings. Fugue might not be farfetched. Could he finally be tumbling over the edge? If it were fugue, was it only a matter of time before he descended irretrievably into psychosis?

But a small part of him, less rational and cynical than the rest, could not believe madness brought him all the way here. His only clear memory was of mindlessly riding a beam wind through sunny day and starry night. It had been a perfect wind, an impossible wind, and his gut, if not his head, told him there was some intent in it. But that was ridiculous. He was a rational man, and the wind did not blow with reason. It followed the whims of sun and clouds and waves. It blew where it would by chance and nothing more.

With an oath, he tossed the scone into the hearth. It shattered and some of the crumbs tumbled into the fire where they sputtered into golden sparks. Coppin said nothing, only watched, his expression unfathomable.

The Island. The Island. Eilwen had said strange happenings surrounded it. Was he just one more story in its convoluted myths? A mystery like this so-called Cottage? Part eye-sore, part wonder, it was ensconced in the forest at the end of the valley, an obscene monument to where Eilwen had grown up, lost her family, and developed an enduring hatred of home. And now the place was his. The will had specified a large home in the wilderness. He had imagined some crumbling lodge recessed in the endless boreal forest of Canada, but this was no less than a lord's manor, and despite its weird architecture the place exuded antiquity and brilliant tradition. It was easy to imagine candlelit halls where once regal balls had been held, and vaulted libraries holding lore in leather bound tomes. It was just as easy to imagine sorcerers' laboratories sequestered behind hidden doors, and a torch-lit dungeon rotting beneath the foundation. And the farmwife had asked him if he was the new Laird, as if she were expecting a lord to bring back the Cottage's former glory. He laughed inside at that. Laird? He was a burned out psychologist who hated his profession. A widower who could not let his wife go. A gypsy who spread his bed upon the sea. In truth, he was only Sweyn the Lost. Sweyn the Mad.

Yet still he could not believe mere madness brought him here.

Fugue or fool, there are all kinds of ways to be mad, a hateful inner voice chided.

True.

Yet it was not for fear of madness that he found himself sitting beside the hearth, not cold but with hands trembling like aspen leaves in a zephyr. What really shook him now had happened only last night. If it had happened at all. What had seemed clear and sure in the dim hours of twilight now hung tenuously within his mind like a veil of mist, fading, fading . . . the way the irrational slips the grasp of an enlightened man, if only given time. But in the remnant of memory he recalled the dark haired girl moving through the apple grove by the light of the first stars. In her white gown she had been only a pale, slender shadow, and it was her willowy form, beautiful but believable, that he still held most clearly within his mind. She had sung something, but he could not now recall the melody, only bittersweet fragments of lyrics. She stepped with liquid grace beneath arching boughs, and seemed more ghost than girl. He watched her as if in a dream spun by the setting of the sun. A moment later she had seen him and fled into the trees. He had watched her go, only a moment, then turned to make his way up the hill to the Cottage, but where the sun had just gone down, now it was casting shafts of ruby over the eastern horizon. He had stood beneath the stars the whole night through.

Delusions. Lost time. His mind was falling apart. Here was the surety of it. He had regarded a hallucination and stood frozen, like a catatonic schizophrenic, till dawn broke and he had staggered, dew-soaked, to the entrance of Dundubh Cottage where his desperate rapping at the great south wing door had been answered by the desiccated form of ancient Coppin.

Back in the moment, Coppin ordered, "Drink. Eat." His voice was as withered as his appearance, and it grated in the old man's throat. With trembling hands, Sweyn lifted the mug to his lips and sipped the tea. Yes, it was just like the infusions Eilwen used to make, but it was heartening and helped soothe his frayed nerves. "Ye have the look of a man who has seen the fetch," Coppin observed.

Sweyn blinked tired eyes, looked at the little man without comprehension.

"My pardon," said Coppin. "Ye're no' from these parts. A wraith, a spirit. A ghost."

"A ghost." Sweyn nodded. "Perhaps I have, at that. Perhaps I have seen too many ghosts."

"Ghosts have a way of draining away those who keep their eyes fixed upon them," the old man said in all seriousness, as if quoting some sacred token of folklore.

Sweyn was not a superstitious man, but there was a lot truth in what Coppin said, in a metaphorical way. Persons who could not let go the dead, they became . . . well, they became like him. He took a deep breath and willed himself to calmness by thinking of the sea.

"No' often these days do I get visitors to this broken house," Coppin said. "Who is it comes knocking at Dundubh's door?"

Sweyn took a sip of the tea, holding the mug in both hands, soaking the warmth into his dew-wet hands. "I am Sweyn. Sweyn deSauld."

Coppin sucked in his breath, a brief sound like the hiss of a roiling kettle. "By the Lady," he gasped between clenched teeth. "Ye mean to tell me ye're the Laird." He narrowed his gaze on Sweyn, and it was not easy to say what thoughts flickered behind the slits of his bright blue eyes.

Sweyn grimaced, and a single laugh spilled from him, mirthless. He put thoughts to voice. "I was Eilwen's husband, that's all. She didn't want the estate and neither do I. I haven't come to be your Laird, whatever that involves." After a considerable pause, he added, "Besides, there is more of her in these walls than I could bear."

It was then, finally, that Coppin ceased his bustling, for till then he had been occupied with the comfort of his nameless guest. Good Celtic manners required no less than the best hospitality. But now he gave Sweyn his unbroken attention.

"She was a dear girl. I knew her well, and loved her well. She'd been like a daughter to me."

Sweyn regarded him coldly. Eilwen's feelings toward the little man had been mixed, sometimes fond, often bitter. Because of it, the psychologist within Sweyn suspected the old man was a classic abuser, most of the time endearing, but for tempests of vile temper and violence. Perhaps Coppin had simply been too firm a disciplinarian. Whatever the case, Sweyn was none too concerned for his feelings. It was only out of honor for Eilwen, who had had some regard for the little fellow, that he did not fire him on the spot and send him packing from the Cottage.

"It's odd," said the old man, feelings still concealed behind the blue slits of his eyes, "that she never brought ye home to visit. After all, I'd expect she'd have wanted ye to meet the Island folk, get to know the Cottage." There was a none too veiled message in Coppin's statement: Why had Eilwen never presented him?

But Sweyn, who had never been one to mince words, responded frankly, "I expect she had every intention never to see this place again. She hated this place." He regarded Coppin directly, driving the next statement right at the old man. "She hated everything here."

Sweyn meant it to sting, but if it did, Coppin did not let it show. He merely continued to study Sweyn, his leathery face a cipher. As a psychologist Sweyn had been trained for years in how to read people's every little gesture, every tick and nuance of behavior. He had even learned to decode the behaviors they were suppressing. But Coppin was a closed book, his inscrutability baffling.

A silence descended over the room betraying thickening feelings.

A grandfather clock, tall as Sweyn, began to chime off seven hours. Coppin turned upon the last chime, returned to the fire and picked at it with a brass poker. "I've been with the O'Shees all her days and longer," he said, as if speaking to the fire. "I happen to know her heart was set on Dundubh once. It was as dear to her as sunlight to a flower." He set the poker down, threw in another twig of birch, hard, making sparks dash up the chimney, tracing whorls around curls of smoke. He added, "As dear to her as this rare Island."

Sweyn shot up. There was more to say, to be sure. It burned in his breast like an ember aching to flare, a storm ready to burst, but he dared not say what was on his heart in this moment. If he should release that torrent now, he might not be able to restrain himself. Anger could surge. A flashback might come, or worse. So through clenched teeth he hissed, "I'm off to find a room. Wake me at noon."

"So, ye'll just be staying on then?" Coppin blurted, as if stunned at the guest's audacity at inviting himself.

"Indeed I will. For a little while. It's my house." He gathered his weary bones and set across the immense den, working his way toward a hallway lit only by the light of the sun spilling through an eastern window shrouded by curtains of heavy green. "Let the old villain chew on that," he thought as he made his way through the hallway, looking for stairs.

It was only then that he realized he did not know where anything was in the enormous house. It took him some time to find a room that was even remotely suited for sleeping, on the second story, facing the rising sun. But it appeared more an abandoned artist's studio, smelling of aged oil paint and old canvas. A plush couch was tucked into one corner of the vast chamber, a white sheet having been thrown over it long ago. The sheet was grey with dust. Without bothering to toss the sheet aside, he collapsed upon it, his solid frame causing the couch to creak beneath his weight. But before the springs had ceased their plaint, he was slumbering.

After he was asleep, the door slipped quietly open and slits of bright blue eyes regarded him. Untold thoughts swam in those eyes, but the face they were set in was no longer impassive. Yet the intent in the expression was lost in a muddle of wrinkles and leathery skin that did not seem to fit over the skull quite right. It might have been bitterness in that face. It might have been suspicion. It might even have been something brighter. Maybe it was a bit of all. The morning shadows shortened and the door softly clicked shut, leaving the sleeper alone with unquiet dreams. Coppin crept down the hall, tending the O'Shees' Cottage as he had done for ages.

*********

Time passed on the Island like the torpid waters on the outside bends of twisting streams. In those places, the water runs deep and slow, and lazy eddies spiral along the outer bank, in no rush to go anywhere. All the while, the water on the inner bank flows briskly over hectic shallows, racing downstream to lose itself in an unknown ocean.

The Island was just like that, out of the flow, off in some lackadaisical eddy. Ignoring the headlong rush of the rest of the world, the island spiraled endlessly around where it had been, content with the time proven good things of the past. The fishermen fished. The farmers harvested. Wood made good heat and clay and logs good shelter. And no machine was ever needed to do what a good strong back and a hard day's work could accomplish all the same. So the Island's folk held dear to what they knew and the rush of the world across the sea passed them by unnoticed.

Some might have called the Island's time patient, or even staid. But to Sweyn it was only backward, and he prowled the estate impatiently while he waited for the shipments of the materials he required to repair Starry Sea. His sailmaker had informed him it would take four weeks to get his new mainsail: two weeks to complete the order, two weeks to ship it, for it had to come by sea. And to make sure he never faced such a dilemma again, Sweyn ordered a spare set of all three of his cutter's sails, and an extra trysail for storms, as well as a light gennaker to back up his previous spinnaker, which had grown quite weary from years of the harsh sun of the tropics. The mast boot was a matter for a crafty metalsmith, but fortunately Man-by-the-Sea had several, what with the need to maintain plowshares and fish weirs and the like. In fact, the young man from the chandler was a decent metal worker, and Sweyn had contracted him to fashion a new boot of aluminum using the old, fractured one as a model. That job required complex cutting and shaping, and the youth had previous commitments, but he promised to have it ready by the time the sails arrived.

The real problem arose when Sweyn returned to Starry Sea—which turned out to be a day later than he had planned, for he had slept though the first day at Dundubh Cottage—and discovered there was other damage overlooked in his first tired survey of the vessel. Several timbers halfway between keel and waterline had separated slightly under stress, but the damage was disguised by a crusty growth of barnacles. He found the damage while sanding the bottom in preparation for a new coat of bottom paint and cursed as only a sailor can when he saw it. The clear cause of it was the anchor. When it broke loose of the bowsprit and first hit the water, it had banged viciously into the hull on its way down, gouging and tearing at the thick oak timbers. This was just the kind of damage he had feared, but he knew he was lucky the damage had not been worse. It could have sunk Starry Sea.

Now it was clear. Starry Sea was beached well and true. To repair this damage, he would have to find suitable timber, cut it to shape, mold it with steam, and fit it precisely to the hull where the old timbers had been. He had the skills to do such work himself, but it would take time. And to pull it off, he first had to see if the tools he needed could be found back at the Cottage. It was doubtful they all would be there. He would need to order some.

Later that evening he did find many tools in the Cottage's carpentry workshop, but there was nothing for steaming hardwood. That was to be expected. The next day in Man-by-the-Sea (Dundubh Cottage had no phone) he ordered what he would need to fashion a steamer. The equipment would itself take several weeks to arrive, and he could not begin molding the timbers to the hull until it did.

There was nothing to do but settle in and pass the time, a chore that would not have been half so difficult had the villagers not taken to calling him "the Laird." He made it clear he wasn't, but they persisted despite his protestations. It frustrated him to no end. They spoke deferentially to him, and showed him favor whenever he was among them, yet when he turned away he could feel their stares and hear their whispering. He was the outsider heir of the house of the O'Shees, the Laird who was not of their number. He may well have been the first outsider to reside in the Cottage since the original inhabitants first settled, long before Canada was even a nation.

In response to their attention, he showed only indifference. If they wanted to believe him their aristocratic alien, so be it. Neither their traditions nor rustic suspicions were his problems. He merely wanted to carry on day to day, surviving the memories Dundubh Cottage thrust upon him while getting Starry Sea shipshape. When she was repaired, he would depart the little Island of Manannan and leave the people whatever fond memories or resentments they chose to keep of him. It was all the same to him. He only wanted the sea, and its promise of oblivion.

It was on his sixteenth day on the Island that he found himself at the shipyard where Starry Sea and a smaller, thirty foot fishing trawler, stood on cradles of broad wooden beams, supported at the sides by stout poles. Starry Sea rested soundly on her heavy full keel, making her stand significantly taller than the almost keelless, squat trawler. With nothing else to do and aching to keep his hands busy, Sweyn had spent the day sanding away the brightwork on her deck and polishing her fittings, even the hefty sailing winches that sat port and starboard of the binnacle, which he used to control the genoa and spinnaker. The sun was going down and nearly all the old varnish around the cockpit was sanded to the point where bare, bright teak could be seen underneath. He sat up, basking in the satisfaction of sore muscles which comes only after a hard day's work. He stretched luxuriously and dropped the worn sandpaper into a five gallon bucket at his feet which he was using at the moment for a garbage pail.

It was only then that he noticed the unusual quiet that had fallen upon the streets of Man-by-the-Sea. Down in the salon, the Weems & Plath Atlantis clock, an elegant gift from Eilwen on their second anniversary, struck four bells—six o'clock. Around this time of day the village shops tended to just be closing, and the streets were bustling—as much as they could bustle in a small village of six hundred souls—with shopkeepers and their families, and smiling farmwives and their children, all heading home for the day. But today the village was quiet. It was May the first, and as the sun drew near the horizon a sense of expectancy hung in air which had grown chill though the sky remained clear. He reached over for a hand towel lying on the starboard bench and wiped sweat from his brow and face. He smelled of old teak and sweat and the clean sea, an aroma that was pleasant or unpleasant depending on one's perspective. He remembered Eilwen's fondness for his mariner's musk and did not bother to go below for a shower. Rather, curiosity drew him from the deck and he climbed onto the transom, then down a stepladder past the enormous rudder trailing behind the keel. He stepped onto solid earth and made his way into the heart of the village, wondering where all the people were.

He passed several lanes of cozy cottages—some made of stone and some of squared and plastered logs, all whitewashed with colorful trim—till he reached a small park of green grass just south of the main business area. There was a smell like beer on the air, but different, and that was his first hint that there were, indeed, folk about, somewhere.

Then from further down the street he heard a growing chorus of children's voices, singing, their lyrics sprinkled with giggles and impish bursts of laughter. As they drew nearer, he could hear their many steps, marching, marching up the empty lane, and the occasional scatter of running feet accompanied by shouts of fright and glee. He took several paces more down the road till he caught sight of the village's children around a corner. They were all there. Toddlers who could barely walk, supported by older brothers and sisters holding their hands. Young lads and lasses nearly adult, who pranced and glided among the little folk, the girls elegant blossoms in snug gowns of wool, the boys sleek in tight leggings and green leather jerkins. They weaved to and fro among the smaller children, dancing to the tune of a piper, a drummer on bodhran, and a skipping fellow playing a tiny harp held in one arm. The musicians were adults all, though their faces could not be seen for masks carved of hardwood. The masks were of beasts of the forest and the hunt: the bodhran player a stag, the harper a hound, and the lithe female piper a swan. They led the procession of running children and skipping, dancing adolescents up the main street in his direction, and between them wove another figure, so tall he must have stood on stilts, though his cavorting was fluid and so expert it could not be told. He wore no shirt and his abdomen was hairy and tightly muscled so that he resembled some great wild man of yesteryear. Skins of moose he wore round his calves, fastened with leather thongs, and a loin cloth covered his waist and groin. Epaulets of thick deer's fur covered either shoulder, giving his muscular form an even more imposing appearance, and vambraces of boiled, hard leather added to the effect of a wild beast-man of the wood. But upon his head was the masterpiece of the costume, a crown of dark, shiny holly leaves and crimson jewel-bright berries concealing a headdress that supported great stag's horns which rose like boughs of trees from either side of his brow. The horns must have been incredibly heavy, yet the dancing man weaved lightly beneath them, so smoothly it appeared he wore no costume nor skipped on stilts. He pranced and danced up the street as merrily as the gamboling adolescents.

As they came, the horned man leapt from one side of the road to the other, apparently picking houses and shops at random, and as he approached a building, the small children flowed around him like a tide and rapped on doors and windows, shouting, "Acorns for the Horned Lord!" And at each door, after a hesitant moment, adults peered out in mock surprise and worry, and quickly poured handfuls of small, round pellets into the waiting hands of the children. Some apparently were edible, and these the children gobbled down. The rest were pocketed or given by the little ones to the dancing teens while the whole grand procession proceeded up the street in his direction.

A door opened at his side, the entry into a whitewashed tavern of stone and mortar. A pair of large, smiling men and a small, giggling woman stood in the doorway. One of the men held up a cool glass of some dark wort as if waving, and said, "If ye dinna' get out of the road fast, they'll be accosting ye for the Horned Lord's luck. And I doubt a stranger such as yerself would have the token to get but the bad." With friendly gestures they urged him into the tavern.

It was not at all like a seedy pub the likes of which he might have encountered on the mainland. Sure, this tavern held its share of pipe smoke, but the fragrance was clean, minty, like the ever-present cloud of herb smoke which clung around Coppin, and the scent of the ale was somehow wholesome, like home baked bread. Someone pressed a mug into his hand.

The woman, who appeared in her middle twenties, and was all smiling eyes and red curls, clapped her mug to his with a hardy, "Bealtaine luck!" Then she tipped back the wort and took a long, deep swig. The men watched him expectantly. He hesitated, but not wanting to offend the locals, he tipped his back too. What he tasted was not bitter, nor dry, nor like any of the watery beers he was used to from taps at continental bars. This stuff had a flavor like roasted nuts and fresh bread, very slightly sweet. There was no bitterness to it at all. It was a hardy beverage, creamy like true old fashioned root beer. And there was some other flavor to it, some hint of herb he could not identify. He swallowed deep and felt the better for it, and though the brew was served at room temperature he did not mind. It cooled and delighted him all the same. "What is this stuff?" he said after wiping foam from his mouth.

"Sweet ale, ye silly," said the girl smartly, who at her full height stood only to his chin. "Ye never tasted a true brew before, I'll wager."

He could only shake his head and take another deep draught of the stuff as the children came by and rapped on the window and door of the pub. A middle-aged man, portly and balding, opened the door and grimaced as if shocked to see them. In feigned terror he shouted for his patrons to help appease the horde and many of the men came forward, drawing forth little packets from jacket pockets. These they poured into a large brown paper sack which they gave to the barkeep who dispersed the contents by handfuls to the waiting children outside. Some of the little round offerings appeared to be ball shaped confections rolled in crushed nuts; others were clearly acorns, doubtless gathered from the transplanted oak woods that surrounded the village. The children ate the sweets and ran off to bring the acorns to the dancing teens, and in a moment the procession was on its way to the next abode.

"What did they get?" Sweyn asked.

A man beside him, one of those who had called him into the tavern, clapped his shoulder and said they were "just ordinary nuts." But some had been leached of tannins and roasted and glazed with honey and spice, and were eaten like candy. The others were live acorns that would be planted later, after dark.

With the crowd of youths past, musicians at the back of the tavern struck up some wild tune on low whistles and fiddles. Their song sprinted along in the rapid, staccato spirals of Celtic reels, and some adults got up to dance. They formed two lines facing each other, men on one side, women on the other. From waiting baskets they drew holly boughs and crossed them over the space between the lines to make arches for a holly hall. Then the couple at the head of the lines lowered their branches, linked arms, and skipped through the holly hall. At the end of it, they rejoined the lines and raised their branches again, and as soon as their boughs were up, the next couple at the head went through. As each couple took its turn through the holly hall and fell in at the end of the queue, everyone in the lines did a sidewise skip that brought them a pace back toward the beginning. So the queue was in constant motion, each couple skipping from head to rear, then dancing in the lines back to the head again. Sweyn watched them as he drank the sweet ale, bemused, when the petite girl with the red curly locks tugged his hand and gestured toward the dancers.

"Oh no, I couldn't" he protested. "I don't know your dances."

But with firm gestures and tugs, and not a few dire glares, she coaxed him toward the dance, held on a partition of polished hardwood floor the hue of clover honey. The girl led him by the hand, weaving smoothly between standing folk chatting lively over earthenware mugs of foamy sweet ale. There was a fruity, spicy scent on the air too, and Sweyn realized it came from cider of apples and pears. But all the chatter and heady aromas blurred into the background when they reached the dance floor.

The girl grabbed holly boughs and handed Sweyn one, then linked arms with him and led him skipping beneath the holly hall. At the end they added their boughs to the arches. The pace of the dance was fast, and Sweyn and the red-haired girl went through the queue time and again, the girl laughing gleefully each time it was their turn to skip beneath the boughs. Even on Sweyn's grim face a smile finally broke through his stony features. He had not known the pleasure of a simple dance in three years.

Then suddenly the music changed and the holly-hall dancers stepped aside. Ladies wearing short green dresses and men wearing black trousers of heavy cloth and white, loose chemises took the dance floor. They stood straight and tall and began skipping in the way of Irish step dancers. The pub folk made a ring around them and cheered them on. Many gleeful mugs were raised to the step dancers, who responded to their encouragement with more daring skips and kicks and broad, proud grins for the onlookers. The musicians responded to the dancers' zeal by accelerating the tempo. Then the musicians exchanged their reel for a faster jig. The onlookers began dancing again, this time forming a ring out of the men, and the women wove to and fro between them. As each went her way, she selected a partner and drew him into the spiraling center, pirouetting as she led him. At the center of the ring, each man and dame danced round and round till centrifugal force sent them staggering out. It was great fun and Sweyn was drawn into the flow by one fine girl and another, who each smiled and curtsied like a maiden of a bygone era. Sweyn learned the art of saluting the ladies with a florid bow from watching the men.

Another dance followed, and another, and still another, and then a faceless man pressed another drink into his hand, "To welcome the new Laird." But Sweyn said nothing about the title. He was all sweat and motion by that time and was only too glad to down the foamy drink. This time it was far sweeter, a cider, with only a hint of potency concealed beneath the flavor of fermented pear and spice. Another man clapped his back and guided him from the dance floor into a small gathering of gabbing bystanders where he was drawn into conversation of small things: farmers' hopes for the coming year, orders of seed, hopes for the annual salmon run, and "Wasn't Sweyn himself a sailor to know the way of the sea?" Some asked if Sweyn might fish with them come the salmon run. Mindlessly, he nodded and gestured and flowed with the conversation, until, at some moment, it occurred to him these people were other than the dull rustics he had first taken them for. They were keen and transparent. And, most peculiarly, they were happy. Really, truly happy. He had never known the simple pleasure of life they enjoyed. His entire life had been struggle and ordeal, but for the three brief years Eilwen had been at his side. Whatever made these people as they were, it was alien to him. Too much for him. He suddenly felt painfully out of place.

He set down his mug, looked desperately to the exit. He rose without a farewell, the chair scudding back, almost toppling, when suddenly the pub musicians quit playing. From outside, where darkness was descending, came another melody, aching sad, piercing the heart. And there were many flickering lights passing beyond the window. People began to drift out of the pub in little groups of twos and fours. They went slowly, the thinning of the crowd almost imperceptible, yet shortly the pub was all but empty, and Sweyn found himself alone at the table where moments before he had thought to make an escape from the endless chatter of the farmers and their wives. It seemed he might have, in only a moment, the solitude he had craved seconds ago, but suddenly it made him sad. He did not know why. But then the girl with the red locks was there, and she placed a hand on his and beckoned him to follow. He did not mean to, but he found himself accompanying her into the street. Just left, up the brick road leading north, a second procession all of grown folk had passed, and they carried torches. At their lead were three folk playing Irish flutes, and he realized the grieving music he had heard spilled from their instruments. The girl led him up the road, following in the wake of the adult procession. Sweyn went as if in a dream, but he became aware that more musicians were coming up behind them, perhaps fifty yards back. Glancing that way, he saw three persons, two ladies and a man, playing small harps strung with silvery wire. The instruments chimed like bells as the players plucked the strings, using their fingernails like picks. And where the flutists played a song of darkness and mourning, the harpers played spring sunbeams.

The adults' procession wound its way up the main street to the edge of the village. At the forest's edge, a tiny, arched bridge, just wide enough for persons to pass two abreast, led over a fast flowing little brook. Torches had been mounted on the bridge and every person crossed there, though the brook could easily have been leapt. But it felt as if doing so would be disrespectful, somehow. Beyond the bridge, a dirt path led into Manannan's oak wood. In the night, owls hooted. The thick canopy of oak boughs carried echoes of the brook's babbling—it sounded like voices whispering in the tall dark of the trees. Sparkles winked from the depths of the woods, sparkles that seemed like fireflies, except Sweyn knew well there were no fireflies in this part of the world.

The procession sang songs as they went, in Gaelic, and Sweyn was disappointed that he could not sing along. The songs sounded old as the ages, full of yearning. They found their way to a moonlit glade, and there they halted their march. The children were just returning from the depths of the forest. Bright young faces glowed in the torchlight, smudged by the forest loam. In earth-blackened hands the children carried fluffy pastries which sparkled like glowing stars, and Sweyn could not understand how the bakers had created the effect. Many of the children chewed happily on the scintillating pastries. Sweyn asked the girl where the children had gotten the cakes.

"From the wee folk in the wood," she answered in her crisp brogue, as if it should be plain and obvious.

Sweyn looked back at the children, and realized they had been in the wood planting the acorns. Doubtless the "wee folk" had been other adults who had come out here earlier and left the treats for them to find as they worked.

Logs for a bonfire had been stacked in the midst of the glade, and an old man stepped forward out of the crowd. His name was Fergus, and the girl explained he was their seanachie. He told the villagers a tale, an old, old tale of how the first forest had bloomed out of the first spring. And in that forest dwelt the Tylwyth Teg and faerie kin, and later came mortal folk who would become their friends and allies. The Tylwyth Teg taught mortal folk that when the sun faded in winter, they should mourn it solemnly, for it meant the Green Man was dying. But when the sun waxed again in spring, they should welcome it gaily, for the Green Man had revived. The way to honor the Green Man, the seanachie said, was to seed life and revel in its bounty. And so to this day the folk of Man-by-the-Sea remember the old wisdom and plant the forest each Bealtaine, and live to the fullest, and remember the old tales.

Then the seanachie said something in a brisk but elegant tongue. "It is Mannish, our old tongue," whispered the red haired girl. She told him he should learn it, being the Laird. For now, she explained what he said. "It is a blessing upon spring. And a farewell to the dark time, when the Green Man died. The words are very old. They say we learned them from the druids, who walk the wood no more." The horned one must have been standing in the shadows of the oaks, for he materialized into the light of the torches as if out of air. The bonfire logs, of elm and holly, had been well oiled. Four men, wielding bows armed with black arrows that had been dipped in pitch, lit their arrows with matches and shot them into the logs from four directions: north, east, south and west. Flame rushed up in a bright flash, momentarily blinding Sweyn. When the brilliant afterimages faded away, the horned man had vanished.

Then people hugged one another, and children ran to parents to show them their glowing faerie cakes, and tell them of their adventures in the night wood. And then, it now being after midnight, weary couples and families drifted from the forest, leaving Sweyn to guard the remnants of the fire as if it were his lairdly obligation.

And so he stood alone by the dying embers of the fire, pondering. Never in his life had he seen anything like this. It left him feeling full, and it left him feeling empty, and at first he did not understand the queer sensation. Then it came to him that he felt as if he had just discovered something he always should have known, but never did. The realization made his heart ache deep within. He leaned against an oak at the edge of the glade and watched the fire burn down until it was smoke and ash fading into a lavender dawn.

The strangest thing was, for the first time ever since the passing of Eilwen, he felt something other than sorrow. He felt . . . right. He did not understand it and it frightened him. And in the wake of that fear, at the back of his heart the direst memories threatened to break like a storm. He wanted to run from them, as he always had, lest the flashbacks take him again. But where had he been running to all these years?

Here, an almost-voice breathed in answer to his unspoken question. It sounded like Eilwen's hushed whisper. He was almost tempted to turn and try to see her. But she was dead, and to look for her was to descend into madness. Ghosts did not walk the earth. No, the voice was from within, his own wishful thinking.

Besides, Eilwen would never tell him "here." Not "here." Eilwen had hated "here."

# Chapter Four

*"They say a ghost comes as a wisp or a shadow, to haunt with cold sweats and dark wails. But I, who have told many tales, say ye may know a ghost by the force of its presence, and the shaping of its purpose."*

*Fergus Kilwillie*
*Seanachie of Man-by-the-Sea*

He stood upon the prow of a handsome sailing yacht, not his Starry Sea, but elegant and winsome all the same. Her lines were full and swept, her hull cutting deep into the sea and tapering to a stout keel. Her shape was traditional, a fine boat that could keep to its feet in a storm. Her deck was all of dark wood, and much beautiful brightwork of stainless steel and brass and smooth-sanded teak gleamed in the noonday sun. A fresh wind whipped cool salt spray from the waves, scattered it lightly over him, like gems of cold in the summer heat.

The little ship was ketch-rigged, and she proudly flew all her sails, but each was reefed so as not to overpower the craft, for the breeze had continued to stiffen all day. The tightly sheeted sails shone like dazzling white wings against the slate sky, and they were filled out elegantly smooth, their leaches so perfectly tensioned they did not so much as rustle. Their telltales streamed straight back, testifying to the skill of the sailor who had trimmed the sheets. He looked back to Eilwen and smiled. She was turning into quite the seawoman.

Now Eilwen stood in the cockpit, holding a traditional wooden wheel a full four feet in diameter by the handholds mounted around its circumference. Her brow was furrowed in intense concentration as she balanced desired course against the whims of wind and sea. Off the bow, to the north and east, the metropolis of Seattle gleamed glassy and grey in the early afternoon sun. They were making for the city on a tight close reach. The little ship heeled steeply away from the wind, and always felt precariously close to rolling. But there was no danger, the heavy-keeled craft would hold its own easily in this minor blow.

They were completing a sea trial and had found this vessel to be all they had hoped for. At a full sixty feet, she was far larger than Starry Sea, but she was fast, nimble and more forgiving, a good ship for the novices who would ride her. When they returned to the docks of Seattle they would buy her. This little ship, to be christened Cerulean—a name Eilwen had chosen—would be Sweyn's living. He had been certified as a captain and they planned to open a charter business with this vessel.

And after they had closed on the boat, they had other business waiting in Seattle. In a few days they would meet their lawyer and complete the purchase of a small cottage in the woods on the outskirts of Glacier Falls. The cottage was a delicate, cozy affair, high gabled with boxed herbs beneath the windows and half wild lilac scattered round about its tiny yard. Vines grew up its stone walls, and great cedars sheltered it, so that the place—yard, cottage and all—seemed on the verge of being swallowed up again by the rainforest. Eilwen had loved it from the first, said it reminded her of home. This fairytale cottage in its sylvan setting would be perfect for Eilwen's tea and herb shop. The previous owner was an elderly matron who desired to move to warmer climes south, and she and Eilwen had already sealed the deal with a handshake. Eilwen had even already begun redecorating it. As far as the ladies were concerned, the deal was done. Only the signing of some papers waited to make it official.

So the coming days held exciting things. They would undertake new careers together, as a couple. For the first time in their lives, they would make livings of their true passions. And Sweyn took this as a good omen, for the changes symbolized leaving their old lives behind, and starting new ones together.

He walked back to the helm and poured a cup of tea from a stainless steel thermos, offered it to her.

"Want me to take over?" he asked?

She shook her head, her untamable ruby locks flailing in the wind. "I'm having fun," she said. Her eyes twinkled.

He fell into the starboard side bench, the side to which the boat was healing. Near him the sea foamed as the boat flew smoothly over it, cutting the waves, breaking the water into tracks around it.

Something had been eating at Sweyn that afternoon, an old issue that resurfaced from time to time. He contemplated it over Eilwen's cup of tea. Discussing it never went well, but everything was so perfect today. Maybe Eilwen would be in more agreeable spirits this time. "We're on a northerly course," he ventured after he had finished half the mug.

"So?"

"So, maybe after we pay for this old lady," he tapped Cerulean, "we should keep on going."

It was a sore point in their relationship and no matter how he broached it, it always had the same effect on her. She took a deep breath and set her eyes firmly on the prow, as if narrowing her attention to the point where Sweyn and everything but the prow and the seaway directly before it was outside her scope of awareness. Unmoving, except for the slight adjustments of her hands on the helm, she stood for a long time. Miles of sea flowed past. At last Sweyn sighed, tossed the now cold dregs of the tea overboard, and made to rise. But then Eilwen spoke, stilling him. In a flat voice, she said, "If ye must go north, we'll plot a course to Alaska. We can sail straight for it and be there in twelve days."

He regarded her, struggling to decipher the hidden things churning beneath her mask of concentration. But he could not. When Eilwen chose to tune him out, she blocked him out too. Finally, he said, "Eilwen, we've been married a year now, and I've never even seen where you come from. I don't know anything about your home. It doesn't seem right."

"Ye're none too fond of ye'r home either," she pointed out crisply. "I dinna' bother ye to go there."

He thought her brogue, even half washed away with years of American living, was enchanting, and when she grew upset it became all the thicker. Sometimes he was tempted to tease her in order to bring it out. But she had a point. All that was left of his home was his father, and he and his father were volatile, best not mixed. Still, she had at least met his father once, and seen Sweyn's hometown. He had never even seen her island, nor did he really know anything of her family or friends or past. It was like she had no life prior to him. And she was determined it should stay that way, which just wasn't fair. Somewhat frustrated, he replied, "Eilwen, you know we can visit where I come from anytime."

"So let's turn south then. We'll buy the boat and make her maiden voyage to Oregon."

He exhaled loudly, rubbed his brow. The debate was over before it had really even begun. But he was still not quite ready to give it up. "I'd really like to do this, Eilwen. Man-by-the-Sea, it's part of you. We've known each other all this time, but sometimes it feels like I don't know you."

Her mood softened. She could never stay mad at Sweyn. "Are ye saying the great Dr. Sweyn canna' figure out a simple country girl?" she ribbed.

"A simple country girl, you aren't." However remote, however bucolic, her home, there was nothing unsophisticated about Eilwen. "I'd really like to know what kind of village in the sticks can churn out such a fine lady as I've had the good fortune to meet. For that matter, I'd like to know what kind of place in North America can churn out folk with a fine Scottish brogue."

"It's no Scots brogue," she said. "It's Mannish. Unique to my island. Trust me, it's different from what ye would hear in the Old World."

He recalled a small rhyme she had taught him once, a bit of local verse contrived to help Island children remember their history:

*'Of all the Celtic folk we be,*
*last of five clans westerly.'*

His thoughts wandered. "It's odd such a colorful place as your island isn't well known. You'd think Manannan would have become popular with the tourists, with all that Old World charm."

She glanced his way, said, "If the tourists found it, it would lose what it is. It would become just be another exhibition. Mannish folk know this. They value that they've been overlooked by the world and consider it their good fortune."

"Well, Eilwen," he pressed, "I'm not the world. I'm part of you. That makes me part of Manannan."

The change that came over Eilwen was unexpected and instantaneous. She was a small woman, with great guileless doe eyes and a natural, sweet set to her mouth, but in the instant Sweyn uttered his pronouncement her entire aspect changed. Her eyes took on fire, her jaw clenched hard. She seemed to grow, not in stature, but in presence, as if reality itself were suddenly swirling into the vortex of the storm of her emotions. She turned and faced him directly, all charm lost to a dangerous and seething feminine outrage. "Dinna' say that!" she commanded. "Never, ever say that!"

The vehemence of her reaction stunned him, hurt him. He stared at her in shock.

Through clenched teeth, she hissed, "Ye'll never be part of Manannan. It'll never happen." But in another instant she changed again, and the dangerous shadow vanished as if it never were, and Sweyn wondered if he had imagined the whole thing. But her eyes testified otherwise, things still lingered behind them. Things he could not, though he tried desperately, understand. She looked ahead again, to the prow, but he knew she was not seeing what lay ahead. She saw something behind her, something dreadful and old, and not yet distant enough. She would never talk of it, but her eyes held anger and fury and hurt all at once, and then she closed them and summoned strength from somewhere deep, and when she opened them again whatever unwanted recollections that revisited her were gone. Now she looked only at Sweyn, regret softening her features. "I'm sorry," she said.

He nodded and accepted it. He always did. It was not yet time; she was not ready. One day, perhaps. He could wait.

That night Cerulean was theirs, the deal sealed, and they had celebrated by painting her new name on her stern straightaway in sloppy, quickly scrawled letters of water paint that would dissolve easily away back in Glacier Falls when Sweyn did a professional job of repainting and refurbishing the old boat. But for now it was dark, and they were tied up to a peer in Seattle. They sat in the cockpit having dinner together on the table that, when not in use, folded down into the binnacle. Overhead the sky was clear and black as pitch, except for the glimmer of a few bright stars that braved the wash of orange city light. They ate simple fair of flounder and chips and washed it down with wine.  Meandering up the companionway from the speakers in the forward stateroom, the soft notes of something classical flowed around them as gently as the harbor wavelets lapping the hull. The Moonlight Sonata.

They were halfway through their meal, chewing slowly and in silence, enjoying each others' quiet company, when Eilwen's eyes took on that distant look, not the twinkle they acquired when some clever scheme entered her thoughts, but the hollow cast that marked when she glimpsed back into her unclear past.

She set down her fork and knife and said in a small voice, "Sweyn, do ye love me?"

Immediately, he nodded. "There's no question."

"Then please, if ye love me, dinna' ever ask to go to Man-by-the-Sea again. It's no' a place I would wish upon ye."

But why, he wanted to ask. Sometimes she talked about the village and the Island, and she spoke of them as though they were dearest to her heart. And on some nights she told tales of the strange history and old legends surrounding her remote home, and her stories sent pleasant frissons up both their spines. Brightly she spoke of the Island's many unusual personages, who managed to preserve a way of life centuries dead elsewhere. Yearning filled her reminiscences at those times. A deep abiding homesickness came through her words. But there were other times she refused even to mention the name of the Island of Manannan, and would brook no reminders of its existence. The paintings she had created of its little village and fields and farms and forest came down from the walls, vanished into the attic, and she swore she would never give the Island thought again. But as if the Island called to her, always, in time, the pictures reappeared on the wall, and Eilwen returned to her teetering balance of love and hate for her remote home. Yet in this moment she was so intense that he could only nod. Though he was hungry to understand the mystery that was his wife, in this instant she appeared so small and focused and . . . afraid . . . he could do nothing else but agree. Could not even recall why he wanted to go to her island.

She leaned across the small table. Her voice was only a hushed whisper now, as if she were afraid something might overhear her words, take them away, and somehow shape them against her. "Do ye believe in magic?" she asked him.

It was absolutely the last thing Sweyn had expected her to say. He cocked his head to one side, his left eye half squinting, his right eyebrow half up, his own unique expression of perplexity. "I . . . I guess I've never thought about it."

"Well, I'll think on it for ye. It's everything in the fairytales," she went on. "It's all sparkles and enchanted woods and faerie glitter." She grew silent and looked around behind her, into the inky waters of the night time bay, full of the silver and orange scintillating lights of the city beyond the pier. "And it's dark too. It's glamour. It gives ye hope and then it steals away what ye hold most dear." She looked back up at him, and her dark eyes were full of phantoms and shades. She was now quite the opposite of that fighter upon the waves he had glimpsed this afternoon. Now she was only a girl, small and afraid. And she continued to glance at the water, as if searching for hidden movement. Her voice dropped even lower, so low he strained to hear her across the small space of the tiny table. "Never ask me to take ye to Man-by-the-Sea. Ye could no' guess what I've lost there. I will no' lose ye, too, no matter the cost."

It was a strange thing to say, an enigmatic thing, and he could not imagine what could possibly frighten this strong woman so. But in this instant, she didn't look strong. She looked only like a lost child, and he felt compelled to comfort her. "I'm not going anywhere, Eilwen," he assured her. "I promise."

That was the last she had spoken of her distant island home, the last till the final year, so near the end. When the letter came.

*********

His eyes flew open and he rolled violently off his makeshift bed, gasping, that drowning feeling again, grasping furiously at sweat-soaked sheets. The dream memory had faded and another had filled the emptiness. A familiar nightmare that always took him by surprise no matter how many times he relived it. It threw him back to a nameless day, a night when breath failed in fire and black brine. He cried out and gripped a sheet mightily, unaware of what he clawed in his fists. In a desperate rage, he tore the sheet in two. It ripped loudly, and the echo of his cry rattled in the small room, the former art studio with its big sun window which he had claimed since that first night as his private domain in the great Cottage. The sound of his own tortured voice launched his consciousness into the moment, and the nightmare stole away, leaving only a wake of chills, and the pain that never fully quit, even hours after the vision faded. He leaned his head on his forearm and draped himself at the edge of the couch. As always, the flashback left him spent, empty of everything but a gaping wound that could never heal. And there he moaned. It felt as if it echoed within, as though he were hollow. For what was left of him inside without Eilwen?

***********

Breakfast was a wholesome affair, yet he had no appetite. Coppin had boiled a kettle of porridge, laced it with honey and bits of apple. A bowl had been set out for Sweyn and he dabbled at it with a wooden spoon but could not down more than a mouthful after ten minutes. He did manage three cups of tea, however, strong and creamy, sweetened with honey. When he finished his last cup, he set the empty mug down on the counter in the cozy kitchen, warmed by fragrant birch wood still smoldering in a grate centered against the outside wall.

Muttering quietly, Coppin collected both their bowls and his own great mug and put them in the sink. Then he walked to the door. He was wearing great trousers of course homespun wool, a green shirt of flannel, and enormous leather boots—dressed for outside work. Coppin turned to the seaman.

"Are ye coming?" he said.

"Where?" Sweyn said, flatly.

"Well, it seems ye've made yerself at home," Coppin said, and there was something mischievous in his eye. "If ye're to be the new Laird, ye've got some learning ahead of ye. There's lots to look after on the estate, and it's high time someone else tended to it. Since I was left alone here, it's more than I can manage to keep up the lands and the Cottage."

"We've had this conversation before," said Sweyn, as he worked stiffness out of his joints and prepared himself for another hard day renewing brightwork on Starry Sea. "I'm not your Laird. Eilwen never wanted the estate, and neither do I. I'd sell it now except for a promise."

"Ah, sell it if ye will," said the old codger. "Ye'll be hard pressed to find a buyer at any price. Others have tried, but the place has a habit of staying in O'Shee hands. That's its geas, ye see."

"Geas?" Sweyn repeated the word slowly, as if marking it and committing it to memory. He had heard Eilwen use the term before, knew it was important to the folk of the Island, but he did not understand it. He said to Coppin, "What does it mean?"

"It is an old word," Coppin replied. "Ye might call it luck, or destiny. I think some would call it karma. But the geas is no' karma. Karma canna' be broken. A geas can, though he who would violate a geas risks its recompense."

"So, the geas is doom," Sweyn said, thinking he had pinned another tired Manannan superstition.

"No' hardly!" the servant piped. "No doom. It marks ye for who ye are, or who ye are no'. And so it serves as a guide. Ill fortune comes natural to one untrue to himself, and thus to his geas. But luck comes natural to one who follows his true self. Ye understand?"

Sweyn shook his head, said simply, "No."

"Good, good. Now come, for Laird or no, it's yer estate now, as ye've pointed out enough." Coppin gathered a pail and an oil lamp and indicated Sweyn should do the same.

Had Coppin been a younger man, Sweyn would have stood for none of his shenanigans, and set him straight on the spot. But he knew enough to respect the old—even the old and half mad—and gathered another pail at the door and followed Coppin into the brisk dawn. If dawn it could be called. It was still dark outside, and the only hint that dawn was coming was the first fading of the night over the mountains east of the vale.

They walked out back of the Cottage and over a hill, down to a barn set far back in the meadows. The barn was a single story affair, though expansive. It was built of vertical timbers painted white, the paint untended and peeling. A roof of thatch was spread over steep faded green gables. Vertical posts marked the corners and these were painted the color of tree bark, a surprisingly tasteful combination, reminiscent of the building style of an earlier day in lands faraway.

But surprisingly they passed the barn and Coppin led Sweyn still further back, past a chicken coop, and a large pond that was home to domestic ducks and apparently fish, for a silvery form leapt from the water and splashed smoothly back into it, leaving dilating circles in its wake.

"We're not going to the barn?" Sweyn asked.

"We are going to a barn, lad, but the building ye passed is no barn. It's a malt house."

"What's a malt house?"

"And ye from the big city and know nothing of a malt house!" Coppin gasped as if every school age child ought to know what a malt house was. "If this is to be yer place, ye must at least know some of the important things, for the worts of Dundubh were once the most desired of the Island, and it was the worts more than anything else that supported the old place. But no one has brewed them in many years. No' since the last O'Shee man left, and that's been . . ."

But Sweyn finished for him, "More than a quarter century. I know. I've heard the whole sorry tale, long ago, from my wife's lips. Your precious O'Shee man left Eilwen fatherless when she was a child. Left her in the care of a weak and scatterbrained woman who did nothing but pine away after her unfaithful husband."

The old man rounded sharply on his heal, a finger pointed square at Sweyn's chest. "Now dinna' ye go insulting the Lady of this Cottage like that, sir! I dinna' care if ye be the Laird or the shepherd. The Lady and Laird suffered hard times, and mistakes were made. Sore mistakes, aye, but nothing more. No ill was ever meant."

"Yeah," Sweyn said, the blood rising to his face. "They made mistakes. And a fourteen-year-old girl was left to pay for them. I guess it was just too bad for Eilwen, wasn't it? One of those things. Just a mistake."

"Things are different here," Coppin said as he turned away from Sweyn and continued up the path that led over another hill, moving with a stiff, brisk stride now. His voice descended to a rasp. "Age means different than it does on the mainland. Fourteen years old here is nigh a lady for a lass, just as it was in the old times."

"I have important news for you then, Coppin. These aren't 'the old times.' And fourteen is a child anywhere. Only backward hicks could fail to understand that."

The insult was biting, and Coppin's pride was sorely wounded. He wanted to retort badly, set the young fool in his place. Sweyn knew nothing of Man-by-the-Sea, neither its people nor its ways. But with age—and Coppin was very old indeed—comes discretion, and he chose to set aside the dispute. Sweyn might have been ignorant, but he was stone-willed, and if a fight was begun, a man such as Sweyn would stay it through to the end. Best not to have that, for the Island did need a new Laird—indeed and sorely—but not this one. It was a mistake this man was here.

Coppin kicked a stone as he walked, sending it flipping off the beaten path. The problem was, by rights, Sweyn should be the Laird. But if it had been Sweyn's geas, wouldn't Eilwen have returned with him long ago? He wished she had. Had she done so and not turned her back on her own geas, ill fortune might not have caught up with her in the end. But she had not, and paid the price. And now this man was left heir to the Cottage and all that came with it . . . and it had to be a mistake, for to be Laird there must first be a love of this people and their secrets. But the outsider held only contempt for the Island. Surely the lairdship was another's geas, probably someone from the village who remained yet undiscovered. And as long as Sweyn remained, that person might never step up.

But Sweyn was indeed the rightful heir of the property through Eilwen, and so Coppin was obligated to put up with him and see to it his wee boat was fixed. But all the same, no harm encouraging him to hurry his departure. The sooner he went, the less likely it was he might develop a greedy eye for the vast domain.

So he topped the next rise with Sweyn, biting his tongue. Below them a wide meadow spread out, already greening after the recent departure of winter. While on the continent, the Canadian north was just emerging from the snow, the Island was warmed by steady currents flowing from far south in the Pacific. Winter was shorter here, the warm months gentler and longer.

At the base of the hill was another building, quite similar to the one they had just passed. This one was a barn, however, and beyond it were forty-four ewes and four rams, chewing grass contentedly in the pre-dawn darkness.

"The sheep are out," Sweyn noted aloud. "It's still dark. On an island this wild, there must be predators. Bears. Wolves. Coyotes. Why aren't they put in?"

"They get put in," replied Coppin.

"Well, who let them out then?" Sweyn wanted to know.

"Well, that's hard to say, exactly," Coppin intoned, and skipped down the hill to the barn with a grace that belied his age. "They seem to have a lucky way, when no shepherd's to be had, finding their way in and out as they need." Coppin put his fingers to his mouth and whistled. The sheep lifted their heads to his call, and then, to Sweyn's amazement, began jogging up the meadow in Coppin's direction. No sheep dog or shepherd prodded them.

"How long's it been since there was a shepherd here?" Sweyn insisted on knowing.

"Well, that, hmmm." Coppin put a hand to his chin and tapped it theatrically, as if thinking long and hard. "Not since old Ciaran passed away. I think that was, what, fifteen years ago."

The sheep gathered now at their shins, jostling to be close to Coppin.

Sweyn exclaim, "You mean to tell me these sheep have had the good luck to find their way in and out of the barn and look after themselves for fifteen years! Would you give it up and make sense?"

"Oh, aye. I am making sense. And they've all been eaten by wolves and village folk many a time." He sounded serious. Then he scrounged up a weatherworn stool from the barn and sat on it, called a ewe over with a low, warbling whistle. He milked the ewe and a few minutes later he was done. He gave another whistle, this one slightly different. Each sheep seemed to know its whistle like a name and responded to its call, and he milked each ewe in turn. He went through five while Sweyn watched. Coppin paused milking after each ewe to dump the full pail into the twenty gallon tub of a milk cart. Then he sat back at the stool with the empty bucket. "Will ye be helping out then, or just gawking the morning away? After all, it's yer Cottage, yer estate, as ye like to say. And these here, well they're yer sheep, now how's that?"

"Help you?" said Sweyn, at a loss. "I don't know how to milk sheep."

"Well, now's as good a time as any to learn, do ye no' think? Unless ye figure to go into the village and find us a new shepherd, as a good Laird ought."

"Fine," he growled. Sweyn went to the barn and found another stool, returned with it. He set his bucket in front of him and tried to entice a ewe to come over.

But they scattered from his strange whistles, darting skittishly around the corner of the barn, and sometimes behind Coppin.

Just then, the old servant rose and poured his near full bucket into the great tub in the cart. He covered the tub and grabbed the cart by the handles. With strength that belied his aged, stringy form, he lifted the back end and began pushing it up the hill, along the path back in the direction of the Cottage. "We've always sold sheep milk too, to the cheesemakers of the Island, ye know," he said over his shoulder. "Of course, we've been out of business now these many years. Since Eilwen left. Now that yer here, I guess we're back in business. I'll just be leaving it to the rightful Laird, then. There is another milk cart in the barn."

And with that he left Sweyn protesting behind him. Over the hill, Coppin snickered. He thought, "A few days' heat and sheep teats and he'll tire of the place, right enough. Then it won't be so attractive, staying at the estate."

And if tending those sheep was not enough to drive the shiftless mariner away, there were the groves, and the hay fields, and the grain fields, and the malt house, and all the rest of the estate's industries. Coppin was willing to wager the outsider knew nothing of farming, and had even less patience for it. It would gall him and defeat him, and in the end he would grow frustrated and leave. That would prove he was right, and the outsider was not the rightful laird. And then, at last, whoever the geas had chosen for the lairdship could step up. The geas had a way of seeing to such things. Still, no harm in helping it along.

He felt so good about his plan he whistled as he went, a brisk tune like one of the reels from Bealtaine night. And the tune had the added benefit of drowning out Sweyn's shouted pleas for help.

*********

The morning grew old and the sun waxed high, until the chill of the previous evening gave way to the dulcet air of spring. In the house it was comfortable, and beneath the boughs of the apple grove the shade was cool and inviting. But at the base of the hill, at the foot of the barn, where the sun shone down bright and strong, it had grown balmy. But contrary to Coppin's expectations, Sweyn did not come staggering back, defeated, to the Cottage, his face flushed and sweat soaking the barrel chest of his T-shirt and long, prematurely salt and pepper locks. "No matter," thought the little codger aloud. "So the mariner is stubborn. By day's end he'll be in and famished and sore, and sure the whole place is more trouble than it's worth."

But Coppin did not know Sweyn well. A challenge, any challenge, only set Sweyn's mind to defeat it.

Out in the field Sweyn worked tirelessly. At first he tried to catch the sheep, who's fleece was remarkably bright despite the neglect Coppin claimed they had endured for a decade and a half. But the sheep were fleet; they evaded all his tricks. They would gather round him and chew the greening grass or their cud, never giving him a glance, and when they looked sufficiently relaxed and unwary, he would leap for them. But each time they smoothly evaded his ambushes. They would scatter then, like skittish deer, leaving Sweyn panting and frustrated, but soon they would gather nearby again to graze the grass almost under his feet. Sweyn could almost believe they were goading him.

By noon it was true that Sweyn was famished and sweating and sore. He stood tall, arms folded, glowering at the sheep who ignored him placidly. And he kicked dirt and cursed like a sailor. He pulled up sods and threw them at the barn wall. He paced anxiously back and forth. But one thing he was not going to do was give up. He knew what Coppin was trying to do. And he would not let the rascal have the satisfaction of pulling it off. Even though the old man had been right. Sweyn knew he did not belong here. Knew he should let the estate go. But he would not. He had made a promise to a dead woman, and Sweyn never failed to honor his promises. So he glowered at the sheep and puzzled over what to do about them.

They sure enough loved old Coppin. He truly had a way with them. They followed him and came to his calls despite that Coppin, by his own admission, had never spent much time with them. The fellow was a domestic servant, never one to tend the fields but when he had to. So what was his secret? The hell if Sweyn knew.

Sweyn plopped down heavily on the greening grass and rested his chin in his palm, exhausted and frustrated to wit's end. In slow contemplation, he twirled a grass blade round and round a finger. He sighed. A sheep came up and nudged his shoulder with its black snout. He ignored it and continued pondering the riddle of how to draw the animals to him. Another sheep came to his side and began to chew herbs by his knee. Absently, he reached out and scratched behind its ears.

"The old man whistled," he thought very intently. "But such a whistle. The old man could warble like a bird. That takes talent and lots of practice." But if that's what the sheep responded to, Sweyn would learn the trick of it, even if it took the whole summer, just to show up the little housekeeper. He tried again to imitate one of the whistles. It was a sincere effort, but it came out sounding like a gagging robin. "Blast," he swore, and wished he had a cool mug of the sweet Bealtaine ale to slake his thirst.

The sheep on his left lay down at his knee and chewed its cud. He gave it a quick pat while he continued contemplating the problem.

"Mahaha!" went the animal whose ear he was scratching.

"Easy now," said he, and patted it soothingly. And only then did he become aware of them, gathered all around him. Intuitively he understood what was happening. Where before he had been stalking them, not unlike a predator, now he had settled and stilled himself, like a gentle shepherd. The sheep had sensed the change and were drawn to it. It was so simple he would never have discovered it had he not stopped to gather his wits.

Laughter erupted from the seaman. At first he tried to restrain it, afraid the noise might drive the sheep off, but he couldn't. The laugh burst through his defenses, full and loud, but it did not frighten the sheep at all. He suddenly felt giddy and unencumbered. He laughed so much his breath fled, till he fell on his back, staring up into the early afternoon sky, ribs aching and eyes tearing. And, lying there, the sheep gathered round him, looking down at him curiously, nuzzling him with their soft black noses, tickling him with quivering ears.

When Sweyn still had not returned to the Cottage by three in the afternoon, Coppin grew concerned, despite himself. And by four, he could contain his worry no longer. He gathered up a small staff from the back kitchen, worn smooth from long years of service, and started down the path to the sheep meadow. When he passed the malt house he heard shouting from over the next hillock. It sounded desperate. "Blood and thorns!" he gasped, and broke into a dead run, shedding his age and frailty in an instant. He topped the next rise and looked down into the vale, holding the staff defensively, ready to use it as something besides a walking stick.

And down there was Sweyn. The raving seaman was chasing the sheep all about the barnyard. His laughter bellowed, and the sheep before him scattered as he pursued them, bleating playfully. The sheep behind him ran up after him, butting their noses against his thighs, and the lot of them were engrossed in some fool game of chase. Never in all his long years—and Coppin had seen a great lot of them—had he seen a man play so with those fey sheep, for the Dundubh breed were not keen to take to any man, O'Shee or otherwise. And yet the sheep played with Sweyn like children.

"By the Lady," he murmured. "The fool mariner's found suitable company." He shook his head and turned back to the Cottage, quite at a loss what to make of Sweyn.

***********

The gloaming had come, land and sky merging in violet shadow. Sweyn walked in the vast apple grove, and an evening breeze soughed through boughs well into budding. Songbirds sang, an evening chorus to bid welcome to the coming stars. He meandered casually, ignoring his stomach which called insistently for the kitchen. A day in the sun, tending sheep, and then carting the milk load back to Dundubh Cottage, and then a walk around the meadows and groves, had famished him. But he was not ready to eat yet. Too many thoughts churned in his mind.

Last night he had laughed, the first real laughter he had known in the three years since Eilwen passed away and his life had faded into the drifting sea. And he had sung, with people who were open and friendly, and asked no questions of him, held no suspicions, demanded nothing. And he had drunk a mug of sweet ale, and danced with a pretty girl. It had been a moment of joy, and when was the last time in three years he had done anything for joy's sake? He could not recall.

He meandered from the grove to a hilltop in the meadow, and from it the sea could be seen sparkling in the west. He stopped, faced the last shining tip of the sun standing above waters glowing the color of foxgloves. Jewel-tipped waves scattered over the surface of the water like dust of gems. The sea called to him, its voice like a distant siren, and he longed for it to the depths of his soul. Down below, far down in the valley, at the base of the bay, his little ship sat crippled in dry dock on the outskirts of Man-by-the-Sea. He yearned for that ship, to hear the sound of crepitating sails rising to catch the wind, to feel the healing of a strong deck beneath his feet, to sense the flow of water along his keel and ride the bow over and through rolling blue waves of thunder. But that desire was denied him, for the moment, and he was grounded here, stranded as surely as any forgotten seaman upon some unknown isle.

But was it truly so bad a fate? He leaned back against the trunk of a thick apple tree, standing alone atop the rise. He bent a leg and rested his foot against a smooth round knot at knee height in the trunk, slipped his callused hands into his pockets. The day's warmth was slipping away with the sun. He did not mind, it was pleasant now. From the dark, surrounding forest—the ever present forest that sheltered and guarded Dundubh Cottage—came the mellow hoot of an owl, echoing haphazardly beneath the trees.

It was not so bad here, he decided, and the realization was hard. At first he did not understand why it should be so. But it was not so hard to puzzle out. He could begin to comprehend the reason Eilwen had found this place so threatening. It was like a drug. It could so easily get beneath one's skin, into one's soul. This was a place out of time, not quite stagnant, but spiraling round and round about its traditions while the world beyond marched hectically on, ever progressing, but to ends uncertain. On the Island things were staid and sure. The future held the past, and there was no fear of unknown hazards beyond the horizon.

And, oh, there was peace to be had here. And it had been so many years since he had known peace. The sea gave him oblivion, that was sure. It filled him with busy days and the intoxication of wanderlust, things to drive grief from his heart. But peace, no, it had not given peace. Once, perhaps, in another, brighter time. But since Eilwen it had offered only oblivion, and with that he had made do.

But there was peace in Manannan. And the thought of it scared him, for he would no more stay and become this Laird the people expected than he would be parted from his beloved Starry Sea. No matter what anyplace offered, if Eilwen was not there, it was not home. And the only recourse he would accept was to drift away and forget. Forget where she had grown up. Forget the dying estate of Dundubh. Forget even himself upon the waves, for the waves were all that could wash away the relentless memories. And he told himself firmly that that was what he wanted.

But there was peace in Manannan.

It was in that still, fey moment, when Sweyn first knew a bit of quiet in his heart after three long years, that the shadow of a slender young woman was to be seen weaving beneath the curling boughs of ancient apple trees down below in the south grove. Sweyn's attention was riveted the moment he saw her. She did not sing this time, but she wore the same moon-pale gown, and ebony hair darker than the plum shadows framed delicate white shoulders. In silence the girl went, from the edge of the grove to the edge of the wood. And though she was distant and shadowed, Sweyn knew in his heart this was the singer he had heard in the twilight.

"Hello," he called out. But if she heard, she showed no sign. She continued to move into the forest, gliding gracefully over the ground. He bounded off in pursuit of her. "Hey! Hello there!"

But by the time he reached where she had been, she had already disappeared into the depths of the wild trees. He worried about her. What would happen to such a slight girl in the darkening wood? But she must know her woodcraft if she wandered so casually in there at this hour. And it would be wrong to pursue her. So he stared quietly into the forest, his forest, and wondered about the nameless girl. Who was she, and what drew her to the apple grove?

Only the growing night sounds responded to his thoughts, and they had no answer to give him.

**********

Coppin stood at the door of the back kitchen and noted dourly that the mariner had not yet returned, yet he knew Sweyn must be hungry. And that was a sign he was not pleased with. It probably meant the mariner was out wandering, becoming absorbed in the estate. His wrinkled brow furrowed as he pondered where that could lead.

He could not let the Cottage grow on Sweyn. Sweyn had to go, else a better Laird might not be able to step up. The geas was funny in its working of such things. Yet if those sheep took to Sweyn, Sweyn was no wicked man. That in itself almost disappointed the old man, for it would have been easier to drive off a wicked man. But here was a good man indeed.

Of course, he should have expected no less. Eilwen would never have taken up with anyone of poor quality, even if she had abandoned her legacy and her own people. Eilwen, for all her faults, had not been wicked. What she had been was hurt and confused, and, by the Lady, Coppin wished he had done more for her. But when she left, she was in such a state as to listen to no one. Neither the reason of Men nor other things could dissuade her. Still, though hurt, her heart had never become wicked. Could never be. She was good, and she would be drawn to no less than like.

So Sweyn was a good man, and Coppin had to face that. Still, Sweyn could not stay here. He was not the right Laird. Sweyn was an outsider who knew and loved nothing here. His very presence broke all tradition. But Sweyn had proven too stubborn to drive off easily. Coppin would have to find another way, a harmless way, to be rid of the mariner, and soon.

It was time to leave out the evening plate. Coppin held it in his hand. On an earthenware dish was a piece of hearty bread slathered with creamed honey and raspberry jam, and some corners of cheese. In his other hand he held an earthen mug full of a foamy brew, smelling of roasted nuts and rich bread. The wee folks' repast. Normally he left it right here, just off the step of the backdoor.

Maybe not tonight.

At first he frowned at the thought, for it was to break solid tradition. And that was as good as inviting a pinch of ill luck, now was it not?

Hmm. Maybe not tonight, indeed.

He took the evening plate to the back porch with him and sat in a rocking chair. In the growing dark, to an accompanying chorus of cricket fiddlers and haunted serenades of owls, he enjoyed the warm bread and the zesty cheese of sheep milk, and the rich ale. And the very roguish act of eating it made him snicker. Oh, and aye, the little folk would be put out, now wouldn't they? And a little ill luck would come this way. Well, it would be Sweyn's problem, for he was Laird of the Cottage and responsible for all that happened here. They never really hurt anyone, but they certainly had a way of letting folk know when they were put out.

And so in the dark the little old mischief-maker finished the plate and the ale. It was very good, in fact. He might have to do this every night for a while! That thought turned his little snickers into dry cackles, which he tried to muffle with a leathery hand pressed primly over his mouth.

# Chapter Five

*In the gloaming the dark oaks tower,*
*In the oaks the old woman toils,*
*In the toil the sharp herbs flower,*
*In the flowers the fragrant oils.*

*From the oils the savory smell,*
*From the milk the slippery lees,*
*From the blend the fetid jell,*
*From the press the sapid cheese.*

*Herbs and Cheese*
*Oak Peg*

In the two weeks since Sweyn had made his peace with the sheep he had milked them regularly, and each day a boy came from the village leading a pony-drawn cart carrying a number of clear round plastic jugs. Most of the milk, but for a small portion kept back for Coppin and himself, was put in the jugs and the boy carted it back to Man-by-the-Sea. Sweyn had thought for a long time that it was taken to the local market to be sold, and was surprised to learn that it was not.

"There are plenty and enough sheep about the Island to quench the folk's thirst," Coppin told him one day. "That liquor's being carted off for cheese. And on all the Island round, for all the time the Cottage has stood here at the edge of the Guardwood, our milk has been counted the best for cheesemaking."

The thought that his milk was being turned into cheese intrigued him, and he wondered why he had seen no equipment on the estate itself for making cheese. After all, the estate needed to earn to carry on, and wasn't it more profitable to sell finished product than raw?

Coppin explained. "We dinna' make cheese because it's tradition. A Laird has to give back to his people, and the Lairds of Dundubh have done so with their milk. We sell the milk and the folk use it to make the finest cheese. The cheese they can sell off the Island, and so we keep a bit of money flowing in."

"But we barely break even selling the milk," Sweyn told him. "It would be much better for us to make cheese. We'd see a better return."

"Heh," Coppin coughed. He knew the mariner hadn't possessed the makings of a Laird. He had no concept of the give and take that allowed people and Laird to coexist.

Sweyn was sitting at the rough wooden table in the kitchen. The fire no longer burned in the grate at the outer wall anymore, day or night. There was no longer need, with summer fully here, but he missed the pungent fragrance of burning wood. Sweyn went on. "And there's another problem. We're not selling enough milk. It's accumulating and going bad. Another reason why we're not doing well with it."

Coppin hung his head and sighed. He wanted to mislead Sweyn and add to his frustration. But he just couldn't find it in his heart to do it in this matter. Even if Sweyn didn't belong, the mariner meant well. But the knowing didn't make Coppin the less dour as he continued. "The reason we do so poor, and sell too little, is because we dinna' sell to the best market. And the best market is Oak Peg."

Sweyn searched his memory, but could remember no store by that name anywhere in Man-by-the-Sea. "Where do I find that outfit?" he asked.

Coppin scoffed. "Oak Peg is no outfit! She's a lady, and a right sour old bat at that. She lives at the end of the path, the very end, out in the Guardwood miles from here."

"Oak Peg is an old woman," he blurted, the words breaking out in half-suppressed chuckles. "What kind of a name is Oak Peg?"

"A very queer one!" Coppin snapped, frustrated with the youngling's ignorance. "It's three miles to her cottage, as the crow flies. A ten mile trek through the wood with all the twists and turns."

"Ten miles. Well, that's not too bad. I'll go see her tomorrow, before we lose anymore product. Do we keep a horse on the grounds?"

"Ah, no horses," he said as he puffed on his long pipe stuffed with mint and herbs. "We have no' kept horses since the last Laird. And we dinna' keep them now because, as you say, we still have no Laird. And. Horses. Are. Expensive."

Sweyn had grown used to Coppin's crotchety manner and ignored it. But he did not relish a walk of a whole ten miles. "That'll take me the better part of a day," he sighed wearily. A day things need to be done here."

"Indeed," Coppin sighed, feigning disappointment that Sweyn's plan was foiled. "But that's the only way to get down to old Oak Peg's cove." And the moment he said it, he knew he should have kept his lips tight, for the eyes of the mariner lit up.

And so the next morning found Sweyn at Starry Sea. The brightwork polished and varnished, the paint redone, there was precious little to do with her till the sails came, and the equipment to fashion new planks for the hull. But he detached a sturdy wooden dinghy from the davits and lowered it down to the ground. He removed from an aft locker a collapsible dolly and used it to roll the dinghy and some gear down to the nearby shore where he put the dinghy in the water. There he attached a small mast through a center-mounted shaft, ran a bit of rigging, and slipped a daggerboard through a slot at the center of the boat. All set, he stepped in and kicked off from the bank. Around the gunwale custom-made foam tubing had been affixed with a strong, permanent epoxy years before, adding greatly to the tiny boat's stability. He put on a lifejacket, made sure he had a bottle of water with him, and paddled the boat out from the shore a bit. The weather was calm, a mild ten knot breeze kicking up two foot waves which surfed up to the beach. His little tender rolled over the waves as he deftly hanked the sail to the slender mast and raised it, the boom angled so the sail pointed into the wind and luffed. He sheeted the sail tight, sat to windward, and angled the sail to catch the wind. The dinghy responded immediately, skipping at five knots over the coastal waves. Manning the tiller and deftly guiding the mainsheet, an unnamable joy filled him—the ancient exhilaration of those whose souls belong to the sea—as he guided the little vessel through wind and over waves, hugging the coast as he made his way to the mouth of the bay. There he turned south and, hugging the coast, sailed in the direction of Oak Peg's cove.

"The sea!" he sighed. It felt like the lifting of homesickness. How he had longed for the sense of gliding over the living surface of the ocean.

The weather was favorable, the breeze coming out of the west and holding steady at ten knots. At one point, half way to his destination and a quarter mile from shore where the water was smoother and the wind less subject to unpredictable shifts, a little band of Dall dolphins stole up on him. He first became aware of them when two of the little dolphins leapt from the water right beside his boat and arched smoothly back into it, splashing cool salt spray across his brow. Such a welcomed sight! He watched the dolphins when he could, but the little boat was nimble and could easily roll if he did not keep a close eye on her handling. But sometimes, when he was trimming the sail and could see them only from the corner of his eye, the submerged shadows of the dolphins seemed to take on the bipedal forms of men. Only for an instant. It was an odd trick of the light and water that made his skin prickle.

It took only two hours for him to reach the place Coppin had marked on a chart as Oak Peg's cove. He guided the little sailboat in and found it well protected. Within its shielding walls of rock the air was summery and still. He lowered the sail, tied it off, and paddled the last three hundred yards up the flat blue water to a beach of grey sand. He beached and pulled his boat up the sand a little way, then led a painter line from the bow to an oak tree at the edge of the beach and tied the tender off, to keep it there when the tide rose. He followed the beach until he came to a little fall fed by a sparkling clear brook. Beside it, just as Coppin had said, he found the path leading back into the great dark wood. He thought it odd the old lady had not chosen to build her home right on the water where she could have gotten a view of the sea, and easier access to boats from the village coming to pick up her cheese. He stepped onto the path and followed it back into the green wood.

The path twisted and wound, meandering between great boulders called erratics dropped by a glacier ages melted. It followed the course of the brook until it came to a tiny, aged footbridge. Sweyn crossed there and the path departed the brook, leading deeper into the forest. It veered this way and that for no discernable reason, but it was a picturesque path and it led the walker through great airy woods of towering oaks, their boughs spreading high and broad, sporting glossy green foliage through which shafts of golden sun pierced to the woodland earth. The uppermost leaves were caught in the brightness of the vivid sky, glowing like lucent emeralds, and they cast the setting beneath the forest canopy in thick sylvan shadow. Moss hung everywhere, and vines wrapped the broad knotted trunks. Ravens and martins and woodpeckers made a cacophony of song and squawks and rattles above.

After half a mile the path ended at her cottage, and it was nothing like Sweyn had imagined. It was surrounded by a stone wall about seven feet high, made of naturally smoothed brook stone and faded red mortar gathered from the banks of local streams. The walls were wreathed in ivy, and broom and gorse grew all around them. And the walls were expansive, enclosing a full acre. He reached a gate of blackened, slightly rusted iron and pushed at it. It opened easily on creaky hinges. He stepped within.

Inside the courtyard, charming little footpaths of loosely spaced flat stone wove through carpets of knee-high herbs, some sporting blossoms of azure and butter hues, some like sharp blades of grass, others tiny thickets of waxy green leaves. A cottage rose up out of the center of the courtyard as if it grew from the earth, and it was a curious affair. It too was constructed of brook stone. The colorful stones were fitted together with the same pale red mortar as the courtyard walls. Large picture windows adorned the front of the cottage, but they were like dark, blind eyes, for heavy midnight blue drapes hung behind them, revealing nothing. Over steep gables was a thatched roof, but the thatch was a pale green and seemed made of some thickly woven living forest vine. A door of heavy solid oak wood was set off-center of the front of the house. A small porch, supported by knotted shafts of willow, sheltered the entrance. The whole place was neatly kept, but had an air of great age. He could feel it in the earth and the air. The years hung heavy upon the forest cottage. The years and countless green-shadowed secrets. Sweyn—the last thing from a superstitious man—thought it felt . . . spooky. He could not explain it, nor rationalize it, but it felt as if powers and ancient presences abode in the green shadows of this place. He found himself wishing to be out of the wood, back in the sun-drenched cove, sitting safely away from shore in the little sailing dinghy.

But he stuffed the awkward feeling down, as he had learned to stuff so many feelings down, and pushed on, up the two steps to the porch, then to the door. Knock! Knock! Knock! His hand thumped the wood, but no response came.

"Maybe she's not home," he murmured to himself, almost hopefully. He would just check around back to be sure. After all, he'd come all this way. But when he turned to step off the porch, the apparition of an aged and withered hag wrapped in faded woolen skirts and shawls of mismatched deep blue and burgundy stood where a moment before there had been naught but the herb garden.

His breath caught in his throat and he staggered back, tripping over the porch step and falling on his rump on the planks, making Oak Peg cackle.

*********

"Ye have the look of a weary man." Oak Peg's brogue rattled out of a throat withered with years of hard living in the deep wood. But there was strength in her speech too. Like a stout old tree, she was all rough bark and deep roots, an indomitable presence. They were sitting at a wooden table in the back of the herb garden. They drank steaming cups of tea from great mugs and the old woman had set out a plate of honey cookies, baked that morning. But he had no appetite, not after the embarrassing escapade of earlier.

And for all her grandmotherliness, she made Sweyn nervous. Something about her made him think of dark nursery rhymes, Hansel and Gretel, the old child-eating witch of the gingerbread house. Recalling Snow White's poisoned apple, his instincts warned him to shun the cookies. Though he chided himself for thinking it, he feared that if he nibbled at them he would fall asleep and wake to find himself in a pie. It was nonsense, of course. Rantings of a subconscious mind overwrought with too many archetypes. A dark wood, a witchy cottage, a leathery old woman with a worn face and a voice like satin tearing on twigs, herb gardens and honey cookies. It would wake the irrational fears of the most rational man.

But however much he might try to tell himself that his fears were imaginary, there was something out of kilter about the old woman, some mystery running deeper than childish fears. He could feel it. It lurked beneath the surface, deep and green as the oak wood round about. It was hard for him not to keep a suspicious eye on her over the lip of his mug. Yet he forced himself not to stare warily as he sipped the wintergreen tea. What harm could there be in an eccentric old woman living in a crumbling cottage all by herself? She was a loner, and probably lonely too. He knew the type, knew it all too well.

Oh, come, Sweyn, came the inner, unwanted voice again. An eccentric old woman who lives alone in a cottage in a dark wood on a backward isle. And it's not as if the Island is remote enough for her. No, she has to cut herself off from the few people here. Why should that give you cause for alarm? Hmm? What's she doing out here? What's she hiding for? Or hiding from? He shook off the voice, tamped it down in the deep cellars where he stowed the rest of his madness.

She was just an old woman. Period.

The voice made one last effort before it was locked away. She's off, like milk that will turn tomorrow.

And then he suppressed it. Like everything else.

But Oak Peg prattled on, oblivious to the storm of his thoughts. She poured herself another mug of tea and said, "Aye, weary man, worn thin by a long road with many a sudden turn. Would that about sum you up, Dr. deSauld?"

Yes, he was drawn to answer. But he stopped himself before he spoke it. He certainly did not want to discuss his personal life with a half crazy old woodswoman. What happened instead was he leaned forward and said, "Mrs., umm . . ." What should he call her? Mrs. Oak? Mrs. Peg? How about just Oak Peg, he decided, just like he heard from Coppin. That way, if he gave offense, he could blame it on the old scoundrel. "Oak Peg, I heard you buy sheep milk, and I just happen to have an abundance."

"Well, of course ye do. I've been buying yer estate's milk for as long as I can remember." She tapped her head briskly. "And that's a long way, Dr. deSauld, a long way."

"Sweyn," he said.

The lines of her time-etched skin turned up a smile. "Sweyn, then." She continued. "And if those fine sheep of Dundubh are still turning out such sweet curds and whey, I'll be buying it again. The cheese hasn't been the same since the last Laird stopped selling and I had to turn to village stock. There's no sheep on the Island puts out milk the like of yers."

That was a relief. At least he could move the extra inventory. "Yes, I heard you make cheese from the milk. Coppin said it was very good stuff."

"Dr. Sweyn . . ."

"Just Sweyn, please," he corrected again.

"Sweyn, then, if ye insist." Regardless of whether she liked his cordiality, she was from a time when titles were more important. It was difficult for her to adopt only his first name. But she went on. "Some people search far and wide for fine wines. Others would trade their front teeth for fish eggs smoked just right, or a rich pâté. And there are those folk who would rather spend their coin on a good cheese as on any of the former dainties. And the stuff I make, well, it is the rarest and the finest."

He nodded, not really understanding.

"Let me show ye." She rose and led him to the kitchen at the back of her cottage. There she showed him how she processed the extracts and essential oils from the secret forest herbs that grew in her courtyard. In the cottage she mixed the oils and extracts with the milk, which she then took out to a shed in the back to ferment. She called the fermenting curds and whey the lees, and explained that when it was half-done she would add another round of secret herb oils. When the lees became gelatinous, she told him that that was the best time to "start turning them into cheese."

She took him to the shed where she let the milk ferment. The shed stood against the garden wall in the farthest place at the far back of the house. Built all of weatherworn, vertically set poles made long ago from young willows, it was a tiny, ramshackle structure sporting a single small window with an oil lamp dangling from a peg behind it. She opened the door to show him how she worked inside. A horrid stench spilled out the open door, reminiscent of Limburger cheese and vinegar. He paled, covered his nose, and gasped. His eyes watered.

"Oh, I do apologize," Oak Peg said. "I've been doing this so long I hardly notice anymore." She explained that the stench resulted from a reaction between the volatile oils aging with the lees. In time, she said, the stench would contribute to the cheese's flavor, but at this point one was hard put to imagine how. Sweyn endured the barrage of odor stoically and allowed himself to be guided through the shed, though he was white and holding back a gag reflex. Inside were some barrels, a simple press made from flat stones held in place by four stakes, and an honest to goodness cauldron which Oak Peg showed him was for mixing. "The heavy black iron is best for even warming," said Oak Peg. "I warm the lees and give them a good stirring. Then they just sit in one of the barrels till they get thick. Then I add the ground herbs and let it all thicken up some more. When it's all good and ripe, I wrap it in cheese cloth and press out the whey. Then it goes to the next shed for aging.

She took him there and showed him how she hung the drained and pressed curds in cheesecloth and let it age for a season. This little shed had a much different scent than the previous one, yeasty and clean, with a fragrance of nuts and unknown spice. She took a hanging cheese from a wrack and handed it to him. "Let it ripen another week, and then you and Coppin enjoy." She cackled and led him back to the cottage.

He had learned a lot that early afternoon about how to make cheese. And he could see now why Coppin had insisted the estate merely sell the milk. It was smelly, tricky business and required a subtle art that could only be acquired with long experience. And, for the love of all, who could endure that smell? No, the estate would produce the milk and let Oak Peg turn it into cheese.

A little while later they had settled the business with a handshake. Well, sort of a handshake. She had flat disgusted Sweyn when she spit impressively into her palm and expected him to do the same in his, then they shook over the ooze. She would buy all the surplus milk of the estate, everything the village did not use. He was wiping his hand on a clay garden pot in a moment when she had turned away to trim a herb in flower, something sprouting pale red bell-like blossoms surrounded by leaves like swords, when she insisted he stay for dinner. It was two hours back to town by sea and the afternoon was already getting on, but he could not find the heart to turn her down. A lonely old woman living far out in the deep woods. Company must be a rare treat for her. Hiding his reluctance, he agreed to stay. She seemed to grow brighter, and all the stranger, as she began muttering to herself and puttering about her garden curiously, tending her herbs and occasionally gathering a leaf or blossom or root "for the porridge." He watched her work and thought about his little dinghy out on the beach. He could not sail it back by night. He would have to walk back to Dundubh Cottage tonight and return for it tomorrow, a long trip.

*********

Dinner had not been what he had anticipated. He had expected strange fare of the wood, as eccentric as Oak Peg. He would not have been surprised to get a platter of skunk cabbage with toadstools fried crisp for a side dish. Instead, Oak Peg presented a large black kettle of ground oat porridge flavored with venison and wild morels. They had a salad of beat greens from her garden. She served a hearty bread made from a blend of barley and acorn flour. They drank cold dandelion tea, made from the fragrant sunshine colored petals of the flowers which blossomed abundantly in a nearby glade. At the end of the meal, they enjoyed a creamy custard of bluebell petals and wild cherries. They had eaten of the abundance of the forest, but the meal was refined despite its wild origins. And it had been surprisingly delicious and satisfying, and somehow familiar. It reminded him of meals Eilwen used to make from her own herb garden.

Now, full dark had come at last. They sat on the stone patio on the benches beside the rough hewn table, each holding a steaming mug of tea to wash it all down. From deep in the wood came calls like Sweyn had not heard before from Dundubh Cottage, bursts of deep baritone, boisterous trills much louder and more musical than any cricket, bubbling whistles that seemed emitted from a drowned flute. Some of the sounds had an imminently natural, comforting quality—night calls of birds and insects. Others seemed unearthly, and they set him on edge. For her part, Oak Peg sipped her tea calmly, reveling in the nighttime symphony.

Once Sweyn had come to look past Oak Peg's eccentricities, he had found her a remarkably pleasant person to discourse with. Since before dinner they had been deep in conversation. At first it was small talk: the weather, the loveliness of the wood, compliments on the meal. Easy things. It progressed to a few brief notes on how the milk would be transported. And then Oak Peg had casually asked how his livestock were faring. Sweyn explained that the only livestock he was so far aware of were the sheep and some chickens and ducks, and possibly some pond fish, if they could be counted. But disturbing things had happened in the previous two weeks since he had made his peace with the sheep. He leaned forward on the bench, folded his hands together and wrinkled his brow, looking thoroughly uncomfortable.

"Ye're no' telling all," Oak Peg observed. "Come on, tell Oak Peg. She knows this Island better than any. She knows how to mend things."

His dark hazel eyes seemed to go a bit darker as he thought back over the previous weeks. "It's the sheep, you see. Well, I guess they're fine animals. I wouldn't know. I've never had anything to do with a farm before. But they seem to me like good enough animals. They give plenty of milk and practically look after themselves"

She interrupted, her tone full of surprise. "Ye milk them yerself, then? I thought old Coppin ought to be tending to that, and no' a novice Laird. Now, that is strange for him. Coppin is usually a hardworking sort, and if he's shirking a duty there is some mischief afoot." But then she paused and studied him intently, as if appraising him. She took a great swallow of tea and went on, her voice dropping, as if musing to herself. "But ye're milking them yerself. Now that is a thing, isn't it? That is a thing, indeed. Those sheep are a fastidious folk. They'd no' be letting anyone untoward touch them." She smiled, addressed him eye to eye, and raised her cup in toast of him. "Well done, Sweyn. Well done."

He cleared his throat, feeling awkward as he was sure he was missing the meaning of just about everything Oak Peg had just said. He tried to sort it out, quickly, so as not to give away his puzzlement, but knew in an instant he could not. So instead he decided to admit that maybe things had not been going so well. "You see, strange things have been happening, and I'm not sure if it's my fault somehow." He fell silent then.

"Go on," she encouraged. "Tell me, then."

"Well . . . " It was difficult for him to spill. It made him sound crazier than he already was. But he had started; he might as well finish. "I know this is going to sound . . . bizarre . . . but I swear it's the facts. Sometimes I milk them and the milk is sour before it hits the pail. Is that possible?"

She frowned in thought, then after a long minute, said, "And what else?"

"I've taken that sour milk and thrown it out. And then I sniff the empty bucket only to find it was good after all.

"And, you know we have over forty sheep between the ewes and the rams. But some of them turn up missing. My best ewe disappeared for three days. I thought she'd wandered into the wood at the edge of the meadow, or maybe a wolf had gotten her. Then she turns up shut in her stable the next morning. Seems like at any given time, more than ten of them are missing that way, these days. And as soon as I've wasted a day looking for them, I find them chewing their cud in the stable.

"And yesterday—you're going to think this is crazy, but I swear it—one of the sheep bit me. Right here." He pointed to the rear of his right thigh. "And hard too. I know I'm no farm boy, but I have never, ever heard of sheep biting before."

As he had spoken, Oak Peg had refilled his mug. But this time it was not tea, but the nutty brown sweet ale he had first tried on Bealtaine night in Man-by-the-Sea. She tossed the dregs from her own cup as well and poured ale into it. She took a mighty swig and scrunched up her face, thoughtful. A chorus of crickets fiddled. In due time she said, "I know what is afoot. Follow me and I will show you the remedy."

She went into the oil lamp-lit cottage and took an earthenware plate. She set a slab of bread on it, and put a few round pellets of cheese beside it. She also took an earthenware crock and poured brown ale into it. These she carried to the door and Sweyn held it open for her. She strode through her garden to the iron gate that guarded the entrance to the courtyard, and he opened it for her too. She set the plate on the earth, along with the mug. Then she took the gate from Sweyn's hand and pushed it shut, making sure the latch clicked. She drew a key from a pouch at a leather belt and turned the lock. Sweyn looked beyond the gate into the darkling wood, where he thought tiny lights sparkled only a moment before.

"Only set this out every night at Dundubh Cottage and yer troubles with the sheep will end," she told him. "Though I canna' imagine why old Coppin's been neglecting the evening plate." But in truth she could well imagine. Coppin had never been keen on the wandering seaman. Eilwen may have loved him, but he was not now the man she had married. A Laird had to be strong, but this one had been broken since her death. Given Coppin's doubts, she could well imagine how he might go out of his way to make things difficult for Sweyn.

But time was short and the geas had shown her no other. And now look at this Sweyn. He had tamed the fey sheep, and that indeed was something. And now he stared into the darkness with eyes like a fawn, enamored of the mysteries of the night wood though he did not know it. Perhaps he could become a Laird of the O'Shees, after all. For all their sakes, she had to cling to that hope. Time was too short to second guess it, and why didn't that foolish Coppin, old as he is, see it.

But Sweyn was entirely unaware of Oak Peg's thoughts. Looking deep into the sylvan darkness, he was sure now that he saw, far off under the trees, little sparkles that came and went like shy hints of fireflies. But there were no fireflies in this part of the world. Unless the early immigrants to the Island had imported them too, along with all the seeds of their bizarre transplanted forest.

Oak Peg began to say something. Her voice was low, making itself known as a coarse whisper grating in the sultry dark.

*Beithluisnuin to remember the Old,*
*Huathduirtinne to hold back the days,*
*Muinngortgetal to ease the fading,*
*Ailmohnur to keep our Ways.*

Sweyn regarded her curiously as she spoke the quiet words. Her eyes were far off, fixed on something long past, or long in coming. The words had spilled from her lips gracefully, and though he could not understand them, he understood they were pregnant with purpose. Here was part of some incredibly old tradition, something so deep and pure it was beyond ritual. It was action conjoined with meaning, magic, if anything was magic. He shook his head, only slightly, but greatly confused. There was such depth here, and he was beginning to understand Coppin's perspective of him. He was an outsider and had no roots in the place. Something was kept in this land, something deep and old, and he could not hope to grasp it. Because he was an outsider, and suddenly, unexpectedly, he hated that fact.

"That's beautiful," he said to Oak Peg, his voice soft and sad as the crescent moon peeping through the oak boughs above. "Is it from a poem?"

Oak Peg nodded. "The Forest Rede, Sweyn, to remind the Island folk of things old and eldritch. We say it when we leave out the evening plates. Each word is the name of a suite of a lost alphabet we call the Ogham. Beithluisnuin was the first suite. Huathduirtinne is the second. And so on. But there is far more to the Ogham than written sounds, for it is the language of the green things of the Old World."

"I don't understand ?" he confessed. The wan moonlight highlighted the silver-brown of his ponytail.

"Ah, well," she said patiently, "understanding would take a lifetime. For every Ogham had its tree or its herb, and every herb and tree has its enchantment, and the Ogham is the key to both. All the trees and herbs our ancestors brought to the island are linked to the Ogham.

"Would ye like to hear the entire poem, though? That we can do now."

He nodded and she recited the rest of the poem.

*Birch for beginnings and paths of silver,*
*Rowan for flames and faerie friends,*
*Alder for shields to guard the milk,*
*Willow for the clarsach's music,*

*Ash for the comely watery women.*
*Hawthorn is the raven to frighten the wolf,*
*Oak is the wren in the druid's tree,*
*Holly is the bright red burning coal,*
*Hazel is the wisdom down in the pool,*
*Apple is the hind in death's lee.*

*Vine travails like the strong ox,*
*Ivy grows like the swan's sweet grass,*
*Broom is like the healing stroker,*
*Blackthorn is like a secret keeper,*
*Elder the walker is like the past.*

*Fir groans sick or sighs with wonder,*
*Gorse calls the goddess of horse or stone,*
*Heather dwells cold or sweetens soil,*
*Aspen knows whether friend or swan,*
*Yew is the elder or eagle's song.*

*Bring the twenty mysteries to the farther shore,*
*Seed them well in the Green Man's hold,*
*Bide the Island of the sea lord's fortress,*
*Hold fey and fair against time's swell,*
*Thwart the doom of the elder world.*

She fell into a stillness then, when her words came to an end. Something had transpired. Sweyn could sense it, but he could not tell what it was. But it was close and real, even if intangible, like the feeling of mist on the sea by night when it is still and cold but the sea is warm and rocking. The crickets continued their night chorus, the owls their ancient calls. The green darkness of the wood seemed pregnant, and in the distance, between the trees, the sparkles continued to weave, little candle flickers of luminous aquamarine.

Oak Peg pointed at the sparkles. She whispered. "The food is out. They are coming. Best we go inside."

"You feed the fireflies?" he asked dreamily, gazing back into the forest. But deep within, where his waking mind refused to go, he knew that whatever was coming was not fireflies. Whatever it was, it was something beautiful and perilous, some elegant remnant of another time, another place, when this world was not at all the world he knew. His eyes were fixed on those sparkles, and the aquamarine flickers wove slowly closer. They were like shards of luminous crystal, living stars come to earth. He wanted to stay and bask in their dance, and witness their wonder, to be found only here, perhaps out of all the world, in this aged green wood.

But Oak Peg took his hand, a maternal gesture. "Come," she said, her coarse voice still gentle, but there was iron in it, strength he could not resist. "Already ye're being pixie-led. And they dinna' take to being spied upon."

He only half heard, but dimly he remembered her leading him into the cottage and barring the door shut. Then she made a bed of blankets for him upon the couch in her small living room. "Stay the night," she ordered him, and refused to let him into the dark without. His thoughts still upon the scintillating forest lights, he lay down upon the couch and drifted into tangled dreams.

# Chapter Six

*She walks beyond the Guardwood keep,*
*In green arboreal shadows deep.*
*Leaves of gold are her garb,*
*Autumn drapes the forest ward.*

*Hair like birch all pale and silver,*
*Shows time's weight like a river.*
*Beneath boughs of enchorial trees,*
*She keeps the wood from low thieves.*

*Then they came from the rising moon,*
*Outcast refugees sure to swoon.*
*The jealous guardian was soft in heart,*
*And gave them place for their hearths.*

*A crescent of land in the wild sea,*
*for mortal folk and fair faerie.*
*And white-foamed surf for the watery race,*
*A half lost Island to keep them safe.*

*Arn'na'sagt'puch was the dame,*
*Aboriginal of the western land.*
*Old Lady of the Wood she is often called,*
*She made the Pact that saved them all.*

*The Lament of Hawthorn*
*Seoridean, Bard of the Westernmost Tuath*

It is a terrible thing when dreams and nightmare weave together. In one instant Sweyn was back in time, at the chalet with Eilwen. She read quietly, sitting before a crackling fire of cedar, and he was watching her ruby locks shimmer by the light of the flames. It was a perfect, timeless moment. It should have gone on forever. Instead, it abruptly faded and he was in his office, and it was the day he came to know he could practice his profession no longer. A youth not quite eighteen sat in a chair and spoke to him. The youth had the heart of a snake and he bragged about the terrible things he had done. It was clear he would do more, for he did not care what pain he caused. The capacity to care was not in him. He had no soul. Sweyn was incapable of stopping him, and it was more than he could bear.

And then Sweyn was in the salon of a listing boat, Cerulean, and the green sea spilled in through fractured planks on the starboard side. He cried out for his passengers, but there came no replies. But Eilwen fell into the sea wrapped in her death's shroud. And a shadow leered from the seawall overlooking the piers.

Then he was at the chalet, in bed, holding Eilwen in his arms, stroking her smooth white brow as she slept peacefully, while he remained awake, brooding in the darkness over the matter of the soulless boy. And the disembodied voice of his father warned him to remain distant from his clients, to be cold but appear warm, and put them behind him when they left. But such counterfeit affect was not an art Sweyn could master.

And then there was a moment of blackness and the stickiness of blood, and it was on his knuckles and his shirt, and a body lay in a dark alley, smelling of alcohol and urine.

And then he was in the sea, knife in hand, frantically tearing and cutting at sail cloth in black, flaming water. There was an explosion and he was stunned. The knife slipped from his hand and disappeared into the brine. He grabbed a cut he had started in the cloth and tore at it mightily, but his strength was not enough to rip it.

The dreams were not in order, the time of events tangled as a crazed spider's web. And that made the dreaming all the worse, for he was storm tossed between moments of warmth and instants of blinding fear and bitter agony, and he never knew what the next instant held. And back behind it all was a brooding rage, growing like a smith's flame in a forge.

Then, suddenly, he was in Oak Peg's cottage. Chaos was around him. He had torn one of her sheets clean in two. Potted plants which had sat on a coffee table beside the couch were spilled, the plants slumped on the hardwood floor, the dark soil scattered. The table itself was kicked over. Something sticky stung his left eye, and he knew instantly he had injured himself. Oak Peg herself had placed both her tough, leathery hands on his cheeks and was muttering something indecipherable in what he took to be Gaelic. When she saw his eyes open, she spoke English and said, "Easy now, lad, easy now."

He gasped for breath. It felt like he was still drowning, down in the black water with the sail that became Eilwen's shroud. But the sight and sound of Oak Peg was an anchor, and he grasped for her resolute reality. Fixing his mind on her, he buried his memories, stilled his thoughts, taking long, desperate breaths, pulling himself inch by inch from the grip of the madness into the moment, till at last he could sit shakily up on the couch and stuff his hands under his knees, for they were shaking like leaves in a gale. Oak Peg went to the kitchen and withdrew a bottle from a cupboard. She came back with it and two shot glasses, set them at a small table and indicated he should join her. His knees were wobbly but he rose from the couch and took a seat at the small dinner table. She poured them both a stiff drink. He took it, smelled it. It was ordinary whiskey. He downed the glass in a single gulp and she poured him another which he sipped more slowly. She sipped hers quietly, observing him.

After several minutes, when he had come to himself enough to speak clearly, he said, "I'm sorry about the mess. I'll see to the damage."

She brushed it off. "I said when I saw ye that ye had the look of a weary man. Yer soul is worn, Sweyn. Yer soul will fail if ye dinna' do something to heal it."

"There's nothing to be done," he pronounced forlornly and looked to the window just at the edge of the table. A memory of aquamarine flickers came to mind and he moved his hand to push aside the heavy curtains.

She shook her head. "No. Dinna' spy." He let his hand drop and she continued. "What ye need to do is unburden yerself."

"Ha!" he chuckled sardonically. "I know all about that. I used to listen to people do it for a living, and it is my professional and estimable opinion that it does nothing for anyone."

But Oak Peg smiled. "I thought ye had the heart of a healer within ye. I just could no' tell which kind."

"Oh, yeah, I was a healer. I sat in an office and listened to folk unload their troubles on me for a hundred dollars an hour. Just like my father. And for a while I really bought into it. But it's all a farce, a money game. I don't know why I ever went into psychology."

"Ye dinna' believe talking is helping, then? How come?"

He fell silent and sipped from his glass.

"Sweyn," she repeated, "how come?"

He pushed forward the shot glass and she refilled it. He downed it quickly. It burned his throat as it soothed his spirit.

"A tale for a tale," he said.

"A bargain struck," she replied.

"Then tell me first, what is this place?"

"An Island. A bit of rock and wood far off the beaten path."

"Manannan is no mere Island, Oak Peg, and you and I both know it. And if you want truth, you'll give the same."

"Clever lad," she intoned. Then she rose and returned to the kitchen, carrying the whiskey bottle with her, which she capped on the way. She poured spring water into a kettle and set it upon a stove, then went to work stoking the stove with wood.

From the kitchen, she said, "The Island of Manannan is no ordinary Island. Have ye ever heard of leys?"

He searched his memory, nodded, holding back a mirthless chuckle. "You're talking of ley lines, like paths of psychic energy? I'm not into New Age stuff, Oak Peg, so talk straight."

"Ye want straight, or ye want what ye want to hear?" she demanded calmly as she prepped two mugs with honey and cream. He fell silent and she continued. "I dinna' know what this psychic energy is that ye're referring to, but I can tell ye enchantment flows in streams like the Northern Lights. Some call those streams leys. And this Island has always been a nexus of many such streams. Because of them, the Island is very precious."

"Why, so a bunch of superstitious Celts can hide out from the real world, practicing their hocus-pocus?" It was a sharp thing to say to his gentle hostess, but he did not care in this moment. He was still bitter from the pounding of the memories.

But Oak Peg carried on placidly. "Two peoples call this world home, Sweyn. Mortal folk and immortal folk. Men and the Tuath, who are known as the good folk, the little people, the gentry, and also by many other names."

"Faeries. You're telling me you believe in faeries," he said incredulously.

"And ye dinna'? Ye, who were almost pixie-led this very evening? Perhaps ye canna' remember. Perhaps yer vision is still too narrow. But if Oak Peg had no' held ye back, ye'd be traipsing through the darkling wildwood this very moment and ne'er a man, woman, or bairn would see ye again for a hundred years and more."

A silence fell. He brooded over his empty shot glass. The kettle sang and she poured hot water into a teapot to steep. Finally, he sighed and asked her to go on.

"Tuath means clan, Sweyn, and a long time ago, when there was less cold iron and cut stone, there were many Tuatha of faerie folk. Their world overlays this one, a part of it but separate. And their realm spread all throughout the wilds of Europe. But the Faerie realm canna' bear the press of too much humanity, yet human numbers grew and grew. Over the centuries Faerie receded till there were only few scattered pockets of it in the far west and north corners of the Old World.

"And so the faerie clans were fading, ye see, passing from this green world. Enchantment flows in the wild woods and the green meadows, and faerie folk may only live where enchantment is strong. But villages and towns and cities sprang up everywhere, roads of cut stone scarred the land, and cold iron was in every household, and every field. Enchantment was choked and poisoned by these things.

"As Faerie died, it was broken up. A faerie glen here. A haunted wood there. In those pockets faerie folk survived, but those caught in the disenchanted wastes between could no' flee, for the folk of Faerie are like the trees. They are bound to a place and canna' depart it. They faded into the distant Dreaming West, far across a shining sea. Faerie folk are immortal, but it was almost as if they had died, for those that faded were never to be seen again. And this was a great sorrow, for though it is said the Dreaming West is a fair and bright land, the hearts of faerie folk are here in the shady places of the green world.

"Soon it came to seem that even the few surviving pockets of Faerie would fail, for always the number of mortals grew. But on the very breath of extinction, it was mortal folk who found a way to save some of it. Long ago, a band of Celts took pity on the faerie folk. These mortals set their hearts on the Old Ways and lived in harmony with enchantment. And when the New World was discovered, they found a way to bring the faerie folk with them to it. The memory of how they did this is lost, and it is a great mystery, for faerie folk are firmly rooted to their places and canna' travel. To leave their lands is the death of them. Yet this mortal band managed it, and they came here with as many creatures of Faerie as they could gather.

"Now, those brave mortal folk went west and came first to the shores of Nova Scotia, which means New Scotland. It was a land of green woods and rolling hills, and it was reminiscent of their home in the British Isles. Some of that folk stayed there, and kept some of the faerie folk with them, but most elected to move on. They were following the dream of a land they could hold forever, someplace far away and long to be safe for eldritch things. They wandered for decades and decades in search of that dream, and it was hard going often. But they held fast their wandering.

"But the home they dreamt of was hard to find, and for more reasons than just the press of Man. Faeries themselves are a territorial lot. They bind to their land, as I've said, ye see, and hold it fiercely. Wherever those wandering mortals went, they found other faerie folk already occupying the land, faerie folk of the New World called Inuqun. And the Inuqun would make no place for the fey refugees of the Old World coming with the mortals. So the mortals always had to press on, hoping for a land free of Man and full of enchantment, yet also devoid of jealous New World faerie inhabitants. It proved to be thin hope indeed, and time grew heavy upon the mortal lot, till they seemed soon to break.

"It was then, at the very end of hope, came the vision from the sea god, Manannan, to the people. It revealed a far flung isle that might become the home they sought, and there was hope once more. The mortals took all of what little they still had and purchased passage on a ship and came at last to this place, a couple hundred tired souls at the end of their strength. But the Island was perfect, for enchantment flowed strongly here, more sweet and pure than anywhere they had seen before, save perhaps their own precious lost lands in the Old World. But, of course, such a magical place was rife with its own enchanted beings. The Island was occupied by ancient, powerful Inuqun who would neither part with nor share their enchanted land with the strange refugees.

"The mortal folk were desperate. They had given their last to come here, and strength and time wore heavy upon them. And their luck had turned evil. The ship passage dinna' end well. If they could no' share this land, they and the faerie folk with them would perish. And so it would have been, but for a single mortal man, an outsider such as yerself, who found the leader of the Inuqun tribe. The outsider appealed to her, a dame called Arn'na'sagt'puch, who appeared as an old wise woman with silver locks and red-brown skin, wearing a dress of golden cottonwood leaves. She could no' find it in her heart to let the last of the Old World faerie folk perish, nor their noble mortal allies. She regarded the band of them as a wonder, ye see, for never had mortal and immortal kin thrown their lots in together as one people. She was touched and moved and showed great pity. And so she convinced her tribe to make a place for them. A pact was brokered. The Tuath was small and weak, and needed a safe, healing place all their own. They were given this little Island, and their own gods of wood and sea were left to keep it. The mainland offered plenty of space and the Inuqun of this place took themselves to those parts, empowered to leave the land by the strength of Arn'na'sagt'puch. And so long as the Pact is kept, the Inuqun will stay away so that the faerie folk here might heal and grow strong again. The people of this Island are the descendents of those brave mortals, and for all we know, this is the last place where Faerie mingles still with the green world."

She finished and the silence fell deep. She poured the tea then, and came back to sit at the table, setting a mug before him. He took it and sipped it. It was sweet and had a rich flavor, reminiscent of coffee. Dandelion roots, she told him. It revived him in a different way than the whiskey. "And now yer tale, Sweyn."

"But that's a fairytale," he objected.

"It is. But ye wanted truth as the folk of Manannan see it."

So that was what this place was all about. These people followed a myth to the Island where they spent their lives keeping the myth alive. On the one hand, he admired their tenacity, and the comfort they found in their reliable old traditions. On the other, time moves on and people must grow, but these people were stagnant. Surely that was why Eilwen, smart and adventurous, had left the Island.

Oak Peg continued to regard him over her mug as she sipped the rich brown tea.

He sighed wearily and committed himself to fulfilling his part of the bargain. But where to begin? She could see he was a burnout, so why not there.

"You said I looked like a weary man. Well, you're not far from the truth, Oak Peg. In fact, you really couldn't be more right. Looking back at my life, I find I don't believe anymore in psychology. I don't believe in anything I ever said or did as a psychologist. And for proof, none of it gave me the power to do even the one person I loved most any good." In an abrasive tone, he added, "Maybe you should be a psychologist, Oak Peg. You seem to have a knack for appraising people."

His voice became flat as he went on. "You see, my father was a psychologist. He was, you could say, imminent, and I admired him. He made a good living doing something meaningful, and I wanted to be just like that. So I followed in his footsteps. I had all these naïve dreams that I could help people, and I followed them right through college and grad school. When I graduated, I went into practice at my father's office.

"I thought I was pretty good at what I did. My clients liked me and kept coming back. I listened to them, and I cared about them. I poured my heart into helping them. But my father said I was overly enmeshed in my clients' lives, not maintaining a professional distance. For my part, I came to see him as far too professional. All his concern and warmth was only a veneer. Everything he said or did was calculated to manipulate people into thinking in whatever way he thought was best. I guess you could say what he did was like psychotherapy poker, where he bluffed his way into his clients' heads. I couldn't do things that way, and it was slowly becoming more and more of a problem between us.

"Anyway, through it all, things were getting slow at the office, so he decided to contract with the court system to provide services to delinquent youth. Most of them were just kids who had gotten a raw deal out of life. They just needed someone to care about them and give them a helping hand. But a few of those kids had far deeper problems. There was darkness in them. I knew a boy who got his thrills burning dogs to death. I knew another who was a rapist and his fantasy life involved holding knives to girls' throats and watching them squirm. Whatever makes people care for each other, those kids didn't have it. They were hollow inside. It was like . . . was like . . . they didn't have souls." He paused, seeming to remember something, shivered. "We were seeing those kids for a few court mandated sessions, then they were going back out onto the streets, out in the world. I knew they were going to hurt more people, but there was nothing I could do. As a psychologist, all the horrors they related to me, I had to keep secret. As a human being, I couldn't live with that. My father called my feelings another example of my distance issues.

"Now that I look back on it, I realize he was right. Because if I had been able to just look away, Eilwen would. . ." he faltered, his voice quavering. He took several more deep breaths, relaxing himself in a practiced way, but he could not make himself continue along that line. He closed his eyes, swallowed, and went on at a different point.

"One day I got a new kid. Marcus. A seventeen-year-old who had killed a girl while driving drunk. He had spent a year in a juvenile facility and they were going to release him in a month when he turned eighteen. My job was to review what he had learned in the past year and make sure he had the skills to succeed in life after he was on the outs.

"The sessions went well. The boy expressed regret for his crime. He seemed disgusted with it, and self-disgust can be a good thing in those cases. He worked on stress management so he wouldn't feel like he had to turn to alcohol in the future. He processed his relationship to alcohol, and reviewed how his failure to manage his drinking caused him to kill that girl. A ten-year-old girl, can you believe it! Damn! A ten-year-old girl that had been walking down a sidewalk on her way home." He paused and shook his head, roiled between fury and anguish. He knew his father had been right, he could not keep a professional distance from these things. But he could not find it in himself to regret it. And that, more than anything else, is what had driven the wedge between him and his father. It took him a moment till he was ready to speak again. "The boy was sharp. He showed he had all the skills to make it. He knew the right words to say. But something about him kept eating at me. And somewhere inside of me, I was angry. I thought, 'That girl won't get a second chance, but her killer will.' And that galled me."

"But I did what I could for him. My mission was to heal. And no crime, I believed, should victimize twice. If he could be made safe, then let him have his second chance. Feeling my discomfort with the boy was a result of my own bias, I filed a glowing report on him the day before the finalization of his discharge.

"On the last day he was to see me, he was all smiles. That was to be expected, given the circumstances. He was about to be released, after all, and I had told him about the report I wrote the day before. But he sat down in his chair, and in a very arrogant tone he told me, 'I've decided I'm not going to hold anything back today, Dr. deSauld. My sentence is up and there's no point.' And then he told me how he had planned to kill that girl. He had wondered what it would be like to kill someone. Drawn to the thrill of the hunt, he had killed countless animals, but it wasn't the same. No dog or cat, no matter how savagely tortured, could make him feel the thrill of murdering another human being. And so he had taken his dad's truck and driven up and down the suburbs until he came across a lone girl walking past an undeveloped wooded block and he had run her down. He described her screams as he chased her with the truck, taunting her. He described her look when he hit her. He described how powerful he felt in that moment, like a god in a steel chariot. And then he told me about how he rapidly drank himself into a stupor with hard liquor and went stumbling in tears to a nearby house to call an ambulance and make it look like a drunk driving accident." Sweyn could not keep his composure. He kept thinking of the child's last moments, the terror she must have suffered. Redness came to his eyes and anger flushed his cheeks. But he made himself carry on. "And then he smiled and very smoothly commented how easy it was to fool everyone: the police, the court, myself. And he said, 'And everything you've heard is confidential, and the court has ruled on my case, and you can't be tried for the same crime twice. So I just thought you would like to know.' Then he rose and he gave me this queer salute, like a kid playing soldier. And he left.

"He said something else too, but not with words, only between the lines. He made it clear he had enjoyed killing, and he would do it again. The kid was a serial killer in the making.

"But he was right. The case had already been ruled upon and there really was very little I could do. He would go out into the world and who knew how many other little girls would suffer. I talked to my father about it. He said sometimes you just lose some battles and to be professional and move on. But I couldn't. He could, but I couldn't.

"So I broke the rules. I stole into the office that night. It wasn't hard, I had a key. I destroyed my old notes. I rewrote everything on Marcus. I changed his discharge summary. I colored all the documentation on him, carefully characterizing him as lacking empathy and sadistic, what they used to call a sociopath. Then I called his probation officer and dropped a hint she should subpoena the records before she signed his release papers the next day. She was curious why I hadn't talked to her about this before, but I think she had a bad feeling about the kid too because she didn't press it. The next day she got her subpoena and the boy's release was reviewed. The boy learned he wasn't as smart as he thought he was, because while he could not be retried for the same case, his current sentence could be stretched out. The judge extended his incarceration to the maximum allowable time, another year. It wasn't much, but at least the world would be safe from him for one more year. Everything I had done to make that happen was a gross violation of professional ethics, but I felt very, very good about it. In fact, it was probably the best thing I had done since I went into the field.

"But my father figured out soon enough what I had done and he was furious. 'You've put this practice in danger!' he ranted. 'This kind of thing could shut us down!' The professional image, that was the nature of the job, and it was all he cared about. I quit that night. I quit and I never looked back."

He stopped talking then, abruptly, and gripped his mug solidly in two hands, sipping at it absently, his mind far away on things best forgotten.

"It dinna' end there, did it," said Oak Peg.

Slowly, he shook his head. It should have. It could have. But she was right, it didn't. "Four years passed and in that time I met Eilwen and started a new life, and put Marcus and my father behind me. But Marcus knew what I had done. He didn't forget." He stopped, bits of unwanted memories flashing dangerously vivid behind his eyes. The dead black of night and orange sodium vapor streetlights shimmering on the black water between the docks. Green seas pouring in through torn planks. A listing hull. Screams and screams and desperate tearing at canvas. The dark shadow of a man watching from the seawall above the pier. The silhouetted image of a familiar salute.

He looked up at Oak Peg and shook his head, his eyes weary and hollow. He had talked enough. She did not ask for more. "And now yer memories haunt ye," she observed instead.

"I go to sleep, and they run over and over in my mind. Sometimes they come even when I'm awake, the living nightmares. It's like it's all happening again. And that happens," he indicated the mess around the couch, the torn sheet. "It's called PTSD, Posttraumatic Stress Disorder. And it's hell on earth."

Oak Peg shook her head. "Ye poor man," she said softly. "It's the blight of a riven soul, is what it is."

But Oak Peg did not know the whole story. He was not entirely guiltless. And his nightmares did not haunt him just because of what he had failed to stop, but also for what he had done.

*Blood. Blood on his fists, his knuckles. The sultry dark of an alley in the black heart of a city. The stink of urine and vomit. The racket from a jukebox in a bar.*

He shivered, and he refused to talk anymore. Oak Peg did not press him. She checked the doors and the windows, making sure the curtains were drawn and the doors barred with iron. She admonished him not to go outside till morning light. And then she went back to the cottage's single bedroom where she must have gone to sleep, for he did not hear her stir again.

As he lay back down on the couch and the hours slowly drizzled by, he wondered why he had told her any of this. He had not spoken a word of it to anyone, ever, nor had he ever felt a reason to. It bothered him that the old woman had been able to draw his darkest history out of him.

Yet the cottage was still and silent and the darkness soft and comforting, the absolute tranquility of the forest. In time oblivion came and he slept again, this time without dreams.

*********

When Sweyn set out from Oak Peg's cove early that morning, billowing cumulous clouds could be seen gathering on the western horizon, far out over the sea. But the wind had still been light and favorable. But during the sail back, rolling waves had grown steadily higher, presaging the arrival of a grand storm. He arrived in Man-by-the-Sea just as the weather turned really sour. He hauled his wooden tender high up out of the water and secured it snuggly to the trunk of a nearby tree by the painter line. By that time the clouds were only a few miles out and the air was rapidly chilling as the wind kicked up. With the first flashes of lightning flickering out at sea, he made his way into the village. Tucked into a shady corner he found the local library, where he hoped to shed some light on the true history of the Island. He wanted the genuine account, not Oak Peg's mythologized version. Only between a grasp of fact and myth, he reasoned, could he understand the complicated relationship Eilwen had had with this place.

The librarian was a tall, spindly woman who appeared the very archetype of Librarian. She was slightly homely, sharp-nosed, and bespectacled. Her salt and pepper hair fell just past her shoulders and was trimmed neatly, and pulled back into a tidy ponytail. But she wore the garb common to Man-by-the-Sea women folk: a long skirt, bodice and blouse. But unlike many of the other ladies, her colors were conservative, the skirt dark blue and the blouse cloud-washed grey. She was courteous and all too happy to help, and led Sweyn to a whole room devoted to the history of the Island and its families. It appeared the locals were keen to conserve the details of their history, for a prolific amount of material was to be found there. Shelf upon shelf of notes were gathered, the older ones written by hand, the newer ones typed and printed. They were bound in covers of sheepskin leather. The village was too small and isolated to support a newspaper, but the mayor's office did put out a quarterly newsletter detailing important business and notes regarding the village, and had done so for more than a century. These too were kept and bound in volumes ordered by decade. In some ways, the room was even like a little museum, for many small artifacts were on display on shelves behind glass, a haphazard collection of trivial jetsam that seemed to share no common theme other than it had once been part of Manannan life. There were also photographs preserved in volumes and a copious amount of sketches. But the centerpiece of the room was a great painting on the outer wall between two large picture windows, mounted in a massive frame of luxuriously carved hardwood nearly black with age and many layers of varnish. The painting depicted a tall ship on great storm waves, billowing clouds, and blinding streaks of lighting. Sweyn's experienced mariner's eye quickly perceived that the ship was listing heavily to port. That could only mean it was taking on water. Of such exquisite detail was the painting rendered that tiny images of the crew could be seen scrambling about upon the deck, and they were clearly panicking. The ship was going down. But one lifeboat could be seen escaping the dying ship. It was approaching the perspective of the viewer of the painting. The lifeboat was large and of the old fat-bodied design, and clearly intended to serve more as a tender than a rescue vessel. A single figure could be seen at the center of the craft, struggling to control a pair of oars. The tender was heavy, laden with several large chests. And when Sweyn drew closer to the great painting, fully six feet tall and four wide, he could make out what appeared to be the shadowy shape of a small head in the craft, tucked low in the bow. The artist had rendered such detail that, if he studied the picture well, he might have even been able to make out the faces of the characters in the lifeboat. All in all, the painting was an amazing, exquisite bit of work and may have been worth a fortune. He suspected that to these people it was beyond price.

He searched the many shelves of the room till he found the section referencing the earliest history of the settlement. He hunted until he unearthed photocopies of documents which must have been originally penned more than two centuries ago. The handwriting was crimped and small, but elegant nonetheless. Sweyn remembered once reading that prior to the twentieth century paper was an expensive and limited commodity. Writers wrote in small characters to conserve it. But what was even worse than trying to read the miniscule handwriting was the fact that the spellings of the words were not consistent and many archaic terms with which he was not familiar colored the record. He went up to the front desk and asked the librarian if she could lend him a magnifying glass. She was only too happy to oblige and commented that she was pleased to see the new Laird taking such an interest in the community's colorful history. Sweyn grunted and quickly returned to the private room where he sat and began to pore over the cramped manuscripts. He explored further and further until he found himself reading what at first appeared to be a ship's log, but a little further delving soon revealed it to be a journal kept by the first lieutenant of an old tall ship, the Mont Royal. The ship had been an unremarkable, tired frigate in the service of the British navy for some years, and it appeared to have been retired from military service and sold for a privateer. Sweyn came to realize it was the very ship that had brought the original settlers to the Island. The journaler was one Raleigh McCavitt, and the year of his entries was dated 1790.

### May 7, 1790

*They are a sordid lot, this pack of wanderers. Were it not for their accents, clearly originating from less desirable parts within the British Isles, I would think the lot of them ne'er-do-well vagabonds and beg the captain jettison them at the next port. Indeed, some are surely vagabonds, for they have the manner of Tinkers, card sharps and mountebanks. But regardless of their appearance, they have paid the captain handsomely in silver for the single favor of transporting them and all their goods to an island they believe lies off the British Columbian coast, which one I believe a witch assures them is where they must settle.*

Sweyn set aside the magnifying glass and sat up, steepling his fingers together and leaning his forehead on them, deep in thought. So that part of Oak Peg's tale was the real truth. Man-by-the-Sea folk had been a wandering clan. They had come to the Island on a quest to find a home of their own. Not a particularly glamorous or noteworthy history, after all. But people like to feel their roots are special, and so the history came to be colored with legends of noble ancestors hiding from the world to guard ancient secrets. He continued reading, and soon discovered the tale grew dark.

**May 26, 1790**
*Diverted to trade in lands two hundred miles south with the Suquamish people. We had intended to trade iron tools for foodstuffs. I was left aboard to command the ship while the captain himself negotiated. Something occurred in the negotiations and a fight broke out. Third Lieutenant Lewis was killed and so was Seaman Christian. The rest of the men who returned with the captain were silent on the matter, but some of them appear haunted. The captain will not even tell me, his first officer, what took place, but it seems there was a dispute over the goods.*

**June 3, 1790**
*We have sailed a week since the battle with the natives and I have learned from one of the men that the captain tried to purchase several of their girls. When the natives refused to sell them, he tried to take them by force and was driven back to the sea. Our stores are low now and we are beginning to feel it as our rations have been cut.*

**June 7, 1790**
*A Russian whaler has been sighted and the captain is making for it. I do not understand his intentions, unless he intends to try to buy some of their foodstuffs. It is unlikely they will sell, as supplies are difficult to obtain this far out.*

**June 8, 1790**
*The whalers refused to part with their foodstuffs and the captain nearly stormed their ship. I was only just able to prevent it, for we all would have been branded pirates. I do not understand his behavior, but there is no doubt the smell of alcohol is often on his breath nowadays.*

**June 10, 1790**
*The captain shot Seaman Ulrich tonight and had his body dumped unceremoniously into the sea. Rumor has it that it occurred after a game of cards.*

**June 11, 1790**
*I am perhaps a mutineer now, or close to it. I have entered the captain's cabin without permission and found letters. He has taken to gambling and his debts are great. He stands to lose much if he cannot repay what seems to me an impossible sum. I can only surmise he tried to purchase the native girls to sell for harlots. If I cannot prevent it, I fear the man will turn next to piracy, and if so, God help us all.*

**June 17, 1790**
*I must choose now between my captain and my soul. He has drawn me into a plan and it is horrible. He believes our passengers carry gold in the three chests they keep locked in the holds. He plans to abandon them on their island and keep their goods. Because we are low on foodstuffs, he does not even plan to leave them with the rations they have contracted for. Without their tools and seed and food to start their colony, they will surely not last the winter. Can I be a partner to such a crime, for it can be no less than murder? Yet what can I do?*

The tale carried on. About two weeks later the Island of Manannan was sighted and approached, and true to his word, the captain deposited the people on the wooded isle. The tenders were returned to the ship and the trusting colonists believed they were to come back bearing their precious cargo of tools and food, and most importantly of all, their three mysterious chests. But the captain brought aboard the tenders and weighed anchor. He meant to leave the colonists to die in the harsh and unforgiving Canadian wilderness. But a violent tempest rose up and the sea was driven mad in conflicting winds. The Mont Royal began to break up under the pounding waves. Raleigh McCavitt took action in the confusion. The next journal entry read:

> ### July 2, 1790
> *In the storm I stole the opportunity created by confusion. I broke into the hold with a trustworthy man and the servant of a family surnamed O'Shee who was to remain aboard ship to supervise the transport of the cargo. Together we brought the heavy chests up and loaded them into a tender, which we lowered into the sea. The captain and his scoundrels caught us then and they shot and killed Seaman Drake. I myself killed my captain with a shot to the head — God save my soul — and at his death his henchman fled. The ship was clearly foundering, and I did not believe she could be saved. The servant was terrified of the sea and could not move when he saw the Mont Royal sinking into it. I had to carry him down the rope with me. He is so light. I cut free the lines to the davits and we fought the storm for the shore in the little tender. I do not know how we made it against the brutal wind, but luck was with us. Many small black and white porpoises surrounded us and leapt from the furious waters, and in their presence the sea broke around us. Coppin seemed to be speaking to them as I rowed.*

Sweyn reread the entry. Then he read it again, coming back repeatedly to the name, "Coppin." At last, he pulled his eyes from the journal and rubbed them. "I must be more tired than I thought," he muttered to himself, then read the entry again. And after that last time it still read "Coppin seemed to be speaking to them as I rowed." Coppin. But that simply could not be.

"Of course it isn't, you fool," he scolded himself and flushed. The true and reasonable answer was so simple, but the Island had a way of disguising the reasonable. Between the bizarre transplanted forest, the maze of myths, the enigmatic people, the unreasonable leapt out. But simple logic held the truth of the matter, as it always did. The Coppin referred to in this journal was not the same Coppin who worked for Sweyn. A forefather perhaps, and nothing more unusual than that. Who knew, but the Coppin in his employ could be Coppin the fifth, or the tenth, or the sixteenth.

Still chiding himself for his momentary lapse into supernatural foolishness, he read on. He was down to the final entries now.

> ### July 5, 1790
> *The storm was furious and it pressed on for six more hours. I saw Mont Royal break up in it, even as I rowed the tender to shore. The waves smashed her hull so brutally that she cracked like an egg, only very slowly. Crates and barrels and dying men spilled out of her, but there was nothing I could do for any of them. This morning, much of the flotsam was to be found ashore. Strangely, none of the bodies were among it. But many of the tools and goods of the settlers survived. With this stroke of luck, these people may yet survive in this wilderness. They have a few tools, some seed, a little food to get them by a while. There is no surety, but there is now, at least, a measure of hope.*

**July 7, 1790**

*It seems I have become something of a hero to these folk. But it is not because I struggled to get their supplies to them, but only due to the three chests Drake and Coppin and myself managed to bring to them. The old woman, whom I know now to surely be a witch, for she sees far off places and possibilities and talks to things not there, proclaimed that I and my descendents shall be given a place of honor till our line has gone from the Island.*

**July 9, 1790**

*I was made the guest of honor at a ceremony at which the three chests I brought ashore were opened. The folk got into their stores of grog and there was a feast of the fruit of the sea: crabs, salmon and clams, steamed on beds of dulse and kelp. Somehow, wild rye and berries in abundance appeared at the feast. Perhaps the old witch gathered them, for I have seen none of the other people enter the wood beyond the shore. But when the chests were opened, I was dumbstruck. I cannot believe I fought and Seaman Drake died to bring this mad gift to these people. For within were nothing more than seeds of trees and herbs. Twenty kinds, the old witch said. The start of an Old World wood was all that was in the chests, and nothing of value or usefulness. I have thrown in my lot with folk as mad as was my captain.*

**July 11, 1790**

*There has been some trouble and the folk have been afraid to press into the woods beyond the shore to build their settlement. Do they not understand that they must begin soon or winter shall overtake them? Yet they bide here upon the beach beneath tents of sailcloth which has floated ashore.*

**July 16, 1790**

*The witch had seemed the strongest of the people, but now even Oak Peg fears to enter the forest. This mad lot will all die here on the shores, for winter presses closer everyday and still they will not begin their colony. I do not know what is back there, perhaps some wild natives who frighten them, but better to face them now and perish swiftly than to die a withering death come winter. Tomorrow I will go to the wood myself.*

Sweyn stopped reading again. "Oak Peg," he whispered, as if underlining the name. It was not a name one heard commonly in any time, among any people. Oak Peg. The old witch. But surely this Raleigh could not be referring to the same Oak Peg who lived in the wood back beyond the cove. He sat back and tried to imagine other explanations. None came conveniently. But he was sure he would figure out a reasonable explanation given time, so he read on.

After McCavitt recorded his entry into the forest, whatever problems the settlers were having simply seemed to stop. The journal did not offer an explanation. It simply went on. A couple more weeks of regular entries followed, until at last, Sweyn presumed, the journal must have been running out of paper, for the entries became scattered and confused, written only every week or two. Some of them were no more than a recording of the date and few words such as, "Connor's steading is neat and good," or "Maire was given a cottage of stone," or "The fruit grove will bear fruit next year." In outer appearance the entries appeared to relate mundane things, the simple development of a rural community. But the abnormal pace of the development of the community was perplexing. Sweyn could not understand how they could, in less than half a summer, create farms and plant groves, and raise cottages of stone. And yet they had, from within the sheltered bay back into the vale behind it. In that short time their village was comfortably established. And they also hunted a place they called the Guardwood, rich in game, but there were perplexing references to odd animals there, including a great deer the size of a moose, monstrous huge wolves and some kind of giant, terrifying boar. But most peculiar was the last entry, in which Raleigh appeared completely transformed. It read:

*October 31, 1790*
*The marvels I have seen cannot be written. I have found a special place and a good life among a strange and wondrous people, and luck is mine. And I have taken a wife from the good folk, which the witch thought good. It is a great honor, I am told. And I have accepted the charge of gillie, and will keep the Guardwood that comes between men and the wildwood. Its care shall be my geas and the geas of my line for all our days. The old forest has grown great now. It covers all the Island from the vale to the mountains. And the O'Shees have restored their house. There is a Laird.*

Sweyn shoved the book away in a fit of frustration. It slid to the far end of the table and fell to the floor. He didn't care. He rubbed his tired eyes again. His head hurt from translating the archaic script. And the worst part was, in the end, it hadn't helped. It had started off making sense, but now he was only more perplexed than before. And the use of the unusual names Coppin and Oak Peg bothered him in particular. He could not escape the feeling that they referred to the same people who now lived on the Island. But that was impossible.

On a whim, he took the magnifying glass and walked over to the great painting. He dragged a chair over from a table and stepped up on it. Eye-level now with the image of the tender paddling away from the foundering Mont Royal, he held the magnifying glass over the image. Now he could make out the forms of dolphins just beneath the waves around the tiny lifeboat, laden with its three precious chests. But a couple of the shadows in the water were not dolphins. They were silhouettes of persons, their genders not apparent because their body shapes were distorted by the roiling sea, but they were persons to be sure. He moved the magnifying glass over the boat. The rower looked over his shoulder, toward land, Sweyn presumed. He had the look of men of the sea, salty and leathery and weather-hardened. It could only be McCavitt. Sweyn moved the magnifying glass over the shadowy figure leaning over the prow. The figure was in three quarter profile, looking down into the waves. And the detail of the painting was such that even though the figure's face was tiny, the features were clear. It was Coppin. Clearly his Coppin.

Sweyn stepped backward, forgetting he was using a chair for a stepladder. He nearly fell but managed to keep his feet at the last moment. He stared up at the painting and shook his head. It was not possible. It absolutely was not possible! The magnifying glass slipped unnoticed from his fingers, clattered noisily on the hardwood floor. Coppin had rowed over to the Island of Manannan with Raleigh McCavitt.

In 1790.

No!

But there he was.

Sweyn could take no more. He left the room and the pile of books he yet intended to research sitting on the table. He needed answers, but he was getting none such here. This whole place and all its people were a confusing morass of delusions and superstitions. The world he thought he knew was falling apart around him with every disorienting revelation. It made him dizzy. He fled the library. The librarian rose and asked if he was all right. He looked pale. He said something rude to her as he burst from the door. The storm which had promised to come was in its glory now, fat raindrops pounding the cobblestone street, accompanied by rumbling thunder and flashes of lightning.

His heart was beating fast. He trembled and it had nothing to do with the weather. He shook his head, trying to drive away demons of memory that threatened to surface whenever stress came. It was hard, confronted as he was with the impossible.

*It could not be Coppin in that painting!*

*It could not be Oak Peg in the journal!*

That Coppin and that Oak Peg were dust now!

It was impossible, and yet the stark certainty that something impossible was going on around him, crumbling his preconceptions of the world, was tearing away his defenses. Scenting stress like blood, the memories rose like a tempest of psychic predators, gathering round his mind, clawing at his spirit, bringing the past to life.

"Make for something familiar," he told himself, or thought it, he could no longer tell. "Ground yourself in what you know is real." Starry Sea was not far away, down at the dry dock. He ran for her. It took only a couple minutes to reach. He ran for her stern and stepped onto the lowest rung of the ladder . . .

*********

. . . and there was fire. The whole deck was ablaze and the companionway was blocked. Four passengers—a newlywed couple and an engaged pair of college students—had been asleep in the aft staterooms. He and Eilwen had been sleeping in the master stateroom at the bow. The fire alarms were screaming and the emergency lighting systems were spilling terrible red light around the ship. He was struggling to push a skylight open, but it held fast, as if jammed.

He tore the backrest cushion from a settee and removed a hefty pair of cable cutters from the storage compartment behind it, and smashed the metal blades into the skylight. The transparent material was nearly indestructible, but at least it cracked. Repeatedly, in furious desperation, he rammed the blades into the skylight.

A second explosion rocked Cerulean and the vessel began to list. Green seawater poured in through the hull as her planks tore under the power of the blast. The passengers were screaming. Eilwen was back near their staterooms shouting for them to remain calm while she attempted to smash the rear skylight. Sweyn realized the skylights had been barred. Eilwen came running into the master stateroom shouting the college girl had feinted. Sweyn didn't have time to deal with it at the moment

A third explosion shook the vessel. It came from the stern and when it hit the screams of the passengers abruptly stopped. They looked at each other and both ran aft. Wreckage blocked the way to the port-stern stateroom, and the sea rushed in. The explosion had happened in there.

"What's going on?" Eilwen screamed, on the verge of panic.

But Sweyn was half in shock, realizing the passengers must be dead. "Oh my god," he breathed. "Oh my god."

Cerulean's hull began to sink from the stern, her bow lifting into the night.

They had been tied off in the pier. They should have been safe. When the first explosion had happened, Sweyn had thought maybe a neighboring boat's propane tanks had gone off. But when the second explosion happened, he knew it was something else. It was like explosives had been placed on the boat.

He came to himself. "We've got to get out of here, now!" He smashed wildly at the skylight. Once. Twice. A third impact, more vicious than any. Water was up to their waists now. To his surprise and relief, the skylight burst open. He lowered himself down, lifted Eilwen and helped her out. He looked again toward the stern. It was entirely submerged now. The passengers. Oh my god. Nothing could be done now. He knew that the moment the third explosion had hit the boat.

"Come on!" Eilwen screamed.

He grasped the lip of the skylight and pulled himself out. Eilwen was standing there, ready to take his hand. There was a loud snap, like a gunshot, but it was not a gunshot, it was the wire rigging which held the mast true. The mast had taken a pounding in the explosions and it buckled now, pulled on one side by the surviving shrouds and stays. With a sickening sound like crunching bone, it bent further over and slowly began to fall. A second terrific bang marked the tearing of the forestay from the mast. The roller furling sail was ripped out as the mast went down. The mast fell into the water, dragging the sail and rigging and a dozen attached lines with it. Suddenly, Eilwen fell over and slid from the deck into the water, a loop of line having wrapped around her foot.

Sweyn launched into a kinetic frenzy. He tore the rest of himself from the skylight, slicing himself viciously on fragments of glass, and dove into the water. In the darkness of the midnight sea, lit only by the weak light of sodium vapor lights on the pier, he could see nothing. But he felt with his hands everywhere, casting about for Eilwen. He found her, struggling ten feet down where she had been dragged by the weight of the mast to the bottom. She was wrapped in the foresail which had sunk down and enveloped her. He drew his marlinspike knife from his pocket, sliced desperately at it, fighting the need to breathe till his lungs seared him. He shot to the surface to grasp a single breath and a final explosion pounded the hull of dying Cerulean, stunning him momentarily. The knife slipped from his fingers. He dove for it but it was lost in the blackness. He abandoned it and grasped the sailcloth again, struggling frantically to tear it clear of her. He tore at it till his hands bled but he knew he could never get it off her. The sail was built to hold up to the worst ocean gales. It would never rip beneath only his hands.

When the fire trucks and police cars came, the rescue workers found Sweyn still thrashing wildly in the water, nearly dead from exhaustion and blanched white from cold. He was still trying to tear the sail open and set his beloved free, though she had long since gone still. And though he was at the bitter end of his strength, it took six of them to pull him from the water, away from the sinking hulk of Cerulean.

When at last they got him onto the pier the rescue workers wrapped him in blankets while two police officers restrained him to keep him from flying back into the water. He hardly had strength to resist them at that point, lost in a numb haze of exhaustion, disbelief and terror. But a single lucid moment came to him when he looked up the pier, in that direction he and Eilwen had walked so many times together before, bringing passengers to their boat, or groceries, or tools, or just walking for the sake of going somewhere hand in hand. And there, at the head of the pier was the seawall, the seawalk over it. And standing at the edge of it, leaning against a guardrail, was the silhouette of a male figure, watching. Sweyn saw him and the figure stood up straight then. It saluted, a queer, familiar gesture. And then the figure turned and faded into the night.

*********

And then Sweyn was lying on the ground beneath Starry Sea. The bulk of his faithful old vessel sheltered him from the rain which had increased to a torrential downpour. Cans of bottom paint were strewn about, and tools were tossed and there was blood on his forehead. He was trembling uncontrollably, but it was not because he was soaked and cold. At least no one had been around to see the flashback take him. But in truth he hardly cared what these people thought. They were as mad and haunted as he.

Breathless, he tried to stand, and finding it too hard, he leaned against Starry Sea's keel, and he cried.

# Chapter Seven

*It was only when I truly opened my eyes that the Island ceased to drive me mad. And somewhere thereafter, it healed me. Only I had never known I needed to be healed.*

Lieutenant Raleigh McCavitt
First gillie of the Guardwood

It passed somehow, as it always did, though he knew not how, for whenever the flashbacks flared to life it seemed they would swallow him up forever. Eilwen, his Eilwen, was gone, gone to a place he could not follow, gone forever where even dreams may not reach. But it was easier for life to pass than pain, and he cried long there beneath Starry Sea, leaning his head against her keel, his only cold, hard comfort. But it was his last link to Eilwen, and the vessel was his old friend. It was the best comfort he had.

The rain poured and the wind began to blow, and the thunder grew louder and the lightning brighter. He was soaked and freezing, for the wind blew the rain beneath Starry Sea's broad beam and water ran abundantly down the hull and trickled over him. His skin became white with cold and he began to shiver violently. Perhaps it was the bite of the weather that at last thrust sense into him. But it did not seem so, for he was too far gone in grief to feel the weather. Rather, some compulsion, some feeble but steady coal of inner strength that originated from someplace within he did not know compelled him to rise and take shelter.

Eilwen, he knew, would not have wanted him to drain his life away in this storm. Eilwen would want him to carry on.

For Eilwen he pushed himself up, leaning wobbly-kneed against the hull as he gathered his heart into him. The hull was wet and slick. He felt woozy, but whether from hypothermia or a sickness of the soul he could not tell. He made his way to the ladder and did not bother to wipe the tears out of his eyes. The storm did that well enough.

He climbed, shoving the pain and the memories further down with each step. Carry on, yes, he could do that, by sheer will. But it was an empty continuance, for he could find no joy in it. Not even though he knew his lost beloved would have wished it. The capability to grasp joy again was beyond him, forever drowned in the tenebrous sea of grief, lying cold and leached in the black depths, wrapped in a salt shroud of sailcloth.

In the cockpit the familiar force of habit guided him, strengthened him. He stepped around the helm to the companionway. He undid the lock and lifted the top two of three slats and stepped over the lowest, stepped within to the companionway ladder. He descended, closing the companionway behind him.

Even the expansive dodger could not hold back the torrent and some of it sprayed into the salon. He did not care.

The interior of Starry Sea was chilly and silent except for the threnody of rain on the deck. Yet the smell of the vessel was comforting, a familiar fragrance of many things at once: old teak and varnish, the salt tang of the sea, the closeness of a dry, airtight space.

He walked to the forward stateroom. Against the portside bulkhead beside a locker a Newport oil heater was mounted. He flipped the switch to power the oil pump that fed the heater. After waiting a minute for fuel to charge the combustion chamber, he lit the oil and started the heater fan to help it go. In a couple minutes a cheery fire shown through the heater's mica window, glowing in the interior of the salon like a small warm hearth.

"What am I doing here?" he muttered, tiredly rubbing the bridge of his nose with a cold half-numb hand.

But he knew what he was doing here. Manannan was getting to him. Too many strange things on the Island. Too many incomprehensible mysteries nibbling at his fragile grasp on sanity. He needed a measure of comfort. He needed the solid, familiar presence of his vessel, the nearness of the sea, the reassurance of the nearby surf pounding the beach. The flame in the heater quietly fluttered as he fell against the settee beside it, and it was very pleasant. It was ambrosia. It soothed better than liquor. It was kinder than the southern wind. It was home.

But he was here for something else as well, and he knew it. He should leave it alone, but for three years and more he had carried it, knowing a day would come he must look into it. Now, if there was ever a time, this was the time.

But he could not summon the strength.

Do it, it seemed a voice whispered. A familiar voice. A voice too briefly known and too deeply loved. Do it.

He summoned what little strength he had remaining. He rose. The heater was already driving the chill from the salon. He opened the door to the forward stateroom and went to the small drawer beside the locker. In the back of the drawer, behind a pile of socks, was a bundle of papers. And beneath the bundle was a single envelope. Long ago it had been opened by the person it was addressed to. And its contents had changed her life, though he never understood it. Eilwen had never spoken of it, and he had never asked.

Open it, came the whisper again, so faint it could only have arisen from the depths of desperate memory. But the feel of the voice was a familiar singsong brogue, and in its wake was a hint of the fragrance of forest herbs.

"I'm haunted," he moaned. "I'm half mad." Half mad, all mad. All the same.

He opened the envelope, unfolded the letter. More than a half year before Eilwen had perished, the letter had come to her. After she had read it she had become moribund, silent, faded. She had not been the same in all their remaining time, and she would never talk to him about it. Only she said, "Dinna' ever go to Manannan, promise me." And he had made the promise. And but for a storm and an inexplicable lapse of self he never would have broken it, for he was sure she had hated this place above all things.

He steeled himself and read the letter.

*Lady Eilwen,*

*The father has taken to hunting Caitlin again and pursues her often into the Guardwood. He swears he will never give up though there is no hope. Still, I fear we will lose them both if this continues. I have seen the elder in their wake.*

*Come back to us, Eilwen. We need you. Come back before it is too late for both of them, and you. Things are drawing to a head and the price of a forsaken geas draws nigh.*

*You are the last O'Shee.*

*O.P.*

Sweyn stared at the letter in silence, gripping it so tightly the corner tore in his fist. It was nothing like he might have expected, and he felt a skein of lies, created not by things said, but things left unsaid, tangling around him.

Lady Eilwen? That was the second time he had come across that title. Who had Eilwen been, truly? It was no longer in doubt that she had been some kind of noble to these people. It was the only way to explain how it was the local folk thought he had come to be their Laird, whatever that was. But why had Eilwen never spoken of this? Did she think it would matter to him?

But what confounded him more was the reference to a Caitlin. Eilwen had had a sister named Caitlin, six years younger. The girls had loved each other dearly, but Caitlin was dead, lost in the wood when the girl was ten. But this letter was not four years old. Clearly, it could not refer to Eilwen's sister. Caitlin was a common enough Celtic name. The letter must refer to another girl of the Island.

But in his heart, he was less than sure.

His head swam, and a pressure began to pound in his skull. Too many mysteries in this place. Too many ghosts that should lie quiet. Too many half truths and deceptions. A tangle of unspoken lies.

He let his head drop back onto the settee cushion, stilling his thoughts by focusing on the roar of rain on the deck. It did not help. A lump grew in his throat as he began to realize how much he had not known about his wife, how much she had kept from him. Oh, Eilwen, why were you not open with me? How could you deceive me?

He rubbed his forehead, pushed stray hairs out of his eyes, and forced his thoughts onto the next enigma, the peculiar reference to "the father." The term was very vague. Eilwen's father had abandoned the family when she was six, just after the birth of her sister, and he had never been seen or heard from since, so the letter had to refer to Caitlin's father. But why not just call him that?

He considered whether the girls could have been half sisters, but that was out of the question too. Eilwen's mother had died of a broken heart a couple years after her worthless husband abandoned the family. The Caitlin of that union had perished in the woods twenty years ago. Yet the Caitlin of this letter was alive just four years ago. There could be no relation. Still, the coincidence of name was uncanny.

But perhaps a more important question was why was this "father" hunting Caitlin, whoever she was. And why on earth did the letter read as if it were sympathetic to him, for how else could he interpret "though there is no hope".

What bizarre drama was being played out when the letter was written? What skeletons was Man-by-the-Sea hiding in its closet?

And what was this Guardwood where the girl had fled? The mutineer, McCavitt, had also written of it in his venerable journals. It must occupy a large portion of the Island if someone could vanish into it indefinitely. But why would Caitlin choose to flee there rather than turn to her neighbors for help?

And what did the reference to "the elder in their wake" mean? Was there some dangerous old codger back in the forest? At this point, Sweyn supposed anything was possible.

But the final part of the letter was the most ominous. Coppin had made the geas sound like fate or karma. But the letter made it sound more like a family curse? It could not be denied that the O'Shee line in the last quarter century seemed doomed to unhappy ends. The superstitious people of the Island could easily enough interpret that for a curse in action. But Sweyn did not believe in curses. And he could not escape the feeling the passage referred to something more. To him, what it seemed to say was that Eilwen had left something undone when she left the Island, and there was a price for it.

The letter contained mystery upon mystery, and revealed that nothing upon the Island was as it appeared. And it brought home the painful truth that he had known so little of Eilwen she was almost a stranger. At the end of the reading, Sweyn was left only with more questions than before. But at least, perhaps, he knew which questions to ask now. And the letter gave him a good guess where to start, for "O.P." could only refer to one person: Oak Peg. Somehow she was at the heart of all this. Impossibly mentioned in McCavitt's ancient journal, reappearing here in this letter, she must have answers. Sweyn was determined she would supply them.

The dull coal of rage, which had smoldered in his heart like an infection since the day in the alley, responded to his fierce intent as if a breath were blown across it. It glowed brighter, more dangerous.

That same hint of a voice warned him to be cautious of Oak Peg. And what lay within himself.

He was folding the letter to slip back into the envelope when he spied script on the back. It was lightly written in pencil, Eilwen's hand. Six words. It read: "O'Shee will never have my Sweyn." For the longest time he sat frozen, staring at the half-folded letter in his hand. There it was: Eilwen had been afraid. Something here had frightened her. And for him, of all things.

The thought that something in this place had frightened Eilwen fed his anger. It took root quickly and grew fast and ran deep. Anger such as this, he knew, was dangerous. Could trigger flashbacks. Could drive him to worse. He turned to familiar, comforting routine to salvage himself. Shutting down the heater took half a dozen steps. Then he had to shut down the ship's power systems. Then he dried the companionway and the area around it to prevent mildew, and wiped clear the Dorade vents to help dry air flow. When it was all done, the comfort of routine had given him back his composure. But still too angry to pay heed to the storm, he left Starry Sea, on a mission. He would get answers. Come hell or high water, he would get answers.

He went to the pub which doubled as the Island's post office and sent two hastily scrawled letters, one to a genealogist in Victoria, another to a title company in Prince George. Then, compelled by a burning sense of resolve, he walked back to Dundubh Cottage. It was his Cottage, after all, and it would give him answers.

If he had to strip it stone from stone and plank from plank, if he had to overturn every piece of furniture and plow every inch of earth, if he had to rend Coppin himself, he would get answers. Before he was finished, he would know why Eilwen had hated this place so much, and what she had been so afraid of that she had felt the need to lie to him.

*********

Ignoring the rain he walked up the north path and soon passed the last of the farms and entered the woodlands. For the first time he understood, instinctively, this must be the Guardwood. It shielded Dundubh Cottage from the eyes of the rest of the Island, though why the O'Shees should desire such privacy he could not imagine. In the gloom of the fading day, with roiling low clouds and crashes of thunder and flashes of lightning, the forest seemed only a dreary shroud, a place where sad dreams and lonesome things must dwell. The trees, now green with early summer leaves, were bent beneath the weight of the rain, their swaying boughs shedding water over the rich black loam at their roots. No bird songs brightened the forest. No shafts of golden sun promised bright hopes. There were only the damp and deepening shadows. The storm even washed the green away.

Without warning, the storm increased its power. It was as if the celestial dams had burst and a deluge poured through the sieve of clouds. Rain sprayed the land so hard it stung as it pelted him. It obscured his way, turning the world into a dark haze of grey. It pounded his shoulders and drove him to refuge, which he sought in the only available place, beneath the boughs of a great beech tree off the edge of the path. But the tree was not the best shelter. Its branches were widespread and water coruscated down the trunk, spraying over him as if pouring from a roof gutter. It was icy. He was driven deeper into the wood, from tree to tree, seeking one whose branches were woven tightly enough to cut back the downpour.

He found a semblance of shelter beneath the knitted boughs of a great cedar, whose green foliage and tightly gathered twigs scattered the falling water round about it. The tree grew on a slight elevation, only a couple feet above the forest surface, but it was like an island at this moment. The forest loam all around had transformed into a black and gooey mud, but beneath the cedar was stacked the brown and fragrant deadfall of many previous years, and at the very base of the trunk was a bed of seasoned cedar needles, soft and inviting and wonderfully dry. The bottommost boughs hung so low they even cut the wind, and the tree offered a sweet measure of warmth. He huddled beneath its branches while the rain poured and poured in endless grey sheets. The sound of it was like the roar of a river's surging rapids.

Sweyn knotted his fists and ground his teeth as he was forced to wait for the torrent to ease. He was impatient for it to ease. His fury made him impatient. He wanted to get back to Dundubh Cottage now and tear his answers out of it. He needed to understand Eilwen. His smoldering fury drove the need like a hunger, and it was changing him, for he no longer was in terror of reawakening the memories. He wanted to know all about his lost wife, every secret hope and fear, for it was clear now that the better part of her he did not know, had never known. And until he did, the only woman he had ever loved must in truth be only a stranger whose life had once touched him.

But the storm carried on oblivious of him, and the day became darker as the afternoon waned. Time passed but the rain did not. Puddles formed over the earth around his tiny retreat, puddles that became a moat, and raindrops splashed melodically into it. They struck a ceaseless tune, like the tapping of fingernails on crystal decanters. It was a sweet sound, and it comforted him despite himself. In the cool melody his anger softened, becoming a dim coal in his breast rather than a furnace in his brain. And with the failing of the anger went his impetus. It faded, faded, becoming weariness, until he was lulled into drowsiness by the ceaseless raindrop chatter, until his lids became heavy, until his forehead fell upon forearms folded around drawn up knees.

*********

When he woke the rain still tumbled down, but lightly, out of grey clouds. But the clouds were smooth now, shallow-curved cumuli that promised only a shower and not the full rage of a storm. Drops had become droplets and the droplets plashed into mirror puddles round about him, creating countless ripples that coruscated over reflections of gloomy sky and a network of forest boughs. The forest remained bereft of birdsong. Only the sound of water, falling, sliding, rolling, plashing, splashing, with a thousand simultaneous voices filled it. There was the fragrance of fresh green and pungent sap, and the sweet, earthy scent of mud. But at least the storm had abated to the point Sweyn could make his way to Dundubh Cottage now. He crawled out from the canopy of cedar and stood in the drizzle. It fell like ocean spray over him, cool and familiar.

He looked for the road and realized he could not see it. The forest shadows were not so deep, nor the rain falling so hard, that it was obscured. He realized he had simply wandered further into the wood in search of shelter than he had thought. It was an easy enough mistake to make, given that he could barely see in front of him at the time of the torrent. But he did not think that he had wandered so far from the road that he would be unable to find his way back. The trouble was, which way was back?

He turned round and round. Oaks and hazels and the odd evergreen were all there was to be seen. The first pang of worry hit him as he realized he could become quite lost should he choose the wrong course at this point. Manannan was not a big island, but it was not small either. Ten miles wide and shaped in a crescent like a quarter moon, it encompassed many square miles of untamed forest. Yet the road was somewhere nearby. If he went the correct direction, he would come to it in minutes. If he made the wrong choice, he could be lost in this weirdly misplaced European hardwood for a very long time.

But try as he might, he could not discern the way back. And the shadows continued to deepen. At last, he drew a deep breath and chose a course while there was still some light. He marched into the darkness. It took him only five minutes of picking his way between trunks and puddles the breadth of ponds to realize the course he had taken was poorly chosen. It took him only another fifteen to realize he was lost. And it took him only another half hour, when the shadows of the brief post-storm twilight were nigh to fading into complete darkness, to begin to worry. He was soundly lost, and the woodlands of this Island were broad enough that he might never find his way out.

The last of the evening luminescence, a hazy, grayish pall beneath the starless sky, had nearly gone when he saw the lights distant in the woods. Like amethyst candle flames, they seemed to promise respite. The last time he had seen such lights was near Oak Peg's cottage, the aquamarine flickers that fluttered and spiraled at the edge of vision back in the dark oak woods beyond her iron gate. These scintillations were not quite the same as those, the hue was off, and they did not zip about so playfully, but wafted, like soap bubbles on a breeze. But the lights were the closest thing to a destination he had seen since well before dark— they at least gave him something to aim for. Perhaps if he went in their direction, he reasoned, he might find his way to Oak Peg's cottage. If nothing else, it would be an interesting sight. He pressed through the wood that way.

But the lights receded as he pursued them, and the faster he went, the more they fell back. He passed great stands of oaks and hazels, a scattering of birch with pines mixed in. He came to a grey acreage of burned out husks of trees, where a lightning strike had scorched the wood years past, and stumbled through it. He ground his shins against the bark of massive fallen branches and charred, broken trunks as he pressed hard through the devastated field, and scratched his hands on the raspberry canes that grew there. But he paid all this no mind. In the chase for the amethyst candle flickers before him, such small hurts did not matter.

And then he could hear the sea. It beckoned him from the far side of the burn, on the other side of a marsh. And the candle flickers drifted above the marsh where they stayed. He approached and they did not fall back any longer.

Had Sweyn been thinking in his right mind, his goal would have been the sea, for on the sandy shore he could have veered right and walked over soft sand until he reached Man-by-the-Sea, surely no more than a couple miles away. But his mind was no longer on getting out of the wood. Somewhere along the way that objective had been lost. Now his thoughts were only on approaching those beautiful living gems that radiated their own inner light, and gazing into them from up close. He stepped into a stand of cattails and wild rye, growing thick and leading down into the brown murk of standing water. At this barrier of green, the ash and black hues of the burn suddenly ended. He paused briefly at the marsh's edge, gazing into the lucid amethyst lights, a dozen, floating quietly, motionlessly, and then made to step into the water.

"Walk no' further, no' if ye value yer mortal life," a deep but melodious voice spoke beside him.

The shock of hearing the unexpected voice startled him back to his senses. He sucked in breath and took several steps sideways, lost his footing, and began stumbling and sliding down into the stagnant pool.

A strong hand shot out, grasped his own flailing arm, held like oak and steadied him. Sweyn turned in automatic reaction to his savior, words at the verge of parted lips, but they did not emerge, for the speaker placed a finger over his mouth. "No, lad. Dinna' thank. Never thank." The figure pulled Sweyn up and away from the standing water, back into the ash of the old burn.

He was dark, this stranger. A head shorter than Sweyn, and he wore raggedy clothing of coarsely woven wool, but the vestments were clean and possessed a fresh scent like a pinewood after a shower. His shirt was cut in the form of a tunic, and had no sleeves. Arms so hairy they were almost furred hung gangling from his shoulders. The same shaggy growth could be seen upon his chest, where the tunic was cut low and airy. The hairy growth extended up his neck to his chin and sideburns, yet he had no beard or mustache, though it did not appear he ever shaved. The shaggy growth was just a rough outline of bristle that grew on his face like an untrimmed hedge. The figure had wizened skin and long curly brown hair. He wore breeches that ended just below the knee, revealing gangly calves as hairy as his arms or face or chest, and around his neck was a necklace of twine laced with the blossoms of clover. Most disturbing about the odd fellow were his eyes. They seemed to flicker, like a cat's eyes in moonlight, except there was no moon this nubilous night.

Sweyn regarded the strange figure cautiously, and for the first time he seemed to become aware of his surroundings, the old forest burn, the verge of the marsh with its boggy, black stand of water, still as a drowned corpse. Out beyond the marsh, a hundred yards more distant, he could see the grey sands of the beach glowing dimly in the night, the black sea beyond, and the phosphorescence of breaking waves rolling over the shallows. But he hardly paid attention, for more distracting and beautiful were the amethyst candle flickers hovering silently over the marsh waters, their cold light reflecting in it like a small scatter of stars. He looked back to the stranger, trying to find words and questions, but nothing came to his hazy mind.

"Come with me," said the hairy stranger, and he led Sweyn away from the stagnant water. Sweyn followed, though often his eyes drifted behind him, to the candle flickers. They seemed to call to him, though they made not a sound. He longed to risk the marsh and peer into their luminous depths.

"They are the wisps," said the fellow. "Some have called them in other tongues the swamp lads and the fool lights. Stay away from them."

Sweyn managed to pull his eyes from them. The growing distance helped. "Are they dangerous?"

"Aye. Though it is no' as if they mean to be. They simply are. It's their nature to glow, and the nature of mortals to be drawn to them as moths to a flame. They dwell in the moors and over bogs, and that is what makes them dangerous to ye."

"Fireflies," whispered Sweyn.

"Now ye know, lad, they're no' fireflies."

Sweyn followed him a long time, in silence. He knew his guide was right, but it was hard to reckon with, easier to deny, easier still to forget. So he said instead, "Are we going out?"

"Indeed, out. And see to it ye dinna' enter this place again from twilight till dawn. It's safer by day."

"Who are you?" Sweyn said as they left the burn and entered the dripping forest where he ducked the low branch of a last fire-scarred tree.

"For a long time I've been called Broom. Some say I'm a gillie, and I guess there is truth to it."

Automatically, Sweyn said, "What's a gillie?"

"A warden. A caretaker of the wood. Do ye know nothing, lad?"

"The more time I spend here, the less I think I know," Sweyn confessed.

"An outsider, then. A newcomer too. I should have known by the speech, though it's been long and long since I've spoken to the folk of Man-by-the-Sea. Right-minded folk, they are, but it is no' my preference to be about their ordered fields and squarish lodgings. But now I see why ye know so little. Then take my word and leave it at that, stay out of the Guardwood by night. And since ye're an outsider, stay out by day too. Folk here are none too trusting of outsiders, and it has been long since one has been among us."

"There's a yacht down in the bay right now, with a cruising couple not from these parts aboard," said Sweyn. "No one has a problem with them."

"They dinna' leave Man-by-the-Sea's surrounds either," Broom quipped.

Sweyn realized the hairy man was walking a straight, unerring path, though Sweyn could not tell the direction. As his guide went, he slipped quietly through the wood, stepping fluidly over every fallen branch, swishing through the thin undergrowth with no more noise than the breath of a moth's wing. Clearly he was an expert woodsman. "You said you're the gillie," Sweyn said. "So you look after all the grounds of the Island?"

"I used to keep the moors," Broom said, "in another country. Here I watch the beach and the narrow marshes, and the lands just above them. There is another who keeps the Guardwood further inland for the O'Shees. He is one of yer folk."

"You mean someone else works for me I haven't met yet?" Sweyn asked.

That stopped Broom quite suddenly. He turned and looked over Sweyn as if newly regarding him. "Are ye saying ye're an O'Shee?" he asked, and his voice took on a new, indiscernible quality.

"Not in name," Sweyn told him. "Though I inherited Dundubh Cottage."

"Do ye tell me that now," Broom croaked, and he looked Sweyn in the eye, as if measuring him.

Sweyn nodded.

"I thought I should know ye, but ye look so different now. Not the desolate wild man upon the water, eh? As ye were in the storm."

"Excuse me?" said Sweyn.

*Some dark thing, almost as large as a man, was crouched on two legs in the pulpit, just in front of the windlass. Long fingered handlike paws clutched at something sinuous and creamy white. A strip of sailcloth. And then with a grace surprising from the gangly, crouching wild thing, it slipped off the bow into the brine.*

Sweyn froze in his tracks, pinned by the memory. His breath fled as he stared at the wild man who led him, his mind trying to reconcile the hairy, upright image before him with the crouched, sea-soaked creature that had appeared on the foredeck of Starry Sea the day he was blown into the bay of the Island. Now Broom was dressed and dry, but there was no mistaking him. This is what he saw at the prow of Starry Sea.

But that was impossible! No man could have swum in that storm.

No man. Then what was this thing standing before him? Ice coursed his veins, then. But hot anger came also. He hissed, "You! You sabotaged my boat! You tore my sail!"

But Broom turned and continued walking, muttering to himself as if he had not heard Sweyn. "So, a new O'Shee has come at last. It seemed the line would fail, but it often seems like that, and it never does."

Sweyn swore and stepped hotly after the burly little man. "I know you! I don't know how, but you got on my boat in that storm. You cut my sail. I could have died!"

Still Broom carried on as if Sweyn's ranting was inconsequential. Sweyn wanted to kill him. He picked up a large fallen branch, hefted it. "I don't know what your game is, but I'm going to get some answers!" he yelled at Broom's back. He closed the distance, but then Broom stopped in his tracks, freezing Sweyn. Still facing away from Sweyn, his head bobbed and his arms moved animatedly. Sweyn cocked his head, realizing the mad little fellow was reciting something. No, singing it. To a tune like a child's song, the wild little woodsman was singing some bizarre nursery rhyme.

*Some are blown,*
*Some are brought,*
*And some just marry into the lot.*

*Some are fallowed,*
*Some are scattered,*
*And some there are who are but shattered.*

*Some will pine,*
*Some do fine,*
*But always works the geas' design.*

Suddenly, the little man returned to the present. He whirled on Sweyn and gazed hard up at him, his eyes full of a fierce emerald light. In the force of Broom's gaze, Sweyn let go the branch. It fell silent to the dark, sodden earth. Broom said, "Now I know the oak witch's game. I thought she was at last full mad when she sent me into that storm, for I'm no merman. But now I see, with ye here, all cleaned up and in yer right mind, where I hardly recognized ye, that ye are the next O'Shee."

"What are you talking about," Sweyn demanded, stepping back warily from the wild man.

But Broom continued to think aloud. "Ye must have been Eilwen's husband. There's no doubt. And ye say ye dinna' like it here in the wood. Do ye no' know the Guardwood is yers. It and the wildwood, they're yer ward. To hold the Pact."

Sweyn shook his head. "I'd sell it all and be done with it, except for a promise."

The little man looked inward and frowned. "A good woman, Eilwen. A shame to have lost her. The geas may bite. Indeed, it may." Then he looked outward again, at Sweyn. "Made ye promise, did Eilwen? I'm no' at all surprised, no, no' surprised at all. In the end, the geas always goes to an O'Shee. Though sometimes the O'Shee doesn't want it. Or even realize what he is."

Suddenly, the little man sprinted into the forest, moving with surprising speed, as fast and fleet as a buck. Sweyn bolted after him, calling desperately after his vanishing, insane guide.

"Ye want out of the Guardwood?" Broom called over his shoulder as he ran, his deep voice echoing beneath the scattered boughs. "Find yer own way. A Laird should learn the going and coming of his own ward."

And then he was gone and Sweyn quit running after him. The little fellow was surprisingly fleet, his endurance astounding. Sweyn himself, whose health was good, found himself leaning over, hands on bent knees, gasping to catch his breath.

Broom's voice boomed behind him suddenly, very close. Sweyn spun, startled, crouched and ready to fight or fly, but he could not see him. "But stay out of the wildwood," the voice bellowed through the dark, the brogue rich and ancient. "No mortal kin goes into the wildwood, no' even the Laird, though it be his in name to look after."

Then there was silence and Sweyn's eyes desperately sought to pierce the night, but if the little man still crouched in the shadows, he could not tell. There was nothing there but the moist dark, and dripping trees, and the sounds of a post-storm forest gently coming back to life.

Time passed, and how much he was not certain. He could not see the ebon sky through the latticework of boughs, and even if he could, a scudding sheet of silent, heavy cloud held back every star. In the dark, with only the accompaniment of night sounds, the evening was timeless and formless, a great leering void of emptiness like Ginnungagap, ready to swallow up anything that stumbled into it.

Sweyn stood there, and he waited. Despite himself, he hoped that his guide would return. But he knew in his heart Broom would not. The crazed woodsman seemed as twisted as every other person on the Island. Whether folk of village or of forest or his own estate, whether greatly odd or only subtly so, everyone on this rock was mad, driven by forces and desires and goals he could not begin to fathom.

Only now he was starting to feel he needed to.

Clearly, Eilwen had understood them.

And the more he learned of these people, the more he began to understand just how much like them his own fey wife had been.

He turned round and round, then, where he stood, searching the darkness for some sign of the direction he should go. If Man-by-the-Sea were an ordinary town full of brightly lit houses, the spilling light might have colored the low clouds and moisture-laden sky a hazy gold, pointing the way out. But no such thing was to be found in this luckless place. Man-by-the-Sea was illumined by oil lamps and candles. What little electricity the village consumed was used only for shortwave marine radios and the community's few phones. It was so little it was all garnered through a few small wind turbines. There was no urbanish glow to light his way.

He was sure he was not yet too far from the road, and if this were some other place he might yet hope to catch sight of a streetlight, or a passing car. But the Island's roads were only frail paths upon the landscape; there were no streetlights. And the only persons on the Island who might drive gas powered vehicles were the farmers, but they were not likely to be out at this hour. They drove only tractors and a few trucks to haul equipment, and there was no need for farm work at this hour. He would languish in the darkness if he only stood here, waiting for vehicle lights to show him the way out.

The situation offered no ready solution. As he had done so many times at sea, he must rely on himself now. Except on land Sweyn was very much out of his element.

There was nothing else for it but to press ahead, simply going one direction and hoping he ran into something useful. But within ten minutes he knew he could not be moving toward the road. The terrain rose, becoming hilly. The trees grew taller, the canopy of forest thicker so that the forest floor became clear and park-like, for in the endless sepia shadows beneath those boughs little foliage grew.

But there were odd noises in the forest, coming from one direction and another. At one point he heard something that sounded like the ringing of crystal bowls. The sound was sweet yet had the power to penetrate to the bone. It seemed to come from behind him no matter which way he turned. He began to fear, then, for it was neither insect nor beast that made such droning. What it was, he did not know, but no rational thought could account for it.

*And if one were beyond reason, anything the imagination can conjure is possible.*

He shook away the thought, for it was not a thing to bear here, alone, in the living dark. He pressed on and in time the crystal sound faded. He ascended a low hill which shortly leveled out, and at last it began to descend. As he descended the hill he could make out what must have been the sound of flowing water. As he pressed on, the sound clarified: fast water dancing over stones and splashing down tiny falls and racing around fallen branches. For the first time since the night came down he allowed himself a smile. A stream could only flow out to the ocean, and on this small Island the stream could not have far to go. He needed only follow it and he would soon be out of the wood.

And he was glad of the stream for another reason. The night was turning warm and muggy since the rain had passed, and he was thirsty. He had been unwilling to drink from any of the scattered puddles he had splashed through, but he might risk a drink from a clear flowing forest stream. He pressed on until at last the hill bottomed out, and at the very root of it, in a tiny vale, a narrow stream no more than eight feet broad coursed down the little glen. The water flowed clear, fast and deep, skipping over rocks and foaming white where stones and branches impeded it. Just to his right, the stream swelled behind a natural dam of tumbled stone into a small, calm pool. He approached the pool and knelt to drink the cool water.

The water was like liquid crystal, deep and clear. He dipped his hands into it. It felt cool, clean and soft. He cupped his hands, lifted and poured water into his mouth, over his head. It slaked his thirst, washed the sweat away. He drank his fill and sat to rest a moment beside the pool, taking comfort in the presence of the familiar element of water. From somewhere above the hill came a sound like soft thunder. He thought it was the dying remnant of the storm and ignored it. He leaned his back against a stone and looked into the darkness over the pool, to where the banks narrowed again and the stream continued on down the glen.

What if it led into the wildwood? he wondered. Why did that crazy Broom warn him to stay out of there?

Probably Broom was a squatter, living back in those woods, technically Sweyn's woods, and he did not want Sweyn going back there and discovering his camp. That's what a more reasonable part of himself argued.

But a less reasonable part argued something other. Bide Broom; beware the wildwood, it urged. Angry at himself for his childish fears of the dark, he kicked a stone. It flew into the still water, disturbing the tranquility of the pool. Rings spread over the surface, then settled. The soft thunder came again, and with it another set of rings, this time originating from his side of the bank.

That was curious. Thunder could not cause such a thing. He leaned over and looked into the pool.

The pale white face of a lady gazed up at him from beneath the surface. She was deep-eyed and her skin was like moonlight. Her hair floated like suspended threads of gold around her white cheeks, framing slender shoulders clad in green. She was still as death, and around her tiny golden radiances darted about, like minnows. Within those watery lights were the nude, diminutive forms of girls

Sweyn's heart beat a sudden staccato rhythm, his breath came in short faltering jerks. The lady — for she could be described as nothing other — was regal and fair in appearance. She lay just beneath the surface, as if on her back, staring unblinking up into the forest night. And she was utterly motionless, appearing in the pool as the reflection of a painting, the frozen essence of a captured, nubile dream. Trembling, he drew back from the stream, pressed his back to the rock.

The soft thunder came again, behind him, and the still water rippled harder.

Turn, a part of his mind demanded.

He ignored it. He refused to take his eyes from the pool.

"Turn," came another voice, only as the faintest whisper. It bore a familiar ring, the fragrance of herbs and sweet tea.

He turned, and the impossible met his vision. A tree glided through the inky darkness. Great and tall it was, its trunk towering high as the massive oaks around it. It could only be seen as a deeper shadow against a backdrop of shadow, but it was plainly no oak. It moved as if upon a writhing storm cloud which scudded slowly across the earth. Its movement was steady, though from time to time it seemed to make a great surge forward, as if it were taking a giant step. As it closed the distance he discerned the tree was traveling on a mass of tangled small roots, its own root system. Thousands of roots were continually lifting and pushing ahead and retracting so that the tree-thing appeared to float over the earth. But at those irregular intervals when it surged ahead, it moved great roots beneath it like spider legs, which heaved the great bulk of it forward.

As the thing drew closer, the air grew colder. Malice surrounded it like a cloud. This thing, whatever impossible thing it was, was old, older than the hills he stood between, and it was no friend of Man. It was no accident that it came upon his path. It hunted the night.

Behind him there came the sound of breaking water, then dripping water plashing upon still water. And a soft breath, smelling fresh like the air about waterfalls. A voice there was upon the breath, delicate as mists, but it was lovely, though cold as the stream that fed this pool. It sent shivers down his spine to hear it. He turned away from the impossible horror of the walking tree to see what had risen from the pool, and there, standing above the still water was the lady, all but for her feet which remained beneath the crystal surface to the ankle, which was impossible, for the bottom was much deeper. "Elderman," whispered she, and her eyes were tortured emeralds.

The great tree that could not possibly be a tree continued lumbering toward the pool, aiming unerringly in Sweyn's direction. It knew he was here, Sweyn realized. It sensed him in the darkness. It was coming for him. And with its approach, the darkness seemed to grow thicker. The air grew so chill he could see his breath, and he shivered. But the thing was slow. He was sure he could outrun it. But for how long? While he would stumble in the darkness and often lose his feet, it would never falter, never fail its pace. It would come relentlessly, like the nightmares that pursued him just beneath his consciousness. And in his exhaustion, or when he sprained an ankle or cracked a knee, it would overcome him.

Still, the instinct to run was strong, overpowering.

A wet hand, chill as the benighted pool, touched his shoulder, and there was kinship between the seaman and the brook lady. "Hold," she whispered.

The tiny golden lights in the pool darted this way and that. "Asrai," she softly spoke to them, and pointed downstream. Suddenly, one darted through the clear water into the current of the stream. Then, downstream fifty paces and all but concealed in shadow, he saw himself, but he was standing upon the surface of the stream.

The impossibly massive elder tree turned in the direction of the doppelganger, started that way. The image of his own self turned and fled downstream. But it did not run on solid earth, only where the water flowed. Its feet never splashed upon the water, never raised a capricious drop. It vanished into the wood, and the ancient, malignant tree flowed and lumbered after it.

"Glamour," came the cold whisper of the lady.

He watched in awe and horror as the tree-thing disappeared into the dark and the distance. And then he turned his attention to the preternatural entity behind him, a word of gratitude upon his lips. But he never spoke it, for he fell toward her, or was drawn toward her, or threw himself at her, he could not tell, and she wrapped her cold arms around him as if embracing him and held him close and tight. Her lips pressed soft and moist against his: the texture was like dulse beneath the tide. She kissed him, softly, repeatedly, about his cheeks, but there was no love in her eyes. They were unreadable eyes, full of unknowable thoughts quite beyond mortal grasp. Down he and the watery damsel fell, down into the cool and silent pool, and out into the gurgling flow of the stream. There, all was cold and fearful and swift, like the world a salmon knows as it fights its way upstream. Around gurgling stones and foam-scudded shallows they went. Weaving between fallen branches and over smooth rounded pebbles, they seemed to glide, fast and sleek and weightless, smooth in their finned movements, like a feather that drifts on a breath of wind. They wound upstream—somehow he knew this. And overhead the latticework of branches coursed by, or they coursed under, and the black shield of clouded sky blocked every silent star so that even the sense of time was broken and he drowned in the eternity of the rushing stream. Water. His element.

*********

If one were to ask Sweyn where the brook lady took him, he would scarce be able to recall a detail, for his memories would soon come to seem no more than a hazy dream. But in the dream there was a small, fair isle, surrounded by lazy lake waters that lapped with tiny blue wavelets upon its sandy shores. And there was a wood there, of apple trees, but the trees were great and tall, like the mightiest sequoias, like the grandest redwoods. Mist hung in their branches, and yet through the mist the light of azure sky shone, so that the woodland of the tiny isle was brightly lit all about. And there were many ladies there. Their hair was long and flowed wherever they walked as if they swam beneath a clear pool. The ladies wore gauzy gowns of caterpillar silk and spiderweb, translucent and shimmering like droplets of dew. Others wore nothing at all, save crowns of gold autumn leaves upon regal heads. And there was music there, for some of the ladies were harpers, and some were flutists, and they played fine instruments of dark ruby cherry wood, the harps strung with wire of gold. The flutes hummed like the wind in evergreen trees. The harps sang with voices of bells trapped in crystal, and the melody was like the plashing of raindrops in tarns, like the chanting waters of brooks, like the melodious singing of ocean waves against the sleek hull of Starry Sea.

And there was food in abundance. Such delicacies as he could not imagine. There were great laden trays of fruits of surpassing sweetness, such that it seemed they must have been basted in honey and spices. There were tables covered with fine marten skins, and upon the skins silver trays of breads light as a feather, white as hoarfrost, soft as down. The bounty of fresh waters was all about too, salmon trussed on spits, pates of trout, rolled spheres of crayfish. These were set on fine glazed clay platters held aloft in the agile branches of shrubs. And in every hollow of a tree, and between every nook of a branch, sweet dainties were stashed—crystallized honey with spices, berries in fragile cups of sweet doe's cream, custard of robins' eggs and stolen cow's milk.

And every lady had at hand a goblet of silver or crystal, filled with sweet wine of muscadine, or ale of heather, or mead of honey and apples, or a potion of minty spring birch sap.

Yet he ate nothing. Some inner knowing warned him away, a faded voice distant but familiar, that rung in his mind's ear with the timbre of his lost beloved. He did nothing but walk the isle and listen to the harping and the fluting, and the fluid melodious voices of the ladies.

But among the tall ladies who were no less fair than fresh bloomed water lilies one who was far different walked. Where the ladies were luminous beauty draped in flowing gowns, this one was tall and gaunt and withered, her skin sun-darkened, the color of a fawn's fur, and tough as parched hide. Her hair was long and white. She wore it in two long braids which fell down either side of her head to her waist. She wore a chemise of autumn gold sewn of cottonwood leaves. A thick leather belt was cinched around her middle. He features were well formed but elongated in the way a warped mirror stretches and exaggerates. Yet for all that she walked among the ladies as a matriarch and they gave her deference.

She regarded Sweyn surreptitiously. He could feel her eyes upon him whenever she looked, but when he turned to her, he always found her facing away, or her eyes in a cup, or talking quietly to one of the brook ladies. Yet without doubt she studied him.

He was surprised to hear what the ladies called the crone—the Old Lady. But they did it openly and she did not seem to mind. Indeed, they spoke it most respectfully. But she called herself by her proper name, Arn'na'sagt'puch, the R spoken like a feral growl, the "ch" coming deep and harsh out of the throat. Filled with alien sounds, he instinctively knew her name did not derive from any Western tongue.

Eventually, the Old Lady left the fair isle by way of a small, wooden door set in a great rock upon the white sands of the shore. When she stepped into it, he saw beyond her a dark passageway that seemed to go nowhere except beneath the sandy shore into the earth.

Later, in the evening, stars came out and the ladies schooled like fishes beneath a vine-shrouded gazebo. Drink in silver goblets flowed freely, and where once they had seemed gay, the ladies' mood became sullen and brooding, and they began to sing soft-hued airs of an era past, another world, old and different and long lost, when they lived far away, across the dreaming sea, in a land they called Cymru. He learned they called themselves the Gwragedd, the ladies of the brooks. Their songs were old and alien as their customs, and when he heard them he grew dizzy, disoriented, feeling himself swept away to places of enchantment so green and shaded his mortal mind could not hold it in memory. The songs reminded him that he was an outsider among them, for when he heard their refrains, he sensed the fair ladies were not of this earth, anymore than he was of their world.

Many songs the Gwragedd sang to pass the long star-bright night, and they all came into his ears like sparkles and slipped from his memory like windblown embers. Yet one song they sang, the last he recalled, which could not slip away. It spoke deeply to him, and burned, and bit hard. It brought tears to his eyes while the harpers played bitter tunes. He wept as he listened, and he did not know why.

*My love has passed the time we shared,*
*And I outlast the fading day,*
*And yet still falls the honey mead*
*In wooded halls of gathered dreams.*

*The honey mead of forgetfulness*
*To blur the need of a forlorn heart,*
*Locked in the pain of cold love's web,*
*Tied to the skein of memory.*

*I lost the sight of the great horned lord,*
*When he took flight of my stately stream,*
*He once was a strong great horned stag,*
*But fell to a throng with arrows of iron.*

*I lost the vale where my elder tree grew,*
*I lost the dale where I drank elder wine,*
*I lost the shard that cut the cluster of my fruit,*
*I lost my lord to iron.*

*Now in the West my lover calls,*
*He keeps the best of whitened shores,*
*And there my lord holds out strong arms,*
*Upon my word I will come.*
*Upon my word I will come.*

He could not remember the melody of the gold-strung harps, nor the tune in the singer's voice. The bittersweetness of the enchanted music was more than a man could keep. But the words would not be parted from his soul. They burrowed deep, deeper than any other memory had ever gone before, save that of his beloved, and all his life he knew the poem must haunt him, for it contained a passion and a sorrow he had himself felt once, one terrible dark night when his dreams flamed upon the black waters of a far away pier, and his own love was buried under the sea in a shroud of white canvas. Yet though hearing the song was painful, it was a good pain, like the sensation when a splinter is plucked. The words spoke true and gathered deep within his breast where they became the very soul of the ghosts of memories which haunted him, and the seal to bind them deep, and through their plaint the painful shard within him was pulled and the wound mended. The sharp memories were still there, but for the first time in three long years he did not feel as if he walked on the edge of an abyss with hungry visions threatening to devour his sanity in flashbacks. For the first time in three long years he did not feel as though he needed oblivion. It was a sensation so unfamiliar that he had forgotten what it felt like not to be tormented. Suddenly, it seemed to him like spring was birthed. It felt to him as though he were flying. And certainly he knew he must be dreaming . . .

*********

. . . and when he opened his eyes the dream had ended and he was weeping, leaning against a tree in the apple grove beside Dundubh Cottage. Behind him a little brook muttered as its waters flowed deep and torpid over submerged stones.

The rising sun was warm in lucent eastern skies, and the first rays cut through the foliage of the apple boughs and touched his face with gold.

*Upon my word I will come.*

He placed his head on his arms and let the tears come. He could not have stopped them had he tried.

A touch as light as a songbird's feather brushed his stubbly cheek. He sucked in breath, startled, but unafraid. He was filled beyond fear at this point. He looked slowly up from where he reclined against the trunk of the great old apple tree. A girl stood there, the girl he had seen the night he first came to the Cottage. She was dressed in a thin summery gown of white that seemed to shimmer and flow with every slight breath of the near standing air. Her skin was pale as cream. Her eyes held summer stars. Her hair fell to her waist and was black and shimmering like obsidian.

"I dinna' ever think to see a lady of the brooks guide a man," said the girl. Her voice was soft, like the utterance of a flute blown low. Then she looked up toward the rising sun, and its gold beams touched the smooth curve of her cheeks. She turned then, stole one last glance at the seaman, and sprang into the forest quick and silent as a hind. He pushed himself quickly up and called after her, but the only thing to call back was his echo, and the notes of the dawn chorus.

And then came the overjoyed sound of a familiar voice, Coppin, who was running down from the Cottage.

# Chapter Eight

*Ogham herbs and Ogham woods,*
*Twenty different kinds,*
*Ogham ciphers and Ogham mysteries,*
*And twenty ways to bind.*

*Ogham cords tie Ogham vines,*
*With witch's eldritch lore,*
*Ogham seeds and Ogham nuts,*
*Bound for the farther shore.*

*Ogham fey and Ogham mortals,*
*One doom have these races,*
*Ogham luck and Ogham land,*
*Sought in yonder places.*

*The Voyage of the Trees*
*Oak Peg*

Sweyn was dazzled. He would have sat in mindless silence beneath the apple trees through the morning and through the day, riveted by the fading recollections of the surreal night, if not for Coppin who pulled and prodded at him and eventually got him stumbling along toward the great Cottage, the wing on the side near to the apple grove which was the only part of the house still in use. Tugging at his hand, using words of encouragement, sometimes peppered with a few invectives of frustration, Coppin managed to propel Sweyn through the kitchen door into the warmth of the morning kitchen. A small wood fire crackled in the stove and the great stone chamber was filled with the aroma of baking bread. Coppin took a wooden bowl from a pantry overhead and cut a great slab of chewy, crusty bread fresh from the oven and put it in the bowl with a dose of honey-sweetened milk. He set it before Sweyn. "Eat," he ordered, and then gathered a mug and filled it with the Island's unique sweet ale. He set it also before Sweyn.

Sweyn had no appetite but wanted to go back outside to the apple grove. He just wanted to sit by the brook and listen to its voice. And maybe see if he might spy a fair form in the wooded shadows.

"Eat!" Coppin ordered him again and shoved the soggy bread into his hand.

Empty-minded, Sweyn took a bite. The milk was fresh from the sheep and rich and creamy, the honey as sweet as sun on buttercups. He swallowed the warm bread and suddenly realized he was famished. Greedily, he sopped up the sweet milk and ate the bread, and when he was done Coppin brought him another helping. This time Sweyn ate slower, allowing Coppin to speak to him as he ate. "Where have ye been?" he demanded urgently. "Have ye no' yet learned to stay clear of the wood by night, ye who dinna' even know Island ways?"

Sweyn made an answer so strange it even surprised him. "There are dreams in the wood."

Coppin clamped his jaw shut and became like stone. Sweyn did not notice. He was occupied with eating the bread and milk, his eyes cast down into the milk bowl. Coppin perceived Sweyn was only half here: the other half was still out wandering with the wild faeries. To shock him into the here and now, Coppin hit him with a fact. "The whole of Man-by-the-Sea has been searching the Guardwood for ye."

Sweyn, still looking into the milk bowl as he sopped up the last of the sweet white cream, said absently, "That's odd. I've only been missing a night."

Coppin leaned forward, low over the table, so his whiskery head was just above Sweyn's bowl, forcing Sweyn to look at him when he declared, "It is weeks and weeks since ye left to visit Oak Peg, ye daft oaf. Midsummer is nearly here."

That did get Sweyn's attention. He set down the remaining crust of bread. "What are you talking about? I left two days ago and saw Oak Peg, just as we talked about. She agreed to buy our milk. Then I came back the next day and spent the day in Man-by-the-Sea. I walked back that night and got stuck beneath a tree in the storm." He thought a moment, and decided to add, "And I have to tell you, Coppin, I don't know what you've been up to to make life difficult around here, but Oak Peg seems to feel you're behind it, and I'm warning you to stop it. Now."

But Coppin said, "Oak Peg herself has been searching the woods for ye everyday. She believed, when ye dinna' get back the third day, ye'd been faerie led. Or worse, maybe found the wisps."

*Amethyst gems floating over black water, flickering like candle flames in a breeze.*

As his strength of mind and body returned, Sweyn was able to sort his thoughts. He began to recall broken bits and pieces of the night before, tiny disjointed fragments of memory. A hairy man. Slender ladies like water lilies. The black shadow of a great, malevolent tree. Sparkles in a forest pool. An old and regal woman. But the memories came like midnight dreams, resistant of recollection, as if they were more comfortable tucked away.

But one memory did stay, lucent as the sunlit sky. The memory bore the face of a girl with black hair and pale skin and limpid eyes like gems. Her alone he could recall clearly, from the dress that seemed made of no more than threads of caterpillar silk to her doeskin-shod feet. Perhaps most of all her voice came to mind, rich, like a flute played in the low register.

There was a haunting beauty about the girl, bound together with a powerful earthiness. But there was something even more peculiar about her than that, something which drew him to her. It was a secret told in her features, the button nose, the high cheeks, the slant of her mischievous sapphire eyes. Somehow, he felt he should know her.

"The village folk are still searching," Coppin had continued though Sweyn's thoughts had failed to track it till now. "Searched the Guardwood from Oak Peg's place to here, they did. Oak Peg would have driven them deeper, into the wildwood itself, but they would no' bide that, no' even for Oak Peg. I dinna' think I'd go to those parts to save my own skin." Coppin paused, shivered.

Sweyn interjected. "Who is the girl that wanders in our apple grove?"

It took Coppin a minute or two to lose momentum and stop talking about the search and the drama and his worries that Sweyn had been lost in a moor, or had foolishly wandered into the wildwood. He had built up so much steam it took time just for his train of thought to change course. And when he did change course, he looked Sweyn directly in the eye and said, "Ye have seen her." It was a statement, but spoken as a question, with surprise.

Sweyn nodded.

Coppin seemed to search for words before continuing. "She is a vagabond. She wanders onto Dundubh lands from time to time and I let her eat whatever she will. Sometimes she sleeps out in the barns. Sometimes I set a bit of food and drink out for her."

"There's no need for that!" Sweyn blurted, aghast that such a fate should befall the girl. "Coppin, how could you? There's plenty of room."

Suddenly, Coppin's voice was very firm. "Now I know what ye're thinking, and I'm warning ye now, quit going down that path. And, blood and thorns, she is never one to invite into the house."

But Sweyn was firm. "Coppin, when you see her you will invite her to stay at Dundubh. And if you don't see her, you will get her a message. Leave her a note. We have plenty to spare and no reason not to share."

But Coppin stood then, his hands gripping the oaken planks of the rough hewn kitchen table so forcefully that Sweyn could see veins rising in Coppin's forearms. "I'll never do it. And if ye could see past her bonny face, ye'd listen to me. I'll never bring her into the house."

Sweyn continued to sit beside the table, unintimidated by the little man's display. When Coppin had vented himself, Sweyn simply said, "It is my house. You will do as I bid."

Coppin simply folded his arms and glared defiantly at Sweyn.

"And you will set out the plates of food for the little people again, Coppin. Silly, I know, but Oak Peg put great stock in that superstition. So what can it hurt? Who knows, maybe it'll buy me a little luck."

Sweyn got up then and made to enter the house. When he reached the door, Coppin said, "I dinna' wish ye to stay. And I dinna' wish to see ye harmed. Yet I want to see ye' go away."

Sweyn turned then, slowly, deliberately. "Are you threatening me, Coppin?"

But the wizened little man shook his scrawny, whiskery head. "Never that."

Sweyn looked him over cautiously. As a psychologist he had long since developed the art of reading people, but he could not read this one, no matter how hard he tried. "Good," Sweyn said, finally. "I'm going to sleep."

Sweyn stumbled to the room he had adopted, collapsed onto the couch. He had been direly tired, more so than he knew. It took sixteen hours for the fog of weariness to lift from his mind. But when he woke to the music of crickets and the salt scent of an evening breezing wafting in off the sea through the open window, his head was finally clear. It was only then that the enormity of Coppin's news drove home. Weeks and weeks! It was almost midsummer. Where had he been all that time? But by now the memories were quite faded, driven deep and denied by a mind not yet ready to face their implications. When he tried to recall them, only bits and flashes came, and less than before. The memories were at best hazy and quickly come and gone, like pulses of distant lightning. All he could recall clearly was an aching sweet-sad air that he had heard in some unrecollected place, some time not too long ago, and the clear bright image of a girl with hair as black as the spaces between the stars in his apple grove.

But weeks and weeks had passed. It was nearly midsummer, and all the Island folk had been looking for him. It was more than he could wrap his mind around, and certainly more than he was ready to deal with at this time. The very thought left him shaky.

He rose quietly and made his way down to the kitchen. In a cool pantry under the floor there was a larder for wine and cider and ale. He took a crock of sweet Island ale and went out to the porch off the kitchen. Coppin was out there, also nursing a mug of something, and sitting in a rocking chair too large for him so that his small form looked like that of a child. Coppin was staring off south, where grew the apple grove.

Sweyn turned to close the outer kitchen door, and it was only then, when his mind was no longer sleep hazed, that he noticed the great oaken table where they had sat earlier in the day. Where Coppin had gripped the hardwood in his anger, indentions of his fingers had been left in the wood. Sweyn stepped over to the table, ran his finger over the scars. They were truly marks pressed by slender fingers, branded in wood as hard as ore. He shook his head and took a deep swallow of the ale. It was not possible, he knew. Not even a large, muscular man possessed strength enough to simply crush hardwood.

He went back out to the porch then, and sat down in another rocking chair with his crock. He too, stared silently south as he drank the foaming wort, staring fixedly toward the apple grove, where sometimes the girl roamed, but not now. And the strains of the ladies' last lyrics went round and round through his thoughts as, from time to time, he stole glances at Coppin, who also stole glances at him.

He had a lot of questions for the little man. Perhaps tomorrow, when he had the energy for it.

Time passed slowly. The darkness had settled over the land like a blanket, and the sky was an ocean of stars with stray cumulus clouds scudding across it like the white foamed horses of waves. He decided to return to bed, for though he was not sleepy he still felt tired in his body. But there was one last thing to do. He rose and went to the kitchen. Remembering Oak Peg's example, he took an earthenware saucer from the shelves and saddled it with cakes and dribbled honey over them. He took a small pot of ceramic make and filled it with sweet ale. Then he went outside with the faerie plate.

"Where are ye going?" asked Coppin, who sat quietly in the rocking chair, now smoking his long pipe of mint.

"To do what Oak Peg bade," he said, and he proceeded to push open the screen door that led off the porch.

"A plate for the Little People," Coppin scoffed. "I'm surprised at ye, ye who know so much more than we simple folk."

"I don't know what I know," Sweyn answered in truth. "But people change."

"Aye," Coppin said. "The Island does that to people. It'll make ye mad or it'll keep yer soul. Best ye escape before the latter fate ties ye down."

Sweyn ignored him, pushed open the screen door.

Coppin continued. "The equipment and supplies ye ordered are here. Ye can repair yer boat and be off in a matter of days."

"It will take weeks to fix the hull," Sweyn said in passing. He would have to carve and shape and mold great planks of oak perfectly to his hull, and that was no small task. At least oak wood could be gotten here in abundance.

"I've had it all taken care of for ye. Galen is the best carpenter in Man-by-the-Sea, and I contracted him to shape the wood. He only awaits yer supervision to fit it to yer boat."

There could be no doubt. The little man was trying to get rid of him. What was his plan, Sweyn wondered. Did he think to get Dundubh Cottage and all its lands for himself?

But Sweyn went on through the door. He would go down the worn grass path to the low pasture where the white sheep rested. But not yet. He turned, faced the wizened little man. "I'll go. In my own good time. Tomorrow you will restore the faerie plates. And they are to be of the best we have. And then you and I are going to have a long talk." Then he went out into the pasture and left the plate and the pot by the barn where the white sheep had tucked themselves into their stables. And from that day the many small problems that had plagued the business of the Cottage ceased.

*********

The rising sun found Sweyn already out of bed and dressing. There was much to accomplish this day. He stopped by the kitchen and found Coppin already in there, baking bread for the day. A small pot of oat porridge simmered over the woodstove and Sweyn spooned a dollop into a wooden bowl, laced it with honey and wild dried raspberries and crushed hazelnuts. He ate hurriedly, wolfing down the porridge in great heaping spoonfuls on his way to the exit, and set the empty bowl down on the last counter before exiting the kitchen, giving Coppin not so much as a "Good morning," or a "Farewell." He started down the path that led to town, looking off to the apple grove for the girl, but of course not seeing her. Things on the Island seemed only to be found when they were not sought. Without pause, he continued down the path to Man-by-the-Sea.

He was met by many peculiar stares as he passed the folk of the town. They whispered amongst themselves as he passed. Sometimes he could hear them. "The Laird has been beyond the Guardwood and has come back." "The Tylwyth Teg have taken the Laird and returned him sound and hail." "Luck is with our Laird, and with our folk." After a while, the mood of the folk grew from dubious amazement to open friendliness. As he conducted his business about the town, people ceased to speak to him with that wary courtesy he had sensed before. It was as if he had passed some right of passage and was one of them now.

The first thing he did—after stopping off at the grocer to leave an order for the Cottage, and the town square to hire a shepherd for the flock and a keeper for the groves—was head down to the dry dock where Starry Sea sat patiently upon her supports. Tarps covered a heap of something beside the little ship. He tossed the blue sheets of plastic aside and found three oak planks ready to fit to his craft, perfectly fashioned. There were also crates with the equipment he would need to steam the wood to shape it to the hull. A note had been left with the crates by Galen the carpenter, notifying Sweyn to summon him when he was ready to attach the planks. Sweyn had been dubious of the carpenter's skills last night, when Coppin had told him what he had done. Sweyn was a perfectionist when it came to his vessel and was rarely satisfied with anyone's work but his own. But there was not the least fault in the carpenter's craftsmanship and he knew the moment he saw the quality of the timbers he would trust this man to finish the job.

Then he climbed the ladder and mounted Starry Sea's transom, stepped onto her deck. Someone, probably Coppin, had been busy aboard while he was away. The little ship's wooden hull had been painted and varnished top to bottom, and the brightwork had been beautifully sanded and polished. An inspection down below soon revealed that the innards of his craft had been cared for as well. She was sparkling clean and smelled of nothing but her timbers and the salt sea, as any good ship ought. The completed mast boot was below, sitting on the navigation station's desk, awaiting his inspection before installation. The workmanship was fine and he could see to the installation as soon as he had a chance.

Over the next week he went through all the motions of finishing the repairs upon his vessel, making her seaworthy once more. And by the following Wednesday she was as ready as ever to put to sea. He need only stock her larders and put her in the water. Then he could motor out of the little bay and bid this rock farewell. He bought groceries and stocked his pantries and lockers with dried fruits and dried salmon and venison and sheep. He filled his fresh water tanks above and below decks. He inspected his sails, especially the new mainsail, and stitched and reinforced them. He went through all the motions of planning a departure, as if trying convince himself it was now exactly his plan to go.

But in the evenings he always returned to Dundubh. There were the new laborers to be supervised. They were tending to the oat and barley fields, the berry gardens and fruit trees, the apple grove, and the sheep flock. The carpenter who had mended Starry Sea's hull had been contracted, along with his three strong sons, to renew the Cottage, reviving the unused wing and making the place appear less the crumbling, haunted old mansion of some demented eccentric.

Another week passed in this way before Sweyn took the time to have the chandler lower Starry Sea back into the water where she was tied off to a peer nearby the fishing fleet which would soon be heading off after the annual run of salmon. The afternoon she was lowered back in the water and all set in order, he sat in her cockpit holding the smooth polished wood of the ship's wheel in his hand. Its familiar touch was cool and comfortable. Anytime he could simply start the iron genny, untie, and motor away, and that thought gave him some comfort. But somehow he could not find it in himself to do it. Somehow it did not feel right.

No. Too many things ate at him now. Too many uncanny discoveries, and unlikely questions. What was the likeness of Coppin doing on an aged painting in the library? Who was the Oak Peg referenced in Lieutenant Raleigh's journal? What did the letter O.P. had sent to Eilwen really mean? And the most recent and stupefying mystery: What exactly had happened to him in the nearly two months he had gone missing in the wood? He could only recall a single moment of it now, an air to pierce the heart, sung by a golden voice, and that memory grew hazier by the day, as he immersed himself in the day-to-day affairs of running the estate. Commonsense warned him best to leave the mysteries unanswered and simply sail away from the strange affairs of this place. But Sweyn had always been one to oppose commonsense, as his coldly reasonable father had been fond of reminding him. More importantly, he knew if he did not come to understand the enigma of this place, then his beloved wife would forever remain a stranger to him, someone he only thought he knew but never truly did. For in the end, despite all she had denied it, Manannan had reclaimed the heart of Eilwen, and she had made him promise to keep the legacy of her family, never to sell the Cottage of the O'Shees nor its lands, and he could not understand what possessed her to ask it of him.

Yet the longer he spent on the Island, the more he understood how deeply it was etched into her. The living knowledge of the Island's old ways was so much a part of Eilwen. Her uncanny knowledge of herbal lore, she had probably learned it from the likes of Oak Peg, who was undoubtedly some kind of witch or herbalist to these people. The dishes she had made, of wholesome foods of nuts and fruits and wild berries, and dried lamb and fresh fish, this culinary tradition she had learned from this people who lived for the most part without electricity and refrigerators, relying on their farms and forest for sustenance. Her unusual habit of leaving plates of food out at night; he understood now she had been carrying on the venerable tradition of honoring the Little People, though perhaps only out of habit. The bizarre practices she had had for the first of May, when they ate acorn cakes and drank cider and raised a toast to the forest sprites, he understood this now in light of his experience at Man-by-the-Sea's Bealtaine festival. Her passion for mournful Celtic airs and lively reels was more comprehensible now — for it was the music of the Island's folk. The Island's character had wrought so many of the pieces of Eilwen, and though he now understood a little of the forces that had shaped her, he knew for certain that he had only scratched the surface of the mysteries that revolved around her, thick as morning mist upon the moors.

And so he sat in the cockpit of his boat, now the only yacht at the pier, for the other one had sailed away weeks ago, and made the decision not to go just yet. There was plenty of time to sail south before winter landlocked him for the season. There were things he must accomplish here first.

But there was more to it than that, he realized. Something else seemed to bind him to this place. Indeed, there was peace in Manannan. He had sensed it once before, distantly, near the apple grove when he had seen the strange raven-haired girl for the second time. It was a sense of rightness that comes with knowing one's center, and finding one's balance. But that peace had never fully caught. It had waxed and waned, a fragile ember struggling beneath a deluge of fear and anguish, for always at his very core the nightmares of the past hunted him: the burning of Cerulean, Eilwen drowning in a shroud of canvas, blood on his fists in an alley behind a seedy tavern. Fueled by despair, those nightmares threatened to possess him body and soul, and he only kept them at bay through an act of sheer will. But they waited, within, threatening to burst into his waking mind with flashbacks at the trigger of a sharp memory, a new fear, a measure of distress. But something was different now, something within. The lyrics of an air of lost love and defiant hope had lodged in his soul like a talisman. Where it came from was now uncertain, a lake island, perhaps. He could barely recall. It seemed fair ladies and an old woman had given it to him, but he was no longer sure. But the lyrics came as a gift, and they shared hurt and hope, and he knew in them he was not alone:

*My love has passed the time we shared, and I outlast the fading day . . .*

And with that knowledge, the power of the nightmares subsided. They were not gone, but he sensed they could no longer overwhelm him with flashbacks. He did not need the oblivion of the sea any longer to survive. That a mere song should possess such strength made no sense, he knew, yet he had changed within, and he dared not question it.

Yet the sea still called to him, and strongly. And he fully intended to answer it and go. Only, he wanted answers first. Most of all, he just wanted to know who was Eilwen, really?

He checked his vessel and secured her and left her floating at her moors and returned to Dundubh Cottage early that day. It was time for that long put off chat with Coppin. As he was leaving he noticed the trawler that made the monthly round to the mainland cities far to the south was coming in. He went to the pub and drank a pint of sweet ale, which he had become quite fond of, and waited for the boat to tie off and deliver its mail. The village pub also doubled as the post office and a sack of parcels and envelops was soon brought to it by a swarthy dark haired lad. The barmaid sifted through the pile of mail and found letters for Sweyn. Both were responses to the queries he had made to the title agency and the genealogy researcher before he disappeared. He thanked the barkeep, tipped her, and walked back to Dundubh, reading along the way.

By the time he reached the Cottage, the sky was graying and rain seemed surely on the way, but he paid it no mind. The contents of the letters occupied him entirely. Like everything else about the Island, they seemed to make sense only if he looked at them out the corner of his eye, and not too closely. The letter from the genealogist described the lineage of O'Shee as so ragged and broken the genealogist was surprised the family name had ever survived. It had been passed at times through males, and sometimes even through females. There were even times it seemed every O'Shee had died of old age or infirmity or simply (and disturbingly) disappeared. But somehow another O'Shee always reappeared to carry on the line.

As to the other letter, the one from the title research company, it revealed a similarly strange history—smooth transitions of the estate from one heir to another despite the broken lineage and dubious origins of many of the O'Shee heirs. And no matter how questionable the heirs, no one ever rose to challenge them, nor had the estate ever been sold, put in trust, or any part of it divided. For more than two centuries the vast lands and assets of Dundubh Cottage had remained resolutely within the family and unbroken. To say the least, in this day and age that was anomalous.

But while the stories the letters told were strange, the title company had also sent a separate package the contents of which were nothing less than unbelievable. The Dundubh estate was huge, and Sweyn had asked for any topographic maps of the lands they might be able to provide. There were no topos available. But they had been able to find some aerial photos, which were included in a folder. They had been taken over several decades, when Canadian survey planes happened to pass over. The portion of the Island belonging to the estate had been outlined with a black marker on the photos. The property was far larger than Sweyn had realized, for it did not merely include the fields and fruit groves as he had expected. Much of the wood was highlighted as well. In fact, it seemed that the O'Shees owned fully three quarters of the Island, from the uninhabited mountainous region on the eastern side, facing the mainland of north British Columbia some twenty miles distant, to the moors and beaches on the western shores. Indeed, all the property to within two miles of Man-by-the-Sea going east and west, and four miles going north and south, belonged to the Cottage. It was more than thirty square miles of land. He was stunned. He had had no idea.

But as he flipped through the photo sheets, his attention was drawn to the deep forest about a mile beyond where the woods abutted his fields. That was part of the area the villagers called the wildwood. A series of photos had been taken of that portion of the wildwood over several decades. The first photo, shot in 1943, showed a hilly topography in that area. The second, taken in 1957, showed a recessed landscape, like a bowl in the same region. The third photo, taken in 1974, showed a flat expanse of forest, dotted by glades and small lakes. He doubled checked the coordinate markings on the corner of each photo sheet, and they confirmed the photos showed the same area, yet in each shot the topography was remarkably different. But that could not be right. Terrain could not just metamorphose like that.

He examined the photos of the Guardwood and local farms. Meadows and ponds, crops and berry thickets stayed exactly where they should. The land appeared changeless and normal.

He pulled out more of the aerial photos from the folder. They gave a pretty thorough overhead view of the south and west quarter of the Island, the inhabited side. The Guardwood was a mile broad and it ran from the south side of Man-by-the-Sea to the north shore of his estate, terminating at Oak Peg's cove, forming a boundary separating the populated lands from the wildwood. He examined a group of wildwood photos shot two miles east of Man-by-the-Sea. Over three decades the land metamorphosed from a forested vale to a grassy plateau and back again. He shook his head, rubbed his eyes, frustrated and perplexed. Then he searched through the bundle until he came to photos of the terrain beyond Oak Peg's cottage. A little beyond her place the land had been swampy in 1981, but had become a glade with many small streams in 1994. He knew from experience that area was swampy again now. It was where he had seen the . . . the firefly things. The things Oak Peg had said do not like to be spied upon.

But terrain simply could not transform like that. It took thousands, even millions of years for the earth to change its face so completely. But the land of the Island seemed to change its shape as often as a lady of fashion changes her attire. Major features such as mountains, lakes and tarns remained steady. But small brooks and ponds, whole forests and glades, and even small hills and glens and hollows seemed to migrate around the Island, or simply come and go. It was as if bits of the world were peeling away to be replaced by others.

But perhaps most peculiar of all was that though the topography of the Island had been photographed for at least sixty years, no one had ever seemed to notice the incredible metamorphoses of the land. Not the aviators who took the photos, not the cartographers and surveyors who worked with them. No one.

He stuffed the photographs back into the folder, the folder back into the large envelope. It was yet another mystery to add to the Island's enigma, one more puzzle to nit and nag. He made it to the Cottage's warm kitchen just as the first misty rain began to drift down. As was his habit, Coppin could be found working near the hearth, preparing a stew of venison and smoking his pipe, making the room smell of fresh mint and unnamed forest herbs. Sweyn dropped the envelopes on the table and sat back in a stout wooden chair beside it. Coppin set a cup of fragrant herbal tea in front of him. Sweyn said, "We have to talk."

*********

The meal had been simple, hearty, and good: turnips, carrots, and venison in a pasty broth thickened with barley. They had washed it down first with ale, and then with tea. Now they sat quietly, listening to the rain. As is so often the case in the north country, when clouds hide the sun it becomes instantly chill, even if the day till then had been quite hot. Coppin had stoked the fire that seemed always to be smoldering in the kitchen's woodstove. Now Coppin smoked his mint pipe and Sweyn fingered a crock of elder blossom cordial while he contemplated what to say. But it was Coppin who spoke first.

"So, ye will no' leave, and now yer wanting to know more of the Island."

"So much more."

"And yet yer mind canna' even accept what it has seen. Ye lose the memories like smoke that drifts off in the autumn night's gusts," said Coppin. "Oh, Sweyn, such a mind bides best in ignorance. There is history here, aye, so much of it. No' all right on this rock, mind ye. Much of it we brought over. But native or brought, it is with us all the same."

"Brought?" said Sweyn, raising his eyebrows thoughtfully. "As in on Mont Royal, all those years ago?"

Coppin smirked. "Oh, no, lad. That's only one tale. An instant within the grander spectacle. What ye think ye know is but a grain upon a shore of stories that go out deep as the cold black sea. And when learning history of that kind, it's best to learn from the stories. For they convey the heart of the truth, even if cold history might be more fussy about the details."

Sweyn leaned forward. "Coppin, I saw a figure that looked just like you in the painting at the library. I read about a Coppin in Raliegh McCavitt's journal. Was he your great, great, great grandfather?"

Coppin tilted his head to one side, slyly, and there was an unearthly gleam in his eye. "Lad, I think ye know the answer to that, if ye will but be honest with yerself. And if ye're a stubborn fool enough to stay here, despite I've been trying to see ye off, then ye best be honest with yerself. This Island has a bad way of dealing with those not honest, least of all with themselves."

"You're actually trying to say it was you?" Sweyn whispered.

But Coppin replied, "I think what ye would do better to ask is why this house, and why the O'Shees, and why ye are called Laird." Coppin set the pitcher of elder blossom cordial on the table, and set his pouch of mint there too, and stoked the wood fire in the stove, for he had a long story to tell. "And when ye've heard the telling of it, ye must choose whether to stay or to leave. And whichever choice it is, the Lady give ye luck, for ye'll need it either way. Hearing is binding, and if ye must know, ye weave yerself into the geas of the tale, lad."

And so he began . . .

*********

"They were the Hundred Horsemen, and they were magnificent. But they had no soul between them. And they lived in the old time, when the west lands of the old world fell to one petty king after another, and invaders came to the British Isles in a ceaseless torrent of clashes and blood. In that time the clans of the Celts struggled to hold fast their own, for the invaders grew in number all around them.

"The origin of the Hundred Horsemen is unknown. They first enter our memory as a band of mercenary knights serving a failing Pictish kingdom—which is now no more—though they were none of them Pictish. They came from many lands. Cymry from south and west of Britain. Gaels from Scots clans and as far north as the isle of Uist, and as far west as the kingdoms of Ireland. They were wild knights eager to prove themselves in battle, and they had come to this dying kingdom for rich pay and not for honor, and so it is said they had no soul. Mighty warriors the Hundred Horsemen were, and they were as beautiful upon their steeds in full armor as they were when they walked at court in green and white tunics and cloaks, among fair ladies who were as colorful ornaments amidst them.

"This company always had a leader. Currently, their leader was a man named Angus. He was the strongest and the best among them. His claymore could hew down an elm. His javelin could skewer a boulder. His lance could throw an enemy from his horse and break him like a dry branch. All the folk of the Pictish lands respected Angus for his battle prowess, and the Pictish king paid him dearly for his skill both in the fight and for his talent for strategy, for in the wars he conducted against the Pict land's many enemies, the armies led by Angus never ceased to triumph.

"But Angus also had no soul, and he was too proud. Some said that a knight should espouse humility, for the way of the knight was to guard justice, hold safe his laird and lady, protect women and children and small animals, and keep the peace. But Angus valued none so much as himself, and he was always eager for a challenge to prove his greatness and add to his riches. So Angus fought many tournaments with other proud men, and the losers of those tournaments lost their treasure, and sometimes their horses, and now and again their lives. But it was nothing to mighty Angus—he was the bravest and strongest and swiftest. None could stand against him and always it was he who came away the victor.

"Then one day a dark knight rode into a Pictish keep on the borders. He rode a great sable warhorse and his armor was all stained black, and his hair was black as the night and fell to his shoulders. He wore no helm, and all the folk could see he had eyes like a hawk. He had the manner of a raven, the beast who hungers for war so it might feed upon the corpses. 'I have come to be numbered among the Hundred Horsemen,' declared he. Angus himself was with the company at that time and he came out to meet the wayward knight.

"'Be off with ye,' cried Angus to the knight. 'For our number is always a hundred and no more nor less. And we take new blood only when a comrade has fallen in battle.'

"'I do not wish to wait for a battle to join the company,' the unknown knight said. 'I have come to find action and seek my fortune in war. I have not come to sit on a hill and look over the bloodletting as a king who fears to enter the fight he sends his men into.'

"'So ye will ride off then,' said Angus in his great, gruff bear's voice, 'and it is as well, for it is rare enough that one of our Horsemen falls. Ye could wait a long time, if ye had the patience, and the belly for it.'

"'I have a belly for war and for glory!' declared the knight. 'And not for patience. And I would have none but a place among the Hundred.'

"Now Angus saw the wayward knight's steed was an exceptional mount, strongly muscled and sleek and fast. The warhorse bore his knight's armored burden as lightly as a bird. And Angus saw that the armor of the knight was of exceptional craftsmanship, indeed the finest quality. And his weapons were no less than the best to be had. Clearly, this knight was a callow youth who had come from a family of some wealth and had spent a goodly portion of that wealth to acquire these things in hopes of finding greatness. Angus had no real respect for the young man, but he did much envy his accoutrements. So he decided he would add them to his hoard.

"He declared to the young knight. 'There is but one way to become one of the Hundred, and that is to prove yerself in battle. And even then, there must be a place among our number. And as I see it ye have done neither, boy. For a pretty sword and stout pony do not a knight make.'

"Clearly he had intended to insult the newcomer. But the black knight was cold-eyed and calm as he responded. 'Then I shall have to prove myself, and make my place.'

"Angus smiled. 'Then I will contest ye. And may the best man win.'

"That day the folk of the keep made preparations for a tourney, to be fought on the morrow. All the Hundred Horsemen came to witness it, for with Angus doing the fighting the leadership of their company was at stake. And the people came to see, for the battles of Angus were the stuff of legend and each one wanted to witness his skill.

"So the next day the people gathered on a flat hill not far from the keep. The grounds for the battle were marked out, and the people watched anxiously while the knights regarded the coming belligerence with some interest. None knew who this wild, dark knight was, but stories circulated that he was the last heir of a small Irish kingdom far to the south and east which had fallen to Norse invaders and been utterly destroyed, wiped even from history. And now, having no home and no wealth but his steed and his armor, the knight wandered the lands having no greater cause than seeking fortune from the incessant wars with invaders. But none was sure if this were true, and the young knight said nothing of himself.

"At noon the tourney began and Angus and the young knight met in the field, the leader of the Hundred Horsemen in magnificent white, his challenger in gleaming black. They clashed on horseback at first, using sword and buckler, and fought till their horses were too tired to hold them. Each wanted the prize of the other's steed, so neither sought to disable the others mount. When the horses were in a lather, by mutual consent they dismounted and continued the battle. They fought now with broadswords and great shields. Angus' shield bore his device, a griffin with spread wings. The young knight's shield bore no device. It was dyed all black.

"Metal rang on metal and smacked wood for minutes that dragged on, and no victor seemed to be surmounting the other, for they were evenly matched. For his part, Angus was surprised at the skill of the young knight, and knew in the battle that this youth with the callow appearance was no simple lad with star bright dreams of glory. He had survived his share of war, and plenty of it, else how could he fight so skillfully.

"But both knights were tiring and it happened that Angus tripped upon a small stone unseen in the grass. Immediately, the young knight seized his chance and knocked Angus' sword from his hand and put his own sword to Angus' throat. But he did not kill the leader of the company, for it would not have been an honorable death. Yet all could see that he was the victor.

"'Yield,' commanded the young knight.

"'Never,' his opponent roared from the ground. 'For warriors do not join our number without the letting of blood.'

"'I will not let your blood,' said the young knight. 'For we are kindred of the British isles and must stand together against the enemies pouring into our lands or we all shall fall.' And he withdrew his sword from Angus' throat and extended his gauntleted hand to his opponent.

"Angus lay upon the ground and stared agape at the proffered hand. In offering it, his dark opponent made himself vulnerable. He could pull him from his balance and skewer his enemy upon his dagger. But there was no honor in such a death, and he would mete out no less courtesy than his enemy had done for him. So he took his enemy's hand and stood up. And for the lad's honor, he reckoned then that he had met a noble man. 'Who is it who asks me to yield to him?' he demanded when he stood upon his feet.

"'I am Dylan of the House O'Shee,' the dark knight declared, and so all the people and Angus knew the rumor was true. This was the last heir of the fallen Irish kingdom, a land smote so painfully even its name is now forgotten.

"Angus knelt then upon one knee. 'If ever there was a man worthier than I to lead the Hundred, it is ye.' And that day the leadership of the Hundred Horsemen came to Dylan's hands, the first time it had ever passed or one had joined their number without the letting of blood.

"They were a motley lot, wild mercenaries from every Celtic land, with no other purpose than to travel to whatever kingdom paid best for their formidable skills. They cared not who they fought, nor who they killed, so long as their enemies were not other Celts."

*********

Coppin fell silent and Sweyn regarded him a long time. The rain outside had increased and brought with it wind. Droplets made their way under the porch and plashed against the plate glass window. Sweyn sipped the elder blossom cordial and thought long on what Coppin had just told him, while Coppin paused to tamp fresh mint and herbs into his long pipe and light it again with a flaming twig he stole from the wood- burning kitchen stove. While Coppin was up and lighting his pipe, Sweyn said, "So you're saying the first O'Shee was a deposed prince of a fallen, forgotten kingdom of Ireland. And he became leader of a medieval mercenary band. That's a far cry from telling me anything that I want to know."

Coppin sighed, an act bespeaking incredible patience and longsuffering. Through the sigh he said, "The problem with youth is a terrible lack of patience." He returned from the stove and looked directly at Sweyn as he sat in his chair and puffed on his minty pipe. "Often the best way to the truth of a matter is the roundabout path."

"Coppin, there are things I need to know. Things you and I need to settle."

"And I am settling. Close yer mouth, lad, and listen."

Sweyn bit his tongue, sipped his cordial, and did as the old man bade. He may have disliked and distrusted the wizened rascal, but he respected age.

*********

Three years passed since Dylan took the leadership of the Hundred Horsemen, three years of battles and adventures and long wandering, until one bright autumn day found seven fine riders racing through the hills and vales of Cymru, a mountainous land of endless oaks and beeches on the west coast of Britain, a misty, green-shadowed forestland so dark and vast a squirrel could travel from Caernarvon to Cardiff, more than a hundred miles, without ever setting paw to earth. The riders were now in the service of one Maelgwn who held an old kingdom in the north of Cymru. Maelgwn was not widely liked, but he was widely feared, in part due to the services of the Hundred Horsemen. And while neither Dylan nor his fast friend Angus had any liking for the king themselves, in serving him they had opportunity to keep the invaders from the north out of this region of Britain. So well did the Hundred Horsemen do their work that there had not been cause for their services in two summers: the invaders feared them and tried for easier pickings—weaker kingdoms—further south. Having no sport of battle to occupy them, the Hundred Horsemen were growing restless and thinking of moving on. For now, seven of their number, Dylan, Angus, and their five sergeants, occupied themselves with riding the deep forest and hunting.

But Old Man Winter was already breathing his chill breath over the land. Autumn was descending and the forest was surrendering its leafy summer skirts for veils of gold and ruby. And where none of these bright fall hues shown, there was either the rare evergreen of an elder or holly tree, or the bare scraping bones of a willow struggling for the sun beneath the drapes of interlaced forest canopy.

The riders raced down the face of a hill, beneath massive oaks that tented them with firestorms of amber leaves. They guided their valiant mounts with their left hands and in their right they held bows. Quivers of iron-tipped arrows were ready upon their backs. They were in pursuit of a small group of deer, a stag and his autumn harem. This stag was mighty, for many does went with him. And he was bold, this one, for he went heavily through the wood. His tracks were easily spotted, even from racing horseback. The company of riders had not yet seen the deer, but they knew they could not be far off, for the tracks were deep and sharp edged.

At the base of a hill the company stopped. Horses' nostrils flared. Sweat-wet long manes fell over sable and piebald necks. Saddle leather creaked as the warriors leaned far over, reading the tracks.

"They've split up," said Angus.

Dylan swung himself quickly from his mount. He wore no armor except a boiled leather vambrace upon his left arm, and gloves of soft leather, all for shooting. The rest of his clothing was soft cloth of sable and forest green, silent and hard to see in the wood. He knelt and examined the tracks closely. The other warriors awaited his interpretation of the sign, for there was no better tracker among them than the young knight. "They have indeed," he answered Angus. "The lot of them has gone west, but the stag has gone on alone to the south."

"Then let us divide our company and men," said Angus. "And I will pursue the does, and you shall have the stag."

"No," said Dylan. "I will give you the chase of the stag, my old friend, and I will content myself with a doe of the harem." And before his friend could contest the honor, Dylan leapt upon his steed and kicked its ribs. The warhorse heeded the will of its master and bolted ahead, fast and fleet and unstoppable as a tempest. The warriors watched their leader vanish into the forest.

"Let him be alone, for it appears to be what he wants," Angus commanded, and the men rode after Angus as the chase resumed for the stag.

The afternoon was early, clear and bright, and the chase had not lasted long when Dylan came to a place where the does' tracks ended. In fact, he had hardly split from the company when he found it. In the distance he could still hear his men crashing through the wood after the stag. He slowed his own mount's pace to a slow trot in order to better study the spore.

The earth beneath his steed's hooves was strewn with amber and scarlet leaves, and the does' hoof prints were clear and legible as ogham scribed on tablets of yew in the soft soil. With no difficulty he followed the trail they left behind. The way was so clear it disturbed him. It seemed they wanted him to follow. Cautiously, he pursued them through the forest.

Then he came to a place where the prints of hooves ended. And what he saw at that place sent shivers up and down his spine as no horrid battle ever had, and he had seen many. For continuing from the very place the tracks ended were the small imprints of slippered feet, having the narrow, light step of damsels. He dismounted and knelt to the earth, touching the tracks lightly with his hands, feeling for the imprint of deer tracks within the human tracks. But they were not overlapped. Where one instant there had been five does, now there were five damsels, and they had continued to proceed into the forest. And they did not run. The steps were closely spaced. The damsels had walked, confident, or perhaps exhausted. Instinct warned him turn back, but he was well versed at suppressing instinctive fear. He had learned that trick in countless wars. Instead, he drew an arrow from his quiver and knocked it, followed the light tracks. "Aval, follow," he whispered, and his steed went with him, stepping lightly behind him despite the warhorse's great size.

He continued silently into the wood. As he went, he could hear the growing voice of a babbling stream. The tracks led down now, into the midst of a small vale. He passed through a thicket of blackthorn and emerged from it to find a massive stand of birches and willows growing thick beside the stream banks. And beneath the shade of the graceful trees was a gazebo of stone. It was built in circular fashion with eight round pillars of smooth white stone standing round the perimeter of a floor of smooth, brook-polished stone. White branches of birch laid precariously over the pillars served to support a roof of ivy that grew thick over the top of it, shading the structure in cool, green shadow. The build of the whole thing was unearthly, for it was held together by no mortar or notches. No tool had ever touched it, not to carve the stone nor trim the ivy. Indeed, the whole structure seemed fragile, as if it had tumbled together, as if a breeze might collapse it. Yet it also bore the appearance of great age, the stones seeming to have settled comfortably into place over eons. And if that were not wonder enough, five damsels reclined beneath the interlaced ivy. They were dressed in cloth so thin and fine it must be woven of spider's web. The cloth was dyed in autumnal colors of gold and scarlet. It shimmered translucently so the ladies' willowy forms could be seen as lithe shadows beneath. They were tired, as if they had only just ended a long run.

Clearly, this was an enchanted place, and Dylan held his guard. The bow was clutched in both fists, an iron tipped arrow ready upon the string.

One of the ladies, the only one dressed in violet, leaned against a pillar. Her hair was black as a cold winter's midnight when no star shines, and her skin was the soft pale hue of cream. She spoke to the knight. "Sir, you have given chase and caught your quarry. Stay your hand now, for you have won the sport."

Dylan stepped closer to the gazebo. "Who is it who asks the captain of the Hundred Horsemen to let down his guard?"

"I am Elidurydd. And you need not fear, for I was once as yourself, a mortal of the green world."

Dylan's bow slipped low, and the arrow of iron no longer was raised against the dame. As his caution waned beneath her gentle eyes, he released tension on the string. "I have heard tell of a mortal maid by that name," he said. "It is said she fell in love with one of the good folk and took him for a husband. She has not been seen in the green world in long ages."

She said, "Perhaps she has not been seen, yet she has walked here often, in the lonely places where times and worlds mingle."

But Dylan shook his head. "My lady, forgive me, but ye cannot be she. She was in the world in the old time, when my grandfather's great grandfather was not yet born."

She smiled, and slid her graceful back down the pillar so that she now sat reclining against it, legs folded to one side beneath her long, shimmering skirt. "Sir, time in the faerie realm is not that of the mortal realm. It is neither faster nor slower, it simply does not matter at all. And those mortals who are long there take on the character of the elfs."

Dylan felt no threat at all from this gentle lady, nor her companions, who sat like potted flowers and whispered in soft, gay voices as they regarded him and listened to the converse. He replaced the arrow in the quiver at his back and hung his bow from the warhorse's saddle. He made to step toward the gazebo and speak more appropriately with the gentle wild ladies.

But their aspect became fearful of a sudden. "Step no closer, sir, for we cannot bear your cold iron!" Elidurydd warned. And the damsels with her recoiled.

Then Dylan did something he had never done before. He removed his belt and hung it, with his dagger and sword, from the warhorse's saddle. For the first time in many long years, he was unarmed, and then he stepped closer to the gazebo. The ladies relaxed and allowed his approach. He sat on a step, an arm's length from Elidurydd.

"My lady, do you mean to say you are the same mortal maid who disappeared from the mountains of Cambria all those years ago."

"I am indeed," she said. "But I am no longer mortal. I have lived beyond the green world far too long to retain mortality in me. I am of the Tylwyth Teg now, and it was in my nature to join with the Gwragedd, the ladies of the brooks of the land. Their geas is my geas now. Yet you and I are still kin, by dint of our common mortal heritage." And she added, "And I have come to ask you a boon."

Now Dylan was struck by the lady's beauty and her grace, and he could find it within himself to give her no other reply than what he did, for he said, "Ask, my lady, and it shall be done, you have my word upon it."

She rose then and walked the breadth of the gazebo over to where the edge of it met the flowing stream. Small, bright things glittered back and forth in the shadows of the living water, barely discernable from the sparkles the sun woke upon the surface. Then she touched his hand, and in that moment he could see more clearly. The sparkles were not the jewels evoked of sunlight, but the tiny nude forms of girls, slender as willows, only inches long. They were nearly transparent, and even with the gift of the Second Sight, the elementals could hardly be told from the water unless one looked closely.

"The Asrai are fair little maidens," said Elidurydd. "And there are few waters free of iron and wares where they may yet dwell in the land. They are delicate, you see. And if they are touched by iron or kept in captivity, or even near to watery beasts in captivity, such as fish in wares, they return to the substance of water, and do not enter this world again, for their spirits go quickly far off into the Dreaming West. This is their last valley. My lord, keep it and defend it, and do not let any hunt in this place again. For that is why I and my ladies and my lord have brought you to this place, to ask this boon of you."

Dylan knelt on both knees and leaned far over the clear, quick flowing water. The tiny nymphs darted and frolicked like minnows and tadpoles, and they seemed oblivious to his presence. They were the color of yolk and cream, and their long hair was silver as moonlight, or sometimes delicate green as foils of dulse. They smiled as they played, and they seemed innocent as small children. And they were beautiful to look upon.

At last he stood again and faced the lady. "Who is your lord?" he asked her.

"His name is Mwdr."

"I will go to Maelgwn, and I will tell him the price of five seasons more of the service of the Hundred Horsemen is the eternal solitude of this valley. You shall have rest here from men, and peace from iron."

She smiled, and her relief was wondrous to see, more than worth the dear cost of this boon. He would have served a hundred years to see such joy in her fair jewel eyes.

"Where is your lord that I might tell him this news myself?" he asked.

"He is the stag whom you were pursuing. It is not the way of his kind to assume a man's shape before the rising of the moon."

Dylan's face grew pale then. He withdrew quickly from the stream, and without saying a word threw himself over Aval's leather saddle. He wrapped his belt around himself, set his bow over his shoulder.

"My lord," said Elidurydd, "why such fear in your eyes? No man can catch my horned lord, for that stag is faster than the wind."

But Dylan took not the moment to answer. He clapped his heals fiercely to the steed's flanks, and with that Aval flew through the wood. The wind roared in Dylan's ears and whipped back his long sable locks. He tracked the does' prints to the place where the harem separated and then continued on through the wood, in hard pursuit of his own men. Fear was in his heart now, and a certainty that he must be too late. For there was no huntsman more skilled than Angus, and no one more dogged. Once he had decided to take a beast, he would pursue it without ceasing, and the more skillfully it sought to evade him, the more he would revel in the chase. As would have Dylan.

The day wore on and the captain of the Hundred Horsemen chased the huntsmen the long length of it. Slowly he gained on the lot, and the sun was drawing low in the sky when he topped a great hill crowned in hazels. The air was growing chill and his breath frosted in streamers behind him. But his valiant steed was tiring, pushed to the limit. At the top of the hill a lonely stone stood, planted lengthwise into the earth. And it was at this fateful place that noble Aval fell, stumbling over an unseen log in the failing light. Dylan was thrown from his equine companion and rolled over and over on the ground. He was bruised and battered, and black dirt thrust into his mouth. Bits of leaves and twigs pressed into his hair. His body hurt sorely, and he cursed every moment he lay there trying to regather strength to stand. It seemed an eternity when at last he could. He turned and saw Aval lay upon the ground, still. His great chest no longer rose and fell. Dylan limped over to the steed and saw his neck had twisted in the fall. He fell to his knees then, and the mighty warrior hugged his old friend, and kissed his still brow, and closed his great brown eyes. So he bid Aval farewell, and with Aval went his last link to his fallen kingdom, for the horse was a king's horse, his father's horse, and the last bit of that land he still held to his name.

He rose to his knees then, his hand still on the steed's mane, and slowly his wits came back to him in full. The chase! The promise! He slung his sword belt over a shoulder so the sword was sheathed across his back. He tied the bottom of the sheath to his waist belt so the sword would not flap wildly as he ran. Then he took his bow and his quiver in his hands, and he started through the wood again. The sun had fallen lower, and the black, bare fingers of the trees were dark against a chill plum wine sky.

But he was not far from where the chase would end, for at the bottom of the great hill with the menhir, the standing stone, he found his men. They were gathered round the place where a mighty, white stag had fallen, pierced by iron-tipped arrows. But no man had moved to touch the beast, for on the spot where it had fallen a mighty elder now rose into the night.

Angus saw his captain descending the hill, limping as he came. He turned wild eyes toward him. "The tree was not there when we shot," Angus rasped in wonder. "There was only the stag. And when the arrows took it and it fell, a vista opened up behind it: a shining sea, and beyond it white shores, and beyond that the mountains of a far, fair land. And there was a man with long snowy hair standing upon the shore. His eyes were like those of a stag and horns with many tines were upon his brow. He looked wistfully back at this world. Then the vista faded, and where we had witnessed it, there was only to be seen this great elder, where no tree had stood before."

Dylan let fly a great cry and flung his steel sword into the night and never retrieved it. A fury came upon him and he pounded the earth while his men stood about, perplexed and saddened and helpless to do anything for him. The fury did not subside until dusk had fallen in full. Then Dylan and his men began gathering stones to bury the fallen stag.

In the darkness the ladies came, and they were weeping, but the tears of Elidurydd were ardent. She could not be consoled. The damsels with her recited this poem:

*A horned lord has gone into the Dreaming West,*
*far beyond the green world and fair Faerie,*
*where our spirits dwell away from mortal kin,*
*and we are left with bitter tears of loneliness.*

Through the night, around the mortals a great host gathered. Some were of the resplendent Tylwyth Teg, wild and graceful and beautiful. Some were of the Gwragedd, the brook ladies, as was Elidurydd. Some were diminutive, little more than tiny sparkles of light and flashes of glittering wings. Some were barely discernable from the land, appearing like vague faces in knots of trees and half-seen flits of shadow amidst earth and stone. They held silent vigil round the elder tree which had grown in the span of twilight massive and twisted so that it appeared burdened with many years.

In the midnight darkness some elfs came who resembled children, male and female, with impish eyes and pointed ears, and long straight hair of red and black. They were nude except for belts and purses of leather. They carried flutes and pipes and small harps, and in the night they made such bitter music as the men with Dylan could barely stand. Beneath the power of the elf music, the men wept sorely for the fallen stag, as if he were their own dear laird, while the faerie folk showed their sorrow in their own peculiar ways, some by weeping, some by laughing, some by gaily skipping between the trees, some by howling into the night like angry wolves, some by drinking elder wine till they could not stand straight, some by making love in the shadows.

Near dawn the faerie folk began to drift and fade away, each to its own daytime haunt. But Elidurydd remained, seated at the roots of the great elder tree.

Before the coming of Dylan, Angus and his company had had valor but no honor. But since Dylan had come they had learned to respect the chivalrous ways of this prince who held no kingdom, and no inheritance. They had learned to value honor, and so gained their souls. Now, there in the morning twilight, when the faerie music had faded and they regained their minds, they conversed long with the brook lady. And they each made their pledge to her, and to Dylan, for their hearts were bitter over what they had done.

Then Dylan spoke as captain of the Hundred Horsemen to the lady of the brook, the Gwragedd, who had once been a mortal lass. "We will hold this valley, my lady. We will keep it ourselves for you and your kinfolk. And we will guard the elder tree all our days. And our children will keep it after us."

But the lady said, "Bitter and ephemeral are promises made in the green world of mortals. Hold this valley as long as you can, and keep the Old Ways and shun cold iron so the land might remain pure and heal. Faerie kin will stay among you and aid you as you keep the land. And now I must remain near this place, for it is as close as I can ever hope to be again to what remains of my horned lord in the green world, because biting shards of cold iron have driven his spirit into the Dreaming West without me. And I, who was born among mortal folk, can never hope to follow him. For, being of mortal ancestry, my lot beyond life is the Otherworld and not the Dreaming West. And yet even death is denied me, for I share the geas of the brook ladies now, and they know no mortality."

And so the oath was made between the Hundred Horsemen and the faerie folk, that always the one should keep the other, and a place shall always be guarded for Elidurydd and the fallen faerie lord, Mwdr, deep in the enchanted wood.

*********

Coppin rose from the table and went to the stove, where a great pot of stew boiled to feed the new-hired hands who would soon come in for dinner. "But the story does no' end there. Yet it is enough for now, lad," he told Sweyn. "It is perhaps more than ye can bear, and certainly more than ye will yet believe." He stirred the pot and tasted it, and nodded approval.

But Sweyn had listened raptly to the tale, a poignant bit of fiction. But fiction is powerful and it touched him deeply, leaving a bitter ache within, for the loss of love was familiar to him, as familiar as the instinct to eat and breathe. And he found he was not ready for the tale to end. He was hungry to know more. "If there is more, Coppin, tell it," he said.

Coppin smiled as though he knew something the seaman could not fathom. "I'm glad to hear ye taking interest in our heritage, lad. It is no' a tale we tell to outsiders. But I canna' seem to get rid of ye."

"But the Hundred Horsemen," Sweyn pressed. "You are saying they were the first of this people." He made a sweeping gesture, indicating the folk of the Island.

"Indeed," said Coppin. "But the folk are neither knights nor horsemen any longer. The sad green world has no more place for either. Now the folk simply call themselves the Company, and the Cottage is the house of their Laird. And mind ye that the hearing of their stories is dangerous for an outsider, for one must have the mindset for it. And coming to that takes time."

"Tell it," Sweyn insisted. "I need to know, what is this all about. What drove Eilwen to hate this place so direly and yet love it so much? Why did she make me promise never to let Dundubh Cottage go?"

"That is another story entirely," said Coppin. "And if ye do stay and I canna' get rid of ye, ye'll hear it, in good time. But no' now."

"Coppin, I am your employer and your Laird. Tell the tales."

At that pronunciation Coppin studied him thoughtfully. "Be careful before taking on that title, lad. The geas binds and does no' let go. But be ye my Laird or the Old Lady of the Wood herself, I would no' tell the tales until ye were ready, for to perceive before the mind is ready is to find only madness and death."

"Don't be ridiculous," Sweyn spat, frustrated with the stubborn little curmudgeon.

"And the very fact that ye canna' understand it is proof enough ye're no' ready to hear more. As well as the fact ye canna' remember what happened to ye in all the weeks ye were in the wood." Sweyn started to say something, but Coppin cut him off. "Some things must simply be said in their own time." Coppin pointed a spindly finger at Sweyn, wagging it with each syllable. "Accept that wisdom, lad, and ye'll do better here. And now, here's another bit for ye. Winter will come in a few short months, and we need firewood." And with that, he busied himself setting places for the staff who began to trickle in.

Sweyn had a thousand questions for him, but somehow he knew to set them aside and wait till the time was right for the asking. Coppin would never give him answers otherwise.

# Chapter Nine

*On evenings just before the fainter stars,*
*when the west sky is bound in plum,*
*and owls hail from farther beeches,*
*the chill air gathers in the shadows*
*beneath the rustling bones of trees.*

*Men are gathered to boil oat sprouts*
*warmed and smoked from the malt house,*
*in a black cauldron upon cherry coals,*
*to make the wort and blend the spices,*
*and brew the ale that makes folk smile.*

*Round the fire of burning cherry*
*murmur voices of the brewers,*
*holding to hand the finest sweet ale,*
*telling tales and sharing laughter*
*reaping memories in the glade.*

*Autumn Wood Brewing*
*Donald McCavitt*

Sweyn was no one's fool. Being a doctor of psychology who had treated many resistant clients, he was well versed in knowing when someone was brushing him off. Why Coppin was doing so remained a mystery, but less and less he suspected duplicity on the part of the wizened little man. There was something else driving Coppin's peculiar behavior, Sweyn was sure of it. Coppin was worried about something, and wished to talk about it, but for reasons Sweyn could not discern he was refusing to do so. However, patience had proven a useful tactic with Coppin. Indeed, the only successful tactic. The little fellow was stubborn, he would reveal no more to Sweyn than what he was ready to. Sweyn could not prod him into it by being the directive boss nor by supplications.

"Still," Sweyn muttered to himself, "an employer shouldn't have to put up with that kind of behavior from his employees." He went out the kitchen door and stood in the yard immediately behind the south wing and looked over the estate, trying to decide just what he would do to go about procuring firewood. Of course, the entire place was surrounded by forest. Where the wood would come from was no mystery. But Sweyn had never cut firewood in his life and wasn't sure just how to go about it.

"Tools," he decided first off. He stalked off to a tool shed atop a hillock and found a wheelbarrow, a large axe, and a pair of leather work gloves. He tossed the gloves and the axe into the wheelbarrow and exited the barn, pushing the wheelbarrow before him. The rain had lightened by now to a heavy mist. It turned the air muggy and if not for the surety that winter must indeed follow summer, one would be hard pressed to imagine the need for firewood ever coming. Yet, when he thought about it, midsummer was only a couple days away and that meant autumn was less than two months behind at this latitude. A house the size of Dundubh Cottage would need a good supply of firewood, even if he only heated the rooms actively used by himself and Coppin.

Standing in front of the tool shed at the top of the hillock, he regarded the grassy fields round about Dundubh through a haze of humidity. Under the care of the new-hired farmhands, the meadows and groves were once again becoming neat, well-groomed, and productive. But beyond the fields were miles and square miles of untamed woods. His woods, unbelievably. It was odd, but till now he had scarce given thought to the immense forest. And such a peculiar forest, where the land seemed to change its shape with the passing of years, and where Old World trees of beech and hazel and oak dominated where once American northwest coast rainforest had grown. How could European trees, most of which were deciduous, even tolerate the soil and climate here? How these people—the Company, as Coppin referred to them—managed to make it happen was beyond him.

So he returned his thoughts to the more immediate matter: firewood. From this vantage he espied what appeared to be an old dirt path leading off to a stand of trees that stood out somewhat from the general line of forest. The path had two narrow ruts in it, a sure sign that carts or motorized vehicles often made passages into the stand. He lifted the handles of the wheelbarrow and pushed it down the hillock onto the path. The day was already drawing on, and the weather was not fit for working out of doors, and he had no real intention of doing any serious wood gathering today, but he thought he might as well get an idea where he would go about it, and what the job would require.

It took him a good fifteen minutes to reach the stand. The dirt path proceeded into it a ways. He followed it. Faded memories of a recent and less than pleasant encounter with the wood left him wary, but he had no real recollection remaining of the event to hold him back. Just the distant ringing words of the air, moments of fear and joy, and that was all. Everything else was only the blurry after image of a long lost dream, no more than enough to give him pause. Besides, somehow Sweyn felt Coppin would not send him to do something which would bring him to harm. Coppin may not have wanted Sweyn at Dundubh, may not even have liked him, but he wasn't malicious.

As he walked into the stand pushing the creaking wheelbarrow, he saw signs that this portion of the wood did indeed serve as a woodlot. There was little undergrowth and here and there could be seen the ancient stumps of long felled trees. Most of the trees in the stand were birches, a fast growing species which burned long and hot. Given the abundance of these trees, it was no wonder this area had been chosen for the Cottage's woodlot. After walking a bit he found a likely silvery birch near the path, growing tall and straight and stately. He looked it up and down and thought it a shame to cut it, but it had to be done. He put on the gloves, hefted the axe, and began hacking into the base of the tree. The leaves rattled with each jarring blow; chips of white wood flew.

After ten minutes Sweyn was dripping sweat but the tree was not a lot closer to falling. Less than perhaps a tenth of it had been bitten by the axe. "So this is Coppin's latest plan to get rid of me, is it?" he grumbled. "Wear me out on woodcutting." Sweyn hacked a few minutes more. He was healthy and, while no Olympian, was fairly well in shape for being in his latter thirties. Yet the work was wearing him ragged. Huffing, he leaned the axe against the tree and turned around to sit down and use the trunk for a backrest.

A tall, lean elderly man met his vision. He leaned against a nearby tree, one of the few beeches in the stand. Surprised, Sweyn made to rise quickly, but the old man smiled reassuringly and made a gesture with his hand that said simultaneously hello and rest easy. Sweyn relaxed and waved back at the old man, studying him carefully.

The old man's hair was thin, white and wispy, but long, tied into a ponytail. His skin was weatherworn like comfortable old leather. He was dressed in jeans and a plaid shirt, the sleeves rolled up and the top two buttons undone. His arms were slim cords of strong wire. Over his shirt he wore a dark oilskin cloak. He wore gold rimmed wire spectacles, yet he did not have the look of a reader. His entire image portrayed a vigorous man comfortable in his current environment. Without a doubt, this was an experienced and capable woodsman.

Sweyn waved his hand and said hello, and it occurred to him that maybe he should ask the fellow what he was doing on his land.

With a nod, the old man approached Sweyn, looking down at him with a sort of curious bemusement. He brushed his hand against the handle of the axe, then glanced at the wheelbarrow Sweyn had intended to use as a wood cart. Then he stood back, folded his arms, looked down at Sweyn and said, "Ye dinna' have the faintest notion what yer doin', do ye."

It was a statement, though it rang like a question, and Sweyn knew it was true. But it incensed him, nonetheless, and he grunted, "Sure I do. I'm doing my best."

The old man stepped back to the beech, leaned against it and watched Sweyn inquisitively, as if waiting to see what he would do next.

Feeling more the outsider than ever, and fed up with it, Sweyn rose to his feet and gathered the axe into his hands. Knowing full well his behavior was sophomoric at best, he began chopping furiously at the tree. White chips of birch flew everywhere, and bits no larger than sawdust managed to cling all over Sweyn: on his clothes, in his salt-and-pepper ponytail, to his sweaty brow. Sweyn's heart hammered in his breast and his clothes were quickly soaked in perspiration, yet he did not let up the assault on the tree. In ten minutes more half the breadth of the trunk had been cut away. In ten more another quarter had been removed, and then, with a protest of groans and snaps, the tree fell ponderously over toward Sweyn who barely sidestepped out of the way in time.

Once the tree lay still upon the ground, Sweyn huffed heavily, wiped sweat out of his eyes, and looked at the old man with a victorious grin. It was the first time in his life he had felled a tree, and it felt somehow as if he had proven himself to the woodsman. He dropped the axe with the intention of preparing the wood to haul back up to Dundubh Cottage when the second problem occurred to him. Now that he had a fallen tree, he had to strip the thing of branches and cut the log into transportable pieces of a size suitable for use in the stoves and grates of the Cottage. He looked at the axe in despair as the thought of chopping and rechopping the trunk into fifty small logs wended through his mind.

But the old man perceived what vexed Sweyn and approached him a second time. This time his eyes were softer, as if Sweyn had proven his metal—if not his wisdom—and earned a measure of the old woodsman's respect. Despite his apparent age, his gate was efficient and smooth as some hunting forest creature. Once beside the fallen tree, he set a foot upon it and rested an arm on his bent knee, so that he seemed both relaxed yet coiled. He gave Sweyn the impression of a fox, full of supple energy and cunning. But he looked Sweyn in the eye and said with a kind, deep voice, "Dinna' worry, lad. Ye did all right for yer first time. I'm no' hear to criticize, believe it or no'. But ye clearly need some help and I thought it best ye figured it for yerself." He extended a hand. "The name's Donald McCavitt. I'm yer gillie."

*********

Evening found Sweyn and Donald seated upon ancient unsplit firewood logs stood on end in a tiny clearing just in front of Donald's small log cabin. Around them, woodland shadows deepened to pools of elderberry wine. Between them a small fire of seasoned birch crackled, and they drank cool apple cider from earthenware mugs. The night was not at all chill, and the stars had come out. The only purpose of the fire was to keep the mosquitoes at bay, "and other things away" Donald had added enigmatically.

Donald's cabin was a modest affair tucked into the trees. It consisted of a lower level with living room and kitchen, and a loft with two tiny bedrooms. The place was primitive. For water there was a clear spring. For facilities there was an outhouse. But Donald had showed Sweyn about it earlier as if it were a mansion.

It turned out Donald was an employee of Dundubh Cottage, and had been so all his life, as had his family as far back as the founding of Man-by-the-Sea when his ancestor, Raleigh McCavitt, mutinied and threw in his lot with the Company. Donald served as caretaker of the wood and wild animals; such was the role of a gillie. It was the traditional post of the McCavitt family since the day they joined the Company. He also assisted the Cottage by bringing in firewood for the winter. As woodcutter, his cabin was located at the back of the square mile of forest that served as the Cottage's woodlot.

Despite their initial awkward meeting, Sweyn had soon come to feel comfortable in the company of the old woodsman. They had talked easily all the way back to Donald's cabin as Donald had guided Sweyn among the many forks of the meandering forest path. Along the way, he had explained that the woodlot was carefully managed, and only the oldest birches and wind fallen trees were harvested for firewood, saplings immediately planted to replace them. Under such judicious care, the Cottage had been able to fulfill its need for firewood for centuries from this single plot of land, and the forest still stood strong and healthy. "But it's a mundane wood," Donald had added. "Iron axes keep most things away."

Sweyn had regarded him quizzically. "I don't understand," he had said after a minute.

Donald's reply had been terse. "Animals come through here. Us. Little else, except sometimes." Donald had added nothing else to the bizarre statement all through the remainder of the walk to his cabin.

Aside from that baffling statement, Sweyn found Donald to be the most reasonable person he had met since coming to the Island. He seemed somewhat aloof from the Island's strange beliefs and traditions, aware of them but not immersed in them. That was not to say he disregarded them entirely—he certainly had the Man-by-the-Sea folks' concern for things that go bump in the night. But he was more open and interested in ideas from the world beyond. It soon seemed to Sweyn that he had found a kindred spirit in Donald, someone he might call a friend, and by the time they were sharing cider together by the fire, he found himself speaking openly with him. Sweyn admitted to Donald that he had never meant to the come to the Island, and did not want to be this Laird everyone thought him to be. Sweyn explained he would have as soon sold the estate but for a promise his wife had made him vow only days before her death.

"So now yer boat . . ." Donald said, but Sweyn corrected, "Cutter." Donald began again. "So now yer cutter is repaired and yet ye have no' left. I'm no seaman, now, but I do know a thing or two about the weather, and I'd guess that if ye dinna' set yer sails soon ye'll be passing the winter here, whether ye mean to or no'."

Sweyn nodded. "I have time yet. I figure I can leave as late as the beginning of September and still run south faster than winter can come down out of the north."

Donald shrugged. "Ye're the sailor, but I'll warn ye, the weather can make funny turns in these parts on a moment's notice."

"I noticed that when the gale blew me into your bay this spring." Sweyn took a long swig of the cider. It was potent stuff, more alcoholic than the sweet ale.

Donald observed him and shook his head. "Slow down, lad. Careful with that stuff, or ye'll be wobbling and winding yer way home. And it's best no' to do that come dark in these parts." He looked cautiously about into the darkening wood. "Ye have a lot to learn about the Island if ye dinna' plan on leaving," Donald observed. "It does no' take a keen mind to see it."

Sweyn could only agree with that. "Look, I don't know anything about this place. Not about being Laird, not about a forest of beech and oak on a Pacific coast island, and nothing about how this throwback to prehistoric Britain got tucked into this corner of the world. And, honestly, Donald, I don't want to know either. But I feel obligated to, if I'm ever going to understand who my wife really was. Still, what I'd really like to do is just get away. I feel like I'm being sucked into something too big here, and that worries me, because I have no idea what it is."

Donald said, "I'll help ye understand as I can, for I know some of the tales of this place." Then Donald took an earthen pitcher of cider and refilled his mug and Sweyn's. "Drink that slow now," he warned Sweyn again. Then he began his tale. "The forest was brought here, as I am sure ye have already realized. It was brought here well over two centuries ago when a fool lot of Celts came west following the vision of an old witch who claimed to have scryed out a message from an ancient god. The god's name was Manannan, hence the name of this Island. He was supposed to be the lord of the sea and its islands."

Sweyn said, "You sound as if you don't believe in this god."

"Bah!" spat Donald. "I dinna' have time for gods, and I would no' have time if I did."

Sweyn raised an eyebrow, but Donald continued without pause. "The old witch had come to be their leader, so to speak. In truth, the descendents of Dylan O'Shee led the Company, but the witch, it was she who had the Second Sight. She was the one who could see the faerie folk and the gods. It was she who knew the path the Company had to take . . ."

*********

The old witch, it was said, had even been with them since the ancient days of Dylan's men. She it was who had encouraged the Hundred Horsemen to take wives and create a small village in the enchanted valley of the Asrai. She urged them seek their wives from all the stock of the British Isles, from Kernau to Cymru, and north among Scots and Picts. She even urged them to seek west all the way across the sea, in the emerald land of forests and mists called Eirne. And also she sent them to the refugees who fled the Norman invaders, east in far off Brittany, a little Britain then in its infancy. Dylan had heeded the old dame's advice. For reasons known only to him he had esteemed her highly from the start. Of his men he had chosen ten and sent them in five pairs to wander the dispersed old kingdoms in search of damsels willing to settle with his retiring knights.

"You must take the damsels from their disparate lands, showing favor to no kingdom over the other," the witch had said. "Your folk must be a joining of all the elder peoples of the isles, united in common purpose to keep their flame alive.

"These damsels must be those who treasure the Old Ways of our people. Their eyes must be open and clear; they must be those who do not fear and shun the twilight. They must be chosen for their hearts and not for blood or lovely eyes or fair skin."

Said the envoys: "We will do your bidding, witch." And they rode to the far lands and were gone, some more than a year before returning with damsels and sometimes their whole families of fathers, mothers, brothers, sisters, and kinfolk with them. They returned with those who were dissatisfied with their lands and their lords, who feared the many invaders pressing from all sides, and sought new lives and new opportunities. None of the folk that came into the valley with the envoys were without merit. All honored the ways of the elder times. All were friends of faerie folk. All were fit to the purpose of the Hundred Horsemen, for the old witch had given the envoys clear instructions what to look for in the hearts of people, and she had set charms upon them, and the hazel nut of wisdom, to give them eyes to see true as a bard.

But in the years following the founding of the Company, after the valley was lost and the Hundred Horsemen vanished, the Company had nothing left to defend. They became a wandering folk, and fell into the questionable habits of Gypsies and Tinkers. But whatever their dealings in business, they kept their old ways, and they always sought the remaining enchanted places in their travels. In such places they encountered the remnants of the faerie folk whom they befriended, and so they were always kept by faerie luck.

The old witch stayed with the Company through all the difficult centuries of wandering. The Company needed her to keep them strong and united, for it goes hard on a people who have no place to call their own. She became their strength and their center, and she counseled the O'Shees who led the Company. And in this way many generations passed.

Then one crisp day, when the air was chill and spiced with autumn, the Company was camped far in the north of Britain. In a glen amidst a grove of hazel the witch sat alone beside a pool, and salmon swam deep within the crystal water. There in the cool depths the god Manannan appeared to her, for he is a sea god and does not walk upon dry land. He showed her the far shores of a strange continent and told her that a time would come when the Company must go to

136

those shores, "West, go west, and always west," the sea god said. And he gave her instructions. "Before you go, you must wander yet farther here. Travel all the lands of this Old World. Find all faerie kin who have not faded and bind them in the trees. For fair Faerie is fractured and sundered with the coming of iron and mortal folks' endless spreading roads and cities of carved stone and plowed, ordered fields which undo the wild places. Faerie will fade in many places and faerie kin will vanish with it, for they are bound to the land and cannot flee. Take what you bind with you and my sea folk will follow, and go into the new world. Trek until you find a lonely place where enchantment flows abundant, and there rebuild the world that is slipping away."

Then the witch told the O'Shee who was then the reigning Laird of her meeting with the sea god. That O'Shee led his people after her vision, and so the Company wandered ever more widely throughout the Old World. They went beyond the British islands into far European lands. The wandering was long and hard, and they called that time the Binding Years. Their generations saw the great snow-covered Alps, and the deep German forests of magnificent pines. They saw the flooded lands of the Dutch coasts, being drained and turned to farms. They saw the falling Belgian forests, being turned into cottages and firewood. They saw the green places of France, where once a sprite had dwelt in every spring, but now every spring was given to watering crops and horses. They wandered all these wide spaces, careful to omit no place, and they found every wild glen and spring where Faerie had not yet faded. And the faerie folk of those scattered hidden places they gathered and bound into the trees so that they should not leave this green world once for all and drift forever into the Dreaming West. And when Columbus found the New World and the settlers began to pour into the new western lands, the Company went also, and faerie folk traveled with them, far across the sea. And there they began a new season of wandering, following the witch's vision, looking for a land where magic flowed. But their only guide was the god's parting words: "West, go west, and always west."

*********

It was full dark when Donald had finished the tale. With the end of it he tossed the dregs of his cup into the fire which sizzled and spat and smelled for a moment of apples and burned sugar. Donald refilled his mug from the earthenware jug. "Ye have the look of a man who does no' believe," said Donald.

Sweyn shook his head. "It's a myth, that's all. It has all the classic elements. An immortal witch. Magical visions of pagan gods. A quest. Tragedy. Gypsies. All it's missing is a big bad wolf."

Donald smiled and chuckled at that. And he nodded.

"You don't believe it either, do you," Sweyn suggested.

But Donald nodded, to his surprise. "Oh, I believe it well enough. But believing and being impressed are two different things."

"You're saying you don't care."

Donald shrugged and sipped his cider.

"So why stay? Why live in this backward place, in this cabin with no power or plumbing if you're ready to move out of the past."

"Well," said Donald, "that's because I've nowhere else better to be."

Sweyn did not understand, so instead he took a big swallow of the heady cider. For the life of him, he could not figure out these people. But at least Donald seemed to make more sense than Coppin.

"Now Coppin, that servant up at yer Cottage," began Donald, startling Sweyn with his uncanny use of the name at the instant Sweyn had been thinking it, "he'll no' be telling ye this. Coppin likes to leave folk to 'grow into the mysteries.' The old fool is a mystic and ye'll be an old man before he sets ye right about the ways of this place. So I'm filling ye in now."

Sweyn nodded. "Much appreciated."

"Of course, there may be wisdom to Coppin's way," Donald said a moment later, contradicting himself. Donald leaned forward, resting his elbows on his lanky legs and looked Sweyn directly in the eye. "I'm telling ye, lad, this Island's got a way of keeping folk and losing folk. And if ye dinna' intend to stay, best ye leave before ye become to tangled up in its geas."

"I've heard this term," said Sweyn, "this 'geas,' over and over. But I still don't get it?"

"Well, that's another can of worms entirely, and explaining it puts me between a rock and a hard place" Donald said, stroking his chin and looking thoughtful. The appearance of the two contemporary American expressions within Donald's archaic brogue caused Sweyn to wonder at the peculiar heritage of this people, who in their wanderings had merged bits of many cultures into themselves and emerged from the joining something singularly unique, yet distinctively Celtic as well.

Donald tried to explain, trying to find some analogy, some metaphor that might enable Sweyn to relate to the concept. "Some folk believe the geas is like a taboo. Keep the taboo and luck is with ye. Break the taboo and good luck fails. But that's a very simple perspective and hardly adequate." He paused, sipping cider and staring into the fire for a long time. He must have drunk half his mug in that slow way before he spoke again. Staring into the fire, he spoke almost dreamily, carefully choosing each word. "More perceptive folk understand the geas goes deeper. It is part of the skein of reality, and it winds folk into its fate. But that does no' truly explain the geas because it gives the impression the geas drags one into a predetermined future. But the geas does no' follow a set future. As far as this folk believe, there is no set future. The future is made by the nature and actions of the persons who live in the present. So I guess I'm still not helping ye. Let's see here . . ." He stopped again, reconsidered the direction he was taking the discussion, then seemed to settle on what he was going to say. This time he looked Sweyn in the eyes as he spoke. "What the geas truly is is a brand. It is built on a person's individual character and brands those traits. It demands a role in the world for the person according to his own unique attributes, and if the person stays true to the geas he'll have the luck for it, for he has stayed true to his own right self. But if he breaks the weave, he does no' stay true to himself and luck will be his no longer. Often things go bad for such a one. This doom is not a curse, mind ye, but the natural consequence of breaking how ye should weave into the world. Folk say on the Island, "Cut the skein and yer world unravels."

Sweyn regarded Donald with obvious confusion. Donald seemed at once to disdain the Company's beliefs yet be an expert on them. He could not understand why one who did not hold to these superstitions would be so knowledgeable about them. Donald guessed his thoughts from his eyes and shrugged. "The geas is common knowledge here," he said. "We learn all about it when we are lads."

Sweyn nodded, indicated with a rolling gesture of his hand that Donald should carry on.

"The Company believes there are many levels of geasa – that's plural for geas. One level of geasa define individuals, and these may be redefined over time, for as people age they grow and become more complex. Who they are changes, and their geasa may grow with them.

"Then there are the greater geasa, those of households and families and villages. Those are more stable, but they too may change over generations.

"But then there are the great geasa, those of regions of the earth. Such geasa are too big and complicated to be fully understood by any individual, and they are nearly changeless. Ye might think of these things as the order determined by the numinous powers and presences of the world. The Company believes this Island to be an enchanted land under a great geas which binds the Island to protect things of mystery. Since the Company is sworn to protect their faeries, they were naturally drawn here."

Sweyn said, "You can't believe this stuff."

Donald flipped a hand palm up, swept it aside, a gesture bespeaking uncertainty. "Some more, some less, and I'd be lying to confess any different. I've seen things on this Island that would send shivers up and down yer spine, and as ye were missing so long, I've no doubt ye have too."

*Lights hovering over bogs. Some impossible walking thing like a tree.*

Sweyn nodded, and the doing was almost like a confession. But though the memories came to him now only as broken dream fragments, though everything in his rational mind denied their reality, deep in his bones he just couldn't quite dismiss them.

Donald continued. "But what I believe is unimportant. The Company believes it, and here we must live by their rules."

"You don't like them?" Sweyn observed, according to the tone of Donald's voice.

"I like them well enough. I dinna' respect them."

"A subtle difference."

Donald stared wistfully into the dark as if he were looking for something. Sweyn gave in to temptation and looked also, but all he saw were fire-licked shadows dancing beneath benighted trees. Donald turned back to him. "It seems to me ye've already made yer choice. Ye're staying."

"For now," said Sweyn. "It's pleasant here." He hesitated, realizing something, and then added, "It seems I have to do something here."

A frown creased Donald's weathered skin as deeply as the folds of a wind-dried apple still hanging from the tree. "It is the geas binding ye. Go now or never."

Sweyn nodded.

Again they sat quietly a long time, each lost in his own thoughts. It was Donald who broke the silence a long while later when the fire had nearly burned to coals. He simply said, "It's on yer shoulders then."

"I suppose so," Sweyn replied, but he had no worry. He did not believe in geasa.

There was another prolonged silence, not as long as the last, then Donald said, "Assuming ye will be staying a while, would it be fair to say ye know nothing of running a farm, let alone Lairding?"

Sweyn pursed his lips and nodded.

"Well, sir, I guess it's a good thing we met up today for more reasons than tapping my vast reservoir of Island lore. For I am going to teach ye the secret of O'Shee wealth and perhaps ye can get the old place on its feet again."

"I thought I was already doing that," said Sweyn.

"Oh, ye'll barely make ends meet with sheeps' milk and apples. It's Dundubh ale the folk want, and they haven't had it in more than fifteen years. Why do ye think there's a vast field of oats growing in yer yard? Why do ye think ye've a malt house?"

"Frankly," Sweyn admitted, "I don't even know what a malt house is."

"I see," said Donald. "Wait here." He rose and went to the cabin. He returned with two iron horseshoes, one of which he handed to Sweyn, then pulled a hefty branch from a vat where the end quarter had been soaking in kerosene. He lit the torch in the fire and started up the path. He turned and called to Sweyn. "Come on, then, lad! This is as good a time as any to learn the art of making yer estate's income." Sweyn rose and followed. "Keep iron about ye by night," the woodsman instructed as they strode down the dark path. "The woodlot is given to the O'Shees to take care of the needs of the Cottage. Still, despite iron axes things walk here sometimes, in the darkness, and some are no' always seelie. And half the time even the seelie canna' be trusted."

Sweyn sighed as he rose and followed. He would never understand all of what Donald was saying. Just as he was coming to accept that he had never really understood Eilwen, who always related to the world in her own curious Island way. She had seemed at times . . . witchy. It was a peculiarity that lent her an air of mystery, and yet that very mystery, he realized, had drawn him to her.

That brought another thought to him, though, a recollection of the journal of Donald's distant forefather, Raleigh, who had mentioned a witch with the settlers more than two hundred years before. Walking beside Donald, struggling in the flickering torchlight to pick his way over roots twisting across the half-wild forest path, he said, "The witch you spoke of, does the story still have her name?"

"Oh, sure. It was Oak Peg, of course," said Donald, who pressed on quickly and warily through the wood, holding the torch aloft.

Sweyn blinked heavily, a gesture which cost him a misstep and nearly tripped him flat. Hopping for his balance, he almost stumbled into the dark off the path, and only just regained his footing when Donald lent him a steadying hand.

Chagrinned, Sweyn said, "The name of Oak Peg keeps cropping up everywhere, even in the oldest stories of the Island. Now, I'm no historian, but Dylan's time must have been fifteen hundred years ago. Maybe more. So, is there a tradition of calling the Company's witches Oak Peg? Or is it a title, like a witch is something strong that keeps things together, like an oak peg?"

But in answer Donald admonished Sweyn always to keep his feet upon the benighted path. "Always."

*********

By torchlight they made their way through quarter-moon-lit Dundubh lands, stepping lightly through calf-high emerald grass that whispered softly as they passed. The gentle hills rolled up and down and Donald led Sweyn along a roundabout route, along ancient wooden fences, toward a great waving expanse of oats that soughed gently as the night breeze combed invisible fingers through the waist-high foliage. Beneath the pale moon all the colors of the world were silvered, except those within the sphere of torchlight which took on the tinge of molten gold.

"Surely ye've noticed ye have nearly two hundred acres of oats growing here," said Donald.

Sweyn nodded. "Yes, but there are all kinds of things growing around the property. There is a field of barley turned half wild up by the seaward side. There're a grove of elders down off the front of the house. There're acres and acres that seem devoted to various vegetable crops, now overgrown with weeds and gourd vines. And, frankly, I don't quite know what to do with any of it."

Donald said, "Coppin should have filled ye in long ago. I've never known him to hold back like this. He's taken a right disliking to ye, I'd venture."

"I don't know why I put up with him," Sweyn said.

"Ye put up with him because he comes with the Cottage," Donald stated flatly, as if the house and Coppin were a package, as if one could not have the one without the other. He turned and faced the direction of the elder grove. "The elders grow blossoms and berries which are both useful. We use the blossoms to make a strong syrup for the elder blossom cordial. One of the few unspirited beverages we like to drink here on the Island." They both laughed. Donald turned toward the apple grove. "The apple trees have all kinds of uses, and that's why the grove is so large. We use many of the fruit in cooking and for cider. And the wind fallen branches, those we use to spice the malthouse wood." He turned toward the barley field. "That's yer hayfield. That's fodder for those fine sheep of yers come winter." Finally he turned to the oat field, spread out before them. "This here, this field has a special purpose. It's the starting place of the finest wort made on the Island."

"The sweet ale."

Donald nodded approvingly, hearing the fondness for the drink in Sweyn's voice. "Aye, lad, the rich, thick brown sweet ale. Nothing like it, I'll wager, is to be found among the watery stuff they call ale on the mainland."

Sweyn shook his head.

"Well," Donald continued, "several households on the Island make it. But the Man-by-the-Sea folk have been pining for the O'Shee brew since the last O'Shee male left us. And the secret of O'Shee ale starts here, in this field."

Donald pointed to the forest beside the field. "Over there a spring flows from the Guardwood. The waters are the sweetest on the Island, and the soil here is the blackest. Oats grown in such have no comparison." He led Sweyn back through the darkness to the malthouse, a barnlike building whose purpose had always stumped Sweyn.

"Now, when the oats are matured, ye bring them here to the malthouse. On the second level they'll be laid out like so . . ." He made a scattering motion. "Laid good and thick, but not so thick as all of it canna' breathe equally. A cool, smoky fire will be built below, and the wind fallen apple branches, and many dried apples, will be used to feed that fire. It is what gives the ale that faint smoky-sweet flavor.

"The oats are laid to rest here till they've sprouted, and they must be turned as they lie, for even though the heat is low, the sprouting process also gives off heat, and so much oat sprouting in such a small space can cause them to cook. We dinna' want that. Ye just want them to grow, all nice and warm and coddled.

"When the oats have sprouted, ye'll carry them to the foot of the wood at the back of the sheep field, where there is a malt shack. There the sprouted oats will be boiled in a huge black cauldron of iron, and the water drained from the cauldron will be thick with the oat sugar and flavor of the malt smoke. Three times the oats will be boiled, each using half the water as before, and the sum of all the liquid will be kept together.

"But it's in the second boiling where is the secret of O'Shee sweet ale. For in that batch ye'll add the herbs of mint, elderflower, sweet clover and bluebonnet that give the ale much of its unique flavor. And there is a secret herb, which only Coppin knows, and he'll tell ye it or I'll wring his scrawny neck. But when he does, ye must never tell a soul. No' even me. It is said it is the luck of the O'Shees to keep the secret of their ale.

"When the water has cooled, ye'll set it aside with fresh elderberries in it. The yeast in the elderberries will start the fermentation and it must ferment the span of one moon. Then, and only then, it may be primed, barreled and shipped to town."

"You make it sound so simple," said Sweyn.

"Dinna' worry lad, I'll walk ye through it when it's time. There's been a Laird in the Cottage all these months now and the folk will be wanting their O'Shee ale. The harvest will begin next month and we'll have everything ready to go for then. Then yer house will prosper again."

"But it's only two hundred acres of oats to make the ale. I imagine that might make enough for Man-by-the-Sea, but why don't we grow more oats and export it. Surely it would do well beyond the Island."

"Maybe, maybe no'. But the ale does no' keep well beyond these shores. It has to be made fresh only weeks before it is consumed. There would be no point in shipping it out."

Sweyn nodded, then said, "I'm surprised there is no hops in the ale. You can't find a beer on the mainland without it."

Donald spat at the word "beer." "That watery, bitter stuff!" he exclaimed. "Manannan's cauldron, lad, why would ye consider putting beer hops in fine O'Shee sweet ale!" He put an arm conspiratorially on Sweyn's shoulder. "Let me tell ye something about hops, lad. Beer is ale with hops, and the reason they put hops in it is to keep the ale from spoiling. And that's it. Folk here dinna' want a preservative in their ale, they'll take it fresh from the brewer, thank ye very much."

"But if hops keeps the ale, we could export it."

As if affronted, Donald turned and regarded Sweyn, eyes round, mouth agape. He exclaimed, "But if ye added hops, ye'd no longer have sweet ale! Ye'd have nasty beer, wouldn't ye?" He stood back from Sweyn, arms folded in front of his strong but wiry frame, and looked him up and down, as if measuring him. He seemed to come to a decision after a moment, and said sagely, "Do ye need to get rich, or do ye need enough to continue? The Cottage is already wealthy enough, what with the rents and the milk and ale it produces. Be content, lad." And then he added something Sweyn would not have expected from him. "Keep to the Old Ways, lad, and they'll keep ye back."

Sweyn studied Donald when he turned away to look out over the oat field again. Here was a complicated man. He gave at first the impression that he looked down upon the Island's ways, yet suddenly it was apparent that this was not the case at all. Whatever his reason for dissension, it was more complicated than mere disdain.

Donald fingered his cold iron horseshoe and eyed the nearby wood suspiciously. This did not escape Sweyn's notice either. He knew the Islanders had strange beliefs about things dwelling in the wood. However enlightened, however aloof Donald may have been, he was of this folk.

So Sweyn nodded agreeably and they started back to the Cottage. It was very late and they had not yet eaten. Sweyn invited Donald in and he sat on the porch while Sweyn went into the kitchen and fetched leftover bread, some of Oak Peg's cheese which Coppin had stocked in the larder, and a bit of mutton bought from a neighboring farm. He set it on a brass tray and brought it back outside. Then he went back in and came back a few minutes later with another tray with a pot of steaming tea and two mugs. They sat in silence on the porch for a while, eating and drinking and listening to the night sounds, the hoots of owls and the chirruping of crickets. The sky was a dizzying sea of stars and the Milky Way was a ghostly river coursing its zenith. The quarter moon hung just above the treetops in the west.

After the meal they sat in silence for a time, soaking in the evening tapestry. Sweyn was leisurely sipping warm tea when Donald began quietly intoning something, his voice so soft and low it took Sweyn a moment to realize he was singing.

*Always in the West our path lies,*
*Not in the future,*
*Nor in the past,*
*But among other stars of other skies*

"What is that you are singing?" Sweyn asked, his voice low and full of thoughtful curiosity. Sensitive song was yet something else not expected of this at-first-glance gritty woodsman.

Donald waved his hand, brushing away the question. "I dinna' know. I heard it a long time ago, when I was a child. It's something the old timers sing. A nursery rhyme for old folk." He laughed then. "Old timers like I'm getting to be. It's funny how the years sneak up upon ye when yer no' looking."

"But surely it means something?" pressed Sweyn.

"Aye, surely. Something to do with the Binding Years, I'll wager."

Sweyn looked from the old woodsman out into the night. The trees of the Guardwood stood like a silent siege wall, shielding mysteries indecipherable. He thought, "And out beyond those trees, the wildwood. And where does that lead?" And for the first time he was possessed of a palpable curiosity, an almost irresistible urge to trek off into the Island's great, deep forest and discover what wonders lay hidden in the misty, green shadows beneath its forbidden boughs.

While keeping his eyes on the wood, Sweyn said, "The Binding Years. That's just one more thing I don't understand."

Donald nodded. Sweyn could not see it as he faced the wood, but he felt the woodsman's agreement.

"If someone doesn't help me to understand, I'll go mad," Sweyn said.

"Coppin would say if ye understood too much too quickly, ye'd go mad."

"It's all very complicated," Sweyn said. "I need help."

"Coppin's a fool," Donald stated tonelessly. "I'll help ye."

Sweyn turned to face him. "I'm trying to put it all together. The tales I've heard about the history of this Island. The Hundred Horsemen. The Company.

The stories of fairies. The strange mysticism of the Man-by-the-Sea folk. Donald, when I came here they were celebrating Bealtaine, an ancient pagan holiday. I've sailed all over the world, Donald. Several times. I've seen May Day celebrated in the Old World, in Ireland, and even in Wales. There's dancing and festivities, and I think even a mass. But these people, they had none of that. There aren't even churches here. These people, I think they celebrated Mayday pagan-fashion."

"Here, the Old Ways live on. The Island is a place that never took to the course of the rest of the world."

"You're saying the Island is a world apart? Like I'm lost in some strange other-earth?"

Donald shook his head and sipped his tea. "No, lad. Ye're in yer own right world, sure enough. The green world, the Company calls it. But they say there are three other worlds beyond this one—three at least. There is Faerie, where faerie kin come from. It is like the dream of the green world, and wherever enchantment is strong, Faerie mingles with the here and now. But Faerie is no' quite a world apart. Its fate and the green world are tied to one another.

"And there is the Otherworld, where mortal folk go when they leave life. No one is sure what lies down that path. Some say it is a bright place of light and green grass and blue sky, where we meet all our loved ones who have gone on before. Others say it is only a place we rest a while before continuing our journeys.

"And there is yet another place, they say. A realm all alone for faerie kin, though so wondrous it is that mortal folk pine for it. They say it lies in the west, beyond the setting sun. Some call it Tir n'an Og, the Land of the Young. Some call it Tir n'an Beo, the Land of the Living. The Company calls it the Dreaming West, and it is only for faerie kin, if life should somehow fail their immortal kind in the green world.

"They say that wherever enchantment is weak, Faerie becomes less real, and the faerie kin who dwell in those places are half-hidden and half asleep, unable to mingle with reality. In those places, the things of Faerie are in danger of vanishing forever. But in places where enchantment is still strong, they say the worlds touch. Faerie and the green world come together and men and faeries must share the land. Man-by-the-Sea folk believe the Island is such a place. It's very complicated and I dinna' understand the half of it. I'd tell ye more, otherwise. There is a man on the Island, our seanachie, a storyteller. He is wise in the old lore, and if Coppin will no' fill ye in, he might. His name is Kilwillie."

Sweyn nodded, though in truth most of what Donald was trying to explain went over his head. It was just superstition, anyway, not really worth the effort of figuring out. Yet he could not escape the feeling that it was important, at the very heart of what was going on on the Island. Maybe this Kilwillie could give him a different perspective and clear it up. In the meantime, he tried for insight on another matter. "What about the binding of faeries your story talked about. What is that supposed to mean?"

"I dinna' know lad. It's been so long since the Binding Years the meaning of it has been lost even to the mind of this long-remembering people. All I do know is it once was the guiding purpose of the Company. But these days it is just words in a story the village folk tell to remember our roots."

Frustrated yet again, Sweyn fell darkly silent and slurped tea while staring sullenly into the night. A black, brief shadow swept over the yard beyond the screened porch. An owl, Sweyn tried to convince himself. But the shape had not been that of an owl. It had been childlike, but long and spindly, though small as an owl. Too much, too much! His mind reeled away from the perception and wrapped itself around the image of an owl. It was only an owl.

Yet even reeling from the strange night vision, Sweyn could not still his mind. He was hungry for answers. He had so many questions. And a burning one remained the matter of the timeless witch. "Your story. You said the Hundred Horsemen had an old witch named Oak Peg. And centuries later there was an Oak Peg guiding the Company when they lived like gypsies. And there is an Oak Peg in Raleigh McCavitt's (your ancestor's) journal, written just two centuries back. And now there is an Oak Peg dwelling in a cove in a lonely corner of the Island. It can't be the same Oak Peg, Donald."

"Sure, lad, it canna' be. I'll agree with ye on that. And yet I have only heard tell of one Oak Peg in all the stories from the old time till now, and in the stories Oak Peg is the selfsame witch who lives in yonder cove. Do I believe it? I doubt it. But, ye know, it's funny, but even when I was a wee lad she was an old woman. Kind of makes ye wonder."

Sweyn let go a long, frustrated exhalation. He felt Donald was being forthright with him, but his answers explained nothing.

Sweyn said, "I read other things in Raleigh McCavitt's journal."

Donald raised his eyebrows.

"Well, Raleigh wrote a lot that makes me wonder. He wrote about chests of seeds the Company risked their lives to bring over. He wrote about wonders in the wood, too. Something so wonderful it made him decide to live on the Island. And he also wrote about a Coppin. There's even a painting of this Coppin in the library, and it looks just like the Coppin who lives in my house!"

Donald grunted, but it might have been the briefest laugh. "Ye've asked the old coot about it?"

"I tried. He skirted it."

"Heh! He would. One step at a time, Coppin would say. No' more than ye can handle. And he'll make ye wait a lifetime to actually hear his rascally tales."

"So, is it supposed to be the same Coppin, Donald?" Sweyn demanded.

"Lad, all I can tell ye is the same I told ye of Oak Peg. There is a Coppin in the journal and in many of the old tales. And I only know of one Coppin, and . . ."

" . . . and he was old when you were a wee lad," Sweyn finished.

"Aye. That's about the sum of it."

Sweyn looked off into the treetops and said, "Damn," under his breath. He stared off into the benighted forest as if he sought to find reason there in the dark.

Donald rose, then, and excused himself for the night. At the porch step he turned and said, "I like ye, Sweyn, I really do, so I'll tell ye this. If ye're smart, ye'll go, now, while ye can. Ye look like the smart type. Yet if ye stay, ye'll make a fine Laird, and ye'll love the Island and the Island might do ye good. Either way, ye're sorry ignorant and I guess there's none but me to cure ye of it. I'll come by tomorrow morning and begin yer lessons, for ye've got a right piece to learn if ye plan to guide this Cottage."

Donald left then, shambling off tiredly toward the trees and his cabin a mile away, holding a horseshoe of cold iron in his right hand, a loaned oil lamp in his left, and whistling as he went. Sweyn watched him and knew, somehow, everything Donald was doing as he walked had purpose, and he knew equally well he understood none of it.

But a hunger to know was growing in him, gnawing maddeningly at his bones.

"Damn," he muttered again. When Donald disappeared over the hill, Sweyn went to his room, the converted studio, and dug out the aerial pictures of the woods which had been sent him by the title company. He regarded their weird shifting topography a while, then pulled out the chart of the O'Shee family tree, as far back as it could be traced. The haphazard family line hardly seemed connected from one ancestor to the next—some folk marrying in, some born in, some appearing as if out of the blue. Yet the inheritance of the O'Shee legacy had transferred smoothly from one disjointed heir to the next across the generations. Never a challenge. Never a problem. It was the most unusual way for a family's legacy to be passed on, especially as it dated back to medieval times—an era when blood relation meant everything.

The enigmas of the photos and the genealogy vexed and riveted him. He pored over them both into the wee hours of the morning, until, at some unrecalled time not long before dawn, he drifted off to sleep and dreams which he could not remember.

# Chapter Ten

*"There is a mountain in far off Cymru; the name of it is Snowdonia. And if one climbs it and spends the night in a certain enchanted cleft in the heights, when that one wakes he will find he has obtained the Sight. If he has the mind for it, he will see wonders. But if he has no' the mind, the wonders will bring him only confusion, and madness, and death."*

*Fergus Kilwillie*
*Seanachie of Man-by-the-Sea*

The next day Donald arrived early in the morning and Sweyn invited him in for breakfast. They ate oatmeal with bits of dried apple and laced with honey in the kitchen, ladled from a huge pot Coppin left simmering on the woodstove. While they conversed, Coppin puttered about the kitchen, arranging herbs to dry, stacking dishes and cookware, and generally making a noisy nuisance of himself. While he spoke politely to both Sweyn and Donald, he gave them plenty of sidewise glances and Sweyn saw that his glares were mostly directed at Donald. Plainly, the wizened little man did not approve of Dundubh's gillie. Sweyn paid him no mind and he and Donald capped a pleasant breakfast with tea laced with sheep milk and honey. When they had had their fill and were pleasantly revived by the tea, they rose and made to leave. Donald led the way out, grabbing his woolen jacket and cap from the peg by the door. Sweyn lingered a moment longer as he made to help out Coppin by carrying their used dishes to the sink.

Coppin joined him there, tugged at his sleeve. Sweyn turned to him. "Yes, Coppin?"

Coppin whispered, "He's no' one to spend time with, Sweyn. He's no' one to abide."

"He's helping me, Coppin. There's a lot to do to get the Cottage on its feet again, and so far he's been more helpful than anyone. Including you."

But his words failed to make any kind of impact on the little man. "Donald knows how to be a fine gillie, sure, and he's lived at the Cottage long and long. He knows the work of all Dundubh. But there are things about him ye dinna' know. There is history between him and the Cottage and the woods, mind ye, and ye best leave him to keeping the Guardwood and the woodlot."

"You care to fill me in, Coppin?"

Coppin scowled at him, taciturn.

"And here we have the problem, you see. I need to run this place, and to do that I have to understand it. But you're as tightlipped as a monk who's taken a vow of silence. Donald's the first fellow to offer me a real helping hand since I got here. And I like him. I trust my gut instincts about people, and, frankly, I get a better feeling about him than I do about you, Coppin." With that Sweyn turned on his heel and left the little man glowering behind him.

Sweyn spent the morning with Donald at the malthouse. Donald took him through the many complicated steps of making the sweet ale, from boiling down the malt to the fermentation process which, he explained, must be done in carboys of glass with bits of the tender parts of birch twigs mixed in. At noon, they had lunch together in the great dining room on the south wing of the Cottage. It was the first time the dining room had been used since Eilwen had left, nearly two decades ago. That morning, before Donald had arrived, Sweyn had left instructions for Coppin to prepare it, and Coppin had grumbled it was too big a job to handle along with making the king's luncheon Sweyn was expecting, but Sweyn had paid him no mind and Coppin had spent the day dashing between the kitchen and dining room, tending the meal in the former, dusting and cleaning and airing out and rearranging in the latter. At least the old villain was finally earning his keep, Sweyn thought. He intended to bring the Cottage out of the moribund dormancy to which it had descended with the death and departure of the last of the O'Shees.

Lunch was steamed brook trout in a chestnut and cream sauce, with leeks and parsnips on the side. Simple, yet tasteful. Donald commented that it was a meal befitting a Laird and wondered aloud if brighter days were on the verge for Dundubh, after the long grey time when there had been no O'Shee to keep the land.

Sweyn leaned forward, a bite of trout halfway to his mouth. "This whole Island seems overjoyed that the estate has a Laird. I don't understand why they should be. I'm not even an O'Shee, not by blood, and I never took Eilwen's surname. And if Eilwen had had her way, I would not be here, would never have set foot on the Island. She despised this place."

But Donald shook his head. "I knew Eilwen well, when she was a wee lass. And she was a fine girl, Sweyn. Please dinna' take offense at this, but I knew her many more years than ye, and while I have no doubt ye were a fine and devoted husband, I believe there were things I knew about the girl that ye did no'."

It was true, Sweyn knew. He had had the privilege of knowing Eilwen only three years. This man had known her since her birth. He envied the years the old woodsman had shared in her life, here at Dundubh Cottage, and he asked him to go on.

"I have no doubt Eilwen despised the events of her life, but I also have no doubt she loved the Island. This place," he made an encompassing gesture, a grand sweep of his arms, "it gets into yer soul. It binds ye to it. It's hard to let it go. I dinna' think Eilwen left because she wanted to let the Island go, but because things happened in her life here that she could no' bear. And the Island was a constant reminder of them."

"But in all the years I lived with Eilwen, she never said a kind word about this place. She called it backward and superstitious. She was filled with venom. I never knew her to hate anything except the Island."

"When people are hurt, they often lash out against the things they love the most."

Sweyn pondered that. Slowly, he ate the trout and realized the old woodsman could be right. Dr. Sweyn deSauld, psychologist, was receiving an education in human nature from the folk wisdom of an old woodsman.

It was hard for Sweyn to voice the next thought that came to mind, but he had to. Donald, who had known Eilwen so long, might be the only person who could help him figure out the side of her he had seen just before the end. He said,

"Before Eilwen . . ." he swallowed, ". . . before she died, only days before, she made me promise never to sell the estate. I was floored, Donald. I thought she hated it, and I couldn't understand why she just didn't put it on the market to be rid of it. But what struck me more was the way she brought it up. Sometimes she had these brooding periods, but this time she seemed morbid, as if she smelled disaster in the wind."

Donald set his fork down. "It sounds as if she was worried."

Sweyn's appetite suddenly failed and he pushed his plate away. The half-eaten trout grew cold in the middle of the table. "She was worried. We both were. I guess we had a little reason to be, but we didn't really think anything would come of it. But she became quiet in the final days. Dark. Then she made me take that oath, as if she had . . . had somehow known things would go bad." This was terribly hard for him to talk about and he regretted bringing it up now. But there was no going back, and Donald had a way of drawing words out of him.

Donald said, his voice low and gentle, "Sweyn, it is eating at ye, lad. Talk now, to me. How did she die? All we of the village know is we got word she had drowned. But there was more to it than that, wasn't there?"

Sweyn nodded and closed his eyes, stealing himself to repeat the story he had already told Oak Peg. There was immense pain in the recollection, but the memories did not writhe like demons in his heart this time, they did not threaten to surface in tortuous flashbacks. A gentle song sung by unknown fair ladies ghosted out of memory and soothed his spirit and gave him strength. He opened his eyes, found his voice, and told Donald of the murderous youth he had treated at his father's clinic, and what he had done to keep the kid off the streets. Donald listened, quiet as stone.

Sweyn had not been able to continue beyond that point of the tale with Oak Peg. But now, comforted by the strength of the song, he carried on.

"I should have done more, Donald. More to stop him. I should have seen through him and known what he was capable of. But by a year later, I was no longer practicing psychology and I had all but forgotten about him. And it's so, so rare clients ever attack their therapists — it's almost unheard of. So I had no real concern for it anymore.

"So Eilwen and I were spending the night on my boat. Not Starry Sea, another boat. Cerulean. I was teaching sailing and running a charter business then, and we had passengers spending the night, too. That night he sealed the exits and set the boat on fire."

But those memories were harsh, and not even the power of the ladies' song was strong enough to diminish them. Sweyn's lower lip trembled and his eyes reddened, yet he found the wherewithal to continue, talking faster and faster, trying to hurry through it. "I tried to get them out. We were asleep when the fire broke out, and it all happened so fast. There was an explosion and the boat was sinking and the staterooms were blocked." The recollections came cold and fast as the rushing sea, washing over him, making him gasp for breath. He began to stutter. "I couldn't, I couldn't, I couldn't . . ."

"Slow down, lad. Easy." Donald rose and went to a venerable liquor cabinet which had not been touched in decades. He opened it, removed a bottle of ancient Scotch and poured Sweyn a stiff drink. Sweyn downed it swiftly, and with the soothing warmth of it regained a measure of his composure, though sweat dampened his brow.

Tremulously, he went on. "I couldn't save them, Donald. I couldn't save her. They all died and somehow I made it out. Those people, my wife, they all died. And it was my fault. I didn't see what kind of monster that kid was. I should have. It's what I was trained to do."

Donald sat near him and set a hand on his shoulder, a fatherly gesture Sweyn would never have received from his own father. "Ye canna' see every path, lad, no matter what ye've been trained to do. No' even witches can see so well. It was no' yer fault."

"It was," Sweyn insisted. "I knew the kid was sick." He looked directly into Donald's eyes. "But I failed to see how much."

Sweyn looked away and a profound silence settled over the room, broken only by the rhythm of a stately grandfather clock in the corner. Other memories gathered behind his eyes, dark and hateful recollections best never revisited, never spoken. He cringed at them.

But Donald summoned them when he said, "But that is no' the end of the story either, is it?"

Slowly, shunning the darkness of the hateful memories, Sweyn shook his head. "Later, I . . . I stopped him." His eyes were turned toward Donald, but they did not see him. Glassy, they looked back, back upon a terrible, haunted day.

In the present, Donald said, "So Eilwen is avenged."

Sweyn's gaze returned to where he was, to Donald. Sweyn shrugged.

"And the world is a little safer," Donald added.

Who knew, thought Sweyn. Men like himself still walked in it.

Donald nodded. The set of his jaw was grim, but there was a spark of approval in his eyes.

And from that day it seemed they would always be friends.

*********

The afternoon passed in much the same way as the morning. After they ate they went round about the fields again and Donald explained what work the farmhands must attend to. He taught Sweyn what was involved in raising the oats, from fertilizing the fields with sheep dung and seaweed, to harrowing and threshing. He explained how the fruit trees must be topped and pruned so they did not grow too tall to be harvested, nor so thick that the fruit became dwarfed. He explained that the great apple trees of the grove must neither be pruned nor clipped. "They will give plenty of fine apples, trust me. The old Apple Man will to see to that."

"Is he a hand?" Sweyn had asked.

Donald chuckled. "No, lad. He is the friend of the apple trees, of course." Donald left the explanation at that, and Sweyn assumed the Apple Man must be yet another of the imaginary creatures so plentiful among the Island's myths.

Donald went on to explain how the wind fallen branches of the apple trees were soaked so they would burn slow and smoky when warming the oat sprouts for malting. Then he led Sweyn through the elder grove, where already great clusters of small white blossoms gathered bright on the sunlit boughs. "When ye gather from here," said Donald, "ye must say:

"Elderlock, permit me to take a bit of yerself,
and I will give a bit of myself

when I become a tree."

Sweyn squinted at him, perplexed. "It's the Old Way," Donald offered in way of explanation. "Ye dinna' have to understand it. But some say elders are enchanted, and ye dinna' want to upset the treewives that are fond of them"

In the afternoon, Sweyn invited Donald over for dinner.

"I would be pleased to join ye, but we're none of us taking dinner at Dundubh this night," said Donald. "It's midsummer eve, Lughnasadh, and there are festivities in the village. Everyone goes." They made plans to meet up at Dugan's Pub, where he had first tried Man-by-the-Sea's sweet ale and witnessed the Bealtaine festivities, and then Donald took his leave. Sweyn went back to the Cottage, ignored Coppin's sullen looks of disapproval as he ate a quick sandwich of garden vegetables and sharp sheep cheese, then went up to wash and change.

Two hours later the sun had drawn near the horizon and the shadows of the wood were stretching long and deep over the meadows when Sweyn came back down. He was on his way out, and all the farmhands save Coppin had already gone down to Man-by-the-Sea. Sweyn passed Coppin on his way out through the kitchen. As he went by, the little man grabbed the sleeve of his light jacket. Sweyn made to remove Coppin's hand but the little man was startlingly strong. Coppin hissed at him, "That one does no' keep the Old Ways as he ought. He'll fill ye more full of witchlore than ye're fit to bear, and yer soul will burst for it!"

Sweyn glared at the little man, who let go after a moment. Sweyn pushed out the door and stepped off the porch, bound for Man-by-the-Sea, and determined not to let the little old man's griping bother him. "He is half senile," he told himself, by way of excuse for Coppin. But senile or mad, Coppin was no easier to cope with.

*********

It took Sweyn several minutes to walk down the winding path of the expansive front yard, with its gone-wild shrubs and tangle of unkempt herbs, and reach the creaky gate where he had first laid eyes upon the Cottage. To either side of the gate, an aged wooden fence, the whitewash long since weathered away, kept the bounds between Dundubh land and the Guardwood. Past the gate, the tangled wood grew right up beside the dirt path to Man-by-the-Sea, the towering trees casting pools of shadow over the way. The forest air was fresh with summer blossoms and luxuriant foliage, and the evening promised to be sultry. Sweyn found himself standing motionless at the gate, absorbed in the sight of the great wood, as if truly seeing it for the first time. On either side, and for a ways down the path, grew a thicket of holly and rowans, their red berries and dark glossy leaves creating a darker contrast against the lighter shades of oak and beech further back. He recalled Coppin having said holly and rowan were trees of protection. Bright red berries from the previous year still clung to the holly. Sweyn felt comforted in the presence of these friendly trees. He smiled after a moment, feeling foolish, and lifted the heavy plank that served as a catch, keeping the gate shut.

As he swung the gate wide, a delicate sound wafted over the still summer air, sweet and fragile as the fragrance of the forest. It was coming from his right and he immediately recognized the fluty voice. It belonged to the girl who sometimes wandered the apple grove.

He forgot the gate, his thoughts drawn entirely into the intricate weave of the song she sang. Her song set his mind at ease and made his thoughts fly all at once. To hear her lyrics was to shed in a moment the burden of the cruel decades, and all the hardness that a bitter life could instill, and he found his feet following his heart in the direction of the apple grove.

It was not far, less than twenty yards to the first of the apple trees, and he had little memory of the steps that brought him there. He seemed to have just flowed that way, like a wraith drifting the course of its ancient haunt. He went in silence, not meaning to spy, but he went cautiously as a spy, for he had come across the skittish girl thrice already, and each time she had fled in an instant, wary as a deer. He passed the outer trees of the grove, following her melody, and it came to him then that his ears registered another sound, even more delicate than the girl's voice. The sound was like the chiming of bells of crystal struck beneath clear water. And sometimes the sound was like the staccato patter of raindrops on spring hay. Other times it was like the notes of many songbirds. And once even like the soughing of wind in autumn leaves. The instrument was very finely played, and somehow sounded familiar—like something he had perchance heard upon a dream, maybe not so long ago, though he could not recall. Its clear strains accompanied the girl's voice in perfect unison, flowing up with each rising note, cascading down with each plunge of melody, sometimes wandering away in elegant countermelodies.

Then he passed another great old apple tree and he could see her just ahead, a slender form in a gown of moonstone white, seated upon the great fallen branch of an ancient beech that had been allowed to grow in the midst of the grove. The branch was so old it was smooth of bark and bereft of leaves, a natural bench fit for the singing damsel. The sun touched the distant trees of the west, and wine shadows lengthened across the grove, and with the failing light the air grew sweeter, as if the nectar of summer was emerging from a moonflower. The girl's hair fell in a midnight curtain past her shoulders. Her skin was so pale it glowed in the forest shade.

Near to her, seated in the lowest branches of a great apple about as high as a man stands, a spindly fellow held a small, triangular instrument. A harp, Sweyn realized, a small, many stringed harp. The man was tall, disproportionately thin. His hair was shorter than Sweyn's, yet it fell to his shoulders. It was a tangled mass of curls, the color of smoke from wood burned wet, and it carried the twilight within it. Yet the skinny man was not handsome. He was spindly, and his cheekbones were too high, giving him an impish look. His skin was the color of tanned doe hide, rugged and wrinkled. He had the appearance of a man used to long hours of exposure to the elements, much as did Sweyn, who had spent so much of his life in the wind and waves. The slender man plucked masterfully at the little harp, the closely spaced strings gleamed metallic in the wan light, and the sound he evoked from it was as beautiful as that the girl cast with her living voice.

The girl sang in a tongue he could not understand. He was sure he had never heard any language like it before. It had an ancient quality, like the Mannish the Island folk sometimes spoke. Whatever the words, they carried a bittersweet feel. Her eyes were closed and she was embraced by the melody, as was the tree-borne harper. Sweyn, feeling it wrong to spy, stepped into the open where he could be clearly seen. He made no move to approach, and every attempt to convey harmlessness and appreciation.

The thin man noticed him first, and the moment he did the harper ceased to play. In a single, blinding quick movement, he leapt from the tree and grabbed the branch of another and pulled himself up into it, so that he never touched the ground. Leaping like a squirrel among the boughs of the trees, quiet as an owl, he made off into the thicket of apples in this inhuman way, all the while holding the harp beneath the crook of one arm. The girl ceased to sing, eyed her companion's flight, then turned wary eyes upon Sweyn.

Sweyn stood frozen, gaping at the harper vanishing among the high distant treetops. He had never seen anything like it in all his days. He took a step forward, as if that might help him peer more clearly into the tangling boughs. "Did you see that?" he gasped, more to himself, momentarily forgetting the girl was there.

But she replied, "Of course, I did! He was sitting right here." She patted the tree trunk at her side.

Sweyn remembered the girl, regrouped his thoughts. "I'm sorry. I didn't mean to startle you or your friend. I heard the music. It was so beautiful. I just came to listen."

She sat stone still and scrutinized him. He stood equally still and endured it, though her gaze was piercing. "Ye startled the Apple Man," she said then, most seriously. "He's terribly shy, ye know."

"The Apple Man? Was that the harper?" He held out his hands in a gesture of sincerity. "Hey, I'm really sorry. I didn't mean to."

"Now how am I to practice for the Midsummer ceilidh?" she snapped sternly. "Ye must play for me. Get yer harp!"

"My harp?" he stuttered. "

"Indeed. Go on, now. Go get it!" She sounded as if she fully expected everyone to play a harp.

He pursed his lips, pondering how to explain. Finally he just settled for simplicity and said, "I don't play harp."

"Is that so?" she gasped, as if this were the most preposterous thing she had ever heard. "Well, go get yer fiddle, then! Your whistle. A bodhran even would do."

Sweyn only regarded her, at a loss for words.

She stood, put her hands on her slender waist. Sounding flustered, she demanded, "Just what do ye play then?"

"On a really good day, if I'm really focused, I might be able to carry a tune," he replied in all earnestness.

"What! Ye mean ye canna' even sing?" She looked profoundly disappointed, and Sweyn had visions of her stalking into the forest, never to speak to him again. But then her eyes gleamed and an impish crooked smile turned up a corner of her mouth. He grew at ease then. It was a good sign. She was teasing him.

"Seriously, though," he went on, "that was beautiful. I wish he hadn't bolted off like that. I'm really sorry for it. I would love to have heard more. Should I go try to find him."

"Find the Apple Man?" she said incredulously. "Ye're either arrogant or sorry ignorant." Smiling again, she said, "I would wager the latter. And I'd also wager ye're the new Laird Coppin's spoken of."

"Coppin told you about me, did he?" he said tightly. That wasn't a good sign. The rascal could have little decent to say.

But she surprised him by saying, "He say's ye'll make a fine Laird, if ye can ever decide whether yer heart belongs on land or sea."

That took Sweyn so unawares the only response he could find was a quiet, "Oh." And then words escaped him. Silence drew out. She continued to watch him with mixed measures of curiosity and caution, yet she did not seem afraid. Here, so close, he saw her eyes were as blue and bright as sapphires. Stars glittered within them.

"I've heard you sing here in the grove before," he finally thought to say. "I kept hoping to meet you."

"And now ye have," she replied gamely.

He nodded. "Why were you singing tonight? I've never heard you sing to a harp before."

"Oh, I've always sung to the harp. The Apple Man is a fine harper and I come here to share tunes with him. He plucks the wires like no other in the wood. I'm surprised ye've no' heard before."

"The instrument is not loud."

"Still, most folk can hear it. It carries on the verge of the wood." She rose and studied him. "But ye're no' from the Island, are ye? Ye've no' the ears, I imagine." She began to step from trunk to trunk, lightly, lovingly brushing a hand upon the bark of each stately giant. Her movements were graceful and whimsical, as if a dance were barely restrained in her steps. Bit by bit, her path took her toward him. "No matter about the deafness. If ye stay, the hearing will come, and the seeing. The old folk say that's the way of it."

She passed Sweyn, and he turned and said, "May I walk with you?"

"Perhaps. If we're going the same direction."

He thought, I'm going wherever you are. But he said, "I'm going to the Midsummer Festival in Man-by-the-Sea."

"It just so happens," she answered, "I was going that way too."

*********

There was a meadow on the north side of Man-by-the-Sea. It was large, a quarter mile square, encompassing a full forty acres. Emerald grass and clover grew there, and small violet and scarlet flowers. The meadow was mostly clear, but enormous old rowans and hollies stood here and there in scattered thickets. Within the thickets picnic tables were set beneath small, octagonal pavilions made of pillars of log supporting high-arched hickory shingle roofs. In one corner of the meadow a clear, shallow brook babbled and sputtered past a stand of oaks that stood like sentinels against the Guardwood. Barbecue pits of smooth, round brook stones stood beside each picnic table, and each smoked like the cobbled chimney of a village cottage. The fragrance of sizzling mutton and venison was borne upon the lazy midsummer air.

The meadow trees were adorned with paper streamers the colors of sky and sea and summer blossoms. So brilliant were their hues they glowed in the waning light.

All the folk of the village had gathered in the meadow. Voices rose in laughter and friendly discourse. Older adults sat at tables with their spouses and family and friends. They drank sweet ale and cider from earthenware mugs. Young lovers in their latter teens and early twenties walked hand in hand around the grounds, the girls gaily dressed, their blond and red locks laced with bright ribbons, leaning heads on their boys' shoulders and laughing carefree. Children ran about, playing chase and skipping games, flying kites and tossing balls. The little girls were like the petals of daffodils, wrapped in smocks of bright pastel hues, with garlands of clover blossoms and dandelions woven into their long, gleaming plaits. The little boys were like puppies, dressed in the practical canvas trousers and white shirts common among the village folk. None of the small children wore shoes, and they ran playfully through the soft sweet grass. It was an idyllic scene, a scene from another life, another world, thought Sweyn as he entered Man-by-the-Sea with the raven haired girl at his side.

The day was getting on, it was nearly ten in the evening, and the sun teetered above the horizon in the west. Candles glowed on tables and oil lanterns were suspended from trees. The whole of the meadow glittered with score upon score of tiny, flickering gold lights.

No picnic tables were unoccupied but it was no bother. Sweyn and the girl knew they could find comfortable enough seating beneath the boughs of one of the great trees later on. They walked around the park to take in the goings on.

The center of the park seemed to be the locus of activity. Two great piles of logs—oak and hawthorn, birch and elm—were stacked ten feet high one beside the other. A hundred feet away from the firewood piles a great tent pavilion had been set up. There was only a single chair within, set center of the far wall, clearly awaiting a guest of honor. Opposite the tent pavilion a great round area a hundred feet in diameter had been covered with a layer of sawdust and marked off with a fence of saplings laid on their sides and supported by tall stakes.

The girl regarded it all with wide, bright eyes, her expression full of wonder, like a child who has just seen a great birthday present wrapped up and mysterious beside a candle-decked cake. "There will be music and singing, and sweets and meats." She spoke rapidly, as animated as any of the playing children around them. "And there will be dancing, oh, the dancing." She bobbed on the balls of her feet. "The musicians are very skilled. They are not the Apple Man, but they play from the heart. And there will be stories under the tent, and friends will talk and . . ."

She was speaking so breathlessly Sweyn had to restrain himself from laughing. But then she said a very unexpected thing. ". . . "and I can stay till the morning twilight."

Puzzled, he said, "You're a grown woman. You can stay as long as you like."

She said nothing but led Sweyn by the hand to a very unusual cooking pit. A great hole had been dug and a fire built in it much earlier, so that now it was burned down to coals. Stones had been laid over the coals and seaweed heaped over the stones. Over the seaweed many kinds of seafood had been scattered: huge prawns, greenish razor clams big as chicken thighs, ling cod, halibut, and many large silver salmon. Another, thinner layer of dulse had been laid over the seafood so that it steamed in the seaweed. Upon a table beside the fire pit earthen plates had been stacked, along with wooden forks. She handed a plate and fork to Sweyn and neatly picked out a hot clam with her fingers. Handling it carefully so as not to burn herself, she plucked out the meat and popped it into her mouth, smiling mischievously as she chewed. Sweyn shook his head in mock disapproval of her lack of etiquette. She giggled and reached for a long serving fork stuck into a pile of seaweed beside the fire, meant for skewering and serving up the fishes. She was looking at him, just swallowing and about to say something, when she wrapped her hand around the metal fork. Her eyes widened suddenly, and she yelped and whipped her hand back, sucking at her fingers.

"What, did you burn yourself?" said Sweyn immediately. He glanced at the fork, still stuck in the seaweed. It was long and forged of black iron, with a small wooden handle sandwiching the end. Though the pile of seaweed was set beside the fire pit, it must have been close enough to be heated over time and the metal conducted the heat up and down its length. "Let me see that," he said, and reached for her hand, but she withdrew from him anxiously, shaking her head. "It's ok," he said. "I just want to see. There must be a first aid kit around here. We'll get it fixed right up."

Biting her lower lip, she held out her hand for him to see. A nasty white mark of seared flesh ran across her palm to her ring finger. Already it was blistering. He sighed. "Ah, that's not good. We'll have it tended to. But you'll be fine."

A boy of about eight approached the fire with a plate that still had some scraps of food on it. He meant to get seconds and reached for the fork stuck in the seaweed. Sweyn saw and whipped around, thrusting out his arm, meaning to knock the boy's hand away from the searing fork, but he was too late. "Hey, don't! It's . . ." But the boy had already picked up the fork, taking it in his small hand by the metal stem before the wooden handle in the careless way of children. The child speared a hunk of salmon with it. He put the meat on his plate and dashed back off to where his parents were seated upon a white blanket. Sweyn watched him go, dumbfounded. Then he turned back to the fork. The boy had returned it to the pile of seaweed. Gingerly, Sweyn touched the fork. It was not hot, not at all, but it could not have cooled so quickly. He pulled it out and turned to the girl, holding it by the wooden handle in his right hand.

She recoiled from it, taking a step back, loathing marring her features. "Iron burns," she hissed.

"It's not hot," he said.

"Iron burns," she repeated more emphatically.

He did not understand, but she was growing upset seeing the thing in his hand, so he stuck it back in the seaweed and led her by the elbow off to find a first aid kit. A festival official at a pavilion in the oak grove had one, mainly to treat the skinned knees and scraped elbows the children were sure to get. She was a plump dowager of one of the wealthier families of the Island. Her late husband had left her a small fishing business the management of which she gave over to a nephew, while she occupied herself volunteering at village functions. But the girl was extraordinarily skittish about addressing the village folk. She held back at the verge of the grove, so Sweyn went to the old woman himself and asked for some burn cream and a bandage for the lady with him.

"Oh, it's lovely our Laird has taken a liking to a village girl?" she chirruped in a singsong brogue as she rummaged through the contents of the ample first aid kit. "Might I ask who she is?" she said as she turned and handed him the items.

That got Sweyn thinking about the obvious fact that he did not even know the girl's name. They had seemed to get on so well without that bit of formality passing between them that he had not thought to ask. "She's a neighbor girl," said Sweyn, in answer.

The dowager grinned mischievously, as if she thought Sweyn were keeping secrets. "Oh, it would no' be the lovely Maire girl," she prodded, "who lives just down from the Cottage. Hair like spun gold, that one. And such a sweet girl." The old matron smiled approvingly and handed him the items.

But Sweyn shook his head. "No. She's a black haired girl. I met her in my apple grove, of all places. I'm not sure where she's from yet."

The blood drained from the dowager's face. "The girl who sings in the grove?" she asked.

Sweyn nodded.

Tonelessly, she said, "Oh. I see." And she closed the kit and carried it back to the pavilion without another word, moving in the way of a person who has narrowly avoided an accident, with a cautious uncertainty in her steps. Sweyn concluded the old woman probably disapproved of the girl's bloodline or some such nonsense. That was no doubt important to the conservative Island folk, but for him, he could not have cared less. He turned and made to go back to the girl, but she was nowhere to be seen.

At first he thought she had vanished again, as she had in previous encounters. But then he spied her in the shadows of the oak thicket, further away from the pavilions than he had left her. And Coppin was there with her. They were deep in quiet but heated discussion about something. He could not make out a thing from this distance, but he could see Coppin's animated gestures well enough. The girl seemed nervous, glancing quickly from Coppin to the persons who passed them by. Then Coppin took her two hands in his own, looked as if he were pleading with her. She shook her head and Coppin let his hands drop to his sides, clearly frustrated. And then she seemed to deflate, like a child from whom all happiness is drawn out.

Enough. Sweyn walked over. "Hello, Coppin," he said curtly. "I see you've met."

Coppin turned to Sweyn, nodded in greeting and farewell, and left without saying a word, disappearing into the crowd.

"Good riddance," muttered Sweyn.

"Coppin doesn't believe I should be here, around these people, or around you," she said.

"Is that so?" He would have to have a chat with Coppin when he got back to the Cottage. "Why?"

"He won't say."

"Was he bothering you?"

"Oh, no. Coppin's always been very kind. He's taken care of me more than once. But he has his own way."

"'His own way.'" Sweyn grunted. "I'll agree to that. Now, let's see to that hand."

"Oh, no, I'll be all right," she objected, but he insisted and got her to give him her injured hand. But there was no mark on it. The skin was soft and white as if nothing had ever happened.

"But I . . . but I saw it," he stammered. He looked at her intensely. "I saw the burn."

She shrugged away the question implicit in his eyes, and withdrew her hand. He started to speak again, but she laid a finger to his lips. Her eyes implored him let the matter be.

Then she tugged him back into the meadow. She led him to a barbecue pit where they gathered plates and got something to eat. She was delighted by the fare, a little salmon, a little pork, a little of Oak Peg's cheese and cabbage on the side. For dessert they had elder blossom pie. After the meal they sat comfortably leaning against the trunk of a rowan, talking idly for a long time, about the food, about the merry colors of the women's dresses, how pleasant the evening was proving to be. But there was a sense of effort in the conversation, as Sweyn tried to keep from pressing the matter the girl had asked him to leave alone. But in the end he couldn't. He had to know. He sat upright, looked at her.

"I don't understand how the burn healed," said Sweyn, who could contain his wonder no more.

"I heal fast," she replied.

"No one heals that fast," he stated. Then he added, "I don't understand how you got burned in the first place. The serving fork wasn't even hot."

"Iron burns," she said again, as if that in itself contained all the answer he should need.

But he sighed in frustration. "I keep trying to understand this place," he said, "but it's no use. The more I try, the more it perplexes me. It doesn't make any sense, the things that happen here, the things you people talk about."

"It is no' the same in the rest of the world?"

He turned to her. "You've never been off the Island?"

She shook her head.

"Yeah, then I guess you wouldn't understand. No, it's not like the rest of the world. Not by a long shot."

"Iron does no' burn elsewhere?" she said.

"Cold iron doesn't."

Her voice tightened. "Cold iron burns worst."

Sweyn tore a blade of grass from the ground, crumpled it in his fingers. Then he pursed his lips and seemed to ponder the ruined blade of grass after a moment, looked sorry for it, and tossed it away. Then he turned to her and said, "You know who I am. But I don't even know your name."

That brought a sudden change to the air of the conversation, and a sly smile to her lips. She seemed to glow, and it was like the rising moon. Raising her eyebrows, she intoned, "True, ye dinna'."

"So? Would you tell me?"

"Tell ye what?"

"Your name?" he said, drawing out the latter word in exasperation.

She giggled. "There is power in names, Sweyn. The wood folk hold their names very close."

"You live in the wood? Is that where your family is?"

The smile faded then, and she said, "I dinna' always live in the wood. It used to be better."

"What did?"

But her eyes became distant and dolorous. She was not seeing the here and now, memory was taking her. Memories best left untouched. Sweyn knew the look well. "I'm sorry," he said. "Forget I asked."

An uncertain moment passed. Then she nodded, glanced out upon the meadow. People were beginning to gather toward the center grounds. Whatever was planned next, it would begin soon.

Sweyn became aware of the bleating and lowing, and even the grunting, of farm animals. And some of the girls were leaving the grounds, and some of the young men too.

He was pondering wandering over to see what would happen next, when, quite unexpectedly, she said, "I suppose it's only fair ye have a name for me. How have ye thought of me till now?"

"I only knew of you as the black haired girl who sang in the apple grove," he said.

"Then ye may call me Dubh," (she pronounced it like Doov), "for my black hair."

"Dubh means black?"

She nodded. "Aye, Dubh. As in Dundubh, the black hold, for that is what yer Cottage's name means."

"But that is not your real name," he said, disappointed.

"In time," she told him. "Real names come slow. Names have power."

"Okay . . . Dubh," he said, trying the name on her. It didn't quite seem to fit. "So, my home is called the black hold, is it? I've heard something like that before. Does it have some kind of dark history?"

She shrugged. "I dinna' think so. Its history is grey, like the past of everything else I know of. But I think the place is so named because of the rich black earth there, which grows the best of everything."

"Well," he shrugged, "that, at least, is a good thing." His mood began to lighten.

Time was getting on and the light was failing. More and more of the village folk seemed to be disappearing. "Where are they going?" he asked.

"To get ready," she answered. "It is midsummer, after all. Lughnasadh. It's a day for green and growing things, and lovers, and farmers. Ye'll see."

They brought their dishes to bins where folk were to leave the vessels for the morning, when volunteers would tend to them. Then they made their way to the center of the field where the crowd was growing thick. Folk parted around Sweyn like water, some making way out of respect for the man they took to be their new Laird, others seeming to skitter away, with eyes locked on Dubh. Sweyn was quick and keen to notice this and understood that whatever had so bothered the old dowager about the girl also irritated some other people. But he could not for the life of him imagine what they found so troubling. None spoke ill to her, none were discourteous or disrespectful, but some were clearly uncomfortable around her, and most simply looked the other way. In this they treated the girl worse than an outsider, worse than a criminal—they shunned her. It angered him. No wonder Dubh was so skittish. Yet he could imagine no reason for their cruelty. Dubh was almost childlike in her innocence.

Sweyn decided he couldn't care less for their superstitions or their reasons, and he would brook no rudeness to the girl while she was with him. Ignoring the sidewise glances, he led Dubh toward the center of activity.

Beneath a starry welkin, the two piles of wood were set ablaze by a man dressed in a cape of green, whom the folk referred to as Jack-in-the-Wood. He looked like Robin Hood to Sweyn, in his medieval woodsman's garb. He carried a longbow and a broadsword, and wore a vambrace of boiled hard leather dyed the color of holly leaves. He lit the fires by shooting flaming arrows into them. The logs had been doused in kerosene earlier and quickly the flames leapt into the sky.

Then fiddlers and bodhran players scattered playful summer melodies into the dark, and farmers came, driving their livestock toward the bonfires. Many farmhands stood to either side of the fires, forming lines to trap, prod, push and pull the frightened beasts between the leaping twin flames. But it was long work, and won many a laugh from the onlookers as the young farmhands struggled with the animals. The boys chased them and called after them, but the animals had an instinctive terror of fire, and they were not in the least cooperative. Most of the time, the boys had to resort to wrestling the farm animals into line. One young boy was seen being towed away from the meadow as if on skis by an old sow as he clung to its tail. Another had somehow straddled a cow backward, and was last seen galloping off toward Man-by-the-Sea! Dubh explained that the ceremony of driving the animals between the Lughnasadh fires was for their own luck, and it was very ancient. "Passing between the fires makes their future bright," she said.

Sweyn grunted and mentioned something about some traditions obviously surviving for their entertainment value.

When the last farm animal had been chased through, a wild-eyed sheep dragging along a young boy who had gotten a foot tangled in its rope tether, the next procession started. These were the maidens and young men of the village who had taken vows of betrothal to one another. They were teens and not yet engaged. Rather, they had taken oaths to remain faithful to one another and become engaged when they came of age. The maidens wore simple homespun gowns of white, with pale sashes wrapped around narrow waists. Their long locks were braided and festooned with varicolored ribbons and garlands of tiny white flowers like baby's breath. The couples skipped merrily as they went between the fires, dancing in step to the tunes. With smiles on their faces, they were the hope of Manannan, and the older folk on either side, their parents and relatives and friends, cheered them as they passed.

The next group to pass were the engaged and the young, married couples. Sweyn was at first stunned by what he saw, but quickly grew to accept it as simply part of Man-by-the-Sea's ancient culture, for the young couples were nude. Those engaged were painted blue, from their faces to their feet, and their hair was matted and spiked, and bleached with lime, so that they looked feral as the wood and wild sea that ensconced the Island. The newlyweds had no body paint upon them, no bleach of lime in their locks. Rather, their bodies were partially covered by brief kilts that fell to mid-thigh. The newlyweds also wore torques of silver round their necks. Sweyn did not entirely understand the symbolism of the ceremony, no doubt some blend of ancient Welsh, Irish and Scottish ways, and perhaps even a bit of lost Pictish tradition. But clearly the nudity had something to do with fertility.

The young couples moved between the fires to the encouraging cheers of their friends and family standing to either side. The young men strode strong and tall and proud, showing off the musculature that years of hard work on farms or on the sea had developed. The girls moved sensuously, waving their hips, full breasts swaying. Each couple walked side by side, and they looked at each other often, though they did not hold hands.

Dubh explained, "This is so when they come together, they will have the summer's fertility inside them."

When the couples had passed through the fire and moved off into the darkness, the rest of the villagers began to walk through. Old men and old wives went hand in hand, middle aged couples arm in arm, younger families with their children all close together. Each family passed between the fires. "To burn old bad luck away," Dubh told him. Then she surprised Sweyn by taking him by the hand and leading him between the fires. "I've always wondered what it would be like," she exclaimed, smiling radiantly.

"You've never done it before?" he asked, surprised the lovely girl would never have had a boy ask her to do the ritual with him.

"I've never been to the festival before," she said. "Only watched from the edge of the wood." She said it as if it were an ordinary thing, but it made Sweyn's blood boil to hear it. How dare they! How dare these people exclude her! But he said nothing of it. He wanted her to enjoy the night.

After all the village folk had passed between, they gathered again in the midst of the meadow, the young maidens bright and fair in their fancy homespun gowns, the young boys who had chased livestock in farming garb back in their best festive attire, the young engaged and newlyweds dressed and standing close to one another and talking with friends and family, though a few couples seemed to have disappeared into the dark woods. The evening's activities seemed to have divided up now. Where the great circular area had been fenced off with saplings and covered with sawdust, a makeshift pub was setting up. A group of folk musicians had gathered there with whistles, bodhrans, fiddles and uilleann pipes, and they were kicking up lively tunes in a rousing jam thrown together for the simple pleasure of music making. Villagers gathered and danced, while some stood aside and shared sweet ale with friends.

"Oh, I wish I had my clarsach with me," Dubh said.

"What's that?"

"Clarsach. A harp."

"Oh," Sweyn nodded. Of course, she played. What else was she to occupy her time with, alone in the forest.

As the musicians played the dances became more intricate, requiring the participation of many persons, not just couples. To some tunes dancers formed aisles while others skipped between. To others, the dancers went round and round in circles, floating from partner to partner until, by the end of the song, they were back with the person they had started with. And on and on it went, faster and faster as the musicians challenged their own skill, and the dancers came up with more intricate patterns and weaves, forming rows, bridges, and even at one point a net of arms so that ladies could be tossed by a pair of men and caught by others who then paired off with them in a spiraling romp. But the choreography was spontaneous: there was much skipping and laughing and stumbling until, every now and then, a misstep threw all the dancers off and they stumbled into one another, whereupon they paired off with whoever was closest and started the whole tomfoolery again.

Opposite the makeshift pub other folk were gathering under the great awning of the tent pavilion, sitting down all around. Their eyes were fixed upon the person sitting in the sole chair at the far end who was animatedly speaking to them. "They are taking turns telling stories," Dubh told Sweyn. "When the seanachie comes, we must surely go there."

"And what would you like to do till then?" Sweyn asked her.

She looked wistfully, yet anxiously toward the pub. It was clear what she wanted, but she was afraid to go there.

"Let's dance," he told her, and made to lead her there by the hand. Let them try to deny her, he thought to himself.

But she pulled back, shaking her head briskly. "I can't," she said.

Gently, he said to her, "It's okay. We don't have to go there. Trust me. Let me teach you a new way to dance."

They stood alone in the warm darkness, and the copper light of the fires shimmered over them like their own twin suns. The musicians in the pub had slowed their songs to airs, and to their liquid melody he tugged her gently by the hand. She allowed him to draw her close. He slipped a hand behind her waist. She glanced down at his arm, startled by the intimacy of the gesture, then looked up into his eyes, full of trepidation. But he smiled reassuringly and began to lead her in simple steps, the easiest movements of a waltz. She looked down again, this time observing the unfamiliar movement of his feet, matching them with her own. The firelight forged rubies in her ebon locks, and cast gems in her sapphire eyes. He could detect the scent of her hair, so close was she. It smelled of all the good things of the forest, wild blossoms and the tang of evergreens.

She caught on quickly, matching him step for step. He moved more intricately, showing her how to twirl and dip. She laughed like a young girl, her face aglow. The brightness of her eyes lit a long dead spark in his heart, a spark that only one other woman had ever lit within him.

*Eilwen.*

Three years she had been dead, yet he felt guilty for enjoying the presence of this woman.

He missed a step. Dubh looked into his eyes, wondering what troubled him.

He would have stopped then, but it felt as if a hand laid then upon his shoulder, the touch fleeting but familiar, approving.

He did not know how or why, but somehow it suddenly felt all right to dance with this girl. It did not feel like betraying his long lost wife. He danced with the raven haired girl until the twin bonfires burned down to cherry coals, and in the slow sweet airs she leaned her head on his shoulder, feeling so small and fragile against his sea-hardened frame.

In time even the coals grew dim, and their white smoke sailed off into an expanse of bonny stars, more numerous than the sands of beaches. He looked up into the star-strewn night, into the deep spaces between. The sky wavered behind the veil of smoke, liquid and marvelous as clear water. His mouth opened in wonder. Beauty he saw above; beauty he held in his arms. Never since he lost Eilwen had he known a moment like this, a moment of perfect beauty. For three years, he had believed that was over for him.

*********

In time the musicians at the pub needed a rest, and Sweyn and Dubh ended their long dance. Then they walked round the circumference of the meadow, doing no more than talking idly. He spoke of tall ships and the wind and the sound of waves. The sea called to his blood and it filled his thoughts and dreams, and it showed now, when he let his guard down.

She spoke of forests and misted hills, and strange people with names like the Apple Man and Sprig and Cailte, the latter which, she said, had horns on his head like a stag. Surely a metaphor. Or a birth defect. Perhaps they were the rejects of the Company, as this girl was, and lived alone, away in the Guardwood, like the outcasts of ancient societies. Indeed, he thought, perhaps that was the purpose of the Guardwood: to keep the villagers from those persons who could not fit the social order.

But the wood was in her heart and soul as the sea was in Sweyn's. She brightened when she spoke of it. She smelled of it. Often, her eyes glanced wistfully to the line of dark trees east of Man-by-the-Sea in the way a person long away looks toward home.

Around midnight the last of the village storytellers finished her tale. Then the official storyteller and lorekeeper of Man-by-the-Sea came into the tent. This was the seanachie, a man who had been raised to tell stories for his trade, and whose purpose was to keep alive the lore of the Island folk, so that it would not decay in musty books on dusty shelves, where it would be forgotten, save as an artifact. All the villagers came to hear him, and Dubh led Sweyn by the hand beneath the awning where he would speak.

The man's name was Fergus Kilwillie and he had been the Seanachie for fifty-three years, taking over the role from his father, as his father had taken it from his father before him, and so on as far back as anyone could remember. The old man was neither short nor tall, thin nor fat, but somewhere comfortably between. He wore a long white beard upon his chin, and his bright blue eyes were lively and full of wisdom. Unlike the other storytellers, he chose not to take a seat when he related his tale, but walked about the tent, watching his audience keenly, gesturing vividly. Sweyn saw Coppin sitting on the floor in the front row, and folk had made a space around him too, as if out of respect or wariness. It perplexed Sweyn.

The old Seanachie spoke:

There was a man named Durus, and he was a peasant who lived in Cymru far off in the east. It is in the Old Country, and is the homeland of many of the folk of the Company.

Durus worked for an old landowner, and the landowner was no' a kindly man. He had many servants at his call and he pushed them long hours in the hot fields. They ploughed from the time the sun rose till the time the moon set. They tended the flocks of sheep with no huts in the hills to stay warm from the rains in. They rarely had enough to eat, and they were no' paid half the value of their work.

Now in Cymru there is a high mountain, far to the north, where the wild sheep still roam. There is a still tarn there, with a surface like mirror glass. It is said a dragon dwells beneath that tarn, but that is another story. It was the mountain that interested Durus, for he had heard that the one who ascends it will receive enchantment according to his courage. This mountain is now called Snowdonia.

Durus packed food one day and snuck away from the farm. He made northward until he came to the great mountain, and when he reached it he began to climb. He ascended halfway up its formidable height when there he came across a small creature. She looked like a girl, but half the size of a grown woman. Her hair was long and blue like the sky, and it flowed behind her as if in the wind. But there was no wind. She wore no clothing, nothing at all but a chain of silver around her neck, and a bright garnet set within.

"Ye have shown a measure of yer courage," said she, "and what enchantment would ye have for it?"

"I want to know the secrets of the alchemist," said Durus, "so that I can make gold, and set myself and my good mother and sister free of the landowner."

"It is granted," said she.

But when the knowledge of the alchemist came upon Durus, and he knew all the complicated formulae for the making of gold, he realized that all the other alchemists in the world had failed because they lacked a key ingredient for their potions. An ingredient he could only obtain in Faerie. So he said to the magical damsel, "I must also know the way into Faerie."

And she said, "If ye must, ye must, but I have given ye a boon. To earn another, ye must climb higher."

Now, the higher he went, the steeper became the mountain, and though he had herded sheep in his laird's hills, he had no skill for such treacherous country as this. Still, he deemed he was too far committed to do less than go on, so he climbed higher still.

Two thirds up the mountain, he came upon a wizened hag. Frightful was her appearance, for she glowered from the rocks at those few who passed by her way. But the lad summoned his courage and approached Gwyllion and said, "I need another enchantment to set my family free of the landowner who is cruel to us."

"What is it ye needs?" said she, and her voice was a cracking grate like branches scraping in the cold winter wind.

"I need to know the way to Faerie."

"That I can give ye, for ye have earned it right."

And then he knew the way into Faerie. It was no' hard. But when he understood the way, he also understood that he would never find it because he dinna' yet have eyes to see. "How then shall I find it if I canna' see it?" he told the old faerie hag.

"If ye wait and are patient and look diligently, ye will learn to see the way," she advised him.

"But we need to be free of the landowner now, for surely he will be angry with me for having left his service without his leave."

"If ye goes to the top of Snowdonia and spend ye the night in that place betwixt earth below and stars above, in the cleft in the rock they call the Giant's Couch, the Sight will come upon ye. But this is a boon better earned than awarded."

Careful no' to thank her, the lad took his leave of her and proceeded up the mountain. It was a steep and difficult climb now, and the air grew thin and terrible cold. Still, he had courage and pressed on. And he came to the Giant's Couch and there spent the night. And that night he dreamed.

He dreamed the way to Faerie was beside him, a door up in the air over the Giant's Couch. And beyond it were verdant meadows and fat sheep and trees that grew like towers. There were crystal rivers and merry folk who skipped and sang and ate their fill from a land that gave to them abundantly and without toil. He knew if he could enter this land he would need no gold. He would find happiness and all he sought there. So he stepped from the Giant's Couch into the Faerie gate.

The next morning Durus was found dead at the foot of the mountain. It appeared he had taken a great fall. But the wise folk understood what had truly happened. Durus had sought to look deeper than his wisdom allowed, and he was beguiled by a prize too great for his novice spirit. And caught in Faerie glamour without the wisdom to bear it, he found only his end though he had sought only rest and good things for those he loved.

And so it is said to this day that if one climbs Snowdonia and spends the night upon the Giant's Couch, one will find the way to See into the Otherworld. And a reward it is to him who is ready. But few are. For all others, the boon of the Sight brings only madness and death.

The seanachie finished the old tale and the villagers were quiet in the steady gold light of the oil lamps. All eyes were rapt upon him, save one pair which seemed to capture and hold the evening light like a cat's. Coppin stared across the heads of the gathered crowd, looked directly at Sweyn. Listen, his eyes warned. Learn, they commanded. Patience, they implored.

But Sweyn paid him no mind.

They stayed on and listened to the old storyteller relate more tales of eld. The seanachie told of how the Hundred Horsemen had met the Norse invaders in the Pict lands and turned them away like a storm. He told them how Dylan O'Shee had defeated a band of spriggans by leading them into a moor while holding a torch, pretending to be a wisp. He told them about Angus' beautiful, faithful wife who was pursued by a faerie courtier, and how she thwarted his irresistible advances by building around herself a cottage of iron. He told them how the Hundred Horsemen had made peace with the Faerie folk when they agreed to keep the valley of the Asrai. He talked about how Dylan's knights had turned back invasion after invasion of the greedy King Maelgwn who believed the Hundred Horsemen had found gold in the hidden valley. He told them of how the Hundred Horsemen vanished, and no one could now recall how, yet from them emerged the Company who went a-wandering long centuries in search of the seeds of Ogham herbs and trees. And he told them how their ancestors had come to the New World, bearing three chests of those magical seeds, seeking a land where they could be sewn, and found that land here on the Island.

And when the tales finally drew to a close, the light of morning was coming and many folk had already drifted away.

"I have to go," said the girl, and Sweyn asked permission to walk her home. She agreed to let him walk her "a ways."

They returned in the direction of Dundubh Cottage, and there, just before the gate in the morning twilight, she turned and kissed him lightly on the cheek, the gesture of a shy girl toward her first love. He smiled at her. "What was that for?"

She blushed and seemed perplexed by her own action. "Because," she answered, short of anything else to say.

But he knew why. It was simple. Because I treated you like you exist. As much as he could almost like the Man-by-the-Sea folk, he could not forgive this. It was cruelty beyond reason to ostracize the girl, and for what? Because she was different? Because she did not have the right blood? Oh, if they only knew the secrets their Laird harbored in his closet of skeletons.

*Blood, the smell of blood. Blood on gloved fists.*

He shivered.

Keep it deep, he thought to himself. Don't ever let that side come back.

She touched his hand lightly, unaware of the darkness swirling inside him. "Caitlin."

Suddenly drawn back into the moment, he said "What?"

"Caitlin." She pronounced it like *Cawtsleen.* "My true name is Caitlin."

And as the rounded crown of the sun came over the east, she slipped into the shadowed wood to the left of the path at the foot of the gate, moving as swift and quiet as a leaping deer.

Sweyn stared after her in profound silence, still as a statue. Time passed. It became brighter. The dawn chorus commenced. Then his knees became water and he leaned, unsteady, on the gatepost.

*Caitlin.*

The hunted girl who might have been Eilwen's sister.

But Eilwen's sister was dead.

# Chapter Eleven

*He keeps the moors 'tween land and sea*
*And wards the beasts of each country.*
*Hard upon every passerby*
*He lends a watchful, wary eye.*
*Hunters, fishers take no more than ye must need,*
*For he sound avenges each beast, herb and seed.*

*The Brown Man of the Moors*
*From the oral tradition of the Island of Manannan.*

Caitlin. She had said her name was Caitlin.

On wobbly knees he proceeded up to the front entrance of the Cottage and opened the door. The house was quiet. It was early and all the hands, even Coppin, were still asleep, resting in after the long night of the midsummer festivities. He passed the entryway, with its dark walls of polished, aged cherry wood inlaid with spirals and intricate knotwork patterns. He slipped through the halls, past the unused living room and the ballroom which had not seen a ball in nigh two decades. He passed the dusty studios and sitting rooms and sewing rooms. Passed the solarium and the armory. Passed the conservatory. Down the aged passages, musty with the scent of dust and disuse and abandonment, he went. The morning twilight was yet dim and the shadows were murky pools. He ignored them and found his way to a great double door of darkly polished oak. Scenes were graven into the three panels of each enormous door. He had never thought about their significance before, but now he understood these panels illustrated the history of the Company. In one a knight on horseback addressed a fair damsel in a wood of mighty trees. It was the encounter of Dylan O'Shee with the mortal maid who became a faerie, Elidurydd, far in the misty past, at the dawn of recorded history, when the tale of the Company began. In the next panel a village of simple cottages was set beneath the trees, with folk going contentedly about their daily affairs. It was the community of mixed Celts that had gathered around the Hundred Horsemen in the valley of the Asrai, and these were the people who eventually became known as the Company when the Hundred Horsemen vanished. In the third panel the engraving depicted a ragged folk plodding through deep-forested wilds with packs on their backs. It was the Company during the Binding Years, when they wandered like tinkers throughout the Old World. A wizened figure led them, hunched, walking with a knotted staff in hand. He looked closely at the panel. The image was clear. It was Oak Peg. He had not recognized her before, and the realization sparked a flame of frustration in him.

"Why does nothing here make sense!" he roared into the darkness.

166

*An image appeared before his eyes. A face, a familiar face. Lean features, but boyish, a youth almost but not quite a man. The face was white with fear, blue with bruises, red with blood. He struck that face, the deceptively handsome murderer's face.*

His bunched fist impacted the oaken door, for one cannot assault a memory. The heavy door rattled on its hinges. He was breathing hard, his breath coming in furious rushes of wind.

"What is happening to me?" he wondered aloud. It had been long years since such anger had taken him. He had never been a dark, angry man. Only once . . . that black night when he had hunted.

He closed his eyes and breathed deep until his mind began to clear. It took several minutes and many desperate gulps of cool, dusty air, but it worked. The blood stopped rushing, his heart ceased pounding in his ears. He regained his thoughts. But the fury was still there, just beneath the surface. Ever since that song it was always there, as if, if his nightmares could not explode in flashbacks, they must roil in fury, building pressure like magma beneath a volcano. Such a thought scared him more than the flashbacks, for if such fury should ever surface, what might happen then? He had once done terrible things in his fury.

Determinedly, he focused on the moment, and brought himself back into the here and now.

The panels of the next door continued the long tale of the Company. They had wandered as nomads across the British Isles and Western Europe. A small group of people, they were often confused with Tinkers and Gypsies. A tiny clan of three hundred souls, they were overlooked in the annals of history. Forgotten.

In the topmost frame of the right door, the panel depicted Oak Peg and several of the Company holding converse with some faerie denizen, something that resembled a tiny man made of sticks. They parleyed beneath a great tree and Oak Peg held out her hand. The creature was giving her something in its palm. It looked like an acorn.

In the next frame a tall ship sailed across a sea. Either the Company was coming to the New World from the Old, or they were coming up the British Columbian coast aboard the Mont Royal, and would soon find the Island.

In the final frame, a man paddled a small boat away from a sinking tall ship. The stern of the ship was visible, lifted high as her bow plunged beneath the waves, and the name Mont Royal was visible upon it. In the boat were three great chests. This was an image of Raleigh McCavitt when he mutinied from the mad captain. At the prow of the little boat, a wizened little man sat. The image of the face was clearly carved.

Coppin.

"Oak Peg," he whispered. "Coppin." They kept turning up. From the depths of history they appeared over and over, like a theme that binds a tale, like a thread that unites a people. Their impossible presence had continued so long the Island folk treated it as ordinary. They took it for granted that these two enigmatic personages survived generation after generation, century after century, leading the Company. But to what end? This far-flung and forsaken Island? To preserve a collection of seeds?

And now there was Caitlin, a mysterious girl who lived like a fawn in the woods round about Dundubh. And according to Eilwen, she should be nothing more than dust and a ghost.

"It might not be Eilwen's sister," he told himself. "It's a common enough Celtic name." But his gut told him otherwise. However, he was not much inclined to trust his instincts anymore. His instincts helped him very little here. Still, he would find out the truth now. He had never before been in the room behind the great double doors. He had never had the courage to enter. Eilwen had spoken of it often. The family library. It had been one of her favorite places as a girl, before she had left the Island. She had said the room contained thousands of old books, photographs, paintings, and journals all about the O'Shee history. In the absence of her parents, the room had given her a sense of heritage and continuation. It had kept her going. And so he had never entered the room before because there was too much of his dead wife in there, and he feared he would not be able to bear it. But now he had to enter. If he was going to understand what was happening here, on this Island, he had to. Answers were not forthcoming elsewhere.

But still, he hesitated. There was so much of Eilwen in that room, so much she had touched and been close to. A part of her lay beyond those doors.

He shivered before the oaken doors, though it was not cold.

Came the whisper in his mind again, the whisper that could have been the soft echo of desperate imagination, or the distant breath of something familiar. Go in.

There was a sudden, warm sense of familiarity about him. Of love and concern. He turned quickly, looking around him as if expecting to see . . . something . . . he wasn't sure what.

Go in.

"Eilwen?" he whispered into the dawn shadows.

But only silence replied.

The Island is making me mad, he feared. He had thought once there was peace in Manannan, but he had been wrong. The Island only seemed to offer peace. But what it really was was a playground of dreams. Reality and imagination blended here in an unbearable way, and it was cutting the fragile thread of his sanity.

Go in, came the soundless whisper within.

"All right!" he roared, furiously, and threw the double doors open wide. They crashed into the walls on either side of their hinges.

A great room a full fifty feet in diameter, walls joined in octagonal form, was revealed before him. The room was three stories high, the full height of this wing of the Cottage. Each level had a balcony around it, and against each of the eight walls were shelves from floor to ceiling. A single spiral staircase joined each tier. The roof was a dome of glass panels, revealing the last withering stars of dawn. Countless tomes lined the shelves, some bound in leather, some in modern hard covers with printed paper jackets. The whole place smelled of aged paper and ancient ink. A great dusty table of oak, octagonal, stood in the center of the room with eight chairs of cherry wood, upholstered in scarlet, set around it. The table's sides were aligned to the eight walls. A lead crystal vase of time-dried wild flowers ornamented the center of the table. Countless paintings hung on the walls in spaces between the shelves, each having a protective white sheet hanging in front of it.

This was a room full of history, and elder lore, and aged ghosts. It was a chamber of memory dead and living. He felt as if he crossed into a timeless space when he stepped into the chamber. There were answers in this room. Eilwen's heart was in this room, and he would learn of that heart if he had the courage to explore it. And if he didn't have the courage, he had the anger to drive him. Anger whose source he did not fully understand, but it was welling up in him, brighter, stronger, with each passing day since the song. By his strength or by fury's fire, he would have, now, the mysteries of this place.

And he would start with the images on the walls!

He pulled a sheet from a painting. It was the oil-rendered face of a man he did not recognize. He had black hair and dark, penetrating eyes. His skin was fair but used to the sun. He read the name, graven upon a bronze plaque beneath the painting. Elphin O'Shee. He stood back from the large painting, surveying it up and down. So, this was Eilwen's father. She had never spoken much of him, except to say that he had abandoned her family when she was just a girl, and he had gathered from her stories that it was from the time he left her and her sister and mother to fend for themselves that things turned bitter for the last remnants of House O'Shee. He disliked the image immediately and lifted it from the wall. With a mighty thrust of arms long hardened from handling the sheets and helm of Starry Sea, he tossed the heavy painting through the entry. It half sailed, half tumbled through the air, and clattered loudly to the hardwood floor of the hallway beyond, the heavy frame cracking like the sound of breaking bones.

He stepped to the next painting and pulled the sheet away. A woman was depicted on the canvas. She was lovely and delicate as a bluebell blossom. Her hair was a deep red, like a coal almost spent. Her skin was fair and her bright eyes were emeralds. Eilwen's face was in hers, in the lips and the twinkle of the eyes and the glowing locks. Perhaps it was his imagination, but there seemed to be a bit of Caitlin in her features too, in the high cheekbones and the shape of the softly rounded jaw. Her name was Gwenllyan and she was the mother of his wife. Eilwen had spoken highly of this woman who had done her best to keep her broken family together, but who had died young, of a broken heart, pining for a worthless man.

"Your picture will honor the library," he pronounced.

He went to the next painting and tore down the sheet. His breath caught and he stepped back. A lovely girl, red haired, with the dark coppery eyes unique to some redheads, looked back at him from the canvas. She smiled sweetly. Her skin was fair as cream and dimples highlighted her smile. Longing filled him till he had no room for breath as he regarded the painting. Gently, he let forth a hand, extended a finger, traced along the frame. Eilwen, his Eilwen. The engraved brass plate beneath the painting read, "Eilwen O'Shee."

He stood and stared at the image long minutes before summoning the strength to move on. But then he made himself go, and he stepped to the next wall, grasped the sheet, and pulled. And there she was. Younger, perhaps only ten, but there was no mistaking her. She bore the same night-sky hair, was bejeweled with the same sapphire eyes with the impish twinkle. This was Caitlin O'Shee, youngest daughter of the O'Shees, last blood survivor of a dying house.

Something dropped inside him then, like a stone falling upon his heart, except the pain was worse. It left him feeling empty, hollow, like a dark cleft in the cold earth through which only barren wind howls. He wilted beneath the weight of the emptiness; he faltered beneath the chill wind's wail, for it cried an ugly truth of which there now could be no doubt — Eilwen had lied to him — and he could not come to grips with it. Her sister still lived, and Eilwen had lied to him. The only person he had ever loved, ever trusted. How could she have done that? Why?

The minutes ticked by. Through the great skylight above the sky whitened, becoming a glowing cerulean sea. It was not until the sun came full over the trees that he found the strength to carry on, for he feared if he dug further, everything he thought he knew and loved and believed in would crumble to dust, leaving only a lie built upon the foundation of this cursed Island.

But he had to carry on, for he could not believe malice drove Eilwen.

One other painting hung on the wall on this tier of the library. He tore himself from the image of the girl who could only be a ghost, the girl he had passed the midsummer festival with, and walked to it. He expected it to hold an image of Dundubh Cottage, or perhaps the previous generation of O'Shees. He lifted his arm, pulled the sheet away. What met his eyes struck him as hard as a blow, and it seemed in that instant the earth fell away from his feet, and he was being pulled down into a merciless pit of delusion. For what met his gaze was impossible. Upon the dusty canvas was the image of a man, tall, solidly built, with leathery, sun-browned skin, youthful in appearance but for prematurely salt-and-pepper hair that grew long and was tied behind him in a ponytail. The small bronze plaque beneath the image read, "Sweyn O'Shee."

He stood frozen, and a terrible silence settled over the room.

And then he bellowed, "Coppin!"

But Coppin was already there. Standing quietly at the double doors. And he brought with him a tale.

*********

"Gwenllyan, wife of Elphin O'Shee, was lovely and beloved of all the folk of the Island. She was raised in the ancient lore of her people and knew all the eldritch trees, and all the mysteries of seeds, and the ways of herbs and potions. She was a friend to Oak Peg and myself, and we thought highly of her even before Elphin, the Laird of the O'Shee line, took her to be his wife.

"And she was a good wife. Gwenllyan loved Elphin and they shared many good years together. She bore him a lovely daughter, your Eilwen, and they were the happiest family I ever did see of this long lived house. Together she and Elphin kept the Island prosperous. They kept safe the division between the Guardwood where faerie and mortal kin mingle, and the wildwood where no mortal may trespass. They presided over the villagers no' as Laird and Lady, but as true and trustworthy friends in good times and in bad. And all and sundry on this Island were devoted to them.

"Now there was a man of the Island who owned three fishing boats and it was summer, in the time of the year when the salmon run. The man fell ill and could no' captain his vessels. Elphin was his friend, and an experienced seaman, and he offered to lead the small fishing fleet for him. So Elphin set out one bright morning to set the nets, and he was only to be gone two days, three at the most. But the weather turned foul. A terrible storm arose and the vessels were driven far out to sea, and the sight of them was lost. Days passed, and the days turned into weeks, and still no one had seen the wayward fleet. In time, Elphin was taken for lost.

"Back on the Island, there was a woodsman who lived nearby the Cottage, and he had always had an eye for Gwenllyan. And she had once had eyes for him. They had been childhood sweethearts long before. But the hearts of youth are fickle, and their affections waned and wandered, as is the way with the young. But when it looked certain Elphin would never return, this young man went to Gwenllyan. He had no other thought in his heart than to offer her his condolences and be of what help he could to the shattered family.

"But Gwenllyan was fragile in that time, and no' herself. She was full of grief, and sure her husband was lost, for now her husband's fleet had been gone a moon. Old dead feelings rekindled within her, and her heart turned toward the woodsman. It soon came to pass that they were lovers, and so she found respite from her grief.

"But within a fortnight Elphin returned. Only one storm-battered vessel of the fleet remained, saved by the Laird's skill upon the sea. It had lost its engine and drifted many weeks, until it was found by a passing ship and towed home to the Island. But while the other two fishing boats had foundered and been lost, Elphin had managed to save all the men. So the Laird was given a hero's welcome, and the villagers rejoiced to have all their lost folk home. The Laird returned overjoyed to his wife, and she was dearly glad to see him. But now she was haunted by her unintended betrayal, and kept it secret—as did her erstwhile lover.

"Weeks passed and Gwenllyan discovered, to her horror, that she was with child. In secret, she went and told her erstwhile lover. He was delighted and said he would love the child secretly from afar. But she felt that her betrayal was embodied in the child and spurned his kind words. She fled into the forest and there she found the Tylwyth Teg among the trees, the fairest of all faerie kin, who are of a very ancient kind. Young among these folk are rare and mortal children are highly valued by them, for their vitality invigorates the ancient race. Gwenllyan, in the bitterness of her heart, swore an oath to give her child to the Tylwyth Teg.

"But her erstwhile lover was frequently in the wood, and he was respected by the good folk that dwell there. He was the woodsman, Donald, ye see, and it was his own forefather, Raleigh McCavitt, who saved the chests of seeds from the treacherous captain of the Mont Royal. But for Raleigh's valiant deed, there would be no Ogham wood upon the Island, and no faerie kin either. So in respect of the descendent of Raleigh McCavitt, the Tylwyth folk found Donald in the wood and told him of Gwenllyan's request.

"He thought about what they had told him many days, and he knew he could no' bear to lose the child. So he returned to the wood and found the Tylwyth Teg and asked them to undo her oath. They vowed to honor him, for his forefather's sake, and he left them. But what Donald did no' reckon is that the minds of faerie folk are no' like those of mortal folk. What is right and good sense to the one is no' necessarily the same to the other.

"The months passed and the child was born, a fine dark haired mortal bairn. Gwenllyan named her Caitlin, and she laid her in a crib of elder wood as the Tylwyth Teg had instructed her, and she made sure no amulet of rowan or holly was near the window of the bairn's nursery.

"That night they came for the child, but when the morning sun rose Gwenllyan did no' find the crib empty. Instead she found a child in the crib, a child in the very likeness of her own bonny bairn. But this girl was flawless as a perfect gem—there was no blemish in her at all. Her beauty was wondrous to behold. Then Gwenllyan perceived she had been deceived by the Tylwyth Teg. They had done her no favor but left her worse than before, for they had taken her own true bairn and left her a changeling in its likeness.

"Yet no ordinary changeling, this. No' at all, for ordinarily changelings are shriveled, poor and short-lived copies of what has been taken. But Gwenllyan and Donald were each much loved and respected of the Tylwyth Teg. And each had asked a contrary boon. To make it right, the Tylwyth Teg took Gwenllyan's child, as they had pledged to do. And then they took all their eldritch craft and secret art and poured it into the making of a changeling like has never before walked the green world. It was created so full of perfect beauty it might have seemed better than the mortal it imitated. In this way the Tylwyth Teg, who for all their wisdom dinna' understand mortal hearts, thought they had kept both their pledges.

"But Gwenllyan was devastated. She fled her home and found Donald and told him what the Tylwyth Teg had done, and he, too, was left desolate by the news. In his mind, the Tylwyth Teg had deceived and betrayed him. He raged against the faerie folk and swore he would get his own right daughter back. But he had no chance, of course, for no' since the elder days have mortals been allowed to pass unbidden through the gates of deepest Faerie, where the Tylwyth Teg reside.

"Now, as to Elphin, he was an observant man. He perceived, then, that something had passed between his wife and Donald. He inquired of Gwenllyan and, broken by the tragedy of it, she confessed her trespass to him. One part of Elphin understood. He had been gone weeks and it seemed certain he had been lost to the sea. But another part, the greater part, could no' forgive her. Her deed festered in him, and the wound grew sore over a score of months till he could bear it no more. So came a day he left his wife and daughter and legacy, vanishing like a wave upon the sea, and was never seen or heard again by anyone on the Island.

"Gwenllyan pined away after that, and whether for her lost child or her lost husband no one knew. Nor would she take Donald back. She punished herself, ye see, and she faded over the years, becoming thinner and thinner, and fainter, as if the love of life had drained away from her. Seeing this, Donald buried his anger, and was kind to the changeling girl for a time, hoping to ease Gwenllyan's heart. For a few years it seemed to work, and Gwenllyan persisted, though only as a shadow of her former self. But it seemed when Elphin left, her soul went with him. At last came a day when no' even Donald's kindness could succor her, and she just seemed to fade from that time. In a matter of months she became an empty shell, until she passed in death. And on that day Donald spurned the changeling with all the vehemence his bitterness could muster. He tried to destroy the changeling, which of course was foolishness, for changelings are products of Tylwyth enchantment, and nigh immortal. Yet he kept at it, over and over for many seasons. And so the girl took to keeping away from him, and though she was only a changeling, I could no' bear to see how he treated her, so I looked after her.

"But through all this, Eilwen, the eldest daughter, did no' know of her changeling sister's eldritch origin. I saw to that, hoping to spare her, and so Eilwen loved her well. Perhaps that was my mistake, not being forthright with her from the beginning.

"But Eilwen was strong. The loss of her parents bit her bitterly, but she bore it, and as the eldest by six years, she did her best to fill the role of mother for the girl, and I did my best to care for both of them. But one day, by sorry accident, she learned of right sister's fate, and the nature of the thing she believed to be her sister.

"It was then that what remained of the O'Shee house fell apart. Eilwen had loved the little girl, but now she understood this was no' her right sister. The girl she knew as Caitlin was only a deception, for changelings are made of the wood of living trees, deep stone, and black growing earth. All they are is bound in a net of faerie glamour which has the power to make mortal minds perceive what they desire.

"Her own right sister was lost forever in the realm of the Tylwyth Teg, and the thing she thought was her sister was only a golem, neither of mortal nor faerie kin, with no true life of its own. It was the walking evidence of a lie and a tragedy, and a sign of the loss of all Eilwen held dear.

"From that time Eilwen recoiled from the changeling girl. All the tragedy of her house heaped upon her heart at once and she could abide the Cottage no longer. She abandoned her home to dwell in Man-by-the-Sea for a season, but left the Island soon after. She left no word and was never heard from again, save once. And that was when she sent me word of her marriage, and a photograph of the man she loved, a man named Sweyn deSauld. And Oak Peg said she saw in that man the eyes of a true and just Laird, and had this painting made from the photograph."

*********

"And that is the sorry story of it," said Coppin, sitting in one of the chairs of the great oaken, octagonal table opposite Sweyn. His frame was slight, and he seemed a child seated by the great dark table.

"Sure it is," hissed Sweyn, scowling. "All you forgot to throw in were pixies and fairy dust. And maybe a wicked witch and a big bad wolf. Why can't I get a single straight word from you?"

"Perhaps ye simply will no' hear truth when it comes by ye."

Sweyn shot up, and the chair he was sitting in clattered away behind him. He clenched his fists, trembling angrily. Coppin eyed him calmly. Pity was in his eyes, and no fear of the large man. But Sweyn was no bully. He never had been. He merely said, "You're a damned liar, Coppin." And he stormed from the room and house. He found his way out front to the gate which he threw open with such violence it broke partly from its rusty hinges. He strode past it and turned left, plowing into the Guardwood, through which the sea was only a mile to the south. In the full light of the morning sun it was easy to pick his way among the trees and find his way.

He soon came to a great burned out area, where a fire had devoured several dozen acres of trees a decade earlier. In the daylight new life could be seen taking over, young, slender birches, abundant wildflowers and wild raspberries. He felt he had been here before, but his recollection of it was now quite hazy. Amethyst candle flickers shining in the distant darkness. And a short, burly, brown skinned man. He shook off the memories. They made no sense, and in his rigid way of thinking were best done without, for they did not fit the paradigm of the world as he was willing to know it.

He pressed on toward the sea, and came shortly to a bog on the other side of the burn. This place also had a familiar feel which he dismissed as déjà-vu. A bank led down to black pools of standing water, partially covered by lush green bog plants. Dangerous ground, he knew instinctively. Ground where one could step in the wrong place and disappear beneath the black water never to be seen again. But in his foul mood, such danger did not seem to matter much. He picked his way through, stepping and leaping from stone to clump of solid earth, finding his way more by luck than skill, until he passed the bog.

The ground beyond rose a little, and there was a verdant line where beach peas and wild rye grew. Then the land descended again and became the grey sand of the Island's coast. This place, among all the lands of the Island, felt normal to him, for it was an ordinary Pacific northwest beach. He walked to the very edge of the water and plopped down onto the sand just beyond the reach of the rolling waves. The familiar song of their endless passing eased his spirit, even if it did nothing to provide answers. But it was the only salve he had at the moment, for everything else here was maddening.

He let himself fall back onto the cool grey sand and eavesdrop upon crying kittiwakes and chatting sea ducks. He spread his arms, intentionally relaxing. In time, the anger washed away with the tide, and peace came with the warming sunbeams that fell over him. For a brief moment, when his cares fell away, he was able to doze.

The rest was sorely needed, but he could not enjoy it long. Before the early sun had risen much further, there came a distressed tumult, the bleating of some creature upon the beach. Wearily, he opened his eyes. Overhead, the sky was so clear and bright it made his tired eyes sting, and he quickly looked away. A sparkling sea met his vision and he experienced a sudden pang of yearning.

But then the urgent bleating came again, on his left. Certainly it was the panicked cry of some animal. He rolled on his side and squinted that way. Not fifty feet distant a seal lay upon sand still glistening from the tide's rapid retreat. The animal was bound in a strong net of thin cords and weights were attached to one side of the net, floats to the other. It was some kind of gill net, and it was a wonder the seal had not drowned in it. Somehow it had made it to the Island where it had washed up on the beach.

Sweyn pushed his weary body up, drained from a long night and a wild flight of emotions, rolling his neck to try to ease the kinks from it. Then, slowly, he approached the seal.

"Easy there," he said in a low voice, not sure if seals knew enough of the ways of men to be comforted by a calm tone.

The seal watched him approach with wild eyes, struggling desperately in the net, but it was bound and twisted so fast it was all but immobilized. When Sweyn drew near, he drew a marlinspike knife from a small leather sheath at his belt and opened the blade.

"Take it easy, I swear I'm not going to hurt you."

The seal barked in terror as Sweyn lowered himself slowly to his knees. This isn't a bright idea, he thought as he leaned his body weight against the animal to keep it from struggling and injuring itself as he worked. Careful to keep the sharp edge of the knife away from the animal, he sawed with slow precision at the lines, cutting the net away one strand at a time. Bit by slow bit the seal was freed, and with each line cut loose it became harder to manage the animal that barked and nipped doglike at him. When he figured he had cut enough of the net away, Sweyn rolled quickly off the seal and grasped one end of the net so the seal could not tangle itself up in it again. But the seal twisted out of the net, and as soon as it was free it waddled rapidly down into the rolling surf. But just before the surging waves, it looked back at Sweyn with impenetrable black wells of eyes. It seemed to be saying, in its way, thank you. Then it slipped into the surf and was gone.

"A kind thing a mortal does for a wild thing is twice a mystery," came a deep, unexpected voice behind him. "Rarely seen but from Man-by-the-Sea folk in these degenerate days." The voice was course and familiar, though Sweyn could not place it. Sweyn turned to face the speaker and found himself regarding a short, burly man, hairy all over, his skin browned from long exposure to the sun. He was hunched with his knees drawn up to his chin in a thicket of beach peas just above the sand, from which he must have been spying on Sweyn. "Had ye made to hurt the sea beast, I would have tossed ye into the water and a net yerself," he said and rose, approached Sweyn. He was dressed in coarsely woven wool, and the style of the garb was old. He also wore a tunic, and breeches that ended just below the knees. Sweyn was sure he should know this fellow, yet try as he might to recall, the memory was blocked. Yet he felt he should be wary of him.

The fellow stopped just before Sweyn, watching Sweyn watch him, and he folded his burly arms. "Aye, ye've seen me afore, when we met just on the other side of yonder bog the night ye was lost." He pointed up the beach to the boggy barrier beyond it. "But I ken ye canna' recall it. A bad sign, that, meaning yer of a mortal mind, like most outsiders. Yet ye remain here, and if ye canna' open that head of yers," he rapped Sweyn's forehead with his index finger, "the Island is likely to be yer end."

*A burly man in the dark, holding him back from stepping into black waters over which floated beautiful, flickering amethysts.*

Recollection began to dawn in Sweyn's eyes.

The burly little man saw, and a corner of his mouth rose, forming an indecipherable half-grin. "Ye start to remember, do ye? That's a good sign, it is. It means ye're at last starting to open. But opening may take long and long, and time grows short, short for the changeling, short for the Pact. It may be best to give ye a thing, though whether it will turn out to be a boon or a curse, I canna' tell."

Sweyn stepped back from the burly little fellow and began to speak, his voice rising with each word until he was shouting. "All you people speak in riddles! Would someone just talk plainly and tell me what on earth you mean! It's driving me mad!"

"Aye, mad, that's the worry, ye see. In the past, when new blood has come among the O'Shees, there was more time. Plenty for the new blood to learn our ways, and our secrets, and make peace with the Island. But no' this time. Now there is so little time. The old powers and presences, those here before we came, want their enchanted Island back, but where else have we refugees to go? And without our Laird to keep the Pact, we canna' stay.

"Now, there is a gift which may speed yer growth, though if ye canna' bear it, there is no way to undo it, and it will surely drive ye mad, maybe even kill ye. But these are desperate times.

"Still, Oak Peg would have me wait, and so would Coppin. Wait till ye are all open and ready in yer own length of time. For if we lose ye, the Pact will surely fail. Take no chances, they would say. Yet waiting itself is a chance.

"And even if ye were to open yer heart and face the mysteries of this place, and be ready by the last possible day, by then it will be too late for one under my care now. For I ward all the creatures of these wild parts, be they mortal beast or faerie thing. And one much loved will fail and fade if a way canna' be found to prevent it. I dinna' know if there is a way; I have no' the wisdom to see it. And no folk of this Island will help her—they dinna' see the true life in her. My only ally, her only chance, is ye yerself."

175

Sweyn sighed in exasperation, turned to face the sea, and plopped into the sand. "Thanks for clearing it up," he spat acidly. He put his elbows on his knees and rubbed his hands over tired eyes. They felt better for the imposed darkness.

"Ye proved yerself a good lad, helping my seal. Ye proved yerself a gentleman with yer kindness to the changeling girl, who has known neither friend nor company in many a year. Ye even won the favor of those surly faerie sheep of the Cottage that dinna' approve of any mortal kin."

"I'm so glad to hear you approve of me," said Sweyn from under his palms. "Now go away. I need to sleep."

The hairy man approached him. "We dinna' give our true names easily," said he. "But as ye are a good man, I will give ye mine. I am called Getal, which means the broom herb. And Broom was the name ye knew me by the night ye lost yer way in the wood. And I am a Brown Man. Once I kept the moors in the north and east of England. Now I keep the space 'tween land and sea of this corner of the Island."

"Pleased to meet you," said Sweyn. "Go away. Unless you have a straight answer to give. And some aspirin." He fell tiredly onto his back, one arm thrown over his eyes to block out the day, and wished for the oblivion of sleep.

But Getal ignored him. "Ye dinna' believe in the old tales, I know. Ye dinna' believe in enchantment and ghosts and faeries."

"I believe in what I can see," stated Sweyn. "I believe in straight answers. Neither can be found on the Island."

"Aye, to believe only in what ye can see, that is the way of outsiders, sure. But ye canna' have such simple things on this Island, Sweyn O'Shee, for on this Island enchantment flows strong enough to bend reality to Faerie ways."

Sweyn chose not to remark upon the surname Broom had bestowed. He did not have the energy for it. Instead, he repeated, "Show me, or go away," still hoping the nuisance would make off and leave him to rest.

Getal raised his eyebrows. "So ye accept the gift, then. I hope ye be such a man as can bear it." Then Getal touched Sweyn's eyes.

Sweyn shot up, thrusting Broom's hairy arm away. "Hey, keep your hands off ..." But his voice caught in his throat, for he was not looking at a hairy little man. The creature that met his vision stood upright on two legs like a man, but there the resemblance ended. It was all lean and lanky, yet its bones were bound in tight cords of wiry muscle. It was hairy, but the hair was like a course pelt. But his face, that was the most alien of all. It was generally shaped like a man's, but it was too large for the body, and stretched. A long nose protruded from it. The ears were large and long and pointed. And the eyes were slanted almonds as black and impenetrable as the seal's.

Instinctively, Sweyn rolled away from the creature, scrambled to his feet, watched it warily. It gazed back at him, curiously, and said, "Some mortal folk die by now, at the shock of seeing the world all topsy-turvy for the first time. Some run off screaming and ne'er mutter a sober word again." He grinned, parting lips revealing sharp teeth and fangs, and now Sweyn knew for sure this was the thing he had seen on Starry Sea's bow the day his sail was torn and he came to the Island, when in a moment of storm-driven desperation he had seen clear and true. The creature carried on. "That ye've done neither is a good sign, eh?"

"What the hell are you?" Sweyn rasped.

"Ye said ye would believe if ye were shown. So I've given ye the Sight. Now see a faerie."

Sweyn blinked. "It can't be."

"Would ye no' believe yer own eyes, man?"

"It's a trick. It must be some kind of trick."

"Ye're trying to work it out. There's a sage lad. Go and prove it to yerself, what ye see. For with the Second Sight no glamour may deceive yer eyes, and ye must forever perceive the world without its veils. I hope ye can bear it. Most mortals canna'.

"And when ye are satisfied of the truth of what ye see, turn yer eyes back to the changeling girl, for Coppin and Oak Peg have sent her to her doom because they believe they must keep her from ye to save the Island."

Without ever taking his eyes off the thing, Sweyn shook his head, unable to believe what it was telling him. "I don't like Coppin, and I distrust Oak Peg, but I'm sure they aren't murderers."

And who could imagine you capable of murder, Sweyn deSauld, psychologist and healer, and yet a murderer you are. And with the memory, uncertainty came into Sweyn's mind.

Getal saw him struggling, trying to work things through, and he took that for a good sign too. The Sight was a hard gift, yet Sweyn's mind was still sound. There was strength in this man, perhaps even enough to be Laird, and enough more to save a forlorn life. Still, the full impact of the Sight had not yet come to him. But there was no point in dwelling upon that. There was only point in hoping, and preparing Sweyn.

"What ye have to understand is to them it is no' murder," Broom continued, and desperation came into his voice. "Changelings are but puppets of the Tylwyth Teg—they have no real life, after all. They are creations of magic, having less vitality than seeds and spores. They dinna' truly live, all they do is imitate life, for they have no souls of their own. To slay a changeling is no different than splitting firewood. No more a crime than cutting hay. And that is the sad truth of it.

"But Oak Peg and Coppin, for all their eldritch wisdom, dinna' fully understand the lesson of Dylan O'Shee when he came to lead the Hundred Horsemen. The Hundred lacked souls till Dylan showed them how to have them. For a soul is more than a birthright. Ye canna' get one just for being mortal or faerie. A soul blossoms when the heart is full of love and honor and all good things. Then life fills ye so full a soul takes root.

"Still, there must be the seed of a soul for a soul to take root, and changelings have no such seed. None at all. I dinna' understand it. Yet a soul is in Caitlin, I am sure. That damsel of the wood has more love and honor in her heart than many a plotting faerie or mortal can claim. It is a natural mystery, and perhaps it takes a creature of the wild such as m'self to perceive it.

"But now she is beginning to fade, for no changeling lasts very long, and soul or no, she is a changeling. And she has already outlasted any other changeling I ever heard tell of. The fading took long to start, but now that it has begun, it is happening quick. The enchantment will leach from her body until naught remains but black earth, stones and twigs, and a drop of dried blood. And then she will be gone, soul or no, as if she never were. For if one of faerie kin should perish from this green world or Faerie, there is the Dreaming West for it. And if one of mortal kin should leave the green world, the Otherworld awaits. But what place has a changeling, who is neither of the one folk nor the other?"

He sighed then and sat down hard upon the sand, wrapping his gangly arms around his knobby knees. It was a very human, disarming gesture, yet it seemed out of place for this half animal wild thing. But aching grief was clear in his dark eyes as he stared off in the direction of the sea, which stretched far off to meet the cerulean horizon.

Getal continued. "Though I dinna' claim to be wise in the ways of eldritch lore, I have given much thought to the matter, and I have seen how love binds. If it can impart a soul, perhaps it can even bind a changeling to life. It is a desperate hope, I admit, but all I can find for the girl. So I have gone to the Tylwyth Teg and asked them to take her to them, where she might find love among her creators, but of course they will no' do it. Fair they are, but too proud. They would no' have a changeling in their twilit country. And there are no mortals of the Island to take her. All mortal folk loathe changelings."

Now he looked pleadingly into Sweyn's eyes. "There is only ye, Sweyn. Ye are no' from this place, and have no' the instincts that hold sway over the Company. I have seen how ye care for her, and how she cares for ye. Aye, she does. And perhaps if ye were to lend her yer love, it would give her the strength to cling to life."

Sweyn found himself listening raptly to what this thing who claimed to be Broom was telling him. It almost moved him, but of course it was impossible, all of it. Just as much as this animal-person talking to him now. All that was before him was a hallucination, and the tale he thought it conveyed no more than a paranoid delusion. Still, if he had already plunged so far into madness, there could be no more harm in addressing the thing, though he felt sure that if anyone were watching, they would see only a madman talking to the empty air. "You've come to the wrong man, my hairy illusion. I'm not a fairytale wizard. I can't save your changeling. Now go away and let me go insane in peace."

The creature shot up then, snarled like a hound, grabbed him by his shirt, dragged him to an inch from its hairy, wild face, so close he could smell the sap upon its breath, feel stray hairs of its wiry beard scrape his chin. It was unbelievably strong, like a bear, and he was handled as easily as a boy would handle a toy soldier. The creature shook him several times, violently, then threw him back into the sand. From his back, Sweyn stared up at it, white-eyed, all fatigue gone, heart pounding. Getal snarled at him, "Did that seem a dream to ye? Do I no' feel like a hard and living thing? Or will it take a few bruises and a cracked rib to convince ye, Sweyn? I can bestow those easily enough.

"Open yer eyes and see, man! The Sight is given; there is no going back! The fate of us all hangs on whether ye will see, and if ye canna' the girl will fade, and the Pact will fail, and ye will be bereft of yer own right mind in the end."

Still lying in the grey sand, his arms held up defensively, Sweyn pleaded with him. "None of it makes any sense. Changelings and knights and faeries and magic. It can't be real. You can't be real!"

"Sure it is, lad," Broom growled. "Just look at yerself, lying in the sand where I m'self threw ye."

Sweyn shook his head, refusing to accept it.

Broom saw the desperation in the seaman's eyes, fear borne of coming face to face so suddenly with an unknown reality. This was his doing, he knew. To thrust the Sight so quickly upon an unready mortal was cruel. Yet Broom was not cruel, only desperation drove him to such lengths. But he could feign cruelty no longer, not with Sweyn, the first right good outsider he had ever met. He crouched beside Sweyn and his voice became gentle. "Sweyn," he said, "look." He pointed and Sweyn turned his head in that direction. Broom indicated the sand, back up to the beach peas where he had been crouched only minutes before. "If I am no' real, then what made those tracks."

Through his shielding arms Sweyn regarded the tracks. Bare feet, humanlike, but too narrow. In a moment he lowered his arms. There was no more ferocity in Broom's eyes. Still cautious, Sweyn rose, and watching Broom carefully, he walked over to a print, knelt, and felt the rim of it with his finger. The indent in the sand was soft and real to his touch. From up close, he could see the detail in the tracks, the creases of every toe, the rounded depressions of the balls of the feet. No hallucination could hold such detail.

In wonder he looked up at Broom. He croaked, "I think you're real."

Broom smiled. "There may be hope for ye," he said.

"There is so much I don't understand," Sweyn voiced in desperation, still crouched at the track.

Kindly, Broom said, "Aye, lad. I'm sorry for it. Normally, when new blood comes, years pass before the Second Sight is given. But this time there are only days."

Sweyn stood up, then, facing Broom. Something was changing inside him. Not quick, but it was beginning. His fierce unwillingness to accept a deeper world was crumbling. Still, it was not easy to give up old ways of thinking, and every little shattered preconception went painfully.

"This may be real, but that doesn't mean you're honest," Sweyn told Broom. "I still cannot believe Coppin and Oak Peg would let the girl come to harm. Coppin himself told me he used to care for her after Eilwen left."

"Aye, true enough. He would set food out for her, and walk in the woods and talk with her. He did these things when no one else would, before I ever found her. Dinna' misunderstand me, Coppin is no' cruel. Oak Peg is no' wicked. But they know Caitlin is skillfully made, beautiful and appealing. They fear she will win yer heart before she fades. They know how much ye suffered after Eilwen passed, and they have sent Caitlin away to spare ye from more pain, fearing more might break ye. For if ye are lost, the Island is lost, for the Laird is the surety of the Pact."

"It's quite a story," said Sweyn.

The Brown Man glowered at him. "Aye, and ye dinna' believe. Some terrible thing must have come to pass to put such distrust in ye. No matter, ye will believe. Go yerself to the old witch in the oaks. Seek the truth for yerself. But, mind ye, she will turn your words to inane things and tell ye to be patient. She will mother ye and feed ye cheese and ale and tell ye bright stories until all yer worries have faded 'neath the haze of faerie glamour. Ye must no' let her delay ye. Demand she tell ye of Arn'na'sagt'puch. Tell her to tell ye of the Pact, and why the Island needs a Laird, needs an O'Shee. Make it clear . . ." he swallowed nervously, hesitant to say the next thing he must, "make it clear ye will leave the Island once and for all if she does no', for only then will ye hear so soon the whole truth from her."

Sweyn chuckled then, but there was no humor in the dry sound of it. "Fugue brought me here and a storm blew me into your bay. And if half what you say is true, then I doubt either happened by chance. And I doubt equally as much I will be allowed to leave here so easily."

Surprisingly, this made the creature smile. "Perceptive, ye are. Eilwen chose well. Now listen. It is true no accident brought ye here. The design was Oak Peg's, when she swept yer thoughts away and steered ye like a puppet to our Island. But ye surprised her with the strength of yer will when ye started to come to yerself quite before ye arrived. So strong were ye she had to call upon the Merfolk for a storm to drive ye into the bay, and still ye resisted her, such that she commanded me to go to sea and rip yer sail, otherwise ye would have outfought her storm and gone back to sea. I did as she commanded, and then I rode yer prow and set loose yer anchor and saw to yer safety."

"But ye have strength, Sweyn, such that even she canna' stop ye leaving if ye determine it, and she knows it. She will bend to ye. And I give ye my word, should she call up a storm to stop ye, I will see to yer safety and beat back the storm. My word is oak and canna' be broken. Ye may count upon it.

"Now go, time is so short, and the girl and the Island need a Laird."

And with that Broom the Brown Man dashed into the thicket above the beach and was gone, quick and silent as a hare. Sweyn stood there upon the beach a long time, his back to the sea, looking where the Brown Man had vanished. In one night and day he had changed so much he was not sure who it was who stood there in his shoes, at the very brink of the rolling surf. "A Laird," Broom had said. But he doubted it. His home lay behind him where the waves foamed upon the sand.

# Chapter Twelve

*Culled from silver moonlight when the orb is ripe and full,*
*Lulled from green shadows where trees are black and broad,*
*Bound in hawthorn where faerie magic sighs,*
*Found in willow roots which walk the eerie night,*
*Bairn for Tylwyth to keep just the midnight trade,*
*Cairn for the girl who bides without a soul.*

Tears for the Empty Girl
Broom the Brown Man

The salt wind blew fresh and a sun-drenched sea sparkled with the lucent fire of aquamarines. Fifteen knots the wind blew, out of the west, and Starry Sea rode a fast beam reach south out of the bay before Man-by-the-Sea. Sweyn piloted the vessel just south of the easternmost point, three hundred yards beyond a dilapidated, bobbing buoy that marked dangerous shoals. There he rounded the point hard, veered east to follow the Island's coast, and as he made the turn, so the wind shifted with him, now blowing fifteen knots true out of the south. He never had to leave the helm to change tack, and the wind came perfectly abeam, moving the gallant cutter along crisply. He knew then the wind was aiding him, as Broom had promised it would.

From starboard came noises like powerful bursts of steam. Sweyn turned just in time to sea several gouts of white vapor erupt from the water, from the blowholes of black and white dolphins resembling small orcas. They moved through the sea like swift and graceful shadows, and in an instant they dove deep again, swimming an easy six knots to either side of Starry Sea's keel. To his mortal eyes they appeared to be only an escort of Dall Dolphins, but his new Sight showed something other. Two of the three had within their enchanted shape the forms of men, slim and muscular, with skin the hue of kelp. The third was the color of a stormy sea and contained within it the shape of a youthful girl, slender and strong, with emerald hair that flowed after her to her thighs. These were the Merfolk, and he had heard of their like once before, a long time ago, when he had voyaged around Scotland and spent a score of nights in the remote, northernmost isles where the old tales still lived. One hand on the helm, he leaned far over the toerail and peered into the waters, shivering for reasons he could not discern. Fear. Wonder. Both, most likely, and the reckoning that never again would the world be as he thought it. It felt to him like he was just realizing the earth was not flat, and at the same time like he had sailed over its edge.

But the wind kept with him, blowing him steadily on. And any seaman would have recognized it was no ordinary wind. It smelled of the salt sea, to be sure, but its strength did not waver, not by a knot, nor did its course vary by a degree. No matter his heading, it held precisely ninety degrees off Starry Sea's bow, moving the little cutter as fast as a sailing vessel could. And speed was of the essence right now, every lost minute distancing him from Caitlin.

He activated the autopilot and pulled the gennaker from its locker. He went forward and fastened the gennaker's chute to its dedicated halyard. Once lashed, he attached the forward bottom corner called the tack to the prow. To the clew he attached a long rope called a sheet which he would use to control the gennaker through its tacks. Then he went to the base of the newly booted mast and heaved at the halyard, hoisting the gennaker. All set, he grasped the chute's line and heaved on it. The chute was pulled up and the gennaker, which had been cocooned inside it, was loosed. The bright yellow sail was made of light sailcloth and it filled with wind in a moment. Though the sail was light, it was enormous, and Starry Sea healed another ten degrees under the power of the additional wind it caught. The vessel accelerated to hull speed and beyond. He knew it before he even returned to the binnacle, by the way the water felt as it raced beneath the hull. He returned to the cockpit and rounded the binnacle, regarded the tachometer. Nine knots. For a monohaul sailing vessel, this was a dangerously high speed. He was pushing Starry Sea for all she was worth, but there was no choice. Every moment counted. If he could have gotten any more speed by running the iron genny — the diesel motor — he would have used it too.

Despite his best speed, he could not escape the fear that he was not going fast enough. Anxiety gnawed at him, scattering his thoughts every which way. He released the autopilot and took the ship's wheel. Under the force gathered in the sails, the boat tried hard to round her bow into the wind, and keeping a steady course required strength, vigilance, and constant attention. Still, it was not enough to constrain his thoughts, and he found his mind wandering back to the events of earlier in the day.

*********

Since Broom had touched his eyes only that morning, he had staggered through the forest like a drunken man, making for Dundubh Cottage. But it was hard going, he struggled to get hold of his new perspective of the world, and frequently was confused or distracted. Though he perceived the same world he always had, none of it was as he had known it before. Every sense within him was wide open, clear and true-seeing. He perceived new depths all around him, dizzying and dazzling every sense. Sensuous greens he somehow had always missed clothed the forest. He stumbled as he made his way through the wood because his eyes were constantly drawn away from his path, into the trees, where verdurous sweet leaves moved in the faint breath of wind like waves upon the sea, calling him to climb up into the boughs and rest in the woodland canopy, where songs of birds might envelop him and shifting fingers of sunlight could play over him, tickling him with scattered warmth. And from all around there was the fragrance of the wood, but of such intensity as he had never perceived before. It was a heady potion of wild blossoms of bluebells and starflowers, budding berries and rich loam, full of the power of life. The trees even seemed to ring; it was the coursing of summer sap through their arboreal veins, and the sound of it was like a flowing mountain river — clean and free and strong. By accident, he brushed a hand against an elm and shuddered, for beneath his palm he had felt an undeniable sense of spirit, a slow, green awareness that passed the seasons in peace, gathering mirth and power and wisdom. And he knew in that moment the tree had a spirit. He gazed at it, and from a hollow in the trunk saw a pair of small, glittering eyes gazing back at him. He tilted his head, trying to pierce the shadow, and became aware of a diminutive feminine face, and the shadow form of a body too small and too thin, hiding in the cavity. Breathless, heart thumping, he backed away from the sylph and staggered on through the forest.

Sometimes he thought he saw auras of beautiful color around hawthorns and elders, and over certain places of the earth. Instinct warned him those places were full of wild magic, and he steered clear of them. Once he saw a mouse scamper across the earth, but it was no ordinary mouse. Its coat shone like the iridescent turquoise and emerald of peacock feathers, and the creature stopped to watch him for a while, as he watched it. Uncanny intelligence burned behind its eyes, and Sweyn would not have been surprised to hear it speak. But after a moment the mouse scampered into the underbrush and was gone. He was glad for its parting. It was one less thing to confuse him.

Broom had told him this is what it is to see the world in the way of faerie kin. The Second Sight took away every defense, forcing the mind to perceive all things in their fullness, beyond the limits of preconception. Only by seeing so true could faerie glamour be pierced, allowing Sweyn to finally see and know and remember the mysteries of the Island which had till now defied his mind. But the ability to block out the full depth of reality is an important defense of most mortals, and few could bear to have it stripped away. That was why even most of the folk of Man-by-the-Sea did not have the Sight. For once given, there was no way to ungive it. And if the recipient could not learn to bear it, the Sight would drive him mad or kill him.

Not encouraging, thought Sweyn, who could not even bear the weight of the memories that haunted him.

It was halfway to noon when he came, stumbling, out of the forest at the front gate of Dundubh Cottage. He made his way up the front yard, weaving from side to side, struggling to see straight through his new eyes, and went to the house where he called all about for Coppin. But the old servant was nowhere to be found. Indeed, none of the hands were. He searched from the south to the north wing, and called after Coppin in halls he had never before ventured into, but received no answer save his own echo.

He left the house through the vaulted doors of the central structure, throwing open the great solid oak weight of them with all his might, so that they were scarred on the stone walls they slammed into. He circled the house and went around back. Ignoring the sheep field and the oat field, he strode briskly to the woodlot and down the trail that led to the small cabin where Donald McCavitt had lived all his life.

"Donald!" he bellowed. His voice echoed beneath the shaded forest boughs, and that was as much reply as he got. He went all about the woodlot, and called till he was hoarse. But Donald was nowhere in the woodlot, so far as he could tell.

"I don't have time for this," he growled. Broom had impressed the need for haste upon him. He did not really understand it, but for Caitlin there was no time to lose.

But there came an uncanny sensation, a prickling on the back of his neck, and he spun on his heel. Coppin stood behind him, not ten paces away, rubbing his palms together nervously. But it was not quite Coppin as Sweyn recalled him.

Much the same he was, but a bit shorter and stouter. Yet his ears were long and pointed. He had a stringy beard of curly brown hair, and his eyes were the blue of lapis lazuli, and round and sad, but his pupils were oval as a cat's. The little man-thing looked as if he were debating whether to bolt into the forest or stand his ground.

"You're one of them!" Sweyn hissed, a proclamation that struck Coppin so hard he stumbled back two steps.

"Ye can See!" Coppin rasped.

Sweyn nodded. "Oh, yeah. I can See. Whether you like it or not, whether I like it or not, I can See. And I see you're not what you've been pretending to be."

A deep sense of betrayal and anger swept over Sweyn, then, so profound his hands began to tremble. He had thought once, for a brief moment, there was peace in Manannan, but the ugly truth glared now plainly before him. Nothing here was as it appeared, and even those persons he had almost been close to had lied bitterly to him. No wonder Eilwen had fled the Island so many years ago. And he would have kept his word to her and never come if the oak witch's magic had not forced him to break it. And with the realization his breath came in deepening, broken shudders. His heart hammered in his breast and his face flushed. He wanted to cry out in fury. He wanted desperately to grab something and break it.

Coppin would do. Coppin had lied to him since the beginning.

He took a step toward the little man, and Coppin stepped back fearfully. But all of a sudden, in the rush of his fury, memory flooded Sweyn, all the unbelievable things he had witnessed and put from his mind in his months on the Island: sea creatures that looked like men out of the corner of his eye; deadly lights that hovered like live bait over black bogs; women who floated like fishes beneath clear water; a great, cold tree that crawled throughout the wildwood, hunting. And more. So much more. An island in a lake, somewhere far back in the forest, not quite part of this world, where apple trees touched the sky and the brook ladies feasted and sang, and an old hag walked among them. It was there, yes, there, he had heard the lament for the horned lord, the heartrending love song that burrowed unforgettably into his mind when he could remember nothing else of his woodland encounters.

And all the other memories coalesced upon him at once, flooding into him like a tempest.

This is what it is like to receive such Sight, he thought. It is like having your mind ripped open.

He grimaced and grasped his head, wrapping his arms tightly over it, for it seemed otherwise his skull must explode. Memory and realization and reality filled it so rapidly it was more than anyone could bear.

He fell to his knees.

And Coppin saw the madness flash before Sweyn's eyes, the wild glances as Sweyn was torn by the violent inrush of every lost moment he had experienced on the Island, and forced to face what they meant. Coppin stood frozen, utterly incapable of helping Sweyn. So much rested on this moment. The fate of the Island and Sweyn's very life hung on the reserves of the seaman's strength.

Sweyn's mind was pulled back and forth through time, from one impossible memory to the next. In one moment he relived the terror of finding himself upon the sea, thousands of miles off course, coming to his senses in a tempest blowing him into a rock of land. In the next he wondered at the pixie lights beyond Oak

Peg's iron gate. And in the very next he wept to the bittersweet harping of the brook ladies. The emotions spiraled madly, an intrapsychic cyclone that threatened to hemorrhage his mind, rip apart his sanity. Sweyn looked up into the sky, and let loose an agonized cry.

"Who did this to him?" Coppin moaned aloud, powerless to do anything else. "Who gave the lad the Sight so soon?"

Then came a small, familiar voice, so much like memory, but not. *Sweyn. Sweyn. Dinna' come to me, Sweyn. No' yet, love. She needs ye.*

And in the strength of that faded voice a moment of perfect clarity settled over Sweyn, but not in the present, in the past, to a day many weeks ago, when he walked up the path to Dundubh Cottage for the first time and heard the soft voice of a raven-haired girl singing alone in the apple grove.

*In green glens where flower*
*herbs of bluebell and shrubs of rose,*
*the Lady in her summer bower*
*suffers ne'er when the cold wind blows.*

And that memory was followed by another moment of magic—a different, powerful kind of magic, when a shunned changeling girl danced with him near a midsummer fire, her head upon his shoulder, her night-black locks smelling of the flowers of the forest.

Caitlin.

And then all the missing time, all the forgotten moments, which one not true-seeing cannot hope to recall or to bear, found their place within him and settled. And Sweyn came to understand that reality was indeed far deeper and stranger and eerier, and more wonderful and mysterious than he had ever before dared dream. Than he ever would have let himself believe. And now that he came face to face with that truth, he learned of himself that he could make peace with it.

He slipped his arms from before his face. Coppin knelt before him, chewing his lip, pulling at his beard, his eyes great blue saucers.

He peered into Sweyn's eyes, saw Sweyn looking lucidly back at him.

"No' mad?" Coppin dared ask the fates. "No' dead?"

Sweyn shook his head. "Still here, Coppin," he said. "Still here."

Coppin closed his eyes. His head drooped and he breathed a long, shuddering sigh of relief. So much, Sweyn's life and all the lives on the Island, had rested upon the outcome of that moment. Then he lifted his head and spoke gently to Sweyn. "We would have given ye more time to come to understanding, to make the gift less hard. We dinna' believe ye could bear the truth so soon."

But Sweyn said, "What are you?"

"Lad, I believe ye know in yer heart the truth of it. It is too late to deny."

"Faeries," Sweyn said. "This is an island of faeries."

Coppin shook his head. "No, no' entirely. The folk of Man-by-the-Sea are mortals like yerself."

"But you're not. You're a faerie. Now I understand how you could appear in Raleigh McCavitt's journal, and elsewhere in the Island's old history."

"In time we would have told ye," Coppin said. "After ye had had time to grow comfortable with guiding the Island, and settled into its mysteries. When we were sure it was safe for ye to learn it. But ye have no' been like any outside blood come into the O'Shees before. You were dogged determined to pierce our veils, and we feared for ye." He placed both his leathery hands on Sweyn's shoulders then, looked him in the eye, and demanded angrily, "Who did this to ye, lad? Who risked all and gave ye the Sight?"

Sweyn was surprised at Coppin's sudden and uncharacteristic vehemence, but he told him nothing.

Coppin turned away from Sweyn, fast as a cat, his fists clenched. "Some unseelie thing, I'll wager. Something that would have the end of the Pact for its own designs."

But Sweyn was not yet ready to deal with such complexities as pacts and the relationships between seelie and unseelie. He was still absorbing the truth of the most basic things. "Who are you?" he said to Coppin.

Coppin turned back to face him. "Ye know my true name already. I have never hidden it from ye."

Sweyn shook his head. "No, Coppin. Beyond your name, who are you?"

Coppin held quiet a long time. Then he turned, took several steps away from Sweyn, and looked out into the wood. A light summer breeze blew through the slender birches, whispering secrets, and he began. "By the standards of my folk there are some questions never asked, some rules of etiquette never breached, some things never done. Mortals never thank. We never take gifts. Mortals never pry or spy. We never tell our secrets. And ye would ask for my history?" He began to laugh, a dry, ancient cackle like dead leaves rustling over the forest floor. "And why no', eh? I've forsaken nearly every way of my folk to serve this house so long. And so long I've been with the O'Shees I am sure I think half mortal myself by now. For I have been with the O'Shees since Dylan's days, and I saw to the keeping of the keeper of the valley of the Asrai, and after the Hundred Horsemen vanished I tended to the first O'Shee Laird of the wandering Company. I took care of the Lairds and their families all through the long, hard Binding Years, and through the great voyage to the New World, and during the wanderings when we sought for a place in the North American wilderness to call our home. And I've kept the Cottage since the whole lot of us settled this Island, this last hidden place we know of where the old enchantment flows true and deep and pure. And ye ask who I am?"

He leaned over, whispered in Sweyn's ear: "A Nis, I am."

"A Nis, a Nis," Sweyn repeated, searched his memory, could find no knowledge of the word, until a near forgotten story came to mind, told him one night by Eilwen as they lay abed in their home in Glacier Falls. The memory was faint, whispered in the wee hours before dawn. He had heard it half asleep, spoken in one of Eilwen's rare wistful moments when she waxed nostalgic for home. She said her folk had tales of Nisses, friendly sprites who kept hearth and home for the families of decent folk. They bided only among those families who honored the Old Ways, and even then only the luckiest folk ever kept them about very long.

"A Nis," Sweyn said. "A brownie. A helper spirit."

Coppin shook his head. "No' a spirit. Spirits have no solid body in the green world. A creature of the land of Faerie, which is joined to but apart from this green world."

Just then recollection came upon Sweyn, why he had come out here calling for Donald, and the urgency Broom had pressed upon him. He found his feet, stood up. He kept his balance more surely this time, steadiness increasing with his willingness to accept what he Saw. "Where's Donald?" he barked.

Coppin looked suddenly nervous again. He looked like a schoolboy who had been caught in the middle of a bad deed.

Sweyn articulated each following word so it fell from his lips as if it were a whole sentence. "Coppin! Where. Is. Donald?"

Coppin looked off into the wood, then down at his feet. "Donald is no' here. He heard rumors. He gathered things. He sent the hands home, except for some who are his trusted friends. And he went into the wood."

"Coppin, look at me!" Coppin turned to face the tall seaman. "No riddles, no things half said. Speak clearly. Where is Donald? Why isn't he here?"

"I warned Caitlin no' to go to Midsummer. I warned her beware of mortal folk. I know she is no' quite real, and soon must fade, but I would no' see her suffer more than she must."

"Coppin!" Sweyn yelled.

The Nis flinched. "The changeling burned her hand on iron, Sweyn. The dowager saw. Rumors have spread. It was thought a changeling could no' be destroyed till they faded on their own, having no life within them, but if she can be hurt by iron, she is weakening. The Tylwyth enchantment that made her is failing, and Donald has gone hunting her."

Sweyn dropped to one knee, put both hands on Coppin's shoulders and held him close, looking into an alien face he could scarcely read for truth, into eyes with no humanity in them. "What do you mean, Coppin? Why is Donald hunting Caitlin? Damn, man, she's his daughter!"

But Coppin shook his head. "No, Sweyn, ye must understand. Stretch yer mind, and listen, for ye have the Sight now! If ye dwell in denial, it will cost ye dear. The Caitlin ye know from the apple grove, the one who sings sometimes to the Apple Man's harp, she is no' Donald's daughter. She is stone and twig and moonlight, no more. She is a changeling!"

He recalled a passage from Oak Peg's enigmatic letter to Eilwen:

> The father has taken to hunting Caitlin again and pursues her often into the Guardwood. He swears he will never give up though there is no hope.

The passage made him shiver. He said, "Even if she is a changeling, why would Donald hunt her? I've met the man. He's a descent enough fellow."

"That he is, true. But loss makes craven a true heart, they say. And hope denied brings bitterness. And such ache and bitterness as he has known can make even the best man dangerous." Then Coppin wailed, "Oh, ye canna' understand the ways of the Tylwyth Teg so soon, nor what Donald intends!"

Sweyn squeezed his shoulders and made the little man look into his eyes, keeping him focused. "So explain it to me."

He shook his head. "No' I. A task for Oak Peg, that."

Sweyn shook him. "Coppin! Now! Tell me!"

Coppin fidgeted and glanced away from him, gazed into the green shadows of the Ogham wood where the hearts of all faerie folk find comfort, even domestic sorts like Nisses.

"Coppin!"

Coppin was finding it harder and harder to resist Sweyn's will, even though Oak Peg had direly warned him not to speak of what he knew. They could not afford to lose Sweyn in the wildwood in a futile quest for the changeling, or in a confrontation with Donald, so close to the expiration of the Pact. But it was in the nature of serving sprites to serve, after all, and Coppin was long sworn to this family's service. Coppin shook off Sweyn's hands and stepped back from him, and at last he told Sweyn the rest of the truth.

"Ye must understand, normally a changeling is an inferior thing. Only an enchanted puppet, it has no real life, and a few years after it comes into a household it merely expires, like a lamp that runs out of oil. And changelings are rarely if ever fair. Poor imitations of the livestock and bairns they replace, they are, bearing the shriveled appearance of the dried winter mushrooms sequestered by squirrels in the nooks of trees. These uncouth things are what the Tylwyth Teg have left in exchange for mortal bairns since the eldest times, for it is the code of the Tylwyth Teg never to take a thing unless something like it is left in exchange. According to their fey logic, the quality of what is left is no' an issue, only that what is left is in the likeness of what is taken.

"But the Tylwyth Teg would no' treat the descendent of Raleigh McCavitt in the common way, nor a lady of the O'Shee house. So they poured all their craft into this changeling bairn and wrought a thing the likeness of which has never before been fashioned. They gathered the finest of the forest, the juice of rowan berries for red blood, the sap of milkweed for skin, fibers of raven feathers to weave into hair, and aquamarine ocean drops mingled with starlight for eyes. These they bound with moonlight and songs of bards, and what emerged from their craft was a perfect changeling, one that would last and grow and walk among mortal folk in the very likeness of a damsel.

"But, as ye know, their clever creation dinna' deceive Gwenllyan. No' for a moment. Wise in the ways of Faerie are the O'Shee folk. She knew as soon as she found the changeling bairn in her own right lass' crib they had no' done as she asked. She was devastated. Her sorrow burned her and in time she revealed the whole sorry affair to her husband, Elphin, and it was no' long after he left his family and the Island forever. Gwenllyan herself perished only a few years later, brought low by a broken heart. As for Donald, he blamed the Tylwyth for all the tragedy, and he swore to avenge himself against them and regain his daughter. Only Eilwen dinna' understand what had come to pass. I protected her from it. But that was to change.

"Many years later, one day when the changeling child and little Eilwen played in the wood together, they came across a treewife of the Tylwyth Teg. She was tending a sickling oak of the Guardwood and setting her healing spells upon it. Eilwen was lovely and charming, and she had no fear of the faerie folk of the Island, and this charmed the treewife. In a moment of forgetfulness, the treewife remarked that there was concern among the Tylwyth for Eilwen's true sister who resided with them in their twilit realm. She seemed distant somehow, the treewife said, unable to find gladness or sorrow, and this greatly concerned the Tylwyth Teg, for always before the bairns they took to live among them found great joy. The treewife had meant only to give Eilwen a bit of news of her sister, perhaps ask her advice what to do for the mortal girl in their care. But it was a foolish deed, for it was in that moment what little remained of the O'Shee family finally collapsed. Eilwen fled the wood and the changeling girl, whom she now understood to be only an imitation of her true sister, lost in the Tylwyth realm. From that day she shunned even the Island itself. And, as ye well know, she left us soon after.

"After her departure, the changeling girl had no one, for no mortal folk will bear the presence of a changeling. They are the payment for faerie-nicked children, ye see, and no' good luck to be among. And even most faerie folk would no' have her among them, for faeries seek the company of living things, and changelings possess only the semblance of life. So the changeling girl fled into the enchanted forest, and would have been all alone, but she found pity in some. Beyond Dundubh's borders she was tended by a solitary sprite who lived in the apple grove. The Apple Man fed her the best of his trees, and gave her the sweet sap of spring birches to drink. I myself could no' bear the lovely thing's fate, and I left her bread and milk and honey when I set out the evening plates. And I saw to it soft, warm blankets were left in the forest for her. And on cold nights I insisted she at least sleep in the barn among the faerie sheep who would protect her, if she would no' come into the house, which she never did again. Oak Peg sent herbed cheese for the girl, and ordered her servant to build her a small dwelling of willow logs. The changeling girl had no soul, but we would no' see her suffer either.

"But Donald's determination never waned. His daughter, his own right Caitlin, was lost to him in Faerie, and the knowledge of it drove him mad with grief. Often he went to the deepest wood seeking her, but there was no hope he would find her.

"Now the Tylwyth Teg have a code. If a changeling is found out and revealed for what it is before its magic fades, it is an unjust trade and they must return the mortal bairn to the rightful parents. But the changeling Caitlin, who folk took to calling No-Kin, was powerfully wrought; she had some wit within her, a mind of her own. Finding her out was no' enough to end her. Nor was it believed she could be slain, for changelings have no life within them to end. While their enchantment lasts, they are as enduring as the immortal Tylwyth Teg who create them. So Donald had no way to do away with the changeling and regain his right child, though he tried. While Eilwen was a child and thought No-Kin her sister, his attacks were secretive. But when Eilwen left us he became openly belligerent, and often hunted No-Kin deep into the forest, seeking her with axes of cold iron, but she was clever and always eluded him.

"But always No-Kin pined for mortal company, for changelings are made to dwell among mortal folk. And in her desperation she dreamt that if she could sing as sweetly as a bard, folk might accept her. So she practiced year after year to the Apple Man's harping, and dreamed of having the courage to appear at a festival and win the people's favor. But she was skittish as a deer, and she never found the courage.

"And so the sad years passed, and in time—for it is the way with changelings— her enchantment began to fade. The process was long and hard to watch. For many moons her strength ebbed, returning to the forest from which it was taken, and as she faded she withdrew, even from Oak Peg and myself who had always looked after her. She brooked only the company of the Apple Man, for he had always been closest to her, and charmed her with his harping.

"The sorry tale was, then, almost over.

"But then ye came, Sweyn, and when ye looked upon her she dinna' see trepidation in yer eyes. Ye alone of mortal folk dinna' shun her. Ye gave her the courage to appear among mortals. And then ye yerself accompanied her to Midsummer. It was there she burned her hand upon cold iron. It was a sign. Her enchantment was failing, and she was almost done.

"The dowager saw it and gossiped. Donald heard the tale and seized upon it. He has taken men armed with cold iron, and they will try to track her down.

"Oak Peg sent the changeling into the wood to flee from him, for we would see no violence come upon her. But perhaps Donald will find her. And perhaps better if he does. She has only days left. But even if he succeeds and gets his own right daughter back, this tale is bound to no happy end, for the true Caitlin has dwelt in the Tylwyth realm too long. She will pine for Faerie until she has withered and dried up and perished like an unwatered flower."

Sweyn was for a long time speechless, bewildered by Coppin's tale. But then his eyes flashed hot. He glared at the Nis, appalled. "So that was it? The best you and Oak Peg could do was send the girl into the woodland to fend for herself?" He stood up suddenly, anger flushing his features. "You're no better than killers yourselves!"

That made Coppin flinch. "Now dinna' go giving such names. Ye must understand, she is a changeling, Sweyn. She is no' truly alive!"

"I danced with her. She smiled and laid her head on my shoulder and I held her, Coppin! She was warm and breathing. She was as alive as anything I have ever felt."

"Sweyn, she does that because that is her enchantment. She imitates life, but she is no more alive than your reflection in the water."

"Says you."

Frustrated with Sweyn's refusal to see, Coppin threw his hands out to either side. One more time he pleaded with him. "Sweyn, dinna' put yer heart in her. Wanting her to be real will no' make it so. She will fade, Sweyn! Changelings dinna' last! She will wink out like a candle flame, and leave ye heartbroken all over again. Do ye think ye could bear it, man?"

Sweyn shook his head, clenched his fists repeatedly. Finally, he declared, "I will not let this happen."

He turned and started that moment for the wildwood.

Coppin's eyes became round and wild. He grabbed Sweyn, pulled at him, blocked his way. Despite his small size, he was incredibly strong, and managed to hold the stout seaman back. His voice racing, he blurted, "No! Ye canna' follow there! No mortal may enter the wildwood, no' even the Laird. How could ye hope to survive, ye who dinna' even have the craft to walk the Guardwood?"

Sweyn pried Coppin's hands off his arms, though it took an immense effort on his part. "I don't pretend to understand any of this, but I know both the villagers and your kind need me for some reason. Need me very desperately. I doubt, if that's the case, I have anything to fear in the wildwood."

But Coppin shook his head hard and quick, his eyes bright as moons. "Oh, no. Oh, no, no, no, no. Ye dinna' know what ye say. There are things in those woods, unseelie things, as would no' have an O'Shee on the Island. Walking into there would be as good as setting yerself in their maws. And there are ghosts in there, where the enchantment is so thick the veils between the worlds are worn away. Some of them are very wicked. They have no' been able to accept their passing and move on, and those ye must fear, for in the wildwood they may become real enough to do ye harm. And there are faeries, faeries like the wisps, who will mean ye no ill thing or good, but ye canna' bide in their presence, for their kin and mortal kin are too alien one to another. And ye dinna' even have the lore to avoid those kind. Listen to me, Sweyn. Oh, if ever ye will, do so now, for if ye go into the wildwood ye will surely never come out again."

And he pleaded with Sweyn to look for wisdom and not act rashly. He was so earnest, and so desperate. He quite literally fell to his knees and begged, and that was a thing Sweyn never thought to see from the proud little man. But Coppin's plain fear forced Sweyn to recall clearly his last foray into the wood, and the wonders and terrors he had encountered there. Most clearly came the memory of a malignant tree, a great elder that surely would hunt him the moment he stepped beyond the boundaries of the Guardwood. And with the recollection, deep inside he knew Coppin spoke true. Though he was desperate to be after Caitlin right now, if he marched off foolheartedly he would not last a night, and that would do her no good at all. With that realization, the strength seemed to ebb away from him. He slumped against a tree, feeling powerless. He was a seaman, not a woodsman, after all.

But he would not give up. Surrender was not in Sweyn.

He said to Coppin, "Show me another way."

\*\*\*\*\*\*\*\*\*\*

And so Starry Sea bounded over the rolling waves, and a company of faerie folk swam beneath her hull to see his way was calm and swift. The wind was fair and true throughout the passage to Oak Peg's cove, and sometimes, when he stole a sidewise glance to his prow, he almost saw the form of a hairy, burly man sitting curled up there, looking always into the direction of the wind, fingers dancing over a small reed pipe played carefully and quietly, a song for the elementals of the air. It seemed like Broom. And with the perfect wind and a near flat sea, he made it the full ten miles around the Island in just an hour and a quarter, the fastest his proud vessel had ever sailed. A quarter mile before the mouth of the cove he hurriedly furled his sails and pulled the chute over the gennaker. Under a bare mast the iron genny propelled him the last of the way. Starry Sea clove glass water into the cove, and there in the middle of it he dropped anchor to the sandy bottom.

\*\*\*\*\*\*\*\*\*

Oak Peg's cottage huddled serene and mysterious beneath a canopy of lofty boughs. The "oak witch" Broom had called her, and through the windows of his newly Sighted eyes, the appellation made all the more sense now, for it is said that a dwelling reflects the personality of the occupant, and Oak Peg's cottage was nothing less than the very embodiment of forest mystery. Green shadows lay over the whole of the place, except in the stone-fenced courtyard where Oak Peg grew her precious herbs. There, a preternatural shaft of golden sun never wavered.

The brook stones of which the cottage was made were stained green in the forest light, and ivy grew up and around each plate glass window, so that the house itself seemed to be some great tangled shrub that sprang out of the earth. Indeed, if one were to spy the cottage from afar, the place might be mistaken for a mound of stone and snarled trees, for the structure existed in harmony with the sylvan setting. Around the outer base of the courtyard wall grew flowers of brilliant beauty, shooting stars and delicate bluebells, monkshood and pale lupine. Numerous butterflies visited the blossoms, great delicate things the size of a man's hand, with sable wings traced with knotwork spirals of luminous sky blue. Sweyn was no entomologist, but he did not believe this preternaturally beautiful breed was of this earth—what faerie kin called the green world.

Sweyn approached the cottage and without pause stepped through the iron gates, now cast wide open. Within he found a small assembly waiting for him, Oak Peg and Coppin, who must have run all the way from Dundubh in order to inform Oak Peg of the day's events before Sweyn arrived. And also Broom was there, which surprised him somewhat, for he did not think Broom was getting along with Oak Peg and Coppin, given their differences of opinion on Caitlin.

The three of them were seated at a table of rough hewn lumber in the center of the courtyard. Off in a corner, not far from the small shack where Oak Peg aged her herbed cheeses, a creature not dissimilar to Coppin worked quietly at a heap of brook stone joined with mortar to form a small, stout table with a great concavity set in its middle. In the concavity, boiled acorns were piled and the Nis used a rounded stone to pound them into mast, the flour of oak, an ancient Celtic delicacy.

Sweyn gazed upon the new Nis. Here he was looking at something magical, something fey, something which only yesterday he would have sworn was impossible. He doubted the sensation of wonder and trepidation would ever wear off.

Oak Peg interrupted his thoughts. "He's preparing to make bread for ye to take on yer long journey, for I dinna' reckon we can stop ye, though we shall try our utmost."

He turned his attention to Oak Peg and found himself surprised at what he saw, for given the accounts of her appearance among the Company all throughout their long history, and the obvious high regard given her by both mortal folk and faerie kin, he had expected some queenly faerie thing, perhaps like one of the brook ladies. But she appeared as nothing other than a withered old woman to his Sighted eyes, though sparkles of enchantment sometimes glittered about her like a subtle aura of power. A thought ate at the back of his mind: She is as mortal as myself. Of course, it could not be. The crone was ageless; she had been with the company since Dylan's day, more than fifteen centuries. But there was no time to give thought to it now.

He said to the oak witch, "You have a lot to answer for. You brought me here against my will. You tried to trick me into becoming this Laird of yours. Yes, I've figured out that much. I don't pretend to understand how you did it, nor your reasons exactly—something to do with the Pact. But I know you, Oak Peg, are at the root of all my troubles. And now," he went on, pointing an accusing finger at her, "now you would let that girl die in the wood."

But Oak Peg addressed him smoothly, with a curious twinkle in her eye. "Ye've a keen mind, and it's something I should have taken more account of when I brought ye here. I have never seen a mortal take so quick to Island things and keep his wits or his life."

"Don't be too quick to level praise, Oak Peg," he retorted, "because I don't know frankly if I'll still be in my right mind when all this is through. To tell you the truth, I'm not sure I'm in my right mind now." He kept a wary eye on the old woman as he spoke. She seemed harmless, seated at the table sipping tea, but his instincts warned him otherwise. He continued. "But the flashbacks have gone. Since I got lost in the wood, they have been buried. All that is left in their place is a lament that swims round and round inside me. And a hell of a lot of anger. I can't say the anger wasn't always there. It's been there since Eilwen was murdered. But I've mostly been able to keep it in check."

"Aye," she said, and poured him a cup of tea, slid it across the wooden planks of the table to an empty place, a clear invitation that he should sit and join them. He regarded the cup warily. The old woman knew even more herblore than had Eilwen. Who knew what witch's brew she had laced it with. But Broom nodded, so slightly it was barely perceptible, and Sweyn had begun to trust Broom, the only being on this rock who had not tried to deceive him. So Sweyn sat in the empty place, though he did not touch the tea. Oak Peg went on. "That's the trouble with faerie magic, it's no more perfect than faeries, who, for all their eldritch ways, are no more perfect than mortal folk. When ye went to the lake island of the Gwragedd, they sensed yer broken heart. They are goodhearted creatures, the ladies of the brooks and streams, and they took pity on ye and tried to heal ye as best they could. But in stoppering the one evil, they may have loosed another."

Coppin added, "Ye see, lad, when tinkering with a mortal soul, when one darkness is bound, another is loosed. Sometimes the other is lesser, sometimes no'."

"That's as clear as mud," Sweyn growled.

Oak Peg said, "Faerie magic heals well enough faerie blights and forest ills, but mortals are another thing entirely. Faerie and forest, both are things of nature, and their path is clear. But mortals are as complicated as their tangled cities. The Gwragedd spun enchantment to try to heal ye, but their weave was knotted by yer own complexity. And, indeed, ye are no simple being by any standard, Sweyn."

Sweyn continued to regard her, both dubious and perplexed.

She leaned forward, spoke as if addressing a slow child. "It means, ye daft laddy, they fixed one part and broke another."

"Ah," said Sweyn, "so I just get to discover a whole new way to go crazy."

Broom spoke now. To Sweyn's Sighted eyes, he seemed so much a wild thing it was counterintuitive to see him sitting with Coppin and Oak Peg at a table with a steaming cup of tea before him. It was like seeing a bear dine on wild honey in a fine china bowl with a spoon. "I've been tending mortal creatures many centuries now, wild animals and wandering lost children. Sometimes I have found they carry old and festering wounds that will no' heal. But if the infection is stopped the wound may mend itself."

Sweyn pondered that, and finally said, "I don't get you."

Coppin said impatiently, "He's saying there's hope for ye, lad!"

Oak Peg said, "The thing is, the healing enchantments dinna' create wounds. They are no' so cruel as a surgeon's knife. If the puss of one wound has been cleansed only to allow another to erupt, the other wound must have been there afore, only hidden." She gazed at Sweyn, her eyes penetrating. "What lay beneath your waking nightmares?" she probed.

Fists and blood. The stink of urine and the bittersweet taste of vengeance. A body falling like meat to hard concrete, and the pounding of running steps in the steamy darkness. A memory that haunted more cruelly than any malicious ghost, more hatefully than any baneful demon.

This was not a place he wanted to go, leastwise before these people—things— he could no more trust than his own mad heart. Better to let it eat him up in darkness than spew it here. So he shoved it down, down so deep even cobwebs could not brush upon it. Then Sweyn faced Coppin and Oak Peg, his face hard as stone, and made his feelings plain. "You've used me as a pawn in some game I don't understand. It wasn't like I was doing anything particularly great with my life, but it was my life, and I resent that! So stay out of my head, you understand? Right now, all that concerns me is the girl. I . . . Broom and I will not let her die in that wood."

"Pursue her or leave her," said Oak Peg flatly, "the changeling will fade. The enchantment which binds her together has all but waned. Nothing can stop the end from coming, whether by Donald's cold iron knife or the passage of a few more days, it is all the same."

"How can you say that? It's not the same! I don't believe it!" Sweyn shouted at her.

"I know," she said, her voice softening. "And it is for that reason we tried to keep ye from her. Changelings are superb mimics when they are well crafted, and there has never before been a changeling the like of Caitlin No-Kin. Thus, we knew ye'd see in her what ye lost in Eilwen—for it is the changeling's enchantment to appeal. Yet she is no' real and she must fade, and that could only leave ye with a broken heart in the end. And another wound so grievous might be beyond even the power of the Gwragedd's poems to mend."

Sweyn began a retort, but it faltered before the words left his throat, for the full weight of what Oak Peg said stopped him. She was implying he was in love with the raven haired girl of the wood. Yet, charmed as he was by the girl, he hardly knew her. Could he harbor such deep feelings with so little experience of her? Or was it true that what he cared for was not Caitlin, but the reflection of Eilwen he saw in her?

He could easily see how alike they were.

Caitlin was, after all, Eilwen's sister. They had blood and history in common. They were both children of the Island, products of its strange culture. They both were raised here, in this enchanted wood, and called Dundubh Cottage their home. They both shared a love of Celtic music and dance. They were both full of the fire of life, and so much spirit they glowed. They shared a tenderness that made them at once vulnerable and endearing. And they both carried such sadness within them, yet even in its depths they were heroically resilient.

They even resembled one another, of roughly the same size and build. Caitlin smiled in the way of Eilwen, with a dimple at her chin and lips that turned up slightly at the corners, like a naughty child on the verge of a prank. And she possessed Eilwen's winsome beauty, which she wore unawares.

For such qualities, he could only admire both women.

But did he care for Caitlin only because he saw Eilwen in her?

No, he decided quickly.

Eilwen was in her, it was undeniable. But there was more to Caitlin than just the reflection of another, of that he was certain.

Where Eilwen had been red-haired sunlight, Caitlin was midnight stars. Where Eilwen was a daughter of the Cottage and mortal kin, and could almost pass for normal in the outside world, Caitlin embodied the mysteries of the Island. A child of the enchanted forest, Caitlin lived half wild and fey as Broom. Caitlin was full of faerie song and eldritch lore. She lived alone in a tiny cottage in the Guardwood, like a fairytale princess who must keep the secret of her existence.

And the thought struck him: And why is her existence secret?

Why did Eilwen keep her sister a secret? Why did she let even him think Caitlin dead?

*Iron burned her.*

And iron would not burn Eilwen's real sister, for her real sister would be as mortal as Eilwen.

The color drained from Sweyn's face. He had held the cold spoon himself, the spoon a child had held before him, the spoon which had seared the forest girl's flesh.

*Iron burned her!*

Caitlin, the Caitlin he knew, was not mortal kin. How could he deny what he had seen? And the faerie folk said there was no hope for her, for neither was she faerie kin. She was No-Kin, a changeling, and nothing more.

And yet he must accept that he loved her.

Though she would vanish like smoke in the wind.

The strength drained from him. It seemed something wrapped around his heart and squeezed. He recalled flames upon dark waters, the night Eilwen drowned in a shroud of sailcloth, and there was nothing he could do. This feeling was like that. It made him dizzy, nauseous.

Broom, Coppin and Oak Peg watched him, concern etched in their features. Then Oak Peg leaned forward across the table, took his hand in her dry and withered claw. She said gently, "Ye see now, do ye no'? She is a changeling, Sweyn, and naught can be done to save her. But if ye go into the wildwood after her, we may lose ye too."

He withdrew his hand from hers and sat silent for a long time, struggling to accept what she was telling him. Some part of him told him it would be best if he did. But he could not. Whatever Caitlin was, whether she would fade in a day or a century, he could not find it in himself to leave her in that wilderness alone, with a murderous man in pursuit.

After a while, he drew a deep breath, as if drawing in his strength, and the color slowly returned to him. He sat up straight then, looked Oak Peg squarely in the eyes as he addressed her. "What does it matter where I go?" he said. "The Company has survived fifteen centuries, and they did quite well on this Island long before I ever arrived. Why is it so important I be here?"

"We have always had a Laird."

"Oak Peg, it's more than that."

"These are a people of tradition. Tradition requires a figurehead."

He nodded. "I see." Slowly he stood up. "Traditions survive. They go beyond individuals, and if the Company needs a figurehead that much, they'll find someone else to believe in besides me. They will have to. I belong to the sea." He turned to leave. Broom watched, nodding so slightly no one else could have perceived it.

Coppin stood up suddenly. "Ye canna' leave us, Sweyn!"

Without turning back to face him, Sweyn said, "I've lost my first love who came from this Island, and maybe I've lost another who will end on this Island. I can take no more bitter memories from this place. Find a new Laird."

"Please," moaned Coppin, his voice constricted.

Sweyn took two, three steps from the table. Firmly, without turning, he said, "Then be truthful." Then he whirled on Coppin and Oak Peg. "Tell me why it is so important I stay! Who is Arn'na'sagt'puch?"

Upon hearing the name, Coppin glowered at Broom. Broom cringed, as if expecting to be struck, but Sweyn doubted it was Coppin the burly fellow was afraid of. If anything, he feared Oak Peg who sat composed but glaring at Broom. "No mystery how ye know the name," she said after a minute. "Only that our secrets should flow to the new Laird, who is delicate, so easily. Especially with so much at stake." She spoke slowly, enunciating each word emphatically, and Broom winced with each syllable. Clearly, Oak Peg knew who had given Sweyn the Sight and told him so much.

"Don't be angry with Broom," he said. "He is a caretaker in his nature, and I doubt it is in him to let something perish."

Surprisingly, that brought a smile to Oak Peg's lips. She turned her eyes to him. "Now those sound like the words of an O'Shee."

But he said, "They sound like the words of a man who doesn't want to see anyone hurt." He stepped forward, leaned on the table, both hands open and spread on the oak beams. "Here's the deal. Why am I so important? Who is Arn'na'sagt'puch? The truth, or I sail away this very night."

There was a great span of silence in which only the barest breeze soughed through the trees. Oak Peg and Coppin studied Sweyn to see if he was true. He returned their gaze without flinching, though it was hard, for there was such ancient strength in their eyes, strength like the roots of mountains, especially in the eyes of the oak witch. But Sweyn would not back down, it was plain to see. He meant to keep his threat. And at length it was Coppin who spoke. At first he spoke plainly, or as plainly as Coppin knew how. But in time his speech became a tale, and his tale became a yarn. Stories within stories—myth and legend wove the very fabric of this people, and Sweyn realized he had no hope to understand them apart from their tales. So he sat, and he was patient, and he listened.

"Ye already know much," Coppin began, "though in bits and pieces. Ye know we came from across the sea, from out of the lands of the Old World. And a ragged band of folk we were, too, weary to death from generations of hard wandering and searching after the Ogham seeds. But those seeds were our quest, for we were charged with an oath to the Lady Elidurydd since Dylan's days with gathering them, in hopes of restoring a remnant of the world of elder days. And among the mortals of the Company there was also an ancient witch of dubious origin. It seemed she had always been with them, and she sits across from ye now. And there was myself also, and as ye can plainly see, I am no mortal. A sprite I am, of a most unusual sort, for none other of the faerie kin of the West can travel far save I. And I may do so because long ages past I bound myself to a house of mortals rather than the land, the very O'Shee house of whom ye have also become part, Sweyn. And as long as I serve them, I may go wither I will.

"Now the Company carried their precious Ogham seeds in three chests. Ye have read of them in Raleigh McCavitt's journal. These seeds were taken from all the enchanted trees, shrubs and herbs which correspond to the ancient and magical alphabet of the Celts—their Ogham. And within each kind of seed the spirit of a faerie race slept, dreaming of a new life in a new land. It was only in this way they could make a journey, ye see, for they are bound to their land and canna' depart it. But in the form of seeds, there was hope they might take root and flourish again, someday, in some new soil.

"In truth, the Western clans of faerie folk were fleeing, and the Company it was who were helping them. Carrying them within their seeds. They had to flee, for the places where faerie magic may abound are wild, untamed and green, free of mortal kin's cold iron and carved rock, free of noisy cities and roads which cut the earth like ribbons of frozen, dead stone. In the Old World such truly wild places had become rare. Mortal folk were everywhere, and swallowing up every last lonely place where faerie kin may dwell.

"Now, with the passing of the Old World's wild places, the old green enchantment faded. And in each place it failed, so vanished another bit of Faerie. Ye see, Faerie is a world unto itself, but it exists overlaid upon the green world, and draws its enchantment from the same wellspring. Cold iron and cut stone injure that enchantment. Bleed it away. But the green world is a mortal domain, and it may persist, though lessened. But Faerie is all green magic and living dreams, and without a spring of enchantment it withers like a parched sapling.

"Now among mortals, when a part of the green world is hurt—as when disaster strikes—ye may flee. But Faerie was meant to be timeless, and its folk have never developed the power to flee their eternal places. So when their world withers, they wither with it. As the wild places vanished, so parts of Faerie simply ceased to exist. And when they failed, so did the faerie folk abiding there. Only their spirits went off into the Dreaming West, never to return.

"By the time of the Hundred Horsemen, only pockets of Faerie remained, and only a handful of faerie folk within them. The Company found those pockets over the centuries, and took it upon themselves to safeguard the vanishing folk. These were the Binding Years."

*********

"Long had the Company wandered, following Oak Peg, their ancient witch guide and counselor to their Lairds. Oak Peg led them all across the New World, searching for the right land. But the wildest were too cold and drear, or too hot and dry. The best were soon to be filled by men not devoted to the Old Ways, and the threads of magic winding through those places would be cut and fail. Even in the New World it was proving hard to find a good place for the rebirth of the Ogham wood.

"But the sea god, Manannan, appeared to Oak Peg one day when she scryed in a clear pool, at her wits end and desperate for direction. There, he showed her an Island off the western coast of North America, far in the north. Isolated and rugged, it would be long overlooked. And enchantment was thick as mist over that isle, so thick as to shield it from the notice of ordinary men. Oh, it was part of the green world, sure enough. It could be seen if a ship passed near, for it was no' in Faerie, after all. But it was a place as could keep its secrets. Only eldritch folk might give it a second glance. Safe and distant and green, it was perfect.

"But the trip was hard going and fraught with perils. Many trials the Company faced in their last trek to the very limits of the West, yet the design of the geas grew clearer as they approached their goal. The Company was drawn to the Island, in fulfillment of the sea god's call.

"Now the New World had its own faerie creatures. Made for this land, they were well suited to it, but since the coming of so many colonists out of Europe, even they were finding it difficult to find good places. The uninhabited Island, with its rich threads of magic, was a haven for them, an eldritch cradle to nurture those magical folk. Still, for the New World faeries, there were many places they could thrive on the continent, for they had a power we dinna'. They could go and attach themselves to any land. But for the Old World faeries, who dinna' bear any travel nor change so easily, this was the last good place for the Ogham wood, and our last chance. All hope depended on attaining the Island.

"But every land has its guardian. And the guardian of this place was strange and powerful indeed. She ignored our appeals, and in the face of extinction we even considered challenging her by force and magical battle for the Island. But in truth we were tired and worn, and reduced to but a few. We had no hope of overcoming her. And all would surely have been lost, if no' for one who was no' even, then, of our number.

*********

Morning found an exhausted Lieutenant Raleigh McCavitt asleep in the beached tender. The stern quarter of the boat was half in the water and waves rocked it gently. But the bow of the little boat was solidly grounded. His head rocked back and forth, moving in rhythm to the rolling water that sloshed, moment to moment, against the transom.

A light tapping at his face brought his weary mind to slow wakefulness. A wizened little man stood upon the grey sand, Coppin, looking at him with profound concern. "Are ye hail?" he said.

Raleigh nodded and the little man closed his eyes, breathed a silent word of gratitude. Raleigh was sure that whatever god he had spoken it to had not been the god he knew. But a cup of something warm was handed him, and he forgot about it. He took the cup and drank the warm liquid: tea with honey. It revived him and he stretched luxuriously, yawning like a lion. There came the tinkling sound of girlish giggles and he looked round about him, spotting nearest several young ladies in latter adolescence who gazed brazenly upon him one moment, then looked away coyly when he met their stares. And then he became aware that others were nearby, dozens, watching him in silent awe. He recognized them immediately. The strange folk who called themselves the Company.

A great bear of a man stepped toward him. He had a round face and a full black beard, and eyes like bright coals. He studied the weary seaman up and down, scrutinizing, then offered a hand and helped him up out of the little tender. The moment Raleigh stood upon his feet the big man threw his arms around him and gave him a bone-cracking hug, thanking him repeatedly for saving their beloved chests. This was Bran O'Shee, and he was then Laird of the Company. With the expression of such hearty gratitude, Lieutenant McCavitt wondered all the more what marvelous treasure must lie in those three crates he had salvaged from the doomed Mont Royal.

On the morning tide the flotsam came to the beach, a queer great lot of it, as if every crate and barrel that had been on the ship had had the good luck to be shaken out in the storm and driven into the bay. Most of this should have been dragged down by the ship into the sea, he knew, and he could not understand it. But the folk seemed to accept it as natural that "things in the sea" should aid them, and he helped them get the gear safely onto land. There were barrels of grain and seed, crates of tools, containers of linens and axes and even flintlocks. Supplies were not abundant, but with hard and careful work, there was enough here, perhaps, to start a colony.

That night they threw a small feast in honor of Lieutenant Raleigh and named him one of their number. And the very next morning, before even the aftereffects of the feast had worn off, the villagers proceeded into the rainforest of towering cedars, intent upon their work. They had to build, to make fields, to sow seed. Time was of the essence. It would be long and long before another ship came by this far-flung way and the bitter Canadian winter was approaching. If it found them out before they were set to weather it, things would go sorely, whatever their stocks.

On the very first day seventeen men proceeded into the forest at dawn's first light. They were to scout out the land and determine where to build a ring of cabins and clear the first fields. While they were at this task Oak Peg, with Bran O'Shee and Coppin, gathered herbs and spoke charms and took living wood from the islands indigenous trees and shrubs. Come twilight, they set the wood into a great triangle and heaped the herbs within. The triangle was built with holes in all three sides, facing each of the cardinal directions. A great fire was lit and the fire sent up fragrant smoke, and she spoke charms in words Lieutenant Raleigh did not know, words that had the feel of Scot and Welsh and Man in them. Raleigh blanched, sure now this hag was a witch. What manner of folk had he cast in his allegiance with?

Yet the fire lasted only moments and quickly died, as if smothered. The folk murmured greatly at this. Clearly, they believed it to be some very bad omen.

When the night had grown full dark only fourteen of the seventeen men had returned. The people made brands and tried to set flame to them, but no flame would light. The darkness fell and not a fire dotted the camp, and no one but Coppin ventured into the darkness to look for the men. The Company was clearly afraid. They seemed to understand some devilry was at work, something Raleigh himself could not understand. All he could do was huddle with them in the close set tents and do what he could to keep spirits high. "The wood is only wet, soaked through with these endless rains," he told the folk. "The men will be found on the morrow. They are probably enjoying a roasted deer that luck brought across their path." But nothing lightened the fear of the Company. They knew things were at work in the forest, and its will was bent against them.

Come dawn Coppin returned, hollow eyed and trembling. He went straight to Oak Peg and spoke to her in secret, and only the Laird was allowed in their company. When the council ended, they were crestfallen. The folk of the Company saw the despair in their eyes, and it seemed as if all hope fled them. Some of the Company wept, others drowned their pain in their slim supply of ale. Some only sat and looked forlornly at the three chests. And on this day not even a party was dispatched to search for the three missing men.

Three more days passed in this way, and Lieutenant Raliegh could not understand the cause of the Company folk's despair. And every day wasted was another day closer to winter. The lieutenant, having some familiarity with these waters, knew it was unlikely any ship would be by to rescue them before the seasons turned, so he encouraged the folk lift and work, but the heart had gone out of them.

On the sixth day despair hung heavier still. Most of the folk would not even rise from their bedrolls. The lieutenant was not a superstitious man, but he was beginning to believe some dark curse had fallen over these people. Or the fear of a curse. They were some kind of gypsy folk, were they not, and it was said gypsies were a superstitious lot. He determined to get to the bottom of it and settle the matter, so he found Oak Peg and demanded the truth from her. "Is it the red man?" he demanded. "Does an enemy dwell here?"

Oak Peg answered. "No enemy, not as you would know. Yet I wish it were, for we would have a better chance against a mortal foe. A sprite dwells in the wood, and she has the appearance of an old woman. She wields terrible power and is the presence who guards this Island and all the sea surrounding, even beyond the shores of the mainland. She is angry that we have brought our legacy to her land, and would seed it without her permission first. She has banned us and so condemned the Company and our hope to a bitter end."

"Enough of this," thought Raleigh, and he set his face and determined his course. He went into the camp and took a cutlass and a pistol, a few balls and a little powder, and a little leathery jerked fish. He found Oak Peg again and said, "Whatever this terror is, it is better to face it and perish than to surrender and waste slowly away in winter." And he vanished into the rainforest. Neither Oak Peg nor the Company ever expected to see him again.

Fear set upon the lieutenant soon after he entered the forest. He felt eyes upon him, things watching him from the green folds. They tripped him in the shadows and pinched him when he fell. They would have borne him off to some clouded pool and drowned him, but he bore cold iron and burned away the shadows with his cutlass. He understood unearthly things pressed him. He saw eyes neither animal nor mortal in the thickets, and heard pipes playing pentatonic tunes in corners of the wood beyond sight. But he would not turn back. There lay no hope that way, even if only terror and doom lay before him. He pressed on.

He wandered for he did not know how long. Time seemed to have no meaning in the fey dark wood. Days merged into night and night into night and then it might be day again. Sometimes the moon shone, but never the phase one might expect.

It was after wandering like this a great long while, when weariness and hunger weighed upon him heavily, that he came to a sunlit glade which opened abruptly from the ancient rainforest. In the glade stood a crone. She was very tall, much taller than most men. And she was thin as a willow trunk, and when she moved she made a sound like the rustle of the breeze through broad-leafed trees. Her clothing was autumnal leaves stitched together with spider web. She was Arn'na'sagt'puch, and she regarded with surprise this lone mortal man who came to her with no magic and eyes full of ignorance and wonder, and only a small pistol and a sliver of iron blade to protect himself.

"Have you come to slay the forest warden?" she asked him.

He did not know what peril he faced, but he knew it was very great. He bowed respectfully and made no move for his weapons. "I have come to find the one who will not let the people on the western beach settle the land. Is it you?"

"Indeed, you have found the one you seek."

"I do not know what you are, but I perceive power within you. I ask only that you show them leniency, and allow them to build their hearths and homes, even if but for a season. If they cannot abide here, they will all take a ship from this Island when one passes. I give you my word I will see to it."

She regarded him sternly. "It took courage to pass the things that keep the rainforest, and more to face the Old Lady of the Wood. You I will let pass back the way you came, and I will order the things not to molest you. But your folk may not stay, and they must not build. They have shown no courtesy in storming my Island as they have."

He said, "Forgive them, Lady. I am sure they had no mean intention. Indeed, only a few days ago they tried to build a fire which I believe was meant to honor you."

"That may have been their purpose, but it comes too late. One does not ask to pass the threshold of his neighbor's longhouse after he has already bedded down with his neighbor's wife."

His Victorian prudence stunned by the analogy, the Lieutenant quickly recovered and said, "I doubt they would have come to your Island so rudely, Lady, had they a choice. But they were forced here abruptly by the wicked captain of the tall ship which brought them. The captain forced them here quickly in order to make off with their goods. He would have left them bereft and to die had not a storm destroyed his ship. They had the good fortune that many of their goods came with the tide to the beach, enough to keep them a short while."

And so Lieutenant Raleigh conversed with Arn'na'sagt'puch through the day and explained the sorry tale of the Company's landing on the Island. His tale touched her, and she agreed to dialogue with the leaders of the Company. So Oak Peg and Bran O'Shee were led to her by Raleigh. In the glade the Old Lady of the Wood heard the entreaty of the witch and Laird, and she took pity upon them.

"I will grant you this Island, our sacred Island, for an unnumbered span of years," she told them. "Plant your forest and save what of the Westernmost Tuath you can. This place shall be theirs, their last place, so long as they need refuge."

As for Raleigh, he had shown his courage in defying the black-hearted captain and saving the precious chests of seeds. He showed it again in saving Coppin from the salt sea when the Mont Royal went down. He did not know Coppin was a Nis—he did not have the Sight then—but he saw the terror in his eyes and that was enough to compel him to the little man's aid. And a good thing too it was for Coppin, for Nisses are immortal against all, and even immune to the touch of iron, yet simple brine will unmake them. And then Raleigh showed remarkable courage once more, coming alone among all the folk of the Company to face the Old Lady of the Wood, a New World sprite so great and terrible she was known by one name or another and feared by Native folk from Alaska to Oregon. And Arn'na'sagt'puch could be terrible, but she was not wantonly cruel. She could be wise and compassionate to the worthy. She conceived of the divisions of the Island to keep the balance between mortal and faerie folk, and she named Raleigh and all the McCavitt descendents as gillies over the Guardwood.

But when the other old sprites who had lived on the enchanted Island many long years heard of her concession to the refugees, they were outraged and threatened to unite and assail her. Arn'na'sagt'puch was powerful and none dared, but the threat was truly meant. The Old Lady knew she must set a Pact upon the refugees, a limit to give the old sprites hope they might one day return. Else a war between Native and Old World sprites was assured, and that would surely have been the doom of the Westernmost Tuath.

In the parley, the Old Lady had learned the O'Shee Lairds had always led the people in keeping the Old Ways and Dylan's promise. And so she declared that her gift of the Island would hold as long as the O'Shees continued to guide the people in their ancient wisdom from generation to generation. "A friend to the folk in the wood, a chieftain to the folk in the village," she declared. "Let the O'Shees be surety of this and the Pact of peace between my people and yours shall endure."

*********

"And now," Oak Peg finished, "ye must understand. Ye are the last O'Shee. Through Eilwen, ye alone can be our Laird. And if ye dinna' take up the task, the Pact will end and the last faerie clans of the Westernmost Tuath will be without place. Being sprites tied to the land, they canna' bear it. They will fade into the Dreaming West and the green world will lose them forever."

Coppin added, "And even now, lad, ye may no' know the half."

"But it is enough," declared Oak Peg. "Too much for a mortal mind to bear all at once. Ye must know ye are precious to us, Sweyn. The changeling girl canna' be saved, and going after her will no' change that. Yet if ye try, we may lose ye, too.

"Why?" said Sweyn. "Surely, if I'm so precious, nothing out in the wildwood will harm me."

Oak Peg said, "No faerie of good heart would, sure. And no faerie uninterested in Man will, either. But ye must bear in mind there are some faerie kinds as mean no harm yet will do it nonetheless, for mortals canna' bear even their presence. Yer encounter with the wisps should have taught ye that."

Sweyn nodded in grim silence. He remembered, now, his mindless pursuit of the wisps to the very brink of the deadly marsh.

She went on. "And there are other things to beware of in the wood, Sweyn. Some may no' be so bad, like ghosts that thrive in the leys of enchantment. But they can wake such memories, and draw such vitality from ye. Yet even they are a small hazard. There are more malignant things back there. This forest is enchanted, richly so, and such thick magic is a powerful lure to faerie kind. Over the centuries things from the Old World have found their way to us, terrible things we never meant to bring along. I shudder to think ye should encounter such as they."

Coppin added, "And as this is a time for truth, Sweyn, ye must understand that even among the things we did intentionally bring here, no' all of them were seelie. But the Company was committed to saving every faerie kind of the Ogham."

Oak Peg said, "And there is another matter, the unseelie New World faeries. Such as they will no' be found on this Island. The Pact forbids it and none would dare cross Arn'na'sagt'puch. But they can conspire. Oh, some faeries are better at that, and even more cunning, than mortal folk. They have gained allies among the unseelie things that bide here. They have told them that eventually the Pact must fail, and promised them an eternal place on the isle should they be agents of the Laird's ending. Such offers are sweet to unseelie ears, and if ye were to enter the wildwood with that promise like a price on yer head, it would be like walking into the bear's den."

And with that she concluded. They waited in anxious silence while he digested all they had taught him.

He sat still as stone a long time, thinking hard on it, but the choice was clear, and he pondered only the best path to take. Finally he said, "If you know where Caitlin has gone, if you can tell me or guide me, it might help. But come hell or high water, I'm going after her."

Oak Peg frowned, yet nodded. "I am no' glad to hear it. Ye put all at risk. Yet I would have expected no less from a Laird fit to lead the Company. Of Dylan O'Shee's kin ye are, whether ye know it or no'." And she called for the Nis at the mortar to hurry the acorn cakes.

# Chapter Thirteen

*Beyond the shoulders of grey stone sand,*
*pass the wood that guards and fetters*
*lies the wildwood that sequesters*
*hidden paths and shadow ways,*
*crystal brooks and tarns and springs,*
*a half-lost land of faerie rings,*

*and there is magic both bright and dark,*
*wonders high and perils shear,*
*where joy is sharp and sorrows sear,*
*for here be the last west remnant*
*of divided seelie and unseelie clans*
*revolving round the Elderman.*

*Disparate Dreams*
*Eilwen deSauld*

It was late afternoon and Sweyn was anxious to get going. He had gone to Starry Sea for the packet of peculiar aerial photos of the Island and returned with them to Oak Peg's cottage. He spread them on the table in Oak Peg's herb and cheese scented kitchen. She and Coppin sat at the table and looked at the eight by ten glossy prints. Wild Broom had refused to come inside. He said he could not bear walls, so they held counsel without him.

"Each picture is different," said Sweyn. "What's it mean? How do I find my way?"

Oak Peg pored over the aerial photos. Each one, taken roughly a decade apart, showed different features over the land. Only the major topography — the hills, valleys and mountains, and the large bodies of water — remained consistent. Oak Peg took a print into each of her withered hands and squinted at them a long time. At last she declared, "I have never seen the land from the air, though I have certainly experienced these changes within the wildwood. It is amazing. It seems so subtle from within the forest, yet it is so stark and obvious from the air. The enchantment that shields this land from mortal notice is powerful."

"So powerful it draws faerie kin here," observed Coppin.

Regarding Sweyn over the pictures, Oak Peg added. "And folk bound to the geas." Witch and sprite nodded in unison at the last observation.

Sweyn was none too concerned for their mysticism. He had more pressing matters. "How do I find my way around back there? How do I find Caitlin?"

Witch and Nis glanced at one other. Coppin was clearly perplexed, and Oak Peg simply vexed. She finally took an exasperated breath and told Sweyn, "The land changes. Faerie overlays the land and comes and goes with the waxing and waning of eldritch tides. And those follow the lead of Faerie time, which is no' like time in this world at all. It does no' flow straight nor consistent, and I canna' help ye understand its passing. Indeed, it does no' quite pass. It . . . spirals. It goes and returns, always moving, never changing, for Faerie is an eternal world.

"I see ye're perplexed, as well ye might be. All I can offer to help ye is this: sometimes, in the wildwood, ye will find yerself in the green world. And sometimes in Faerie. And there are between times, when ye may step through both at once."

Coppin shivered excitedly as she described it. His eyes glittered. All faerie kin were drawn to the eldritch nature of their primordial home though they often chose to dwell in the green world where things possessed more substance.

Frowning, Sweyn said, "So these pictures are as good as useless."

"No' entirely," Oak Peg went on, as she continued to study them. "As ye can see," –she pointed to a region of mountains and tarns, south and east– "the major shape of the earth holds true. It is only the lesser features of her face which change. Sometimes she wears a veil of trees. Sometimes she is clothed in grassy meadow. Sometimes she is soaked in moors." Sweyn listened, observing how Oak Peg pointed at the aerial photos, but he did not follow her reasoning, shrugged. She tapped his chest impatiently with each following syllable. "Find ye the mountains, keep to the brooks, stay to the fixed landmarks. It'll help ye keep yer way!"

Of course. He nodded, feeling stupid. Not having slept in a day and a half, he was not thinking clearly.

Oblivious of his fatigue, she went on. "Also, the tides of Faerie time are important to bear in mind, Sweyn. If ye go deep, dinna' linger, for if ye do ye will be long swept away in the spiral. Never sleep! Ye may wake and return to find a century has passed in the green world. Dinna' dance, it may take a moon to end the refrain ye step to. And ne'er eat nor drink anything ye see, for if ye take the stuff of Faerie into ye, ye will become part of it and be bound to that world. It is the mortal lot.

"Whatever ye do, stay on the move and return as quickly as ye can. Arn'na'sagt'puch has set a limit to the span of time between Lairds, nineteen years, which she reckons to be the length of one mortal generation to another. It has been eighteen years and nine months since Eilwen left us. And through her, ye're next in line. And there is little enough time left for ye to step up to the Lairdship."

Sweyn nodded, though in truth he cared nothing about "the Lairdship."

Oak Peg fingered a place on the south and east side of the Island, a place where the land was rugged and several small, tricky coves abruptly twisted the line of beach. "Make yer way by sea back here," she instructed him. "From there go deep into the wildwood, for there is where the Tylwyth Teg dwell. I was there, once, long and long ago. The land has doubtless changed since then. But faerie folk are no' wont to move. They are bound to the land they haunt. Somewhere in there ye will find their hollow hill. That is where Caitlin will go."

"Why?" Sweyn asked. "What would she care about them?"

Coppin answered. "She is fading, Sweyn, and alone. She will be drawn whence her magic came."

"But ye must be careful," Oak Peg warned quickly. "Donald is wise in faerie lore. Since the founding of the Island, only he has entered the wildwood. He has gone there often in search of his own true bairn. And he alone has learned the means to survive that land, and that is no small thing. He is formidable. In pursuit of the changeling, ye are likely to encounter him, and whatever folk of Man-by-the-Sea have fallen in with him."

Coppin said, "He has pined for his right Caitlin these many years. Who can blame him, but now he is mad to get his daughter back, and sore disposed toward Faerie things. The fact that ye are to be Laird may no' be enough to keep ye should ye threaten to get in his way."

Oak Peg barked, "And dinna' risk it! All our hopes rest with ye. Ye are a seaman, but Donald is strong in the ways of the wood. If he finds her first, ye canna' hope to stop him. Give it up and return, for yer cause is already lost. Ye canna' save a fading changeling."

Sweyn nodded, but they all knew his heart was not in her counsel. Come what may, he would try to save the doomed girl—at least from a violent end at Donald's hands.

That being so, it seemed to Oak Peg the best she could do was try to help him get in and out as safely and quickly as possible. So she continued to instruct him. "When ye have arrived in the cove, wait till dawn. Rest then, for ye'll need it. Ye may sleep safe enough upon the water. Dinna' be hasty and try to enter the wood by night, for enchantment is far more potent then. In the night the Elderman will sense yer coming. He will wait for ye."

The Elderman. His newly opened mind could recall it clearly now.

*A great tree lumbered through the inky darkness, as if scudding upon a storm cloud. As the thing drew closer, the air grew colder. Malignance surrounded it like a mist. This thing, whatever impossible thing it was, was old, older than the hills he stood between, and it was no friend of Man. It was no accident that it came upon his path. It hunted the night.*

"What is it, this elder tree thing? Why will it look for me?"

Coppin said, "As long as an O'Shee has led the Hundred Horsemen and the Company, the Elderman has hunted the O'Shees. It is an ancient vendetta, lost in the mists of time. It is sad that ye have inherited it, but the Elderman is of the immortal races, and his memory is long, and he makes no distinction between the generations of mortal folk. One O'Shee is the same to him as the next."

Sweyn squinted suspiciously at Coppin. His reply sounded pat, rehearsed, incomplete.

Oak Peg spoke up. "What matters is the Elderman will hunt ye, and ye canna' stop him. And ye canna' hide from him. But he is no' fast, so ye must stay ahead of him. Never rest, for he will never stop."

"One more enemy I haven't earned," Sweyn sighed. The unfairness of it made him angry.

"Dinna' hate him," Oak Peg admonished, and her voice was full of deep, unexpected feeling. "He canna' help what he is in the green world, for he is less than half here."

What? Sweyn almost barked, but no sooner had his lips begun to form the exclamation than she went on.

She said, "The Elderman long ago failed this world. He was slain many generations back. But when faerie folk are slain, they dinna' die and move on as do mortals. They canna', ye see, for they are innately immortal, and for faerie kin death is an unnatural thing. So they go away to a land where they wait—for what, we dinna' know. But there they wait. It is a land far across the impassible sea—a place we call the Dreaming West, and from its white shores there is no returning. Yet a bit of those lost ones stays behind, the ghost of them rooted inseparably in the green world. But that ghost is only a small part of what they once were. It has no true mind. It is all passion and instinct—the basic essence of life. Among us the Elderman was once great and good and wise. But since he has gone, all that remains is that dim remnant of himself—the faerie ghost incarnate as the elder tree."

Coppin said, "Once his ghost was content merely to exist in the forest. But time has weighed heavily upon the Elderman, long ages parted from his true self and his dear . . ."

"Coppin!" interjected Oak Peg.

Reprimanded, Coppin shut his mouth.

Oak Peg continued before Sweyn could insist upon hearing what Coppin had been about to say. "Once the Elderman was of good heart, the very noblest among us. Time and loss have twisted what remains of him in the green world. Dinna' despise him for it, Sweyn, for his is a sad and cruel tale."

Sweyn shook his head and shrugged. "Sure, fine. I'll hold no grudge. And while I'm running for my life, I'll be sure to feel sorry for the Elderman."

"Dinna joke on these matters!" snapped Coppin, so forcefully it startled Sweyn. "It is a tragic tale!"

"Tragic," thought Sweyn. "A homicidal tree is hell bent on killing me, but it's tragic." Then Sweyn sighed again, deeply, rested his forehead in an open palm and massaged vigorously at the line of his scalp, a tired, vexed gesture. He could not understand Coppin's reasoning, but that, in its own strange way, made sense to him, for Coppin was not a human being. That was plain enough as he looked upon the wrinkled, diminutive form of the little man, with his triangular face and elongated, pointy ears. Surely his thoughts and feelings were not those of a human. But Oak Peg, now she was the real mystery here. His Sighted eyes saw nothing other than a wizened woman, old and haggard and tired. Yet her thinking was certainly as fey as Coppin's or Broom's, but perhaps she had dwelt among the faerie folk so long now she thought like them. And how long was that? If the stories of her held true, she was far more than fifteen centuries old. Surely she could not be mortal, though as far as he could see, she was. He was tempted to ask her about this, for he felt if he could understand her tale, he would grasp at last everything going on on the Island, but he knew before he even bothered with that pursuit he would get no answers from her. Whatever her reasons, she was as private and secretive as her home sequestered deep in the oak grove. Perhaps at another time he would have pushed the issue anyway, but now it had been long since he slept, and so much had happened. The hours were growing heavy upon him. He could not muster the will for the effort, so he confined his queries to the far more pressing issues he was likely to get help on, namely how to find and aid Caitlin. That was all that mattered, really, for once he did—truth be told—he had every intention of taking her aboard Starry Sea and getting the hell off this Island once and for all.

Coppin and Oak Peg carried on for another hour, imparting to him bits of forest lore: terrain to watch for and terrain to avoid, unseelie glamour and tricks and traps, etiquette among the seelie kinds, respect of Ogham seeds. At last, when the sun was westering and the green shadows were deepening over Oak

Peg's cottage, they paused in their education of him. His head was so full of bric-a-brac his temples pounded and his skull felt like it would explode. Bleary of eye and mind, he determined sitting around here would benefit him no more, so he gathered the aerial photos and a few other oddments, including a leather backpack of mast bread and herbed cheese the unnamed Nis had prepared for him, along with a skin of cider. Then he stood and regarded them as if waiting for something, he wasn't sure what. They looked back, equally silent. At last, given the unbelievableness of this whole fantastical situation, he realized what he was expecting. Crazy though it sounded, he simply spat it out. "Isn't this the part where you give me a magic sword or lance or something to help me rescue the damsel in distress?"

They looked at each other, Nis and old woman, confounded.

Sweyn said, "That's how it happens in the fairytales. The knight goes off on a quest, and some fairy godmother gives him some magic weapon to vanquish the foe."

As if addressing a very small, very dim child, Oak Peg said slowly and evenly, "Sweyn, there is no foe to vanquish. Our goal is to preserve the faeries who reside here. We dinna' know for certain, but they may be the last faerie clans in all the world out of the West."

"And what would ye do with a sword or a lance or any such nonsense anyway?" Coppin pointed out.

Sweyn had a quick enough response to that. "Cold iron. You said it kills faeries."

Oak Peg sighed in the way of a despondent mother who cannot control her fledgling adolescent. "Oh, Sweyn. It is like sending the hare to confront the wolf. Please dinna' go." But Oak Peg knew he would not listen, so she did not wait for his response. "Iron burns, sure. Iron is cruel to faerie kin. But these are immortal creatures, and except for a few of the gentlest kind, such as the Asrai, most are very difficult to slay. Ye are no warrior. Wield iron and at best ye might injure some, and then what? Faeries hold long grudges. And those of the unseelie are cold and bitter. Ye'd soon have more than just the Elderman hunting ye in the wildwood. And how would ye then reckon with that, for faerie folk dinna' make combat like a man? They will use subtle enchantment and bend yer mind with glamour and trip yer feet with ill luck. They will conjure darkness and send ye to sleep for a millennium, and hold dances around yer moss covered body and snicker over their nasty prank."

"And worse things," Coppin added with a shiver.

"But I've heard in your own stories that some faerie folk have been killed by mortals with iron," stated Sweyn.

Coppin replied, "Only sometimes can this happen. Only very rarely. Selkies are vulnerable when they shed their seal skins and walk on the beach like a man or a woman. Animal faeries are vulnerable only in their animal form. But some, like Nisses, are no more vulnerable to iron than are mortals. Only the salt sea is bane to us. And then there are the very powerful kind, like the Tylwyth Teg and the Gwragedd, who are vulnerable to nothing. Iron may, at best, only sting them."

"Indeed," said Oak Peg, "that was what protected the changeling girl all those years from Donald. A creation of the Tylwyth Teg, he thought she would have shared their invulnerability."

Coppin mused, "As is usually the case with changelings, till they are found out and fade. A right unusual kind she is."

But Oak Peg did not join in his musings, curious though they were. Instead, she continued educating Sweyn in the faerie lore that might help him survive the wildwood. "Ye need fear unseelie folk, for many of them loath mortal kin, and many others have made deals with the unseelie of the Native sprites. These have been promised eternal place on the Island if they can break the Pact. And the way to break it is through ye, for ye, like it or no', are the heir of the O'Shee's legacy. So they will hunt ye.

"Fear standing water, it is a haunt of unseelie things. Fear the night air. Fear creatures that call with beauty, because they are often seducers. Fear most things which walk upon hooves cloven or otherwise. Avoid especially elder trees in the wildwood, and also walking willows. Tread near brooks and streams and springs when ye can. Stay near pools fed by sweet living water. If ye must rest, rest beneath rowans, deep in their red-fruited groves if ye can find a few of them together. Yet never sleep!

"Even the seelie ye must be wary of. Mortal folk and faerie folk are very different, and the nature of some faerie beings is so contrary to mortals they will harm ye, even though they dinna' mean to, like the willowisps of the bogs who unwittingly draw mortals to their doom. Ye are no' safe among any immortal folk until ye have learned what ye need of faerie lore, and ye have left us no time to teach ye."

Coppin concluded. "Yer best weapon is a fleet gate and a quiet step. Avoid all ye see and go straight to the Tylwyth Teg. They are none too fond of mortals, but they are wise, seelie creatures and will do ye no harm. There wait for your changeling girl. Let her fade in peace and mourn her, for she was a gentle creature. And then return to us quickly."

"I could use a guide," Sweyn pointed out.

But Oak Peg shook her head. "Indeed, but we canna' go, and no' by choice. Ye are the last hope for all the Island's folk, and sure we would go if we could. But I am too frail. I canna' make such a journey. Coppin is devoted to yer house and would gladly accompany ye, but in yer heart ye have no' accepted the lairdship. Ye are no' yet a sworn O'Shee in spirit. Until he is bound to ye through that oath he is bound to his place in the earth, like every other faerie. And that place is Dundubh Cottage. But Broom is of the wilds and will go with ye to the cove, and guide ye a bit into the wildwood, but he can go no further. He is bound to the land near the sea, and the sea near the land round this Island. If ye are determined to go, ye must make the journey alone, the first fool mortal to enter the wildwood in some two centuries, save Donald himself. But then, Donald has generations of gillie lore to preserve him whereas ye have only yer doubtful wits."

Sweyn nodded. That was lovely to know.

*********

The gloaming had come by the time Sweyn returned to Starry Sea. She lay patiently at anchor in the well sheltered glass water of the cove. With Broom seated at the bow of his little tender, he rowed out to her and Broom bounded aboard, careful to avoid the stanchions of stainless steel. Sweyn tossed up the leather pack to the Brown Man who stood motionless and watched it fall to the deck with a hard thud.

"You were supposed to catch it," said Sweyn.

"Was I?" said Broom. "The deck caught it well enough."

Sweyn was reminded again that faerie folk did not think like mortals. He climbed aboard the vessel and secured the tender to lines suspended from the davits. Moving with swift, fluid familiarity, he raised and secured the tender. Then he turned and twisted the key in the binnacle. The iron genny fired right up and, under power, he used the electric windlass to weigh anchor. The anchor was not yet full out of the water when he throttled forward, taking the faithful vessel out into the open sea. As soon as he rounded the point of the cove he veered sharply to port, following the coast as he made for the southeast corner of the Island. Broom took a reed whistle from a long, thin pocket in the breast of his tunic and faced starboard. He played up a fresh wind, and with it came an escort of dolphins and sea otters, some of whom were in truth mermen and selkies.

Sweyn sheeted in the sails and hoisted the spinnaker. Under perfect beam winds and a flat sea Starry Sea made eight knots, the hull speed of the vessel. Eight knots had always seemed fast to him in the past; it was as much as any sailor could expect from a small yacht, but now, with Donald in pursuit of Caitlin, it seemed like a snail's pace.

Throughout much of the voyage he left the autopilot on as he paced up and down the length of the vessel, hands fisting and unfisting at his sides. There was a deep ache in him, smacking of helplessness and fear. The thought of being unable to reach Caitlin was unbearable. It felt like . . . like that night three years ago when he struggled to cut the sailcloth shroud away from drowning Eilwen. The thought stung and he punched the deck furiously. It made no impression on the hardwood, though the pain helped him focus his mind back in the present.

Darkness had fallen full when Sweyn found the cove Oak Peg had shown him on the aerial photo. It was easy to identify, a small indention in the beach, surrounded on three sides by steep walls of high hills and a waterfall on the northeast side. Broom quit piping and the wind died immediately. Under power Sweyn steered into the cove and dropped anchor. He motored ahead a few hundred feet more and dropped his second anchor. Then, returning to the binnacle, he made reverse turns and backed till he was smartly between both anchors. Using the windlass, he took in half the rode from the first anchor, leaving Starry Sea snuggly double anchored in the middle. Broom watched warily as Sweyn worked the anchors and the windlass. In the presence of so much moving iron, he crouched like a wild animal, and a low growl emitted from deep within his throat. Only when Sweyn finished the job and the anchors and their chains were off the deck did Broom's tension ease.

But Sweyn did not pause. He went back to the davits and lowered the tender into the water, threw the leather pack down into it. Lowering the stepladder from the transom he was about to step out of the cockpit and onto it when he felt a hand fall lightly on his shoulder. He turned to see Broom looking at him with deep, sad eyes, shaking his head. "Mortal man," he said, and his voice was a soft bass Sweyn had not heard before, "I want to help Caitlin too, but heed the wisdom of the oak witch in this. Dinna' go aground till the morning light. Unseelie things there be by day and by night, but more by night. Much more." He looked round about at the black hills with their towering trees, suspicion and wariness in his eyes. "With no Laird, their power has grown. And the Elderman comes. Perhaps he is here. He is near, to be sure. Can ye no' feel him?"

Sweyn shook his head. "Time's wasting," he said matter-of-factly.

"Fall among his branches and time will no' matter, and then what good will ye be to the girl? And to the Island which must perish without ye?"

The night was early and Sweyn wanted to get moving now. Who knew how close Donald was to Caitlin. But so far this hairy creature had proven to be the only completely honest being he'd met here, and the closest thing he had to a friend. After a long moment of deliberation, he nodded.

Broom said, "I'm sorry."

Without a word, Sweyn went below, lit oil lamps, and pored over the mysterious photographs with their topography different from decade to decade. And sometimes his tired gaze was drawn to the family tree of the O'Shees. The genealogist had noted it could be traced back reliably only to the early nineteenth century, but even then it was scattered, broken and confusing. Sometimes the line seemed to fail—no children, no spouses to inherit the estate—and then, suddenly, a new heir appeared to take up the line. It made no sense. Nothing here made any kind of sense.

Perhaps if he had a clear head. He closed his eyes and tried to sleep, but sleep came only in broken bits, and when it did the darkness was filled with unkind dreams, drowned corpses of loved ones, broken promises and shattered dreams, a sense of hunting and being hunted. He might have been better off without sleep.

Morning found him restless. The moment the sun showed the first whitening of the eastern horizon, he came up the companionway. Broom was curled up in the cockpit like a great dog. Sweyn handed him a jar of pickled fish from the galley, with a hefty piece of pilot bread. He dined similarly, and the crumbs had not fallen from their chins by the time they were rowing the tender over the glass water to the sandy shore. The water was clear, and beneath the little boat he could see small, translucent jellyfish pushing through the water like living toadstools. Clams and muscles were richly abundant on the sandy bottom, and bright orange and red starfish and many-armed sunfish harvested among them. Yards away, at the edge of vision, something scaled and nubile swam beneath the surface, moving gracefully away from the rowers.

They beached on the sand and dragged the little boat high up so it would be well clear of the impressive tides of this part of the world. Sweyn took a hefty, one inch painter line and tied it from the tender's bow to the trunk of a stout cedar growing just beyond the sand. Then he shouldered the pack and looked about. The sight of the towering oaks and beeches was so powerfully alien on this Pacific Island, where softwood rainforests should dwell in evergreen majesty, that it left him feeling a sense of displacement, as if a carpet had been pulled from under his feet. Fog gathered beneath those thick boughs, and thick, swimming shadows. The sun was low on the horizon, and there in the trees, night yet reigned. It raised goose bumps on Sweyn's arms. "I have a gun aboard Starry Sea," he whispered to Broom. "A shotgun for large fish."

"Leave it," said Broom. "Lead will no' impress faerie kin." He was quiet a while, then added. "We are being watched."

Sweyn felt it too. He had felt it since they anchored the previous night. Eyes regarded them from the shadows, from the water, from the air. The sensation was peculiar, like being caught in spotlights that brought chills. It left him with a cloying sense of violation.

Broom said, "I dinna' think the Elderman is here yet, but other things are about. Some seelie, some no', and some ye must simply avoid."

Broom started then into the forest, and Sweyn followed. Beneath the trees, beyond the light of the open sky, his eyes quickly adjusted to the shadows. The forest was not quite as dark as it had seemed from the shore, and it would brighten as the day progressed.

They moved deeper and deeper into the forest, and as they did it enfolded them, the trees drawing in behind them and closing off sight of the beach. The earth was littered with the leaf fall of many previous autumns, though there was a surprising dearth of deadfall. But forest herbs grew abundantly: nettles, wormwood and chiming bells, ferns and twisted stalk and columbine. Waxy, emerald ivy towered up some of the trees and grew over some of the boulders. Slender rowans grew wherever breaks in the great beeches and oaks fed them sunlight. In one place they found a grove a smallish trees with clusters of white flowers growing abundantly on their branches. Broom gripped Sweyn's arm tightly and drew him quickly away. "Wild elders," he whispered to Sweyn. "Dinna' pass, dinna' cross, dinna' take lest ye offer loss," he advised, quoting some bit of ancient eldritch lore.

They ascended a hill that led up to higher ground. It rose gently, a slope of dark earth and scattered boulders half sunk in the black loam. As they went deeper and further, things changed. The sun burned off the mist still clinging to the shadows, and the forest was filled with a close warm air, scented of fertile earth and herbage. And while the oaks and beeches predominated, they saw more kinds of trees, hawthorn and hazel, holly and scattered wild apple.

At the top of the hill the ground leveled and the oaks flourished in the deep earth, sending out massive root systems and great, low hanging boughs. The beeches rose smooth and noble, and both species grew in size quickly as they went deeper, until it seemed that every tree they walked beneath was an ancient giant's tower. Here the air was thick with the fragrance of the living wood, but it was fresher too, for the vast spaces between the earth and the forest canopy allowed breezes to flow. But here also no more of the sky was visible. The coverage of the forest canopy became so complete that all beneath it lay in an unbroken pale shadow of green. In the poor light few green herbs grew, save those that did not love the sun, like devil's club with its great leaves and bright, cone shaped clusters of ruby berries, and masses of ferns and choked tangles of vines. Bright toadstools were abundant too, and amanitas with their pumpkin-colored, pear shaped tops and white flecks. And there were mushrooms that looked like morels, but when they stepped on them they were filled with white threads like veins devoid of blood.

Without realizing it they had stumbled into a place where fungi grew all about, mushrooms and toadstools all over the ground, displaced shaggymanes and true morels, corals and oysters, bright yellow things shaped like inky caps that held the light like luminous crystal, and sulfur colored growths on trunks of trees, as hard or harder than the wood. Soon hardly a green herb could be spotted. Broom stopped and looked around, eyes squinting. His voice low, he said to Sweyn, "Ye must be careful in these parts. Be wise no' to step in faerie rings, lest ye find yerself dancing a dance ye canna' quit."

Sweyn looked all around him, as if expecting any moment to sight some dark, small goblin leering at him from the preternatural abundance of fungi. "Broom, is there anything here that is not out to get me?"

"Aye, and much?" Broom answered. "No' everything in Faerie is unseelie. Indeed, most of it is good for ye. The thing is . . ." he looked off wistfully, trying to think of how to say it, "the thing is, ye must be ready for each mystery. In the old tales, yer folk always had to pass through trials when they encountered Faerie things, and there was reason for that. The trials prepared them to receive the mysteries, or barred them from them if they were unready. But ye, my friend, have no' had the benefit of trials to prepare ye. There is no time and ye have been thrust into this, ready or no."

Sweyn recalled a tale he had heard long ago, in some Medieval Lit class he had taken on a lark while an undergrad. A great and noble warrior named Ogier was sent to Fairyland where he was to serve King Arthur. But before he could enter that place he had to face many trials to prove his worthiness. He was marooned on a stark island where all his companions perished of famine. Later, at the gates of an enchanted castle he battled magical beasts as a test of courage. After entering the castle he was given poison and survived as a test of stamina.

Then Sweyn recalled the story of the old seanachie, Kilwillie, of the youth who had ascended the slopes of Mount Snowdonia. He had tried too soon for too high a mystery. He had paid for it with his life. Realizing now that tale could well have been a true account, Sweyn shivered, his breath shaking.

Broom perceived Sweyn's fear and spoke again. "Aye, I see ye understand how serious it is, and realize the risks. But know ye this, Sweyn, I believe in ye. I have my own kind of Sight, and it sees deep into folk. I believe in ye."

Somehow, that touched Sweyn in a way he would not have expected, for Sweyn certainly no longer believed in himself. He did not know what to say to Broom for that, so he said nothing, showed nothing, and merely carried on.

They walked beneath green shadow until at last they came to a clear, fast flowing brook. There Broom stopped and crouched low to the ground, staring intently into the waters. Sweyn squinted but saw nothing, but the Brown Man seemed to be looking hard for something. At length he said, "Ah, a brook of the Asrai. Sweyn, this is a good place! Come and see."

Sweyn knelt and looked into the water. He saw a rainbow trout more than a foot long whisking its tale idly behind a nearby stone that shielded it from the current. And while it was a nice trout, he saw nothing more extraordinary than that.

Suddenly, a strong hand pressed down upon the back of his neck, forcing his face down to only inches above the water. "Look!" commanded the Brown Man impatiently. "Look closely into the shadows over there." And he pointed to the opposite bank, two yards away.

The brook was about a foot deep, fast flowing and crystal clear, but its surface reflected the emerald forest canopy like a silver mirror, making it hard to see beneath. But now, his eyes just above the water, he was able to make out a shelf of smooth speckled rock extending from the opposite bank, and beneath it a sandy, shaded bottom. There were the faintly glowing forms of three lovely, nubile creatures. Like delicate girls, they were willowy and only a few inches long. They wore no clothing, were translucent, and fragile in appearance. One had braids of setting sun, the other locks of molten gold, and the third's were glossy and green as kelp.

"The gentle things canna' bear sunlight or captivity," Broom told him in hushed tones. "Nor can they bear the presence of Men things, cut stone and cold iron and plowed fields. These are too much for them. Even a moment's captivity is too much for them, and if ye were to try to lift one of the lovely damsels of the water in yer hand, were even I, faerie kin, to do it, they would dissolve as surely as Coppin would in the briny sea. Dissolve into the Dreaming West, their flower gone from the green world forever." He looked up to Sweyn, and there was a deep reverence in his voice as he spoke the next words. "This is what the first O'Shee pledged his life to protect. That pledge was to be his doom, and the start of the Company, and the oath that saved the Westernmost Tuath. Perhaps," he lamented, "the last Tuath."

Still looking at the tiny maidens who gave them no notice, something Broom had said began to sink in. Sweyn said, "You're sure? You're the last of the faeries?"

"The last of the Old World kind, we think. We dinna' know for sure, but we have had no contact with others since fleeing to this place."

Sweyn regarded the little damsels who hovered in the crystal water beneath the shadow of the bank, luminous as living gems. And a peculiar thought struck him, peculiar because it amazed him that he thought it. He thought, "How shallow the world would be without the Asrai."

Broom carried on. "In old times Faerie spanned the width and breadth of the earth, our world existing side by side with yer own. Every part of Faerie was connected and we could communicate across the vastness of it. But now mortal things are everywhere, cutting off enchantment, and much of Faerie has withered. The remnants of Faerie exist like islands in the sea of man. Are there other islands out there with their own surviving Tuatha? We dinna' know. We have no way to learn of it. We canna' see across expanses devoid of enchantment."

Sweyn stood up then, and for some reason he did not fully comprehend, this saddened him greatly. Not till now did he fully understand why these creatures had come to the Island. He said, "But Oak Peg said faerie folk cannot travel. She said they are bound to places. Like you, for instance, you can't go far from the sea. So how did you ever come to the Island? It's on the other side of the world from Europe."

Broom looked puzzled, unable to understand what Sweyn failed to grasp. He said, "Ye have heard the tale of how we came in seeds."

Sweyn spread his arms. "But I don't understand, Broom. How could you become a seed?"

Very patiently, Broom explained, "Sweyn, yer kind have spirits within ye, and when mortals pass away, they go to the Otherworld to await the next turn of the Wheel. They might progress from there to yet another world, or return to this one, or just stay in the Otherworld and rest a while.

"But we have seeds within us. And if one of us goes to the Dreaming West, the seed we leave behind becomes a herb, or a tree, according to the Ogham of our race. Long ago a mortal found a way to call upon the Ogham enchantment, and gather our seeds without losing us to the Dreaming West. And with the help of the Company, that mortal gathered all of us as could be found and made the dangerous trip here. Otherwise, we surely would have perished." Broom sat up on his knees, looked northwest, in the direction of Oak Peg's cottage. "We owe the oak witch much."

Broom looked sadly, then, at the Laird who might well soon perish here in the wildwood. He truly liked this Laird, he decided.

"I have brought ye to the brook of the Asrai," Broom told him. "Follow it. The Asrai are seelie damsels and will do ye no harm. They are small and delicate, but they have some strength to protect ye, strength of glamour strong enough even to deceive faerie kin.

Sweyn remembered the night he had been lost in the wood after the storm, and the little lights in the pool when he met the Gwragedd. Those had been Asrai. One of the lights had swum downstream, and where it had gone a double of himself appeared a moment later. The double fled and the Elderman pursued it. To make things appear which were not there—this was their magic.

But he had no time to ponder it. Broom was continuing to speak.

"The binding of the sea pulls me sorely now. I canna' stay. Keep to the brook." He rose to leave.

Sweyn put his hand on the Brown Man's raggedly furred arm. "You . . . you're leaving me?"

"I can go no further. Already it hurts to be away." He took a step back from Sweyn. In his sad night-dark alien eyes Sweyn could see Broom did not wish to leave him.

"Tell me one thing, Broom."

"Hurry."

"You said Dylan's pledge was his doom. What happened to him, at the end of his story?"

Broom smiled sadly. Hesitated.

"Broom?"

The hairy wild man took a step forward, clapped one powerful hand on Sweyn's shoulder, looked him deeply in the eyes. "Dylan proved he had a soul. As must every O'Shee. As must ye." Broom tapped Sweyn's chest solidly. "Dylan is within ye, Sweyn. In there, where it was all dark and empty, full of cobwebs and shadows and foul things, I smell a soul."

Then the Brown Man looked long and studiously at Sweyn, nodded once, and bounded off into the forest, moving in the manner of a loping bear. Without a sound he vanished downhill, back the way they had come, back to the timeless song of the sea.

*********

Sweyn continued up the stream for several hours more. Slowly and steadily the terrain rose. Around the brook the trees broke in places, admitting patches of sunshine. Around noon he stopped beside a slowly swirling pool fed by the brook to have a quick bite of Oak Peg's mast bread. The branches parted in this place, and overhead the sun could be seen high in a clean cyan sky. Sunrays fell upon the pool like a downpour of gold, and its surface gleamed with the fire of a gem. A tangible sense of healing and well-being surrounded the pool, hovering like mist beneath the rowans that encircled the area. But though the pool was brightly lit, many large rocks leaned over its bank, offering cool, sheltering shadows. And sometimes, within those shadows, he espied glimmers of light, and quick, nubile forms. The Asrai were here, and he was glad for it. In their presence, with the rowans all about and the sunlight streaming down from above, he felt comforted. The mast bread had an unusual slightly sweet, nutty flavor, with just a touch of tannin's bitterness to it. It was very rich and very filling, and it took him only minutes to eat his fill. Though he was pressed to leave this place, it made him sad when he was done and rose. Without a doubt, this was one of the good places in Faerie Broom had spoken of.

He walked on a couple more hours till he came to the origin of the brook, a dozen small springs gushing from apertures high up a rock wall in the side of a hill. The falling water scattered over jutting stones, becoming a misty veil before gathering in a shallow pool at the base of the wall. The far side of the pool was worn and the crystal water spilled over and fed the brook which raced away. Playful shafts of sunlight fell from shifting breaks high in the forest canopy, sparking scattered rainbows in the veil. The little fall sang as it tumbled, and each stone in its path offered its own voice to the chorus. Mushrooms with broad, sulfur caps grew here as high as his knees, seeming to glow in the deep green shadows. The beauty was exquisite, and drew him in the way of the wisps of the bogs, or the pixies that haunted the night beyond Oak Peg's cottage. It took great strength of will to tear himself away from this Faerie place and move on.

Having reached the end of the brook, or rather its beginning, he had no more landmarks to guide him. He continued from there into the unbroken forest, doing his best to keep going in the direction the brook had led. He might have used the sun to guide him, but so high and thick grew the trees that he could not see it clearly through their leafy boughs. Still, he had a keen sense of direction from so many years finding his way upon the endless vistas of the sea, and proceeded with confidence until the first sign the light was failing. Given the lack of undergrowth in the deep wood, it was not hard going, as long as he could keep himself from being dazzled by the forest's preternatural beauty.

Still, something was wrong. Having kept up a steady, brisk pace, he realized he must have walked miles and miles. And how long had he been walking? Ten, twelve hours? He did the math. He ought to have covered some thirty miles. Yet the Island was not half so broad, and he should have reached the other side by now. Yet it seemed as if he was still only working his way up the first rise.

He stopped then, and pulled the aerial photos from a pouch in his pack. This made no sense. He had to think it through. At Oak Peg's he had been told the village of the Tylwyth Teg was only about two miles or so back in the forest. He should have reached it long ago. Had Broom led him astray? He doubted the wild Brown Man could easily be misled in any wood.

He looked up, then, at the towering oaks and beeches. They were great trees, like the mightiest redwoods and Sequoias of forests south on the mainland. But they were impossibly large for their species, growing so high that mist floated in the air beneath their boughs like small draughts of cloud. The trees were so great they made their own weather, and a gentle breeze blew under the boughs, just enough to move the hair and cool the skin and take away the cloying humidity he had encountered at the boundary of the forest at the beach.

Then a thought struck him. He could not understand how such a wood could be overlooked. Long ago, loggers should have found and decimated this place. Even if it had survived their depredations, the Island would have been marked as a forest preserve or become a tourist trap in more recent decades. It was unnatural such woods as these should still stand alone and untouched.

Then yet another thought struck him. There were no insects. As he thought about it, he realized how bizarre it was. No insects in a summer northland forest? Whoever heard of such a thing?

*No insects.*

And it was with that final revelation that he came to understand part of the tremendous enchantment of the wildwood—it was not of the earth. That was why it had never been discovered. That explained the great trees, the absence of insects, the preternatural beauty. Somewhere back toward the beach he had left the earthly wood behind and now walked in a world that functioned by its own rules. There was no sudden demarcation where it happened; one world had just slipped into the other, the change so gradual it could not be noticed.

And now he walked the realm of Faerie, where Oak Peg had taught him rules of space and time as he knew them did not apply. It seemed as if a great deal of Faerie could be compacted into a small area of the green world. No wonder the aerial photos showed ever shifting topography. Whenever the photos were shot, they revealed only glimpses of scattered corners of Faerie. No wonder Oak Peg and Coppin had feared so much they would lose him back here. Two miles in the green world to the Tylwyth village, that could be dozens of miles on this side of reality. Dozens of miles in a strange, wild country where the universe itself worked in incomprehensible ways. And he, an outsider with no experience, and no guide.

He could well be lost forever in this place.

He shivered though it was not cold.

*********

There was nothing to do but press on, and be careful to keep his wits about him. But it was hard, for the wonders he encountered were many, each more difficult than the previous to tear his eyes from. This morning he would not have thought anything could distract him from his singular goal of reaching Caitlin, but the beauty of this place was surreal, and its effect upon him was like a drug. Every sight was splendor, every sound a siren's song, every forest fragrance a heady ambrosia. It overwhelmed his mortal senses and was perhaps the greatest danger, for in this place he could easily forget the green world forever. He did not understand why faerie folk preferred his world to their own.

But he kept his wits about him, somehow, though it took a lot out of him. Staying focused in this place was rather like a slow physical drain, like walking continually uphill. Bit by bit the exertion taxed him, so that by the time evening had fallen thick and dark hunger pangs bit him sharply. But he did not stop to take his repast. He simply dug out a hunk of cheese from the pack and chewed it as he walked. He remembered all too well the oak witch's warning to stop nowhere, sleep nowhere. But most of all he was aware that if he should spend too much time here in any place, the beauty might overwhelm his sensibility. He might pass untold hours mesmerized, staring at the rainbow hues of some glowing toadstool cap, or the garnet veins of a fallen leaf. So he kept moving.

Sometimes he became aware of shadows beyond his vision, moving like brief, silent pools of darkness. Seelie or not, they chilled him, for they were unknown. He longed to stop, build a small fire and ward away the night, but he had to keep moving, as Oak Peg had told him.

But with each mile the effort cost him more. And late in the evening, when a quarter moon shown bright over the trees and countless stars were scattered across the welkin like gleaming jewels, it became very difficult to keep his eyes open any longer. He had barely slept in almost two days. His mind was growing fuzzy, and he was failing to avoid everything as Oak Peg had instructed. He tripped over branches and stones, walked through a patch of enormous pale moonflowers that grew as tall as his head, nearly stumbled upon and crushed some wild white gourds the size of goose eggs that had tiny windows in their sides and smoking chimneys poking out of their tops.

When he came to the pond in the open place, with ordinary fireflies tracing silver-blue streaks over it, and smelling of sweet water lilies, he seemed to have found a small bit of his own world. Nightingales sang in ordinary sized hazels and elms round about, and an owl hooted from the lowest branch of a birch. Crickets chirruped in the short grass that grew all around the banks, green and thick as carpet. It was a lovely place, but not with the mesmerizing beauty of Faerie. It was just . . . ordinary. It even had bugs. If there were any place in this land fit for a mortal to rest, this was it. In such an earthy place there could be no enchanted things to be wary of. Still, he would heed Oak Peg's warning. He would not sleep. He would just stop a bit, eat a little bread and cheese, and close his eyes sitting up. Just a small break to unmuddle his thoughts.

He found a cool spot on the bank just above the black waters in a place where mandrakes grew. He took the pack off his back and set it beside him, dug out bread and cheese and ate his fill, or at least until exhaustion took him, when his eyes fluttered shut and the food fell, forgotten, from his slackened hands.

The moon had moved a score of degrees across the star-strewn sky when the clouds began to roll in from the north and west. Towering stacks of blackness, they came silent and great and ominous. And when they were overhead, the rain began. The sound of it woke Sweyn, the splashing of heavy drops upon the surface of the pond. He opened sleep-dulled eyes and his groggy mind acknowledged the downpour. Dimly he thought he should move beneath the shelter of one of the great trees at the rim of the clearing. But then he became aware of a most peculiar fact—he was not wet. And he should have been, for he was right out in the open. He forced himself to greater awareness, trying to understand it. All around him was the sound of tumbling water, and the wet smell of forest. The mandrake leaves danced as heavy drops appeared upon them. The few normal sized trees in the clearing swayed beneath the weight of the rain. The whole world glistened wet beneath the moon, which still shone in the east beyond the line of clouds. But he could see no rainfall, and he was bone dry.

He regarded the pond. A thousand thousand scattering rings roiled the surface. But the air above it was clear. Slowly, he lifted a hand and held it up before him. No rain fell upon it. He lowered his hand to the ground and immediately fat, stinging drops soaked it. He marveled. Here was a faerie rain, one moment in the clouds, the next on the land or in the foliage, and nowhere in between. In Faerie one could walk in a downpour and never get more than his boots wet.

Distant lighting flashed. In that instant he could see all the way to the clouds, and indeed no rain tumbled out of them, yet all the forest stirred with the downpour. He began to laugh. Sweyn was a seaman; he had known water intimately all his life, in all its many forms. But he could never, ever have imagined this.

He gazed into the sky, regarding the wondrous downpour in the lightning flashes. As he did, movement stirred unnoticed beneath the surface of the pond. Oily, the movement was, that of something substantial slipping smoothly through the liquid. It began at the opposite bank and gracefully progressed toward Sweyn.

But Sweyn was accustomed to water, and even subtle changes in its nature drew his attention. Before she was half across, he saw her coming, but his sleep-misted mind could not quite recall that the pond was stagnant, which Oak Peg had warned him to avoid. In that moment, the ripple marking her approach was just one more curiosity in a realm of dazzling curiosities.

But then she rose from the midst of the pond, and the sight of her was wonder itself. Her hair was long and emerald and fell to her waist and further, down to the pond surface where it fanned around her like a regal cloak. Nothing covered her save the moisture which clung to her moon-hued skin, and she glistened like the flesh of a ripe and delectable pear. Her eyes were aquamarine jewels from corner to corner, lucent and brilliant, reflecting the rolling lightning with the inner fire of the most perfect gems. There was no white in her eyes at all, no darkening where pupils might be, only the depthless blue. Her breasts were smooth and round and upturned, perfect ornaments upon a slight chest, a narrow stem of waist. She looked at him with the same endless fascination with which he beheld her, her head slightly cocked to one side. Her round mouth, slightly open, conveyed a sense of guileless wonder. Only, her chest did not rise and fall, she did not seem to breathe.

He rose and stepped toward the pond to view the fair creature more closely. The spray of droplets kicked up by the downfall on the pond surface was creating a mist over the water, and such loveliness commanded nothing less than perfect clarity. He stepped down into the water. It was warm and welcoming and came swiftly up to his knees. In no time he would be to his waist and able to swim out to her. Caitlin faded from thought. He could spend all the ages right here with the pond girl.

"Now why go out there and breathe yer life away like that?" came an unexpected, boyish voice. It was difficult, painful even, to tear his eyes away from the pond girl. But by sheer will he managed it and saw, reclining in the crook of a diminutive alder near the water, what at first appeared to be the slight form of a young boy. He reclined against the trunk with arms crossed casually behind his head for a pillow, legs stretched out along a precariously slender branch, his feet crossed casually. The boy wore no clothes save a great leaf twisted once into a cone shape and set upon his head. A feather had been stuck through the leaf. The boy had great dark eyes like Broom, and ears as sharp and pointed as a cat's. In all other respects he looked like a human youth, though Sweyn, beginning to come back to himself, suspected there was nothing human, or even youthful, about this creature.

The boy-faerie leapt lightly down from the tree. A wind began to build and the boughs waved in synchrony with the gusts, the jagged alder leaves rustling in protest of the storm. "Best ye step out of the water and leave the Glaistig to drink the blood of fishes," he said as he slowly approached Sweyn, but watching the pond girl all the while.

Her once innocent face now held the countenance of a woman spurned. Sparks of hatefulness illuminated her jewel eyes. She turned and slipped soundlessly under the water.

The boy-faerie held a pipe of ash wood in his left hand and he lifted it to his mouth. Around it, he said, "Best ye get out of that pond now. And go. And dinna' look back." His voice carried a musical quality that went beyond his brogue, the syllables falling with notes as lively as if they had spilled from his pipe. Then he blew into the pipe and played. Notes emerged in pointed succession, sharp and acrid, clutching at the innards like mis-struck chords.

By the stirring of the music the haze of fatigue fell away, and when it did Sweyn felt the first icy pangs of fear fluttering within as he realized he was now standing exactly in the kind of place Oak Peg had warned him to stay clear of. The pangs sharpened intensely when he felt the light play of delicate hands on his feet in the water. The hands slid slowly, sensuously, up his calves, up to mid-thigh where the slender, pale shape of them came up out of the water, pressing lightly along the flesh of either side of his torso as the girl rose with them, smoothly, as if she were floating up on smoke. Her emerald hair streamed behind her, down her naked back. Her breasts were like fruit ripe for picking. The Glaistig's touch was like that of icy water, and he sensed such danger behind her pure features. But even despite that sense, her appeal was irrecusable. He placed his own two hands upon her narrow waist.

The piping changed, and in its tune were afternoon sunbeams streaming through white, puffy clouds and fragrant apple blossoms. It carried aromas of bread baking in stone ovens and honey yet in the hive. It carried the feel of soft forest earth, where pine needles gather in heaps to make a gentle bed. It bore the sensation of warm creek water tickling the toes and the texture of lustrous damsels' hair. All good things were wound up in the boy-faerie's piping, and it filled Sweyn with warmth and courage, and even here, standing at the brink of doom, it brought a slight upturning of the lips, a hint of smile to clash against unseelie things.

But those very good things were not pleasant to the Glaistig. She winced to the piping, as though each perfect note fell upon her like a blow. The boy-faerie came forward, stepped down toward the water, to its very edge. He watched the Glaistig girl intently, his own seamlessly dark eyes intense in this battle of enchantment, but full of impish delight, while the girl's eyes were bright and utterly unreadable. But the magnetic hold she seemed to have on Sweyn failed, and he found the strength to let her go, step back, back and away, up out of the water, beside the boy who continued to stare at the girl intently. Then a thing happened Sweyn would never forget: the girl became as water, and her form collapsed into the pond as though she had been poured into it. The boy-faerie waded out into the water then, his playing taking on a sultry essence, the notes lengthening sensuously, and the shadowy, smooth movements of lovemaking and sounds of passion were bound up in his melody. He stepped down and down into the pond, still playing, until he disappeared beneath the black water and his song vanished with him. Sweyn did not understand what had just happened, but he knew his life had narrowly been spared. He gathered the backpack and hastily withdrew from the clearing. All around him the faerie rain continued to pour, drops impacting the earth with such force they churned mud and wilted trees. Yet no drops were in the air. His hair and body were dry, save to his knees where he had stood in the pond. He shouldered the pack and made for the forest edge, having nothing other than his nose and the hope of luck to follow.

On through the raining night he trekked, and every step struck him as wondrous and eerie and alien. He was a seaman, almost, one could say, bred for storms, yet never could he recall a storm such as this. The lightning rolled through the clouds like waves, illuminating them with ripples of fire from within. The trees waved their mighty arms as if pounded by a furious blow yet he could not feel so much as a breath of wind. The rain pounded the ground and the foliage, and splashed up in every churning puddle, yet not a drop fell to wet him.

And there were noises in the night wood unlike anything he had ever experienced. Here and there came voices of women singing sad songs, elsewhere came the grinding of rocks being struck and broken, and sometimes there was the whoosh of great wings riding the stormy air. Once, as he leapt over a small brook, he heard splashing further up and saw in a flash of the rolling lightning the form of a skinny, withered hag washing something in the creak: clothing, perhaps, wet with blood. She wailed bitterly as she washed. He did not dawdle but ran on as fast as he dared into the darkling forest.

With increasing alarm he began to face the reality that he was lost. He had no more idea how to proceed toward the Tylwyth Teg village than he had how to make his way back to the sea. Commonsense told him the Island was seven miles across at its widest, fourteen miles north to south at its longest. If he merely held a course for a few hours he should reach the coast and could walk his way back to Starry Sea or Man-by-the-Sea along the beach. But he understood now that if he pulled commonsense out of his head, threw it on the ground, and stomped on it, he might come out the better. For commonsense no longer applied. Faerie was not earth. It was not even in the same reality. All the rules were different. A straight line in this place was just as likely to end him up where he started. The shortest distance between two points might well be a loop.

The simple truth was he was hopelessly lost and in over his head.

He came to a place where, in the lower boughs of the massive trees, bright golden lights flitted rapidly about, so fast his eyes could barely track them. They were beautiful to see, and held his gaze with their rapid maneuvers, leaving sparkling, fragile streamers of blue and gold behind them like dizzy shooting stars. He recalled seeing such lights before, at Oak Peg's cottage. She had warned him then of being pixie-led. He looked away, into the eldritch forest, but the dark of it seemed just as perilous. No worse here among these creatures.

And no better.

He sagged to his knees in despair.

"Trust the pixies," came the shadow of a whisper near his ear. There was a sense of warmth on his right shoulder and he turned that way, expecting anything, yet he could never have been prepared for what met his eyes.

For Eilwen stood there, hazy as a wisp of cloud, barely visible in the flickers of lightning muted by the forest canopy. Her eyes were deep and sad as she looked upon him.

His breath failed. His eyes widened, full of wonder. It was madness and delusion, or it was a dream beyond hope. And whether Faerie had rendered him senseless or contrived some bit of glamour to cast this uncanny visage, he did not care. Here was Eilwen. Eilwen. Eilwen. He reached a hand to her, and she reached hers to his. They did not touch, but seemed to meld into one another the way a ship melds into a thick morning's fog over the sea, becoming faded, then a shadow, then one with the mist. He dared not speak lest he wake from this fragile moment.

"Oh, Sweyn," said the shade, "I have missed ye."

"Eilwen?" he dared breathe.

"And look what I've brought ye to. This is all my doing. I was such a fool, and now it's ye who must right my wrongs."

Sweyn dared whisper more. "I've missed you so much, Eilwen. Am I coming to you?"

She smiled and shook her head, once, the sadness deep in her eyes. "I canna' see the future, but I'll wager ye've long in life before ye. But ye're lost, Sweyn, sorely lost, and ye've stumbled into a between place of the wildwood and stolen a moment for us, where before I could only whisper to ye from afar."

He had stumbled between, the words came to him vaguely, but he gave no thought to their meaning. All his attention was for Eilwen alone. Yet around him was a ring of spotty toadstools, their broad caps phosphorescent in the rolling lightning. And south of the ring was the darkness of his own green world's night. East lay the ceaseless daylight of the mortal Otherworld. To the west the white shores of the Dreaming West glowed. And north lay an endless twilight, the skies of the deepest places in Faerie. He had stumbled into one of those rarest of enchanted places, a gate between worlds where a being might slip body and spirit between the veils of realities. Had he but taken a step, he might have found himself back in his own world. But he gave the matter no thought, and would not have moved even if he had, even to save his own life. For here was Eilwen, and he might live or die happily, if only at her side.

But he was, in the end, only between, and not quite part of any world. Where they touched he felt warmth, and knew she was hale and well, but they could not truly mingle here. They could not be together. He had only this precious moment to cling to.

And such gates are ephemeral. They come and go with their own fey timing that remains a mystery even to Faerie folk, and already the weave of the realities was unraveling. The vision of Eilwen grew fainter.

"Sweyn," she said, "ye've kept the Cottage. Ye've kept yer word. I was always the soft earth and ye were my hard stone. Stalwart Sweyn. And now I've left ye wandering forever, like a nomad spirit, with no place and no folk. But ye are here, on the Island. Sure and some purpose has brought ye here."

"Oak Peg and faerie magic brought me," he said automatically, tonelessly.

"But only ye could make the choice to stay. I should have warned ye of the geas that comes of loving me. It is a dear price."

He lifted his hand to the half tangible mist of her face, stroked his fingers through the shade of her red hair, touched the feathery mist of her sad brow. "I loved you the day I saw you, Eilwen. I wouldn't trade that for any price."

She was only a shimmering haze now, like a faded reflection seen in still, clear water. "Sweyn, I ran." She shook her head, a tear upon her cheek. He could not dry it. "I was seventeen when I learned what Caitlin was. She was only eleven then. But I left her. Our mother was in the ground. Our father was gone over the sea. I was all the family she had, and I abandoned her too. I could no' bear the thought of what she was."

"Shhh," he said to the ghost. "You were young, Eilwen."

"I was her sister."

He nodded. He understood. He looked down to the dark earth, a painful lump gathering at the back of his throat.

"Sweyn, make it right."

The next words Sweyn spoke held such hollowness as had not been heard since he spoke Eilwen's eulogy all those years ago, for with the pronouncement of those words he knew that deep within he believed the oak witch after all. "She will be gone soon, Eilwen. I cannot stop it."

"Make it right," Eilwen pleaded. The soft whisper of her voice frayed then with the unwinding of the realities, and the gate vanished, to return, perhaps, at some unknown time, in some unknown place.

And from somewhere very close, only a shadow or two away, there came the sound of movement. It was a low cacophony really, and it could not at first be discerned as movement. It was more like the rustling of sticks and twigs, then the cracking of great logs as trees might sound when they are felled by the wind. And through it all was the sighing and whispering of countless leaves. It was unnatural, this collection of sound, unlike that of any beast of the forest, or mortal man, or faerie that walks. It was recognizable as movement only when one paid attention and realized it was drawing closer. And with it came the cold, evidence of an ancient malice.

The Elderman was coming for Sweyn.

But Sweyn's own mind was distant and numb, unaware of the world around him. And his own weight seemed too much burden for his knees to bear any longer. He sank to the wet earth, then back, until he sat squarely on the ground, staring into the raining darkness where his love had stood. It was more than he ever could have hoped, one last moment with his lady. But in the end it was also more than he could bear. His heart reeled between new joy and new grief. He had had her again, and he had lost her again. Perhaps the rain became less magical and wet his face. Perhaps tears fell as he mourned in the enchanted darkness.

# Chapter Fourteen

*Once a father ye were to me,*
*Once a kind man to keep to me,*
*Once upon a time ye were good to me,*
*Once I held ye would always love me.*

*What have I done ye?*
*What wound have I caused ye?*
*What offensive song have I sung ye?*
*What reason for scorn have I given ye?*

*I was wrought of oak and stone,*
*I have not blood or mortal bone,*
*I was cast to pretend this wrong,*
*I was sent to take the face of your own.*

*Donald's Bitter Forge*
*Caitlin No-Kin*

Closer now, glittering and darting and playful, were the tiny pixies. Full of boundless energy, they flitted in ceaseless pursuit of fey whims beneath the lofty boughs. Males and females were among them, in appearance like lithe young adults, giggling as they frolicked in the night air. They dazzled him. They enraptured him. They pulled at him. At another time that very allure might have led him stumbling and dazed into the darkness in pursuit of them, but in this moment it was the very thing he needed. It called to him, and drew him back from a bottomless chasm of despair.

Came the memory of the whisper of fair Eilwen's voice: Trust the pixies.

Perhaps he heeded the memory. Perhaps, as is the way with mortals, he only responded to the instinct to follow them. Whatever, he rose and lit out after them, chasing them into the darkness, without realizing it putting distance between himself and the ceaseless approach of the hateful elder.

Somewhere along the way the pixies pushed his pack from his shoulders. Perhaps it was a faerie prank. Or perhaps they meant to hasten his flight from the old elder. Certainly, they meant him good, for whenever it seemed he should stumble over an unseen fallen branch, or injure himself upon an ill-placed stone, or trip over an exposed root, the glittering creatures came close, providing just enough light for him to see his way. But he was not even aware of what they did. All thought had abandoned him. He was pixie-led and beyond mortal recall.

Sometimes some flitted close by, and in those moments he could make them out more clearly. Their forms were full of golden light, as if they were made of light. They did not actually have wings, but held the gossamer wings of

223

dragonflies in their arms. The wings shimmered a luminous blue, and Sweyn realized they were somehow enchanted.

The pixies led him long through the night, further and further from the relentless elder. But even pixies tire, and when they had led him far, they came upon a grove of rowans. There they flickered out and disappeared into the wood, leaving Sweyn suddenly alone, in his right mind, in the company of the seelie trees.

The trees were laden with clusters of bright garnet berries. He remembered Oak Peg's council. In groves of rowan he could let down his guard. These trees were entirely good. They would keep him safe beneath the protective cover of their boughs. Even the air felt better here, as if all tension was relieved from it, and all unseelie mischief banned. Perhaps he could even sleep here, though he recalled Oak Peg's warning against it. But, oh, how he needed sleep. It had been nearly two days, and in the past day he had walked untold miles, stumbled upon dark seduction, fled through a storm that did not fall through the air, experienced the elation of finding lost love, and the despair of losing it again. He was taxed beyond physical exhaustion and he longed more than anything else just to close his eyes. But the ground was wet everywhere, and the storm continued. The rowan trees were not thick enough to provide any meaningful shelter.

But ahead in the darkness he made out a dim, stationary light. Slowly, careful not to trip over deadfall, he picked his way through the wood toward it. Soon he could make it out, a tiny cottage in the forest. It was small and square, no bigger than a dozen feet in width and breadth. Made of brook stone joined with mortar, round windows were built into each wall. A door of solid rowan beams was set in one wall, and it was overhung by a tiny porch. Around the front of the cottage larger, round, flat stones had been laid into the ground to form a simple patio. All around the cottage an abundance of forest herbs grew: raspberry and serviceberry, wormwood and chamomile, and even medicinal devil's club.

An oil lamp hung from a hook beside the door, casting a small semi-circle of warm light over the flat stones before the entrance. A pale, butter-hued curtain blocked the view through the window beside the door, but a reddish light flickered behind it, as from a fire. A slender chimney of stone rose from the steeply cantered roof, and a thin trail of grey smoke curled away from it. The place had the look and feel of Little Red Riding Hood's grandmother's house, right out the fairytale, but in miniature. He remembered the old witch's warning not to be diverted, to go straight to the Tylwyth Teg's village. But fatigue was strong upon him. And though the rain didn't fall through the air, he was now soaked from brushing damp foliage and being splattered from the spray of countless churning puddles. The little cottage promised dryness and warmth and rest, and he was beginning to feel if he didn't soon get those things, he would die. Besides, in this rowan grove the little place ought to be safe. He shook off Oak Peg's advice and made straight for the door of the cottage.

But he froze just before his hand touched the door, listening. Music came from within, the gentle sounds of an instrument he remembered, a unique, unmistakable instrument. The Apple Man's harp, it sounded like. A clarsach, Caitlin had called it, a small harp strung with wire, an instrument which sang with the voice of chiming crystal bells.

He could almost hear the oak witch warning him to be wary. But he was in a rowan wood. What harm could befall him here?

He knocked then, striking the rowan door three times.

Immediately, the harping stopped. There came light footsteps. The door opened. A man met him at the entrance. His skin was fair and he had red, curly hair which fell to his shoulders, framing his face and covering his ears. He was tall and slender and his eyes were the pale azure of a clear noon sky. He might have been faerie, or mortal, Sweyn could not tell. But the man beckoned Sweyn into the cottage with a gesture, then turned and left the door standing open for Sweyn to follow as he would. The man moved with a catlike grace, an uncanny fluidity not common among mortal folk.

In Sweyn stumbled. The man had set his harp upon a great plush chair by the fire, covered in soft furs. He removed it and beckoned Sweyn to take the place. Sweyn nodded gratefully, and he fell into the chair. He was so weary it seemed as if his bones adhered to it.

The red-haired fellow took a seat upon a stool beside a rough hewn table. From there he studied Sweyn, just as Sweyn, weary but not unwary, studied him. He was as tall as Sweyn, though more slender in the shoulders and chest. He wore trousers the color of deep forest, and a tunic the pale shade of oak wood. His boots came to the knee then turned down, made of a soft leather the color of hazel. A silver torque encircled his neck and on each end were ovals the size and shape of wrens' eggs with images of songbirds engraved upon them and inlaid with yellow gold. A belt of leather encircled his waist, and a small purse hung from it. Aside from this, the man wore no other ornamentation. He had the look of a person of wealth who did not flaunt it. He possessed an air of great intelligence. His studious gaze bore, not unkindly, into Sweyn. Eventually, Sweyn decided the man presented no threat and he looked away, into the crackling fireplace which was the cottage's only illumination.

At last, remembrance of manners came to Sweyn. He stood shakily and extended a hand. "I'm Sweyn deSauld." he said. The man rose, clasped his hand at the wrist, then seated himself again. Sweyn continued. "You've no idea how glad I am to find this place. The weather was beating me up." He started to say something more, the words thank you at the edge of his lips, but he recalled Broom's advice. Never thank.

The man spoke then. His voice was melodious, like the striking of the bass strings of a harp. It flowed deep and easy and fluid. "Well met and welcome to Glen Luis, my humble study in the rowan grove. I am glad it has been of service to ye, Sweyn." Then he cocked his head and looked at Sweyn curiously. "Ye are mortal, sure, for only mortals are wont to give away their right names so easily. And it is a curious thing to see ye, I must tell true. For mortals are no' permitted in these parts. No' even folk of the Island dare come, save one who does as he pleases."

"Donald," spat Sweyn.

The other fellow nodded. "Indeed, ye know of him. He is the gillie and is accorded safety because of what his forefather did for us long ago. But in entering the wildwood, he abuses that privilege. Have ye met him?"

"He works for me," Sweyn said.

The harper's features metamorphosed from curiosity to surprise. "Then ye must be none other than the Laird of this Island."

Sweyn was so sick of having that title thrust upon him he wanted hit something, hit it and smash it and break it! The sudden force of the anger was a tangible thing, like a tempest howling through him. It swept him up so suddenly it frightened him, and it was only with the greatest of effort he was able to restrain himself from acting it out. Damn the brook ladies and their lopsided magics anyway, he thought, for now he understood the source of the anger. They had healed the hurt that hollowed his heart, but that emptiness was being filled up, eaten up, with the vengeful anger that followed in the wake of Eilwen's death.

*And what he had done with that anger . . .*

He closed his eyes, swallowed, and took several deep breaths. It was a simple, much practiced anger management technique. It had helped in the past, and it did this time too. But only just. Only just. Soon, he felt, the anger would grow to such proportion he would no longer be able to contain it.

The thought chilled him.

What might he do then?

Finally, he gathered himself together enough to say, "I'm not the damned Laird. My name is Sweyn deSauld, and I've come here to help a person I care about, and nothing else."

"Is that so?" said the harper evenly. "And by 'here,' ye must be referring to the domain of the Tylwyth Teg, for ye are on its very footstep."

Relief washed over Sweyn. "I am?" he asked, needing it confirmed again. The harper nodded and Sweyn sighed. Then he looked at his host and said, "I need to find someone who may be there."

"Well then, I may be able to help ye. I could bring word from ye. I am a bard, ye see."

Sweyn searched his memory for the meaning of the obscure term. "A musician. A poet," he said.

"Oh, aye, those things and others. A messenger among them, for bards are no' bound to a place as are faerie kin. We wander freely from land to land, sharing the news and songs and tales of the places we have been. Our geas is to keep the eldritch lore, and maintain the honor of the Old Ways. And to remember all the tales of the deeds of heroes. And to make the music of sleep, and sorrow, and joy. Folk call me Witch-hazel, but as ye have given me yer right name, and ye are a man of rank, I shall give ye mine. Among bards I am called Seoridean, and I have logged the stories of faerie kin and the Company since before we came from the rising moon."

From time to time, on evenings when Sweyn had wandered into town and sat in the tavern with the villagers, their old seanachie had ambled in. Folk had bought him sweet ales, and gladly, for when he sat among them he recounted wondrous tales of old times, and Faerie magics, things delightful to hear. Sweyn had listened in now and then, and sometimes the seanachie made mention of a mythical harper, an ancient, mysterious figure who wielded all the power of song and knew all the eldritch poems. And his name was Seoridean.

Sweyn stared at the harper in disbelief. "You mean to say you are the Seoridean that Man-by-the-Sea folk tell stories of?"

"I imagine so, unless they have another by that name, which is unlikely as it has no' been given a bairn in long and long. Yet they would know of me. Sometimes I have walked among them, on high days of Samhain and Bealtaine. I have shared lore with their seanachie, and tales with their children."

Sweyn smiled then, for perhaps his luck was turning for the better. "Can you show me the way to the Tylwyth Teg village?"

"I can," he said, "but I dinna' think I should. Perhaps better if I bear only a message. The Tylwyth Teg dinna' appreciate the trespass of strangers, especially mortal folk."

"Whether they appreciate it or not, I have to go there. I have to help my friend. And besides, I don't think they'd harm me?"

Seoridean mused upon Sweyn's words, pondered the reasoning behind them. "Ye think because ye are called Laird they will no' harm ye. Well, let me rest one fear and raise another. Ye need no' fear harm by them, be ye Laird or other mortal. The Tylwyth Teg are no' cruel. But nor are they concerned with the affairs of mortals. Ye may find them unwilling to hear ye. More likely, they will hide the way to their land in glamour so that ye may never even enter it."

Sweyn looked directly at the bard. "Please, I've got to try."

"Why?" Seoridean asked simply.

Sweyn saw no reason to conceal the truth, not here in this place. Though elsewhere in the world the truth might sound a like madman's delusion, here it was credible, as credible as a bard of elder times, harp and all, dwelling in a cottage deep in an enchanted rowan grove. So he said, "I'm after a girl called Caitlin. She is in danger. Oak Peg said she would go to the Tylwyth Teg." He paused, considering, then added, "I care for the girl." Then he looked wistfully through the curtained window, back where he had seen the shade of Eilwen in the faerie ring. Make it right, she had implored him. He had no idea how.

Seoridean held his peace for a long time and stared into the fire. The silence grew, broken only by the crackling of the flames, and the faerie rain which had increased in strength again, pelting the wooden slats of the roof. After some time the bard reached into a satchel and pulled from it a long stemmed pipe and a small leather bag. He took herbs from the bag and filled the pipe, tamped it down, and lit it with an ember from the fire. He puffed and shortly the little one room cottage was filled with the fragrance of summer blossoms. At last, still looking into the fire, he spoke. "There can be only one Caitlin of whom ye speak, for no one of Faerie or Man-by-the-Sea has used that name since that sad tale." He turned then, looked to Sweyn. "Ye search for Caitlin No-Kin."

Sweyn nodded.

"The changelings are things given in trade for mortal beasts and children. The Tylwyth Teg will no' be moved with pity toward Caitlin, even if her story comes from the Laird."

"They had better be!" Sweyn blurted, suddenly furious. "It's their habit of stealing children that started all this mess."

Calmly, Seoridean replied, "It could be said it was Gwellyan's indiscretion that began this 'mess.'"

"You arrogant. . ." Sweyn fumed, suddenly so angry he trembled. He almost rose, but he knew if he did he would strike the bard. He forced himself to stay seated, to close his eyes and listen to the rain till the anger cooled. When he could bear it, he said, "Why? You have to tell me that. Why do the Tylwyth Teg steal children?"

Seoridean smiled, but there was no humor in it. "It's complicated. Fresh ideas. Mortal vigor. Sometimes, out of pity, they take them from unworthy parents. And some mortals have their own beauty which the Tylwyth Teg find alluring. Some even possess fey hearts full of magic, and the Tylwyth Teg take them, knowing they will find no happiness in the mortals' world."

"You are justifying kidnapping," spat Sweyn. "And you say the Tylwyth Teg are not cruel?"

"The Tylwyth Teg would no' call it cruel," said Seoridean calmly. "The taken ones are treated well, adopted into their own households. They receive wondrous gifts. They live in a realm where there is no illness, the best of food, immortality. Even the taken beasts dwell in the finest stables and eat the sweetest grass. Life for them is far better than it would have been had they remained in the green world. And they are no' forced to stay. When they come of age, they may choose to return. They seldom do."

Anger made Sweyn tremble, shook his voice. "Of course not! Even abductors become parents to children who know nothing else."

But the bard continued to address him calmly. "For what they receive, faerie folk would call it a small price. But the Tylwyth Teg have observed the distress caused mortals by the exchange, so they have forbidden the practice these many centuries, save when children have been abandoned or unwanted. And if ye know the tale, ye yerself know the mortal Caitlin was a most unwanted bairn. Her own mother spurned her."

What Seoridean said was true, it was undeniable, and it took a small measure of the flame from his fury. "I know the story," Sweyn said evenly.

Seoridean nodded. "Indeed. But as ye have a care for the changeling who took the mortal Caitlin's place, I will tell ye the full mystery behind her. For changelings fade quickly when the households they are attached to spurn them. Oak Peg has told ye this, yes? It is common knowledge. In old times it was a way to be rid of a changeling and get back a taken bairn.

"But still Caitlin No-Kin persists. Even though she was found out and rejected long ago. For all these years she has carried on, alone, and yet I tell ye such power was no' part of the magic that wrought her." He stared deeply into the flickering flames, puffing long on the fragrant pipe, then added, "I tell ye this as a warning, for ye must be wary of the changeling. She is unduly strong. Perhaps her enchantment has grown over the years, and now she possesses glamour such as can even deceive a Sighted Laird."

Sweyn regarded the sharp-featured, red-haired bard. "I have spoken to her and spent time with her. There's no malice in her, no deception. She is intelligent and warm, and feels just like you and I. She's no different from any mortal girl."

But the bard shook his head. "No, lad, it is no' so. There is no true life in changelings. They are golems only. And this golem was made more than any other to appear alive and real."

"I don't believe it," Sweyn said fiercely.

Sadness was in Seoridean's voice. "I am sorry this tale must hurt ye, for ye are an outsider caught unwittingly up in it. But it is no' as ye think. Best turn yer mind from her and go home."

"Not without Caitlin."

The bard studied Sweyn.

Sweyn said, "Back home, a long time ago, I used to be a psychologist. My job was understanding what people were really like deep down under the surface. I don't know what that girl is made of any more than I know medicine, but I know that within she is as human as I am."

Seoridean shook his head. "It canna' be so."

Sweyn went on. "I have heard that all the Tylwyth Teg's greatest enchanters labored to create the changeling. They spent weeks on her, poured their most powerful magic into her. Nothing like it had ever been done before. I think when they made this changeling, they went further than they planned. Somehow they snatched hold of a soul and put it in her. Unwittingly, perhaps, but if changelings without souls are only shriveled automatons, then I can guarantee you this girl is different."

"No," said Seoridean, looking up at him. "For souls are a heritage of mortal and faerie folk. They are like seeds within us from the beginning, and flourish or wither by our choices. They canna' just be snatched from the air like birds."

"But where do they come from?" Sweyn said.

"Pardon?"

"Where do souls come from?"

The bard gave him a blank look. "Some mysteries even the Tylwyth Teg are no' privy to."

"They must come from somewhere," said Sweyn. "What if the changeling was made so perfectly a soul got confused and went into her."

"But . . . but that's not possible," Seoridean began, but there was the first hint of uncertainty in his voice. He looked back into the fire, pondered it. "Yet if it were so, it would mean someone out in the world exists without a soul." The bard blanched. "How horrible!"

But Sweyn was in no mood to comfort him. "And now that poor girl is dying in a puppet body that is winding down. Maybe the magic is just burning out. Or maybe all the years of loneliness have worn away her will to live. Hell, I don't know. Maybe the fact that Donald — the only man she knows as father — is trying to kill her has driven her over the edge. Anyway you look at it, you have to see why you have to help me get to the Tylwyth Teg. They have to help her."

Seoridean lifted his gaze from the fire, looked directly toward Sweyn. There was a dawning belief in his eyes. Or, at least, belief in the possibility.

But then there came a sound like a crash of thunder, but it did not come from the sky, and the whole cottage shuddered with the force of it. Roof beams cracked loudly. Plate glass panes in windows exploded. The wind and the rain blew in, making the tiny chimney fire sputter wildly.

Another great crash impacted the front of the cottage, and the heavy rowan plank door exploded from its hinges. The whole frame of the cottage tilted several degrees, as if something was trying to knock it over.

Out the front window, through the noisily flapping curtain, Sweyn made out a great black trunk, massive branches writhing about it. And through the window seeped the icy cold of an ancient hatred.

"The Elderman!" he gasped.

It was then grasping branches and tendrils of roots pushed into the tiny cottage, through the aperture where the door had stood, and through the window, reaching, reaching for Sweyn, the hated heir of the O'Shee house. It was then the bard grasped his small harp and struck a harsh chord and the opposite wall tumbled into a pile of broken stone. He grasped Sweyn's wrist, for Sweyn stood frozen, staring in mindless fascination at the arboreal horror, and pulled Sweyn after him. They scrambled over the broken stone wall into the cover of the surrounding rowans.

They ran then, and the Elderman lumbered after them. Sweyn turned to see how close it was, but the bard shouted, "Dinna' look at it lest it hold you in its eyeless gaze! It is slow, we can escape it, if ye dinna' stumble or stare."

Sweyn heeded the bard and turned away, watched where he ran. He leapt over fallen branches and grey stones, followed the bard through openings between thickets he otherwise would never have found. Ordinary branches of thorn whipped at his body, scratched at his face, cut him with cruel, cold fingers wherever his skin was exposed.

"I dinna' understand it," Seoridean shouted as they ran. "The Elderman has never entered a rowan wood before."

Sweyn panted, "Oak Peg said rowans keep out unseelie things."

"Aye, but he is no' unseelie," the bard vociferated.

"Then what is he?" Sweyn shouted.

"He is mad!" came the reply in the dark.

# Chapter Fifteen

*I came to the hidden glen on the ninth day, the first mortal to visit their land in eight centuries. A company of their own lords and ladies greeted me, and knights who rode roan stallions with long manes and tails that flowed in the wind. They said that though Faerie far and wide had faded and sundered into a thousand scattered lands, the realm of the Tylwyth Teg remained as it had been since the primal age, when enchantment flowed free and wild.*

*Bran O'Shee*
*Explorations of the Island*
*From the O'Shee Journals*

Men should encounter the mysteries of Faerie slowly, gently, for each new experience of it brings insight and bears a reward, but it also resists discovery and the cost of seeing is dear. The old lore was not inaccurate in saying that to encounter Faerie unready was to find only madness and death. Surely if Sweyn had had no preparation for the Island's secrets he would have been numbered among the doomed. But what Oak Peg and Coppin—though not Broom—had overlooked was that Sweyn had been exposed to fey mysteries for three years. From the time he met Eilwen, even though she had never meant him to know any part of her world, he had caught glimpses of it through her, for what is fey-touched cannot be untouched. What is enchanted cannot become mundane. Mystery and primal magic swirled around Eilwen like a morning mist. In little ways she had sewn Faerie into his heart, unaware herself of the doing. Her healing potions, her marvelous teas—those came from her eldritch lore of herbs. The way she gazed into the woodland shadows round about their chalet in Glacier Falls, or quietly hummed ancient songs while cooking dinner, or sometimes seemed to regard unseen things from the corner of her eye, bit by bit these small things had begun to open the mind of Sweyn deSauld.

So Sweyn was able to adjust to the Island more readily than most men might have. Yet things had happened this night in such rapid succession and with such intensity that he was sorely taxed. He had stumbled through an otherworldly forest. He had narrowly been drowned by the Glaistig of the pond, and plucked from her cold grasp by a puckish boy. He had met the ghost of his dear lost wife, and run with pixies through the night wood. He had seen lightning roll like waves though the clouds and rain fall upon the land though never through the sky. And now he ran through the darkness with a bard of olden legend leading the way before him. In moments when Sweyn considered it his head would swim, and he would stumble and lose his presence of mind, so he struggled instead only to keep his mind in the present moment, and terror if nothing else gave him the power to do it.

But the going was hard. It was dark and, save for instants when the queer rolling lightning lit the world, he could barely see. Often he would have fallen, slipping in mud or tripping over an unseen branch, but for Seoridean who shot out a steadying hand. Sweyn was agile by any standard, years of living on a pitching, rolling boat having taught him to keep his feet. But the faerie bard ran as if he saw clearly in the night. He seemed to flow around obstacles rather than leaping over them. He moved graceful as a cat, and as silent, and was the very contrast of Sweyn's noisy crashing ahead.

But once Sweyn did come crashing down, when he leapt over a small streamlet and snagged his foot on a tangle of deadfall on the other bank. The bard was a dozen yards ahead then and had not seen him fall. Sweyn had hit the ground so hard he had had the wind knocked out of him and could not breathe for the longest minute of his life, all the while the Elderman looming closer, the sound of his approach like the bare bones of trees scraping wildly in an autumn night's zephyr. When at last he could suck in a breath, he rolled over, and there was the thing only just behind him, impossibly massive and bringing the cold of its hatred with it. Lightning rolled over the clouds, and in the fiery illumination Sweyn saw a terrifying sight, for frozen in its trunk was the tortured face of a man. The image was as perfect as if the man had been imbedded into the tree and overlaid with a veneer of bark. And emerging from the forehead were the great horns of a stag. Thunder shook the firmament and Sweyn might have screamed in that moment, he did not know.

But then the bard was beside him, pulling him to his feet, hauling him along, and they ran on into the darkness, fleeing the Elderman's relentless pursuit.

The bard's energy seemed endless. Running did not even cause his breath to quicken. But Sweyn, already weary, was tiring quickly. "Only a bit farther!" the bard reassured him, and then another wonder, another mystery to assault Sweyn's frayed senses.

For they came to a clearing, and there arose a grassy hillock, not very high, maybe a hundred feet. No trees grew upon the hill, nothing save green grass, except at its summit where a single hawthorn of preternatural size sprouted from the earth. A thousand stars glittered in its leafy boughs, some fluttering round about it like fireflies, some alight upon its branches, some moving purposefully up and down the trunk. Around the tree great luminous toadstools grew, and within the faerie ring a plethora of eerily-lit figures danced. Some were tall and sticklike, and might have been made of twigs. Others were short and stout as tree stumps, and seemed to bear crowns of leaves for hair. Others seemed some melding of animal and man, burly figures upon goat hooves, lithe males with horns of deer, svelte women with wings of swans. Some were nude and wild, others were clothed in a motley assortment of garments, tanned skins and plush furs, pastel-hued caterpillar silks and rough, plain homespun. Some appeared to wear the bark of trees. A trio of faeries that appeared like nothing other than precociously shapely young girls were dressed in gowns of flower petals. To the side of the faerie ring another trio, as motley as the dancers within the ring, played instruments. One sawed a fiddle, another's fingers cantered wildly over a bellows-blown pipe chanter, and the third beat a booming bodhran.

The sight of the faeriemoot halted Sweyn in his tracks. Instantly the Elderman was forgotten and his frazzled mind was immersed in their dance. His heart leapt with the sensuous cavorting of the nude figures. He nearly burst with mirth at the humorous capering of the stout folk dressed in bark. The musicians' jig grabbed for him with hooks, tugging and pulling him into the dance. And he would have gone too, all Oak Peg's warnings forgotten, but for the bard who grabbed his wrist and heaved him along, right up to the hillside, where they met a wooden door made of white rowan encircled by mistletoe set into the very hill! Seoridean pushed it open and beyond was another sight more wondrous than the last. Through the door in the hill he saw a mist-shrouded forest spreading out to the horizon—he overlooked it as from the top of a plateau. The sky above was the clear plum wine of an endless twilight—no storm clouds roiled in it. Night birds called from that forest, whippoorwills and owls and nighthawks. The forest was ancient, each tree as high as a castle tower, but there were scattered breaks throughout it. Indeed, the doorway opened into a such a glade, a break in the sea of trees. It was a tiny meadow of green and perfect grass, soft and sweet as a down bed. And wildflowers grew there—he could smell them from here, like fruit and honey and rare spices. His mouth fell open and he gaped, lacking words, lacking thoughts.

"Go!" the bard vociferated. "Nothing enters the Tylwyth Tegs' land but they invite it. Go!"

But he could not go. He was frozen by the wonder, stunned by the impact of so much of Faerie so fast.

There was no time to snap Sweyn out of it. The bard shoved Sweyn fiercely, pushing him through the door, hoping to the goddess the shock of the passage would not lay the mortal low. Then Seoridean himself leapt through and pulled the rowan door shut behind him, barring the Elderman.

Sweyn stumbled forward, regained a teetering hold on his balance. Mute and dazzled, Sweyn turned slowly around, taking it all in. He and the bard stood at the top of a treeless hill. There were no dancers, no door, no faerie ring. They stood alone in yet a deeper world, surrounded only by the endless forest and the lucid twilight sky. But where in the last place he had felt the chill of danger lurking in a mix of dark and bright enchantments, here there were only seelie things. He could feel it. There was nothing in this realm—this deeper layer of Faerie—for him to fear.

Sweyn sighed deeply. It felt to him as if all his life he had waited for a glimpse of this place, though he had never known it. He breathed deeply the sweet air, soaked in the peaceful twilight. As if for the first time in an age, he did not feel hunted. He could perish now, in this place, and it would be perfect.

And with that final thought Sweyn staggered, unable to keep his feet. Seoridean reached out to steady him, but Sweyn was oblivious of the bard, missed his hand. At last, Sweyn had exceeded his capacity. The realm of the Tylwyth Teg was like a flawless gem, quite beyond the imagination of mortals, and beyond their ability to accept. Its very perfection was overwhelming Sweyn as surely as the Giant's Couch atop Mount Snowdonia had overwhelmed brave Durus. Sweyn shuddered. It felt to him as if he were an overloaded circuit. The world swam out of focus. And then he fell onto his side.

The bard was quick to Sweyn's side, fearing the worst. He had seen it before. When mortal children came into this realm—those who had been exchanged with changelings—they took well to the land, for they were young and pliable. But when adults came, those who had had the green world's relentless narrow reason hammered into them for decades, they rarely did so well. Sometimes they lost their senses. Sometimes they babbled mindlessly till they were returned to the green world, where they came back to themselves with no recollection of what had happened. And sometimes they fell and died in an instant. Seoridean feared for a moment this last fate had befallen his new companion. But when he knelt close by he found Sweyn still breathed, and his heart still beat, though the pulse was weak and erratic. Sweyn was slipping away. The mortal was tired as death, and hammered with Faerie. He needed rest, and time to absorb everything.

Seoridean could give him that; he had the magic to do so. He rolled Sweyn onto his back so he would be comfortable in the bed of grass. Then Seoridean seated himself cross-legged nearby and lifted his wire harp into his lap. Expertly, his fingers created a flawless, sweet arpeggio. Then, with skilled hands, he evoked suantrai, the music of sleep.

Time passed, Sweyn did not know how much. For the longest time, he was immersed in sweet mindless depths, dreams swirling unrecollected. Then Oak Peg's warning flashed through his mind—Ye must no' sleep!—and he became aware he was sleeping, lulled by splendid music that sounded like chiming crystal bells. He opened his eyes suddenly, sat up, found himself atop the hill, lying in lush green grass beneath an amethyst sky. The bard was harping a few feet away. "How long was I out?" he asked immediately.

Seoridean responded, but not to his question. "Ye dreamed," said he.

Sweyn tilted his head to one side, perplexed by the bard's response.

Seoridean continued. "Ye dreamed much, and spoke it in yer sleep. I understand ye better now, Sweyn deSauld. Ye were the husband of Eilwen and through her heir to the Lairdship. But in yer heart ye are no' an O'Shee. Yer soul is tormented and wanders. But ye've the makings of a fine O'Shee in ye, should ye choose."

"I don't want it," Sweyn slurred through sleep-numbed lips.

"Do ye tell me that now?" Seoridean said, still harping lightly, hypnotically.

What the hell, Sweyn decided. Be honest. So he said, "Frankly, I'd like to find Caitlin and just go. I'd sell Dundubh Cottage and wash my hands of this place too, but I promised Eilwen otherwise."

"A promise?" Seoridean said, raising his eyebrows.

Sweyn nodded.

"Ah, a promise." The bard sighed, showing the first sign of weariness. And then he said, "Long hours I have played as ye slept, played ye songs of health and rest and strength. And as ye talked in yer sleep, I have pondered yer words.

"Promises and oaths and bindings and Pacts. Look where the tangled web of it all has brought us, to the very end of all things. The end of the O'Shee house. The end of the Pact. The end of the Island.

"The days of the Westernmost Tuath have faded, and perhaps it is now fit all our kind set into the Dreaming West. I feared it before, but when I think of the cost I feel it might be best. Poor Eilwen, whose family was torn apart by faerie meddling. Caitlin No-Kin, a fair damsel bound to a changeling's husk and doom. And yerself, an innocent mortal dragged into this tragedy."

"I'm not innocent," Sweyn stated. "You don't know what I've done."

"Oh, it is true, I dinna' see the very thing. But I see a blackness within ye, something ye must reckon with. But I dinna' see evil, only black. And sometimes, Sweyn, good men must do black things. But that does no' make them other than good."

Sweyn shook his head. Faerie madness.

Seoridean said, "Whatever becomes of our Island, ye must understand the fate of heroes and good men if yer soul is ever to find peace." Then the harper played with greater strength, a song of sleep and dreams. Sweyn was drawn irresistibly into the inviting dark behind his eyelids and fell back upon his bed of grass. And in his dreams came the melodious voice of the bard, and with the voice, a tale . . .

*********

For seven years the Hundred Horsemen guarded the valley of ancient beeches and towering, twisty oaks. For seven years the fair Asrai swam free and safe in their shining brooks beneath the cool light of the moon. For seven years no iron entered the valley save that worn by the knights themselves. And for the faerie folk of the valley they were restful years, such as they had not known since the first mortal forged iron and cut down trees, since the first king scarred the earth with a winding road, since the first conqueror pushed west and drove the wild Celts toward the sea. In the valley of the Asrai, for a mere breath, they were safe at last.

In the second of those years Elidurydd met Dylan O'Shee in the forest at the elder tree, the husk and ghost of her beloved Mwdr. They had agreed to meet there once a year to remember the brave horned lord who had fallen by sad mistake, fallen to arrows of iron to buy his Lady a moment to speak alone with the valiant captain of the Hundred and try to save the Asrai. On Samhain eve they came together, only the two of them, and an aperture formed there, a momentary hazing of the veil between the worlds when they could peer across an endless sea and catch a glimpse of far white shores. There the Lady's horned lord waited, hoping also to steal a glimpse of her, and that lone moment kept grief from breaking him. But this was all they had. Elidurydd was both mortal and Gwragedd, one of the high folk and truly immortal. She could never join Mwdr in the Dreaming West. Yet they were glad of this moment, and made do. As long as they possessed this enchanted valley, they could come to this place on this twilight and strengthen one another.

But with the passing of twilight, the window frayed. When night fell with a sheet of silver stars it was altogether gone. Then Elidurydd gathered her strength and spoke to Captain Dylan. "Your knights have proven themselves faithful men to keep their word."

"They have souls," Dylan said. "They were mercenaries, but they found they had souls."

"Indeed." She smiled. It was the gentle caress of the summer breeze. Her skin was finer than porcelain, sweet cream and snow blended in measure. She was radiant in the dark. She took a step toward him. "Your knights would follow you to any length, suffer any pain for their captain. But they should not be alone." She turned and looked beyond the silent elder, in the direction the sun had set, where a moment ago there had been the window into the Dreaming West, but no more. "Oh, Dylan O'Shee, your men live in tents and hovels of sticks and mud. It is not right for good men to be thus. Give them a corner of the valley. You are friends and welcome to it, so long as you bring no more iron, and do not cut the land with roads, and do not break stone. Let them make cottages of brook stone and mortar, or logs of deadfall, and invite damsels to be their brides. And if they know folk who long for the eldritch things of old, let them invite them also into this valley. Your number may be nine hundred."

Said the Captain of the Hundred: "Lady Elidurydd, ye speak of the founding of a village. But King Maelgwn presses us hard. He believes we hoard gold and silver in this valley. Soon, he will make all out war to obtain it. How can we found a village knowing he may soon come to pillage and burn."

"That time may indeed come, Dylan O'Shee. Rest assured, that evil king on our border will not rest until he has taken this valley, for there is more between you and him than gold and silver. He hates you for abandoning his service. So doing, you have made him appear weak in the eyes of neighboring kings and shamed him. A bard in his service who is our friend, one Seoridean, known to mortals as Taliesin, has told us. Right now the brave bard confounds King Maelgwn, distracting him from us. He buys us time, a moment to build something lasting. But he will not be able to stay Maelgwn's hand forever.

"In the time we have, gather those among mortals who still love the twilight. Build a village, and become a people. But know that a time will come when you will become wanderers all. It will be hard then. But a wise witch will come from the oaks. She is a treewife, and she will show your people the road they must follow. Heed her. She will teach you the last hope to save faerie kin and yourselves."

After that night, Dylan saw Elidurydd wander the valley throughout the winter. She appeared sad, and when he inquired of her sadness, she told him she was bidding farewell to things she had loved. And by spring he saw her no more, save only upon each Samhain when they came together at the elder tree to look into the Dreaming West and remember the fallen horned lord.

As soon as spring melted the snows and horses could run, Dylan sent riders out far and wide to the dwindling Celtic lands. His riders put forth a call for willing damsels to come. They sought only those whose hearts were in love with old and eldritch things. They accepted no starry-eyed maidens whose hearts were set on sophomoric romance with knights. Their road would be hard, and those that would come must be dedicated. And sometimes other folk came with the damsels, folk discontent with greedy kings and pressing invaders; folk who desired to keep the Old Ways of their forefathers.

Three years later Dylan met with Elidurydd upon a frosty Samhain night. He informed her that his riders had completed scouring the lands far and wide, and had gathered together a company. The village Elidurydd had wished had been built. She was pleased, and they walked the moonlit wood till morning twilight. Then she laid a kiss upon his beard-roughened cheek, and she bid him farewell. "Perhaps we will meet again upon another turning of the wheel," she told him. "I do not believe we will meet again in the green world." And then she strode from the forest path down to the brook of the Asrai she loved. She immersed herself in the icy waters and a salmon swam upstream where she had been. And from that time she was not seen again by Dylan or the Company. One tear the mighty warrior shed for the lady, one tear to pierce his battle-made hardness and say goodbye for him.

But on the day following the fair maid's leaving, an aged mortal crone entered the village. She carried with her two sacks. One was full of herbs and seeds, for she was a witch, a treewife, and a healer. The other was empty. And when folk asked her the purpose of the empty sack she clung to, she said it was carried against a time when they must gather the Ogham seeds. She dwelt only among great oaks and ate the mast of acorns, so the people took to calling her Oak Peg, and no one among them knew her right name.

\*\*\*\*\*\*\*\*\*

Seoridean abandoned, then, the bardic affectations. He moved ahead through the tale, giving Sweyn the true account and not the mixed up recollections of lesser faeries and mortals—whose memories are poor and scattered. Seoridean's tale crossed the years until he came to the conclusion, and there he spoke plainly while Sweyn slept beside him, his slumber full of enchanted dreams of things that were.

\*\*\*\*\*\*\*\*\*

Fog covered the mountainside, a fog so thick it felt like the kiss of rain. Autumn leaves were thick upon the forest floor, bright and gold, but the ceaseless fog had softened them so that even the enormous warhorses of the Hundred Horsemen could trod silently upon them.

Each knight was hid behind a tree, or a boulder, or back in the heavy dawn shadows of the forest. They were ranged atop the mountain that divided the valley from Maelgwn's realm. It was a low mountain; no side of it was very steep, and on the valley side great trees ascended to the very top. On Maelgwn's side was a great meadow that went halfway down the mountain, and then the forest began again.

The knights remained hidden in the leafy cover, for their numbers were few, and to have any hope they must keep the advantages of stealth and the high ground. They were here, and prepared, because only days before the bard Seoridean had left Maelgwn's kingdom once and for all, having effected the rescue of a kinsman, and he had come and warned Dylan that Maelgwn would march against him and arrive this very day.

For five hard years since Elidurydd had vanished, the wicked king had pressed the Hundred. He was hungry for whatever treasure he thought they horded in the valley, but most of all he hated Dylan who had dared spurn him. But each time Maelgwn's soldiers came, Dylan's knights turned them back before even one of the enemy had set foot in the domain of the Asrai. But every year, in the season of autumn, Maelgwn returned, each time with more men, and more steel, and more fury. This time Maelgwn meant to take the valley, whatever the cost. Seoridean had warned Dylan, "He comes with thousands. Ye canna' hope to stop him. Even though all the faerie folk were to stand with ye, his cold iron would cut ye down." The hard choice was made that very day. They must all retreat. But the bard had said King Maelgwn would not have it. He had such hatred for Dylan that he had paid dearly for fast mercenaries on horseback to pursue them. The mercenaries would hunt them down, knight and dame and child, after the valley was taken.

In that night of terrible counsels it was Oak Peg who brought instruction to Dylan. "We will leave all, and take with us only a little grain and what money we have to purchase our needs. And we will become wanderers in far kingdoms." And so that very night, with many sore tears and desperate farewells, and endless rending hearts and cries of children who did not understand why they must bid goodbye to the knights who were their fathers, all the Company left their tiny hold in the northern lands of the Cymry. Only the Hundred Horsemen remained behind.

And now, the villagers having fled three days before, every man of the Hundred had taken his place at the height of the mountain. Each guarded not only the valley, but the escape of a beloved wife and beloved children. They stood their ground to buy their folk time to flee.

Angus, Dylan's oldest and dearest friend, a great giant of a man with flowing red mane and curling beard of fire, was mounted upon a massive sable steed beside Dylan. A cold north wind streaked his red locks sidewise across his green cloak. The pair of them, the only visible of the Hundred, stood at the highest point where they commanded the best vantage. Below them, slipping clumsily through the scattered trees of the meadow, a massive host approached, numbering thousands. Mostly frightened peasants, tired and cold, it was plain they would rather be home in their villages, warming beside a fire. These could easily be turned back. But behind their endless numbers were a company of archers, and behind them a company of horsed hunters, the mercenaries Maelgwn had hired to track and murder the villagers.

Angus shook his head. The visor of his silvery helm was up, revealing grim features. "A hard fight, this," he said in the gruff voice of a middle-aged and stone-hard warrior. "Even peasants sting when their numbers are great enough."

Dylan held his peace and watched the approaching doom. All he had fought for in this place, all he had held dear, would be crushed beneath their numberless boots. He could not keep his promise to the Lady and keep this valley, and it pained him sorely.

And he had a wife now, chosen from among the Company. A fair, raven-haired lady of the last Celtic tribes of Gaul, across the channel. He had promised his heart to the maid and he was a man of his word. He loved her. And she had born him a son their first year, a fine boy now four years old, with hair as dark as his mother's, and skin as fair, and a face that was endlessly lit by the wonder of the faerie glamour of the enchanted valley.

He would never see them again.

It pained him more.

Angus took note of what burned in his friend's dark eyes, and he turned to him and said, "Dinna' think on it, lad. It'll only make it harder."

"They are my own, Angus. Could I do less?"

Angus smiled a humorless smile, clapped a large hand on his friend's shoulder. "Bah, dinna' listen to this old fool. I can do no less for my own."

Dylan looked up and down the line of wood that demarcated the ridge of the mountain top. Even his trained eyes could not see his loyal men, concealed in those trees. But in his heart he saw them. Grim Ian, who rode a piebald horse and had two daughters as bright as sunlight on daffodils. Stout Art, huge as a bear, who held his own wee wife as gently as a ewe mothers her lamb. Valiant Leod, who rode into battle like a storm and spent his evenings carving toys for his three sons. There were so many, each dear to him. And so many memories of good things, green shadows, innocent creatures, bright knowledge, warm family, close friends sharing ale and venison, evening walks with his wife when the nightingales sang.

All slipping away.

"Ye love them, ye do," Angus said to his friend. "And the Company needs ye. Go back to them, Dylan. How will they fare with none but that daft old witch to guide them? I'll carry the battle for ye."

A brief laugh escaped the dark warrior's throat. He turned to his friend. "Ye said to me once, years and years ago, that I showed the Hundred how to have souls. Would ye have me lose my own now?"

The red knight grunted. He shook his bearded head.

"We stood together," said Dylan. "We rode together. We will fall together."

Setting his jaw square, catching a gleam in his eye, the red knight nodded.

The enemy was close now. They could see their king now, riding like a coward behind the endless pikes of his peasants.

The company of archers stopped and fired the first valley from their longbows, testing their range. Many arrows flew into the wood, striking no other home than the sides of trees. Many arrows fell around the dark warrior and the red. They did not move, they did not flinch. They kept their courage. They kept their honor.

"Well, it is time," said Angus.

"For the Asrai," whispered Dylan.

"For our families," said Angus.

Dylan, the captain of the Hundred Horsemen, drew his broadsword from his sheath, lifted it high over his head. It gleamed quicksilver bright in the first sunbeams from the east. The signal. From the forest the calls of many birds announced the Hundred had seen and were ready.

"Remember," Dylan told the red warrior, "the soldiers are nothing, the archers are nothing. We drive through and Maelgwn's horsed hunters fall."

Angus was breathing deeply now, the battle readiness coming upon him. He nodded, his face flushed. He snapped shut the visor of his helm.

"For the Lady!" Dylan yelled. The dark knight and the red knight kicked their steeds' flanks and charged into a tempest of pikes and spears. Behind them, on the left and right came the knights of the Hundred Horsemen like a rush of wind, the colors of their ladies' streaming from ribbons tied round their arms, the device of the Gwragedd burning bright green upon their shining breastplates. Their horses woke thunder on the mountainside and the peasants of Maelgwn broke before them like water as they drove down, through them, through the disheveled lines of archers, into the host of mounted hunters, and their battle cry rushed down the valley like a spear to Maelgwn himself, to strike fear into the empty, greedy husk of his heart. For the words that tore like fire and lightning from their throats spoke of a thing Maelgwn could not comprehend, and never had. Their battle cry, even as they fought losing amidst thousands was unforgettable:

"For our souls!"

*********

Many days had passed and the first snows of autumn had fallen and melted away. What survived of Maelgwn's forces had entered the enchanted valley and found it empty. The village of the Company stood frozen in time, food abandoned on tables, hearths with fresh ashes and pots of water dangling over them, half cooked sides of venison on spits, clothes half in the wash. No gold. No silver. No women to rape or children to steal. No easy blood to spill. Only the silent valley, sighing in the cold wind of winter's eve. It seemed to them as if the villagers had vanished, as if ghosts had taken them. Rumors abounded the valley was haunted and they fled soon after, without dreams of rich plunder to hold their courage intact.

When they were gone, before the next snow fell, an old woman, wrinkled, shriveled, entered the valley. She led by the hand a single small child, a boy of four. His skin was the color of cream on snow, his hair as black as a raven. They went to the mountainside where the battle had been fought and they found the slain lying all about, the abandoned detritus of kings, who throw men into their causes and forget them when their purpose is served. They walked among the dead and the old woman muttered strange, unknown words. Words, the young boy was wise enough to know, like the Gwragedd spoke. She found each of the Hundred, and let fall a little powder of crushed herbs upon their bodies. She kissed gently the brow of Angus, the red knight, and she said a strange thing to him, a thing the boy would never understand the meaning of in all his days. She said, "I forgive you your arrows of iron." And she sprinkled the powder on him.

And then she found the dark warrior. The boy was with her and his eyes were red with tears. He saw the old woman watching him and he was ashamed, but she told him, "Cry, Connor O'Shee. It is good to weep when we lose the things we hold most dear." And the boy hugged the fallen dark knight, and then the old woman did the same. And they built a pyre over him with heavy sticks, as large as their small bodies could carry. And they carved oghams into the trees all about, calling them to watch over Dylan as he ventured out upon the Wheel.

Then they climbed to the top of the mountain, at the waning of the day. When the sun touched the horizon, and the icy sky was a blaze of ruby and flaming clouds, she spoke more faerie words, and all throughout the valley fires spouted, bright and hot, and so the fallen Hundred were turned to ash, and no raven ever came down upon them.

And when the sun fell beyond the horizon and no light was in the sky but the violet that precedes full black, she led the tearful boy by the hand, gently, back into the enchanted valley, what had been the last safe place for eldritch things in the west. But blood and iron and hate had poured into the valley like a plague. The delicate fey things here could not bear them, and the magic of the valley was fading. Soon the faerie folk of even this enchanted place would fade into the Dreaming West.

She took the boy to the stream where the Lady Elidurydd once swam with the Asrai. "Look," she said. She swept her hand down into the clean, biting cold water, and came up with a seed. Wet, it glittered like a dark jewel in her fingers. "Enchantment fades, but never fails. It is like a felled tree which may regrow from the root, if the earth loves it."

"What is it, Oak Peg?" asked the child who cupped the seed and held it in wonder.

She smiled softly at him. "It is a seed. It is an Asrai." She stood, leaning on a slender sapling of alder. The alder broke itself from its roots and gave itself to her service as a staff. They walked up and down the brook and gathered the gleaming seeds. Then they went through the wood, and found hidden places where the brook ladies had gathered, and there found nuts of hazel. And they went further, to the haunts of the horned ones, but horned ones were not there. Yet there were seeds, like gems in the freezing loam. Acorns of oaks. Seeds of faerie hope.

And last in the night they made their way to a great elder tree. Embedded in its trunk now was the sad face of a noble man with horns of a stag. The old woman touched the face of rough bark very gently, very tenderly. Her eyes were full of love. And longing. Her eyes were red. Tears glistened on her cheeks. This was a marvel to the boy, for he had never seen the old woman cry. He had thought she was too strong for tears.

"Why are you crying, Oak Peg?" he asked her.

Still looking at the face, her eyes distant and misty, she told the child, "I am just remembering . . . better times. Good people. Lost love." She leaned forward then, kissed the cold bark face. Then she stood up, sprinkled her powder on the trunk of the great elder tree. They stood back and she spoke the faerie words.

It happened slowly, subtly. First, for a long time, there was only the pleasant fragrance of wood smoke. Then cherry coals were seen in the trunk. In the darkness they worked their way up the tree, lighting it like webs of frozen red lighting. And then the tree was all a great blossoming rose of flame. It burned hot, but it did not burn any other forest tree, though they pressed close about. By the first hint of dawn, when a new light snow began to fall, all that remained of the mighty elder were cool ashes.

Oak Peg led young Connor to the tree's corpse. A seed lay there in the grey-white bed. "Take it," she whispered.

The boy knelt and lifted the seed.

"Will you make me a promise, child?" she asked.

"Of course, Oak Peg."

"Will you gather the faerie seeds all your life? And give the tradition to the Company?"

The child did not understand then. But he nodded. And that was enough for Oak Peg. An O'Shee's nod was a promise never to be doubted. An O'Shee's word was stone.

She took the boy's hand, led him away from the sad heap of ash, through the silent wood, to a place far away, another friendlier kingdom far beyond the valley of the Asrai. The falling snow blew softly, swirling on the dawn breezes. As they walked to that place where the Company was camped, she taught him lore. "They are failing, you see, the faerie folk. Failing from this land. Perhaps forever. This is the only way. I will bind them in their seeds, all that we can find, by oak and gorse and even wicked willow. And we will gather their seeds. And, one day, we will take them far away where they may thrive again."

*********

Seoridean finished the tale and Sweyn continued to sleep, all that he needed. Seoridean sat nearby and harped healing airs to facilitate his rest. And in that rest, in the tale, in the dreams of valiant things gone by, there Sweyn found his soul, and what it meant to be an O'Shee.

# Chapter Sixteen

*If nothing else, mortal folk and faerie kin share this bond:
the things that heal us best hurt us most.*

Coppin
*Keeper of the Cottage*

He awoke to harping in a twilight that had no beginning and no ending. The air was cool and full of the fragrance of elms and moonflowers and dewy nectar. All weariness was gone. The sense of disequilibrium was gone. The world was no longer slipping out from under his feet. He found he could stand and he had no doubt why. He knew who he was and the bizarre twists of a reality that could not bide logic no longer confounded him. He knew who he was. He knew his name. In whatever way enchantment metamorphosed the world around him, who he was was a solid thing he could depend on.

"I am Sweyn O'Shee," he said quietly, gazing into the flaming west, where a scatter of broken clouds branded gold and crimson upon the amethyst horizon.

"So ye have found yer strength," said the bard. He set the harp gently, lovingly, beside him on a soft cloth. "And now it seems ye understand the mystery of the O'Shee line, and how ye fit into it."

A light wind blew, smooth and steady, no gusts. It was the kind of wind a seaman would favor, a gentle but firm breath that could carry a sailing vessel far over a mild sea. Sweyn became aware of cloth snapping in the wind, looked behind him. Tents in the form of great halls and pavilions, made of iridescent cloth, had been set upon the hill. They were framed with poles of pale rowan, and colorful pennants flew from them, and banners bearing devices of ebony fields, intricate knotwork and silver stars. Sweyn realized that while he had slept the Tylwyth Teg had come.

For the most part they were gathered in their tents, but sometimes he caught sight of them, striding purposefully from one pavilion to another. They were tall and beautiful, with flowing manes of amber and sable upon the men, and soft cascades of copper and autumn maple locks upon the ladies. Around their camp were their horses, great roan creatures with long manes that flowed behind them in the way dulse dances with the tide. Ribbons were tied in the horses' manes, and their hooves were as bright as burnished bronze. The horses grazed contentedly on sweet grass atop the hill.

From within the more distant tents, Sweyn heard harpers, flutists and pipers plucking and blowing winsome tunes of stunning sweetness. Silhouettes of ladies dancing with their lords were cast upon the walls of the tent halls by lamplight. The smell of meat and cooking vegetables and delicate herbs was in the air. An evening feast was being prepared upon the hill.

But Sweyn and Seoridean were well away from the encampment. Over them, an octagon of cloth had been set on polls, a canopy to shield the mortal from the intoxicating light of the eldritch moon. Rugs and soft cloths had been strewn all about beneath the canopy, all laid out to help Sweyn rest. There were no wary guards about, and Seoridean himself was quite at ease, for here they need not fear the Elderman nor any unseelie thing. The realm of the Tylwyth Teg was a world apart, even from Faerie, and nothing entered it save by their leave. Not even Man's iron and cut stone could harm this fair realm, and so the world of the Tylwyth Teg had never diminished nor faded. Only, the way to it had moved with the Company to the Island.

Sweyn knelt, picked up a stone from between the blades of grass. He stood and studied it. It was smooth as polished quartz, bluer than a tropic sea. It could have been sand-polished sapphire, for all he could tell. Perhaps in this resplendent world such perfect gems were common pebbles. He slipped the stone between his fingers and threw it hard and away. It spiraled through the air until it thumped against the trunk of a distant silver birch.

Sweyn told Seoridean, "The O'Shee line appears broken because it is not bound in blood. The lineage is held together by the spirit of the O'Shees."

The bard nodded. "Aye. No mortal line could survive so many centuries in the violence of the green world. Yet the line had to survive. A choice was made, and Lady Elidurydd wove a geas. If one had the heart and spirit of an O'Shee in his or her breast, that one could become an O'Shee, a keeper of the fair and fey. Only, one had to be properly exposed to the family in some way, usually through marriage if no' blood, though a few times O'Shees have been adopted after long years of friendship."

Then Seoridean sang a snatch of some ancient lay:

Mortal blood does turn to dust,
like cold iron their flesh must rust,
yet their spirits wax immortal,
of ageless strength forged supernal.
A new way are the O'Shees found,
and only willing are they bound,
by blood or love are they made,
in amity the family staid.

"Elidurydd wove that skein," Seoridean said when he had finished.
"You can say it. Oak Peg."
The bard nodded. "They are the same, as ye now understand."
Sweyn turned to face the bard, though it was hard to pull his eyes from the endless faerie sunset. "So she is faerie kin? But I have seen her handle iron. Cold iron!"

Seoridean said, "She is as mortal as yerself. She was born in the primal days of the green world, long and long before even Dylan, back in the time before Men even had iron. She was a rare woman, born witchy. She had the Sight from the first and could see into our world. She grew to womanhood walking between the green world and Faerie, and she was loved and respected by all for her wisdom and her enchantment.

"One day, while walking in the wood, she met the horned lord, Mwdr. She thought him at first a faun, with his great gentle dark eyes, his moonlight skin.

For him, he thought her more delicate and fair than the brook ladies themselves. Their love was sealed from the first night when they danced together beneath an eldritch moon. Then she forsook the green world to dwell with Mwdr in Faerie.

"Now dwelling in Faerie changes mortals, as yer own ancient lore attests. Time flows in endless spirals. Enchantment sustains all things. And should a mortal come here and spend much time, that mortal will become like faerie folk, becoming like the being the heart most resembles. Elidurydd was beautiful and graceful and of the pure woodland all at once. It was only natural she should come to be numbered among the Gwragedd. And so, over the ages she lost her mortal nature, and became as like to faerie kin as yer kind may.

"But Elidurydd never forgot her mortal kindred, and even wild Mwdr took a fondness to them, for her sake. So often they ventured together into the green world. And in their walks, over the passing of the eons, they saw the coming of iron and the cutting of stone, and the burning of the wild places far and wide to make place for farms and towns. Their hearts went out to fading faerie folk and they conceived a plan to create a place, a last safe place, for them.

"But to accomplish her plan, she would need the help of mortals. Elidurydd chose to ally with a man of noble heart, Dylan, the first true O'Shee, for she knew he would believe in her cause and take it up. But to parley with him, Elidurydd had to catch him alone, for the Gwragedd are sorely shy of mortal men. She and the horned lord found Dylan out hunting one day, and Mwdr took his stag's form and led the other hunters away so she could speak with him alone. And as ye know, he was tragically slain by Angus who took him for an ordinary stag, for the horned ones are vulnerable to iron in their wild form. Cut down by Angus' arrows, Mwdr's spirit went into the Dreaming West.

"Now, Elidurydd achieved her aim and won the heart of Dylan to her cause. She saved faerie kin, and that was a victory. But for it she suffered a terrible tragedy, for no' only did Elidurydd lose her lover to the green world, but she, being mortal, had no hope of ever being with him again. For when faerie folk fall, they go forever into the Dreaming West. But mortals, when they pass this life, go on to the Otherworld where they may stay long or return in time to the here and now and live again."

Sweyn knew well what it is like to lose love. "That's horrible," he rasped.

"Aye," nodded the bard. "And Elidurydd's heart was broken and she swore she would never again enter Faerie, no' out of spite, but out of shame, for she blamed herself for his loss.

"And now she has dwelt so long in the green world that her Gwragedd nature begins to fade. In old times, when she first came to guide the Company as the oak witch, her aged appearance was mere glamour. Ye would have seen through it with yer Sighted eyes. But now she is losing her immortality and the old crone ye see of her is her right self. It could no' happen to a true Gwragedd, but she who was mortal from the beginning is returning to what she was."

"So Oak Peg is dying," Sweyn said. The revelation shocked and saddened him, and the depth of his own feelings surprised him.

"I dinna' know." Seoridean shook his head. "None has ever become so like the faerie folk as Oak Peg, and then left the faerie world. Perhaps she will eventually age and die. Perhaps she has withered all she will. All that is known is that, living beyond Faerie, she has grown weaker over the centuries."

Sweyn listened in silence and frowned, for the tale was bitter. But when it was done he remained puzzled. "But there's still a lot I don't understand. If the horned lord was so good, how did he become that killing thing? How did he become the Elderman?"

"Were you separated from your beloved forever, would you no' become mad and bitter with grief, Sweyn?"

Sweyn ground his teeth. He knew he could. He had.

Seoridean continued. "What ye know as the Elderman is only the husk of what Mwdr once was, for whenever faerie folk fall in the green world they leave a husk in the form of the ogham herb or tree they are bound to. It is a mindless thing that, in other circumstances, might be content only to drink sunlight by day and wander the wood by night, as any proper shrub. But when Mwdr was separated from his own fair love, all that was good and fine in himself went into the Dreaming West. The husk that was left is but a ghost. It has only shadows of his heart, and what it most remembers is the agony of love lost forever, and a dim knowledge that it was caused by the O'Shees. While Elyduridd could see her beloved's spirit on the shores of the Dreaming West from the faerie gate in the valley of the Asrai, the great tree's anguish was soothed. But when the Company was driven from the valley, that gate was lost and the Elder has since dwelt in endless grief. Over the centuries what gentleness of Mwdr remained in the tree ghost failed. Madness grew. Now all it knows is a lust for revenge."

"But then for what damnable reason did Oak Peg bring its seed here? Why didn't she leave it back in Wales?"

Seoridean spoke slowly, addressing a student who was entirely a novice. "Because the Elderman is as much a victim of this tragedy as any of the others, Sweyn. What has become of him is no' his fault. Besides, he is of no real danger to anyone save the O'Shees."

"But it attacked you too in the rowan grove," Sweyn pointed out.

The bard shook his head. "No. It came for ye. I just happened to be in the way."

Now Sweyn understood the thing's hatred of him. Because he was an O'Shee. From the time he married Eilwen. Perhaps, he felt, he had always been an O'Shee and only had not known it.

They sat in silence a while, watching the eternal sunset from beneath the awning while Sweyn absorbed the bardic lore. Finally, he took a deep breath and stepped from beneath the shelter, regarded a titanium moon high in the sky. It was a slender crescent suspended in a wine-hued sea. As he gazed up at it and thought about Seoridean's tale, images passed through his mind. A red knight and a black, racing into a storm of arrows and spears. Men who found their souls and fought for an impossible hope, against impossible odds. His heart pumped with pride and sadness for Dylan's valor. This was his legacy. This was his tragedy.

But in hearing the full of Dylan's tale, he found the story contained another lesson, one these folk had overlooked, perhaps because the faerie mind is quite alien to that of Man's. Sweyn turned to face the bard, and declared, "For all your lore, bard, you are ignorant."

The bard raised an eyebrow. It was said it was not wise to offend faerie folk who are immortal and whose memories are long.

But Sweyn went on. "Your kind talk of this limit and that binding. One thing is impossible and another is forbidden. And yet the man whose sacrifice allowed you to continue till now didn't believe that, did he? He fought and died for what some might have considered a lost cause because he believed if good men hold true, nothing is impossible."

The bard said, "Dylan was a noble man, but mortal folk have long been known to cast themselves into hopeless causes."

"Not hopeless, Seoridean. Hard, yes. Damn near impossible. A hundred men to stop thousands. A single Company to preserve an old world. Dylan believed it could be done. He poured everything of himself into it, and in the end it cost him his life. But he was right. He succeeded. The fact that you are here proves it."

Sweyn reached out a strong hand and clapped the slight bard firmly on the shoulder, pulled him an elbow's span away, looked him squarely in the eye. "What separates mortals and immortals, Seoridean, is not where we go when we die, not enchanted realities and green worlds. What separates us, why you need us, is because your kind accept their limits, and mine will not believe anything is impossible."

The bard regarded Sweyn, and it seemed for an instant awe was in his eyes, as if he beheld not a bedraggled seaman but a towering knight of old come again. At last his ancient, youthful eyes smiled, and he, too, clasped Sweyn's shoulder. "More than the O'Shee spirit is in ye, my friend. Dylan himself is in ye. I dinna' understand what ye are saying, but I sense there is wisdom in it only mortal folk may see." Then he withdrew, lifted his face to the moon and laughed long and loud, and there was a thing in the sound of his laughter that turned every Tylwyth head, and caught the pointed ears of every roan steed. There was hope in the bard's laughter. And through his laughter, he declared, "After eighteen and more years, in the last breath of hope, the Island has its Laird. And such a Laird!"

Then Seoridean bid Sweyn follow. He led him to the encampment where sumptuous foods were cooking in vast cauldrons of silver, and musicians were emerging from the tents to begin an outdoor dance beneath the moon.

"Is this a celebration?" asked Sweyn.

"It is a feast, which is held every day," Seoridean explained.

"There is no special occasion?" Sweyn asked, surprised.

"But of course there is. We are in life, and life is good."

The bard led Sweyn past the cauldrons, past the fires over which spitted venison sizzled, past the tables laden with glistening berries and shining apples and pears. He led Sweyn full across the Tylwyth encampment to a small but elegant tent on its outskirts. The tent was octagonal with a roof that was highest at the center, raised by a single long pole. But unlike the other tents which sported bright pennants and banners of faerie houses, this lone tent was unadorned.

A cold sorrow gripped Sweyn's heart suddenly, for somehow he knew what would happen next.

The bard said, "Laird, for your sake I have bid the Tylwyth open their gates once more, and they have consented. Here is the object of your quest." He pushed aside the tent's entrance, and therein, on a chair covered in soft scarlet, sat a raven-haired girl with sad blue eyes. She seemed spent in mind and body. But slowly the girl lifted her eyes to him. "Sweyn?" gasped Caitlin No-Kin, and for a moment her eyes glimmered bright. But her affect quickly changed to what it had been: empty, surrendered. "You should no' have come," she moaned. But that brief moment of joy told Sweyn she did not mean it, and all the mad chase had been worth it.

*********

A mare of night bore them beneath trunks of trees that rose like towers of Austrian castles, from which leviathan boughs webbed a canopy of endless emerald leaves and flawless summer blossoms. Petals of tree-borne flora fell around them like a fragrant silver snow dancing on draughts of twilit air. Cool shadows gathered heavy everywhere the eye looked, yet always shafts of hoary moonlight found its way through the leafy canopy and graced the forest floor with a soft phosphorescence that flickered and sluiced as through clear water. Round about great flowers like shining fountains spilled opened to drink the endless moonlight, and between them man-high mushrooms crowned with yard-broad caps rose in the shadow pools like tenebrous sentinels wearing great, wide helms. A cloud of fog blanketed the forest floor no higher than the knee, but so thick the loam and fallen leaves could scarce be seen beneath it.

Caitlin No-Kin wore a moon-pale gown of faerie weave, crafted of the fine silk of spider webs gathered in the dawn, when jewels of dew adorn the fragile threads. It hugged her body kindly, neither modest nor leaving nothing to the imagination. A great cloak of sable was wrapped over her slender shoulders to keep her against the chill of the forest shadows. She rode the cantering steed sidesaddle before the Laird, and his strong hand rested on her waist protectively, while his other held the shining black leather reigns of the nightmare. Her hood was drawn up over her head and from within its shadows the fading girl watched the dreaming forest pass in childlike wonder.

They rode to a spring that bubbled out of a cairn of shattered rock and danced and babbled down myriad, glistening faces of stone into a broad, shallow pool which reflected moonlight like a mirror, save where great lily pads drifted lazy and waxy green over the surface. There they dismounted and walked the bank of the pool. Silvery salmon and rainbow-tinted trout swam beneath the cool, clear waters. Caitlin and the Laird did not hold hands; he put no arm around her, but they stood close, as familiar friends, as almost-lovers.

For the longest time they were silent. It was enough to hear the chatter of the spring, the occasional splash of a trout, the fall of an acorn into the crystalline pool. The Laird removed the cloak the Tylwyth Teg had given him, woven of some cloth the color of elm in the gloaming. He spread it on the soft loam near the pool's edge and the fog fled away. The girl folded her legs beneath her and sat primly upon it. He sat upon it near her, but not quite touching. The air was chill but not bitter, as if pleasantly tinged with a hint of autumn.

At last she spoke, her voice like the sighing of wind in wintry willows. She asked him, directly, how he had found her, and why he had come. And he told her how his fey friends had aided him, and he had searched his way through beeches and oaks, past faerie folk seelie and not, and would not be turned away from her. To keep a promise. And for friendship's sake.

"Is that all?" she asked, looking down into the waters, a bit of rose appearing in her white cheeks. "For friendship's sake?"

"I came after you," Sweyn admitted, "because I could do no less. You've had a spell on me since I first heard you singing in the apple grove a lifetime ago."

She held quiet.

"I came because I love you," he confessed.

Time seemed to slow, then, and she turned to him, her pellucid eyes like bright aquamarines and stars. She whispered, as if confessing a secret. "I sang that night for ye."

"For me? You didn't even know me. No one on the Island knew I had even arrived."

"The Apple Man knew. And he told me. 'The Laird. The Laird has come at last,' he said. 'Only he does no' yet know he is the Laird.'"

He almost laughed. Almost. "I suppose I was the last to know."

"Well, the mortal folk of Man-by-the-Sea knew little more than ye, save that ye were the husband of my sister." But then she grew altogether white, like one who has seen horrors. Indeed, she had known horrors. She had seen her mother die, her sister abandon her, her father's hatred. And then learned she herself was a counterfeit. Her voice trembled as she spoke the next words. "Oh, Sweyn, ye should no' have come. I have no sister and I can only break yer heart. Do ye no' know who I am? What I am?"

"I know enough to know that I would have faced Maelgwn himself to find you."

She shook her head, her eyes shimmered red in the moonbeams, creases of bitterness etched her cheeks and brow. "Ye dinna' see me, Sweyn, but the reflection of yer love that was. For it is in my nature to reflect and to imitate. I was wrought to take the face of the true Caitlin."

So the girl knew. She knew the truth behind her making. And who knew for how long she had had to bear it, alone, unloved, shunned. It was an evil worse than anything unseelie, that, and it hurt him deeply to imagine what she had gone through. Tentatively, he placed his large and callused hand over her soft and slight one. It was a touch meant to share camaraderie and comfort. But it conveyed love.

A swift tear like a diamond fell down the curve of her cheek. "Ye should no' touch me, Sweyn. Fall back. Go back. Forget me. Soon it will be as if I never was."

He lifted his hand to her cheek and brushed the tear away. "Caitlin, it will never be like you never were. Never. You've burned a place in my heart, a scar I'll gladly bear forever. And if you should leave me and my heart should tear to pieces, I will never regret the moments we shared. But you can't leave." He shook his head, pleadingly. "You can't."

She leaned her head into his touch. She could do nothing else but, and her own hand rose to brush his. "There is nothing for it, Sweyn. This is the way of changelings." She turned, kissed once his palm, allowed him to run his fingers through her raven locks. "Dinna' give me yer heart, Sweyn, please. I ken it could no' bear another blow."

"Too late," said he.

And she could not deny it, either. Even fading, feelings were strong within her for the Laird of Manannan. "But I'm no' real, Sweyn. I am a dream, a woven fragment of faerie glamour. Ye love me because I reflect Eilwen, and nothing more."

He shook his head. "Every sister reflects her sister. But you are yourself, Caitlin. You are more than you know."

"I canna' be so."

He leaned forward, then, and pulled her gently toward him. She resisted, but only for a moment, and only because she did not wish to entangle him deeper in a tale that could only end in tragedy. But she could not resist more than a moment, the span it took a hummingbird's wings to flutter. And then she pressed forward too, and kissed the Laird softly in the dark. For Sweyn it was first time he had risked loving a lady in three years of sorrow. For Caitlin, it was the first time she had ever been so close to a man, and she believed that if there was a place where a bit of changelings go when they fade, a little place in the universe allotted to keep their memories, then this sparkling moment could carry her through the timeless span of that half-existence.

*********

There was tumult in the encampment when they returned. Another bard of the Tylwyth Teg had come through the door in the hollow hill, and he had brought horrible news with him. Donald had searched far and wide through the forest and had not been able to find the changeling girl. He was waxing senseless, the bard reported, and had begun cutting trees in the wildwood. And he had incensed the young men with him, inciting them to harm against every faerie thing. They were cutting willows and elders, tearing up gorse and heather, and driving iron spikes in faerie rings. Donald had even threatened to dam the brook of the Asrai with explosives if the changeling girl did not hand herself over to him. He and his impressionable youths had, for all intents and purposes, cut and burned a swath from the heart of the wildwood to the cove where Starry Sea lay at anchor.

Such were Donald's crimes that even the gentle Tylwyth Teg were incensed. Had Donald acted alone, they might have ridden out against him. But a band of men wielding iron could break faerie magic and fend them off.

A druid of the Tylwyth Teg exclaimed, "He will tear the very heart out of the Island!"

Seoridean explained the import of what Donald was doing to Sweyn. "Donald is wise in faerie lore, and he knows how to hurt us most. Faerie folk are bound to the trees, for the trees guard mystery and shield enchantment. When the wood is weakened, so are we. And if the wood is hurt enough, many faerie folk may fade into the Dreaming West.

"Iron is the bane of wild magic. With his spikes he kills the living power of the faerie rings, and it is through them enchantment flows and links all the worlds."

"But why?" asked Sweyn. "Why will he hurt the Asrai?"

It was the druid who answered. "Mere bitterness," he said. "Those fair, harmless creatures are most beloved among us, and neither seelie nor unseelie would do mischief to them. Donald means to hurt that which we hold dearest."

Then Seoridean said, "Ye are the Laird. This is a thing ye must stop."

The news-bearing bard said, "He commands ye to bring his own true Caitlin to him, to meet him where Starry Sea lies at anchor."

"Then let's do it," Sweyn told the assembled folk. "She is his daughter, after all. You have no right to keep her."

"But we dinna' keep her!" Seoridean and the others who stood nearby looked appalled. "We have never kept a harmless girl against her will. She has stated she will no' go back."

Sweyn suggested perhaps she might leave the Tylwyth realm just long enough to see her father.

"We have already asked," the druid moaned. "She will no' consent. She says it is none of her concern."

"She what?" Sweyn exclaimed. He could not believe it, and said he wanted to speak to her himself.

Seoridean said he would take the Laird to see the true Caitlin O'Shee. No-Kin said she wanted to meet her double and would also go along. Sweyn tried to turn her away, but she would not have it.

"I want to know how like a mirror I am," Caitlin stated firmly.

The true Caitlin was there, in the encampment, and the bard guided the couple to her. She dwelt in a great tent of iridescent faerie cloth lit by oil lanterns, in the company of other damsels. Clearly a mortal girl among the Tylwyth girls, she was lovely even compared to them. But time in the Tylwyth realm runs different from that of the green world, and she appeared no more than a girl of seventeen years to No-Kin's twenty-nine.

She was seated in a chair combing her long raven locks. The moment No-Kin set eyes upon her she touched her own night black hair, uncut and unthought of since her family left her alone, and remembered a time she cared how she looked.

Sweyn entered the tent and bowed as he saw Seoridean bow. He could see the mortal girl was treated highly, with the greatest honor, because she was the child of a McCavitt and an O'Shee. But No-Kin only stood and stared without courtesy.

When the true Caitlin became aware of them she set her comb down upon a vanity of white rowan wood surmounted with a silver mirror and regarded them, her gaze falling especially upon her changeling double. "So ye are the masterpiece I have heard tell of," she said in a cool tone to Caitlin.

"And ye are why I was made," No-Kin responded.

"A strange fate has befallen either of us," Caitlin O'Shee observed. "I was mortal but now will always dwell in Faerie. And ye are faerie-wrought, yet ye have no real life."

That was biting, thought Sweyn, and there was no need for it. He would have spoken up, but there was something peculiar about the O'Shee girl's voice that gave him pause. It was as if she were numb, feeling neither one thing nor the other, merely commenting upon what she observed.

No-Kin continued to stare as Sweyn addressed the O'Shee girl regarding why they had come. "Your father's heart is broken, Caitlin, for you. It's making him crazy. I think if you would just talk to him, just for a little while, it would help him."

She turned her gaze to the Laird. "He was only a father through adultery."

That took Sweyn aback, and it took him a moment to regain his thoughts. "He loves you all the same," he stated.

She laughed. It was mirthless. "I have more likeness with the Tylwyth Teg now than him. I will no' leave Faerie for him."

In that sudden way that had come to haunt him since the Gwragedd tinkered with his heart, Sweyn grew furious. "But he's your father!" he spat at her.

"Then I disown him," she said simply, shrugging, and returned to combing her midnight locks in the mirror, in preparation for a dance that was to occur later atop the hollow hill.

Sweyn took a step toward her, the anger making his hands tremble. "I'm not asking you to leave forever. Just show yourself to him. Let him speak to you. Let him know you're all right. He needs that. Can't you understand that?"

Still looking into the mirror, she shrugged again.

Sweyn punched the hard white surface of the vanity so forcefully it cracked, and the silver mirror fell from its frame, shuddered on its side, and rolled over the edge, crashing to the rugs overlaying the ground. There girl regarded her precious fallen mirror without expression, then turned to Sweyn and declared with no more affect, "I like it here. I would no' go to him were he to beckon from the very door of the hollow hill. Even if he should kill the Island, what does it matter? The Tylwyth Teg are no' like weak faeries. They and their land would survive and remain."

Sweyn's breath came deep and rapid. His jaw twitched. Seoridean saw it was time to intervene. He laid a hand on Sweyn's shoulder. "Best we go," he said, and half pulled, half ushered Sweyn from Caitlin O'Shee's presence.

But No-Kin stayed behind a moment after the men left. And when they were gone and well out of earshot, she leaned toward her original and whispered in her ear, "It is ye who have no soul." And then she turned and left, leaving only a wake of silence behind her. But Caitlin O'Shee only returned to combing her locks.

*********

Faerie time is not like that of the green world. Time in the wildwood spiraled, moving slowly round and round without origin, tied to but apart from the flow of the green world's time. But in the realm of the Tylwyth Teg the difference was even more pronounced. So tight was the spiral that time never seemed to move. The world was cast in eternal summer and eternal twilight. Words such as hours and days held no meaning, things simply were. Whether one should spend a minute or a week in the Tylwyth realm, it was impossible to know how much time had passed beyond in the green world. Impossible, that is, until someone came from beyond the hollow hill. Sweyn had learned from the second bard that many weeks had gone by in the green world.

In the green world, autumn was beginning to bite. The season of Samhain was close and soon the first snows would fly. But more desperate still, Arn'na'sagt'puch would demand the Laird be installed come the high day, for Halloween is the turning of the Celtic year, and that day would mark nineteen years with no Laird to lead the Island and keep the Pact.

So the Tylwyth Teg permitted a thing they had never allowed, not since mortal folk first shared the green world with faerie kin. They permitted Sweyn the use of the nightmare beyond their borders. She was a mighty warhorse, more magnificent than any green world beast, fast and sure by night or day. They saddled her and gave him a satchel of faerie bread and a skin of their sweet apple wine. Sweyn told them he could not eat it, but they assured him Tylwyth food would do him no harm—it would not bind him to reside in their world as would other faerie food.

He decided to trust the gentle Tylwyth, and ate some of it, and drank a little of the wine. The faerie wine was potent, but the food was rich and energizing. After eating it, he felt refreshed and ready to carry on.

Then the lords and ladies accompanied him to the door of the hollow hill.

Seoridean awaited him there. "Ride swift! The Elderman waits nearby, knowing the O'Shee Laird must exit by this way. Dinna' stop—he will be on the hooves of yer mare."

251

Then they gifted him with a shirt of metal rings, and a shield of rowan, and a sword that shone like silver. It was plain what they expected of him. They believed he must kill Donald McCavitt.

Sweyn remembered sharing ale before the woodsman's cabin, and later walking with him round about Dundubh lands, the leathery old man smiling and sharing his lore with him. He taught Sweyn how to run the estate, and how to stay safe from unseelie things. He did not believe Donald was a bad person at his core, but desperation and grief had driven him to doing terrible things. He recalled his own mad rage after losing Eilwen — and fists and blood and a stinking alley — and he pitied the woodsman. It could easily be him out there.

Could he kill Donald? The thought chilled him. He did not know. But he recalled Seoridean's words, spoken not so long ago in the time of the Tylwyth realm — Sometimes good men must do black things — and he shivered.

Time had spiraled. Donald had become Maelgwn, the enemy of enchantment. And Sweyn had become Dylan, the champion of faerie folk and the Company.

He mounted the steed and waited for them to open the door.

Seoridean sang him a song for luck, and the knights bowed to one knee in homage to the Laird, and the ladies curtsied. And then Caitlin, who had been standing in the company of the bard, leapt upon the great warhorse's back, and wrapped her slender arms firmly around his middle.

"What are you doing?" he snapped at her. "Get off!"

"I will no' let ye go face him alone," she said. "Ye'll need me to guide ye through the wildwood. And perhaps I can reason with him."

"Caitlin," he said, turning to face her, "he means to make the changeling exchange void and force the return of his daughter. To do that, he needs to kill you. Get off, stay here, where it's safe."

"He's my father, Sweyn, in a sense. I must try to help."

"You can't!" he stated firmly, and made as if to force her from the saddle.

But she wrapped her arms full around him and gripped her own wrists fiercely to lock them. "Ye'll have to knock me off this steed to make me stay, Sweyn."

"If need be," he warned her.

That irrational anger was taking him again. It was becoming more powerful, gripping him more easily and more fiercely.

She spoke gently, then, reaching for the goodness in his heart. "Please, Sweyn, please allow me this. My time is gone. I can feel it. I have only moments left. Let me spend them with ye, doing something that matters."

Like sun on ice, the anger melted away. "I'm sorry," he said. And he nodded, once, though it was not easy for him to agree to let her come in harm's way.

Then he nodded to Seoridean who opened the door through the hollow hill. He did not need to kick the nightmare's flanks. She knew what her riders needed. Quickness and silence, for dangers pressed beyond on every side.

The nightmare leapt through the door and into a clear and frosty night, out of the endless twilit summer of the fairest realm of Faerie and into the eve of Samhain on the marches of the green world. They galloped through the wood to the cove, and to Donald. So sure and silent was their steed's gate that if they held their breaths, they could hear behind them the relentless approach of something treeish.

# Chapter Seventeen

*Sometimes good men must do black things, I have been told.*
*It is a kind of doom of heroes.*

*Laird Sweyn O'Shee*
*The O'Shee Journals*

They reached the cove at the first hint of dawn, when the east was kissed by a pale, cool flame. The nightmare stepped lightly over hacked branches and murdered trees, Donald's work. How could he do this? Sweyn wondered. Even vengeance had its fair limit. But now Donald, who had once been the trusted gillie, keeper of the Guardwood, led men through the wood wielding axes, carrying horseshoes of cold iron. No faerie could stop him, for Donald had grown cunning in faerie lore, and he understood all too well that a band of men wielding iron could break faerie magic.

Sweyn stopped at the edge of the wood where trees still stood, and looked up and down the beach surrounding the cove. The waters were a mirror of the sky. All was quiet. No one was to be seen.

"Get off," he told Caitlin, who held tightly to him.

"No," she said.

He looked over his shoulder into the shimmering windows of her eyes. "Caitlin, please," he implored. There was fear in the Laird's voice, fear mingled with a firmness that could not be denied. Smoothly she slipped from the sable horse's flanks, alighting light as a windblown leaf upon the soft forest loam. "Stay in the shadows," he told her. And with the slightest move of his legs he urged the nightmare forward.

Soft as the kiss of a summer night's breeze, the nightmare stepped from the morning shadows of the wood, a pool of equine darkness contrasting starkly against the brightening grey sands. Sweyn paced the steed down to the water's edge and there reigned her back. She turned a full circle before she stopped, as if reluctant to give up the joy of motion.

In the open there was a very slight bit of breeze, just enough to ripple the steed's mane and cause Sweyn's faerie-wrought cloak to shimmer. Beneath the rippling cloak glimpses could be caught of the sword and shield the Tylwyth Teg had given him. He had tied them to the nightmare's saddle. He was a sailor, once a psychologist, and no warrior like Dylan. He would not have known what to do with the things if it came down to it.

He waited and hoped it would not come down to it.

In time the sun came above the horizon and brought with it more wind. Beyond the cove the sea could be seen rolling up into man high waves that tumbled into white horses of foam. The cove was sheltered, but even the waters within it began to ripple, and the wind turned Starry Sea's bow into it, facing the sea.

Starry Sea. It was good to see her again. Faithfully, she awaited him, lying at double anchor a hundred feet away. She was somewhat weatherworn, her brightwork sun-faded and her running rigging gone limp, evidence the vessel had not been tended to in weeks. Somehow, the sight of this impacted him more strongly than entering the autumn wildwood. He had passed the equivalent of a night in the Tylwyth realm and here many weeks had gone by. He shuddered, realizing Oak Peg's warning had been true. Time ran wild in the deep places of the Island. And now it was the very eve of Samhain, and tomorrow he must consent to guide the Island or the Pact be defaulted.

Yet time passed and still no sign of Donald.

At last, sick of the wait, he cried out, "Show yourself, McCavitt! Or will you hide like a coward in the shadows from your Laird?"

The forest fell silent with his cry. All the Island seemed to hold its breath. At long last, the Laird had declared himself.

And then the last thing Sweyn had thought to see appeared. The hatch to the companionway of Starry Sea slid open. One by one the three teak slats that enclosed the entrance were slid up out of their rails and set aside, leaned against winches used to raise and control the mainsail. A grey-headed form appeared, sporting a ponytail much like his own. The person climbed the stairs up out of below, revealing weathered skin, and even from this distance, the hard set of bitterly determined eyes. Eyes of cold iron. He stepped out into the cockpit and took several steps forward, laying a hand upon the traditionally carved wheel at the binnacle.

That dark place in Sweyn's heart began to smoke then, hot and jealous. He felt violated, raped. Starry Sea was more than his tall ship, she was his home. His best memories of Eilwen were bound up in her. And the faithful old cutter was . . . she was his friend. No one else had been there for him after Eilwen's death, but Starry Sea had. She had patiently carried him across the world all those years he needed to get himself straightened out. And now there was Donald upon her. Sweyn's fists trembled.

"Donald!" he called rigidly. The darkness within rose and showed in the depth of his voice. "For two hundred years your family has protected the Guardwood, and now you cut trees? Now you hunt faeries?"

Evenly, Donald answered him. Voices carried easily across the water. "Ye would do anything too, Sweyn deSauld, to make it right when someone hurts yer own flesh and blood."

*********

*It had been only Sweyn's word that young psycho, Marcus, had been there at the burning of Cerulean. But Marcus' girlfriend testified he was with her that night. When it went before the jury, Marcus' previous history could not be considered. He had committed his last crime as a minor and he was twenty-one now. As far as the law was concerned, what he had done as a minor did not exist now. So it turned out Sweyn's word was too flimsy an evidence to cause anything to happen. The burning of Cerulean was arson, certainly. The deaths of Eilwen and the passengers a tragedy, he was sympathetically told. But justice could do nothing, and Marcus was let go.*

*But upon leaving the hearing, Marcus stopped at the street corner and regarded Sweyn, smiling crookedly. Then he winked at Sweyn, and saluted him in that queer way of his, as he had done at the fire, as he used to do in Sweyn's office years before.*

*Something broke in Sweyn then. Civilization wouldn't take this savage off the streets. Justice wouldn't stop him. He would murder again, and again. But Sweyn determined Eilwen's memory deserved better than that.*

*********

Sweyn nodded in grim silence. He could not deny Donald's words. He understood what drove the old father.

"Where is my daughter?" Donald demanded.

"I went to the Tylwyth Teg. I spoke to her. She wouldn't come."

Donald bellowed. "Liar!"

Sweyn struggled to remain in control of himself, but that black anger was growing stronger within him, threatening to swallow him up. Get off my boat! Get off my boat! Get off my boat! he was thinking. He had the sickening feeling the old woodsman intended worse than just using the vessel as a hideout till he came.

Very careful to look Donald in the eyes and keep his voice honest to a fault, he said, "Donald, I spoke to her. I swear it on Manannan."

Donald studied Sweyn from the cockpit, and it did not take much time for him to decide the Laird spoke true. He was the Laird after all, and would answer more than anyone for a broken oath to the sea god who gave the Company the Island. But it did nothing to assuage his anger. If anything, Sweyn's newfound devotion to the Island only incensed him further. "What happened to ye back in that wood, Sweyn? There was a time I liked ye. A time I thought ye were a smart man, no' all taken with the glamour of this place. But now ye would be Laird!"

Sweyn chose his words carefully. "Donald, listen. I'm still the same man you knew. But I've realized some things. I've realized this isn't a bad place, and Eilwen never did hate it. But if you aren't ready for it, it goes hard on you."

But Donald shouted back, "There is no readying for the Island, ye fool! The creatures here, the faerie things, they suck in the weak minded and use them till they're spent!"

Still keeping his voice cool, Sweyn said, "Now you know that's not the way of it, Donald . . ."

But Donald cut him off, crying out again, "Where is my daughter!"

Sweyn paused long, his eyes like stone. There was nothing to say but the truth. "She was taken by mistake, Donald, and an oath to her mother who is dead now forbade the Tylwyth Teg returning her. But now she is grown and can make up her own mind. The Tylwyth have long since given her leave to do so. And I swear to you, Donald, she won't leave Faerie, by her own choice."

A great agonized cry tore free of the old woodsman. He lifted in his hand a massive pair of steel wire cutters, a tool every sailor kept aboard in case a mast broken in a storm should have to be cut swiftly free. He raised the tool, heavier than a crowbar, and smashed it down into the binnacle. The compass exploded, the oil within spraying over the deck, ruining countless electronics necessary for navigation.

Sweyn gritted his teeth. It seemed to him he felt that blow, as if his very bones had been broken.

"They've ensorcelled ye, ye bloody fool! Ye dinna' know faerie ways as I do. They are clever and plotting, every last one of them." He raised the hefty wire cutters again. "Bring me my daughter!" he bellowed.

"I cannot!" Sweyn called back desperately.

Donald swept down to the right, smashing the portside panel holding the autopilot and external radar screen. Then he threw the wire cutters into the rippling cove. They splashed and were gone.

Donald turned to face him again, his eyes mad with fury and desperation. "Then give me the changeling!" he hissed.

"I can't do that, Donald. I know what you mean to do to her."

"Listen to me, ye damnable fool! She's no' a living thing, no matter what ye think. She is just a puppet on faerie strings."

"Donald, you listen to me. She is different. More than glamour is within her. She has a soul!"

"My Caitlin has a soul!" Donald screamed. "A true mortal soul, and she is lost to me forever if I canna' retrieve her by the second night of this Samhain. Oh, I see ye dinna' know that part. Who neglected to tell ye, I wonder, your soulless love, or the faerie things who made her?"

"You are raving," said Sweyn, his voice barely constraining something dark and dangerous now. The woodsman and the Laird were two creatures other than men at this point. They were rabid beasts, mad eldermen themselves, and death was settling thick around them. Blood would flow this day, and trees would fall, and seeds would be left when enchanted things faded from the world in the wake of their mortal fury.

Donald told Sweyn, "This is the season of Samhain, and magic will flow fast and wild for the three nights and days of it. The changeling is weak now. She will no' be able to resist magic's tide. When the worlds touch, it will pull the enchantment from her and she will fade."

"No," denied Sweyn, shaking his head.

Donald's voice took on a pleading tone. "Yes, Sweyn. She has been fading many months now. She is too weak to bear this wild night. She has only hours left, and nothing can stop it. Give me the changeling so I can break the trade afore it's too late."

Sweyn didn't want to believe Donald, but there was truth in his voice, truth and desperation that could not be denied.

*Oh, Caitlin, why didn't you tell me?*

Yet it made no difference. Caitlin's life was her own and not his to bargain with. He shook his head, denying the woodsman.

A cold silence fell between them. The wind increased. The sun rose higher. Donald took a longsuffering breath and said at last, "I had hoped it would no' come to this. I liked ye, once. I've cut the propane line, Sweyn."

The blood drained from Sweyn's face. "You did what?"

"It would be a shame if there were to be a spark." The old woodsman leapt from the cockpit, splashed smoothly into the water, began swimming to a point on the shore opposite Sweyn.

Captains do not abandon their vessels. Their souls are bound up in sails and keels and gracefully arched hulls. And Sweyn was more than a captain, he was a true man of the sea. Without thought he leapt from the nightmare's back, pulling the ringed mail from his breast and dropping it to the sand. He raced into the water, swam wildly for Starry Sea while the old man swam away. He had forgotten the men who were with Donald, and all other dangers as he swam desperately to save his vessel.

He reached the stern, grasped the ladder, and pulled himself up. Exhausted and shivering, he panted a moment clinging halfway up out of the water. As soon as he had breath he pulled himself the rest of the way into the cockpit. He stumbled wildly past the wreckage of the shattered binnacle to the companionway. The whole boat down below smelled of propane. And every vent, every porthole was stuffed with rags to hold the volatile gas in.

An inhuman scream came from the shore behind him. He whirled around. An arrow was embedded in the shoulder of the nightmare. The steed was standing on its hind legs, kicking wildly, whinnying in pain and terror. A man who had previously been hidden in the shadows of the forest edge stood in the open fifty paces from it, holding a spent longbow of old Welsh design. Even as Sweyn watched, another stepped from the wood and loosed another iron-tipped arrow into the faerie beast. The cry that erupted from the steed was terrible, a shriek of agony that rattled the soul. The arrow embedded itself in the nightmare's side and the magnificent creature fell hard to the earth. It lay there a moment panting, rolling its head, then tried to rise again, but half way up its legs collapsed beneath it. The first archer knocked another arrow to his bowstring.

"No!" cried a fair voice, and a raven-haired damsel bound from the forest shadows, soaring down to the beautiful fallen beast to shield it with her own body.

Donald saw her and a terrible bellow of triumph emerged from his throat. The archer who held a knocked bow drew back the string.

"Nooo!" roared Sweyn like a great bear of the wood, his voice full of terror and fury as few mortals ever know.

The archer loosed his missile, the arrow flew, but it was not aimed for the fallen nightmare. It lodged deep in No-Kin's breast, burning iron-hot beside her faerie heart. A single gasp fluttered from her throat, like the last cry of a hunted wren, and a thin line of ruby blood trickled from the corner of her mouth. Then she fell, still and lifeless, upon the body of the shuddering steed.

"Goddamn you, Donald!" Sweyn roared. "Goddamn you!" Tears and fury blended to intoxication. Bellows of rage and bitterness mingled inseparably.

The woodsman roared savagely, lifted his arms to the bluing sky. "The trade is confounded!" he roared, and wild laughter followed.

The Laird stood tall then in the wrecked cockpit of his doomed vessel. "You are a dead man, Donald!" he swore. "Betrayer of oaths! I will hunt you to the Faerie gate. I will never stop!"

Donald turned his face to the Laird. "Today I regain my daughter and put an end to the madness haunting this Island all at once," he spoke, just barely audible. Then he shouted, "Sweyn, the Pact is broken!" He declared it forcefully, slowly, as if savoring the careful shaping of a long held curse.

The two archers knocked their bows, black pitch-covered arrows this time. They held matches to them and the tips caught bright orange flame. They turned toward Starry Sea and loosed. The first went wide of its mark and hissed out in the sea. The second, however, struck into the wooden wall of the cockpit just beside the companionway. But it was close enough.

Sweyn leapt.

The explosion was heard from the cove to Oak Peg's cottage. The thunderclap reverberated among autumnal hills to the very heart of Man-by-the-Sea. It shook the air from the forest's edge to the very gate of the Tylwyth Teg.

# Chapter Eighteen

*The misted Isle*
*of haunted dreams,*
*for mortal folk*
*and fair faeries,*
*binds their lives*
*in every seed,*
*twines their souls*
*in twisted trees.*

*Laird Sweyn O'Shee*
*The O'Shee Journals*

Men from Man-by-the-Sea came in fishing trawlers. Oak Peg came by some other way, and the men could not fathom how the old woman had traveled so fast, though whatever eldritch way she had walked, it had taken much out of her. She was wheezing and pale when they came and found her kneeling over an unspeakable sight.

Their Laird lay unconscious upon the sand beside the changeling girl, soaked in seawater and covered in blood, shattered and battered, burned and half dead. His arm was cast over the still, slender form of the girl and streaks where tears had burned through soot lined his cheeks. Grey sand clung heavily to his damp body. With the last of his strength he had crawled from the water's edge and fallen there beside her.

The girl herself lay upon her back, still and pale as death. An arrow protruded from her breast, and a circumference of burned black flesh surrounded the entry of the wound, the mark of the touch of cruel iron. She breathed only shallowly. Life, whatever life changelings have, was barely in her.

She lay in a depression in the beach sand left by a great beast. None of the men were trackers, but Oak Peg discerned it as the mark of where a faerie steed fell. Such a noble beast must have been sorely injured to stumble so grievously.

In the cove the wreck of Starry Sea still smoldered where she was sinking, still bound to her anchors.

The men were in shock. Such things did not happen on the Island. Folk of the Company did not turn upon one another like this. And faerie folk certainly did not do such things. The seelie would not, and the unseelie would have worked different harm if they could, harm cast by dark enchantments, spells to make one lost and afraid, or bring ill luck. The particularly wicked might try to draw a foolish wanderer into a lair. But they would not have shot arrows of iron nor decimated a mortal's elegant vessel.

Oak Peg stood slowly, requiring the help of the men. She was weary and wobbling and did not seem at all healthy. But she gathered what strength she had and stared angrily into the forest. She shook her head, blaming herself more than anything. "Donald!" She said his name like an oath. "I did not realize hatred could run so deep."

The men followed her instructions. They took homespun blankets from their boats and cut slender saplings and made a tent around the fallen pair. Oak Peg set out more blankets and laid Sweyn upon one, Caitlin upon another. She took her satchel from her shoulder. It was filled with poultices and potions and healing things. She applied salves of herbs, blended with enchantment, to his wounds and made him drink strange, thick liquors. For the girl she could do nothing but remove the arrow and bandage the wound. To Oak Peg she was only a changeling and had no soul. She was a fragile if expertly crafted bit of faerie magic, and now she had been burned sorely with iron. What was there to do? She would fade and there was no stopping it. But Sweyn could be helped. Sweyn had to be saved. So she devoted all her craft to him.

The day waxed high and hot and the men brought Oak Peg cool water from a brook to cool their fevered Laird. The day waned and they built a fire near the tent and she threw up the wall closest to it, so the warmth of the fire could fill the makeshift shelter.

At dusk a sable steed was seen limping at the edge of the forest by one of the men who mistook it for a kelpie and fled in fear. But Oak Peg recognized it right away for what it was. "It is a Tylwyth steed," she told them. "A nightmare." She whistled to it, a high, warbling call like a wren. It came out of the wood several minutes later, limping to her, its head held low. Blood like quicksilver oozed from its wounds. "This one is close to going to seed," she muttered angrily. "But it is no' too late." She applied another poultice upon the wound. It smelled foul, like the sulfurous waters that seep out at hot springs. She spoke kindly to the immortal beast and soothed it, and it understood the painful deed that must be done. She pulled the arrows from its body. It whinnied and galloped off into the forest, where it might heal in pure springs and moonbeams.

For the rest of the night the old witch devoted herself entirely to Sweyn. She stroked his wounds and hummed tunes and spoke poetry in faerie tongues. Half way between the setting of the moon and the rising of the sun the fever broke and many of his wounds were vanishing. Strength was returning to him and it became clear he would live.

But strength fled, it seemed, in equal measure from the oak witch.

Before the light of dawn broke, Sweyn opened his eyes and sat up, hale but hurting. The oak witch lay on blankets nearby and one of the men had covered her. She was shivering, pale and sweating. His shocked mind could not grasp the significance of it, but a young tree was in the midst of the tent, A shining, delicate silver birch, it pushed toward moonlight as if offering mystic prayers. From one branch, suspended just above a man's height, a single silvery seed dangled. It bore the shape of a star and the iridescent clarity of the finest moonstone.

He looked from the splendid tree to the old woman who seemed to lie at death's very edge. And suddenly the full force of the sight of her rolled over him like a wave. "Oak Peg!" he gasped. His throat was dry and the words emerged as a croak. He swallowed painfully.

She was awake. She said, "Is it the Laird of the Island of Manannan who speaks to me?"

"It is. Elidurydd."

She almost smiled, but perhaps she was too weak for it. "So ye know."

He took her withered hand. "I know, Elidurydd, that you and Oak Peg are the same remarkable person. I would not presume to know more than that about you. But what happened to you? You are hurt."

She waved away his question, saying only, "I have been better," and tried to laugh. But laughing hurt and she coughed painfully, tasting smoke in her lungs. Her skin smelled of burned flesh, as Sweyn's had not so long ago.

She ignored the pain. There were other things to be said, now, while there was still a moment of time. A chance perhaps to speak of her own heart's burdens after so many centuries of carrying the burdens of others. "When my beautiful Mwdr fell, my heart perished with him. Yet it was my fault he fell. It was my idea to save the valley of the Asrai. He was innocent and knew nothing of the ways of mortal men, who reek of death and iron. So I forsook Faerie in shame and cast the glamour of decrepitness about myself. I dinna' deserve the good things of Faerie."

But Sweyn shook his head. "Who could have foreseen it? It's not your fault, Lady."

She looked away, to the earth, unable to bear his forgiving words. Millennia of guilt could not quickly be shed.

He said it again. "It's not your fault."

And then he said it again, and held her hand, till, slowly, she looked up to him. Strong, wise, sad and gentle. The Laird of Manannan. His kindness drew words from her, heartrending things she had never spoken. "Mwdr fell for my cause, and I could no' let his loss be in vain. So, though I left Faerie, I looked after the Company and kept our dream alive. But I was no leader of Dylan's quality. So I saw to it there was always an O'Shee to guide the people, to see to the good of the Company and faerie kin."

He leaned over, stroked her silver hair. How sorely he had misjudged this selfless woman. "You did well," he said. "Across the weary centuries, you kept them going. You gave them something to believe in. You brought them to the Island, where it's safe."

She coughed, not hard, but long, and for a while it seemed she could not regain her breath. All Sweyn could do was sit by her side, and his powerlessness to aid her was very hard to face.

At last she found her breath. "Dylan is in ye, Sweyn. Ye've the heart of a warrior and the sensitivity of a poet. I chose well by ye. I believe ye will see well to the Island after me."

That sounded like a farewell and Sweyn was unable to bear it. "You're not going anywhere, you old bat," he said. "We need our witch."

She tried to laugh again but it hurt too much. It emerged instead as a brief cough, and a rasp. "I am sorry, lad, but I have no choice. What strength I had, I gave away. Such grievous wounds as yers could no' be rightly healed. I had to take many of them."

"Why?" he gasped.

"To save the Laird, of course. Without the Laird, there is no Island. And then all hope is truly lost."

His breath failed him, and in its place was left only an aching emptiness. The Laird leaned over then and hugged the old woman's fragile form, and kissed her brow. Redness brightened his eyes. "You cannot leave us, Elidurydd. We need you."

She placed a hand upon his shoulder. "Oh, Sweyn, old I may be, but no' perfect. I reckon ye can find as much wisdom without me, when ye have learned our ways in full."

"I could not. How can I guide this people right without you?"

"Ye already have, Sweyn."

"I've done nothing right since I came here."

"Ye've done great things. And greater to come, I am sure. For ye have the gift of Dylan within ye, the ability to find out souls. Look." She struggled to sit up and he helped her. Propped on an elbow, she pointed with her available hand.

He looked where she pointed, saw the graceful silver birch rising up and out the roof of the makeshift tent.

"That is where ye fell, Sweyn. Do ye no' remember? Ye fell with yer arm around the changeling girl."

*The trees*, he recalled. *When faerie kin fall, they say they go to seed.*

Caitlin.

"Oh, no," he moaned, his voice quavering. He rose and stepped to the tree. He lifted a trembling hand and set it upon the wood. It was cool and hard, like any other tree. The solid form of a faerie ghost. "Oh, no," he gasped again. He shook his head, unable to accept the evidence of his eyes.

"Ye were right, Sweyn. I was so wrong and ye were so right. That poor child. All the years we left her to suffer alone and she was never hollow as we thought."

"Caitlin is dead." He spoke the words, but he could not get his mind to wrap around them.

The silver star of the seed caught his eye then. It shone in the moon as if fire burned within.

"Dead, she is," Oak Peg said, but added quickly, "but no' lost to us, Sweyn."

"Dead is dead," he pronounced. He knew death. Knew it all too well.

She pushed herself up higher, spoke commandingly. "No, Sweyn! For mortals, yes, but no' for faerie folk. Remember Bran O'Shee, Sweyn. Remember the chests he and the Company fought to bring to this land."

He recalled the words of the journal of Lieutenant Raleigh, the first McCavitt and gillie. Within the chests were seeds of trees and herbs. Twenty kinds.

He recalled Seoridean's dreaming story: I will bind them, all that we can find, by oak and gorse and even wicked willow. And we will gather their seeds.

Oak Peg said, "The girl lives. She has a soul. She always had one within her."

It was a good thing to know, that she lived on. But it hurt. Without her he was alone, again. Gently, his hand slid up the graceful trunk to the low branch, touched the star-seed hanging there like a hard gem.

"Take it," she said.

He pulled it from the tree and held it cupped, a precious thing, in both hands. It was warm, warm as living flesh. "A faerie soul," he sighed in sad wonder.

"Oh, no, that's where we both failed to see. A perfect faerie-wrought body had she. So perfect that in its ending it went to seed and birthed this beith, the birch, and caught her soul, keeping it from the Otherworld. But the seed of bound faerie souls, they look and feel no different than ordinary seeds. What ye hold in yer hands, Sweyn, is a mortal soul."

Still cupping it tenderly, he sat on his knees at Oak Peg's side. "Elidurydd, I don't understand. You sound full of hope, but I don't see it, save that Caitlin continues in some way."

"It puzzles me, too. A mortal soul has never been bound in the way of faerie kin before. And a mortal soul in a fey body, that is a paradox indeed."

She began talking about other things. All the technique required to bind faerie souls into seeds, how she had devised the art, how she had come up with the idea of using it to bring this last remnant of Faerie to the Island. But Sweyn did not hear her. The last thing he recalled clearly was hearing that a mortal soul had been bound to a fey body. Somehow, he sensed, that was the key.

"Elidurydd," he said, interrupting her soliloquy, "why do mortals loath changelings as they do?"

"Oh, nasty things they are," the old woman said. "Cruel pranksters. They are poor imitators of the bairns they replace, to be sure. They cry all through the night for feeding, and by day they sneak off and get into mischief at every opportunity. They steal family treasures. They break things. They sneak and hide and hoard things for themselves. They think only of themselves. But they play their appearance well, using it to fool mortals into thinking they are their own flesh and blood. I suppose that's the worst thing about them: they can get ye to love them, but they give no reason for it. So people fear and despise them.

"Yet, that is what always perplexed me about Caitlin No-Kin," she continued. "She was none of those things. She was warm and tender from the very first. She, least of anyone, could have been described as vile."

Sweyn spoke aloud now, but to himself, piecing together the strange magical logic of it. "Dylan found the Hundred Horsemen souls. They stopped serving themselves and served others. Changelings have no souls. They are self-absorbed. Caitlin had a soul, she was full of love and kindness and generosity. But she was bound in a changeling's body."

He turned to face Oak Peg so swiftly it startled her. "I think I understand," he told her. "You said the Tylwyth Teg fashioned a changeling of unparalleled perfection when they made Caitlin."

"Aye."

"Is it possible the mortal Caitlin's soul went into the wrong body?"

She looked away, her eyes wandering far off into those esoteric mysteries he could scarce comprehend. In due course, she said, "I can't imagine how, but it would explain a lot."

"When faerie folk are bound into seeds, how are they brought back?"

"Ye plant the seed and wait."

"That's all?"

"Aye."

"How could I bring back a mortal seed of a soul?"

She thought a moment. "Mortals are no' bound to the wilds, as faerie kin. Ye could no' plant them, therefore. I dinna' see it."

"I think I do," he said, and he kissed her brow once more. Hope gave him strength and he made ready to go. He did not bother with the sword this time, nor the shield, nor the shirt of rings of faerie armor. What could he do with them? He was no warrior. Frankly, after what he had done, long before he ever came to the Island but after Eilwen's death, he never wanted to touch a weapon again. There was darkness in him he feared arousing. But he did wrap his cloak round himself, and wrapped the soul seed in soft cloth to carry with him. Outside the tent the men wanted to question him. "Donald did this!" they fumed, and they swore vengeance. He begged them keep peace, so much as they could.

The faerie steed was out there, too, at the edge of the wood just beyond the firelight of the men's camp. He whistled once for it and the nightmare trotted over, its limp nearly gone, due in part to its immortal blood, due in larger part to the oak witch's potent healing salves. Gently, he placed a hand on the mare's soft black-sky neck, whispered in her ear. "I know you are hurt, my friend. But I must ask a favor. Can you carry me like the wind to the gate of the hollow hill?"

She nudged him with her snout. Bareback, he mounted her, taking her long main in his hands for support. The nightmare turned and raced along the beach in the direction of the gate. She ran with such otherworldly grace she did not kick up a grain of sand. Then she turned into the forest and they vanished as swift and silent as an owl.

After the nightmare was gone and the men beyond the tent were muttering among themselves, wishing they could do something to help their Laird "who seemed a right decent man," a small shadow slipped unseen from the cover of the forest into the tent. The figure looked down at the worn old woman lying in a pile of blankets on the floor.

"Oh, Lady Elidurydd," he moaned. "Ye have overtaxed yerself."

"The price of saving a good man, Coppin," said she. "But perhaps I have at last made good for my follies in other ages."

Coppin's eyes were sad, dark pools. He sat beside where she lay and took her hand in his own. "Ye will never again see the horned one if ye die and go to the Otherworld."

"It is the risk of love between faeries and mortals. Strange. It seems so unimportant in the beginning. Life is so vast in Faerie, death so foreign. But it is a naïve dream. Death finds all mortals, in the end. It is time I accept it and move on."

"But yer word, Lady. Ye promised ye would go to him, into the very Dreaming West. The Gwragedd still sing of yer bold promise."

"Coppin, permit a weary old bat her rest. It was a vain promise, borne of youth and naïve dreams, and I have lived far too long for naiveté. I only wish a quiet grave at the roots of the Elderman, where I can at least be close to Mwdr's husk. Then perhaps I will come across Caitlin in the Otherworld, and somehow make up in the next life for how I failed her in this one."

That puzzled Coppin. He cocked his head to one side. "So, the changeling girl does have a soul?" he asked.

With a nod she indicated the slender sapling tree.

Coppin regarded it, drawing in breath. He knew instantly what it meant; he had seen faerie folk go to seed. Caitlin No-Kin was gone. And with that knowledge his insides seemed to hollow. He could not help recalling Caitlin as a wee child, giggling with Eilwen, picking flowers in a bright meadow, clover and dandelions woven in her hair. He had all but raised her. Slowly, as if pressed down beneath the cumulative weight of so much grief, he gathered his knees against his chest, slumped his head upon them. Doom and doom and doom had befallen this generation of O'Shees, and he had watched all the mortal folk he loved succumb.

Oak Peg set a hand upon his shoulder. "The seed of a soul was in the branches, Coppin. Sweyn always knew what we could no' see. The O'Shees have a talent for finding souls. But hear this now, the changeling girl has a mortal soul."

Coppin lifted his head. "Do ye tell me that?" he croaked.

"Aye, and he seems to feel there is yet some hope for her, though I dinna' see it. Yet in this last hour I have learned no' to trust in my own wisdom too much. I was vain."

"She is dead," said Coppin. "How can there be hope?"

"Go find yer Laird and ask him, ye troublesome sprite, for ye are surely bound to him now. He is an O'Shee, if ever there was one."

Coppin took a strengthening breath and sat up straight. Sorrow would have to wait, for there was more loss to come, and little enough time to profit by it. "No' till ye hear me out," said Coppin. "For if a changeling girl can have a mortal soul, I believe a mortal soul can find its way into the Dreaming West. For certainly this tells us that sometimes mortal and faerie paths can cross beyond this life. But the risk is great and time is short. Comes the Old Lady of the Wood!"

Oak Peg deflated. Her wan cheeks grew paler. "Ye know this?"

"All faerie folk know it. A fey god does no' walk in secret amidst creatures of enchantment."

She said, "But Sweyn has accepted the Lairdship. There is no reason for her to come."

"Indeed," Coppin agreed. "So her coming has brought about many questions. But I believe I ken the answer."

She nodded impatiently.

Coppin leaned forward and whispered, "I passed the brook of the bean-nighe, and she was wringing bloody clothes and wailing."

"Death coming!" Oak Peg hissed.

Coppin nodded. "Aye. And she sang a dirge. A dirge for a lost noble!"

Oak Peg began to tremble, and she became quiet a long time. Beyond the tent, the firelight of the men's camp flickered and cast eerie shadows on the tent wall. With great effort she sat up. "Sweyn is going to confront Donald. Perhaps Arn'na'sagt'puch foresees a bad end to it."

But Coppin shook his head. "She surely foresees a bad end, but however it goes, ye have done all ye can between them. They are mortal men and must settle this without faerie magic. But wherever Sweyn goes, the Elderman will follow. And nothing can stop him lest ye bind him"

She stared, horrified, at the little sprite. "Ye are asking me to take even Mwdr's husk from the green world, Coppin. To remove him as completely as if he were a changeling."

"Aye," he whispered.

"I canna' do this thing. I dinna' even know if it can be done. It is too terrible to contemplate."

"Aye," he agreed again. "No' since the breaking of the world has a faerie shrub left the green world. But what if it were to happen?"

"What are ye getting at, Coppin? Speak plain now!"

"Such magic would cost dear, Lady. Yer life, dear. But were ye able to push the Elderman into the Dreaming West at the very moment of yer own passing, ye might be able to slip into that place before the Otherworld can take ye."

In the amber glow of the firelight beyond the tent wall, she regarded the little sprite in amazement. He was clever, too clever for a Nis, and too bold, for what he was asking of her was to defy the very laws of the sublime. It shocked her to hear one of faerie kin suggest it. "Cheat death?" she whispered conspiratorially, as if agents of the gods might be listening in.

"No," he said, eyes full and earnest. "Cheat the geas."

And be with Mwdr. Again. Was it truly possible?

She listened more to Coppin's plan. She was old and wise in eldritch lore, but he was faerie kin and knew things even she had trouble grasping. They talked till the first light of dawn, conspiring and planning how it might be done. It was a desperate chance at best, with only one opportunity to succeed, for death was certain at its outcome. But death was coming regardless, and it was all the hope she had left for herself.

Then she said some words and scattered some herbs, and as luck would have it the men beyond the tent were soon asleep. They emerged from the tent, then, and she left berries of rowan from her satchel to keep them safe. Then, leaning on Coppin's shoulder, wrapped in her green cloak and many loose skirts the color of ferns and tree bark, they made off into the wood, following after Sweyn. For wherever Sweyn went, hunting after would be the Elderman. And though it was a mad plan that might anger the very gods, perhaps she might grasp one last chance to be with Mwdr.

*********

The sky grew dark across all the worlds existing over the Island of Mannanan. In Man-by-the-Sea a roiling mass, black and opaque as soot, sailed in from the northwest. The village folk came out from their shops and cottages, their bakeries and one-room school, to witness its approach. Never in all their dealings with mortal folk or faerie kin had they seen anything like it. The tempest approached upon shafts of lightning, and furies of wind bellowed before it. Even though it was yet miles off, darkening the distant horizon, massive waves of confused sea, grey and frothing, raced landward before it, and the fishermen of the village knew it would be a mighty blow. As fast as they could, every fishing boat out at sea made for the bay and the harbor, seeking the safety of the piers.

In the first layer of Faerie the tempest came in mostly out of the north. It came as a tangle of blue-black clouds, and pulses of light coursed up and down within the snarled vaporous cords. It was Faerie lightning. It flashed and rolled within the clouds, neither ascending to the heavens, nor down to pound the earth. The clouds were black and heavy with a deluge, but no rain fell upon the Island. Yet all around the sea roared with the downpour that fell like a curtain, obscuring the Island as if wiping it from the mind of the green world. And all across Faerie immortal creatures who knew no fear of death quivered. From the nimblest innocent Asrai to the darkest creeping willow, all were afraid. All took shelter beneath hollow hills, within darkening caves, under toadstool caps, in trunks of trees, in the depths of pools, and whatever other enchanted place might offer shelter.

Even in the Tylwyth Tegs' unbreachable inner Faerie realm the storm came. It rode upon winds that howled like bean sidhes and herded great tumbling clouds of phosphorescent sapphire before it. It drove faerie rain sideways so that it pounded tree trunks and walls of iridescent tents and soaked harts gathered for shelter beneath the great caps of man-high toadstools. Faerie lightning plowed through the clouds, burning the sky with bright cobalt flares, and thunder such as had not been heard in the Tylwyth realm in a thousand years shook the twilight. The Tylwyth Teg called their druids, for even they were afraid.

Arn'na'sagt'puch was coming.

\*\*\*\*\*\*\*\*\*

Donald stood before the doors of the hollow hill and eight men stood with him. They were chosen for the number, three times three, to give his venture luck, for Donald needed to force faerie luck to his own favor. His was the act of a desperate man, and he knew it. But if he did not reclaim his daughter now, he would never get her. He could not live with that.

Then the clouds rolled over the Island, and the glaring lightning flashed down from them, pounding all the land. But the rain and the wind swept around the Island, striking only the realm of the sea peoples. But those people could dive deep; boiling seas could not much hurt them.

But rain or no, Donald's men were afraid. Never in all their years, nor in the years of their stories, had they seen such a storm. There was magic in it, to be sure. Fierce, wild magic. And these men of the Island knew enough of magic to know something wondrous and terrible followed on its heels.

But Donald had no doubt what was coming. He had killed the laird in order to bring her. Driven beyond fear, he raised his face to the storm. He raised his arms defiantly and cried out against the thunder, "It is the end! It is the end of the Pact! The Old Lady comes to drive out the faerie folk at last!"

His men had not known what to expect when the Pact was broken. The faeries simply to go away, they supposed. Or maybe vanish into seeds. But this was more than they had bargained for. This seemed more like the end of the world.

Then Donald hefted his iron axe and tore into the door of the hollow hill. "Bring me my daughter, ye twilight demons!" he cried as he swung. "Children of the Mórríghán, the trade is confounded. I've killed yer sorry changeling, now bring me my right Caitlin!"

The power of the storm sapped much of the enchantment guarding the Tylwyth realm. Incredibly, Donald's cold iron began to bite the door, and Donald grew wide-eyed upon seeing small bits of rowan wood flying off with each blow of his axe. He growled in animal-like fury. Never had he imagined in his wildest dreams of storming the very Tylwyth realm and freeing his daughter, yet with the Pact in shambles even that seemed suddenly within his grasp. He redoubled his efforts, smashing blow after blow into the door, and on the other side the impacts sounded to the Tylwyth Teg like the knocking of Doom upon the threshold. The Tylwyth folk gathered round the door, in terror of their lives for the first time in countless long ages.

At last, one of them said, "If there is doom, then let us meet it with our honor," and he stepped toward the door.

Beyond, Donald saw the knob turn. Slowly, the door was pushed open. Donald swung the axe at the first thing that appeared, a shock of bright red hair, the fine boned face of a man carrying a wire harp.

"He strikes at a bard!" the mortal men gasped. Bards, like seanachie, were the harmless storytellers and songsingers, and the lorekeepers of mortal folk and faerie kin alike. They had license to travel where they willed, and all persons were obliged to show them hospitality. It was the bards who kept the memory of the old ways, without which the folk were not a people, and so no weapon was allowed to touch them. To strike a bard a blow was an offense beyond comprehension.

They knew then Donald was mad, and they had chosen poorly to follow him.

*********

Even injured, the nightmare seemed to glide over the earth, leaping smoothly over every wind-torn branch, dashing between every hedge, sailing over every boulder. Her long mane of soft sable floated behind her, black flame in a race of wind. The seaman who rode her clung with one arm to her neck, but for all the mare's maneuvering she rode smoothly and he needed only one firmly set arm to keep to her back. With the other he cradled the moonstone seed. His faerie-wrought cloak flew behind him, the cloth reflecting rainbow colors in the lightning. The Laird did not understanding the storm, not completely. But deep within he sensed its meaning. The Pact was ending. Something great and terrible was coming. And something wondrous was leaving. Faerie was preparing to depart the green world forever.

"Damn you, Donald," he cursed under his breath and tucked lower. The nightmare sensed his urgency and drove herself harder.

*********

Donald's blow missed the bard. From his side of the door within the hollow hill, where he stood in his own world, Seoridean struck a chord of his harp. All the mortals who heard it were struck with bitter sorrow of such depth they dropped their iron axes. The world was ending, and suddenly they were keenly aware they were at the center of it. All hope was lost for them and they fell to their knees in tears.

But Donald was not so affected. He carried rowan and holly berries in his pockets. The shaft of his axe was carved of hazel. From a leather belt around his waist dangled a horseshoe. But most of all, Donald was mad, and that made him beyond the banes of bardic magic. The emotions evoked by the bard's harping could not sting him the way they did rational men. Donald hefted his axe threateningly at the bard while he shouted at his men, "Quit yer bleating, ye gullible ewes! It's faerie glamour and nothing more." The strength of Donald's words got through to a couple of them, and they began to recover themselves. They stuffed their ears with clover from the turf of the hill and hung their iron horseshoes from their necks. Then they began to help their comrades out of the spell.

Donald turned the full force of his gaze on the slender bard. "My daughter!" he roared.

The bard set down his harp, gave up his magic song of sadness. "Ye will kill her if ye force her from Faerie against her will," he said, glowering at the gillie. "She does no' want to go back to the green world."

Donald swung the axe again, and this time the cold iron edge tore a great chunk from the door. With a tremendous twist, he tore the axe from the door and hefted again, as if to strike the bard. He bellowed, "The trade is broken! My daughter!"

Seoridean glowered at him another moment, then stepped out of sight. Donald did not know what was going on, and he lifted the axe over his head, ready to smash the door to splinters, if need be. He did not know what the consequences might be if he broke the door down, forever opening the way between Faerie and the green world, but he would cut it to pieces and risk all if the Tylwyth tried to deny him even now. He had killed the changeling and earned back his daughter, and by the Mórríghán they would deliver her to him. He struck blow after blow into the door, open and rattling wildly upon its hinges, tearing away great hunks of it, and each time the cold iron dug into it, thunder hurtled through the Tylwyth realm and the wildwood as if all Faerie screamed beneath the assault.

It was a sound which pleased Donald to no end.

But then Seoridean appeared at the open door, dragging a slender, raven haired girl by the wrist. Caitlin, so like the changeling girl, but his own right Caitlin. At last!

The bard held her at the very threshold of the Tylwyth realm. Anger blazed in his eyes. "She does no' wish to go," he pleaded with Donald. "Ye will kill her!"

But the sight of Caitlin had an immediate effect on Donald. The red fury in his face paled, his eyes shimmered. Here at last was his treasure, his own right daughter, and it was all that mattered. "Get back from her!" he hissed and reached for her wrist. He pulled her toward himself, across the boundary of the worlds, ignoring how she resisted coming to him.

When she was all the way through he dragged her several paces from the Faerie door. She looked back wistfully into the twilight land, darkening with storms and flashing with sapphire lightning. "My pretty things are back there," she said.

Donald told her, "Caitlin, I am here, yer right father."

But she only said, "All my pretty things . . ."

He smiled weakly and said, "I will get ye more pretty things, whatever yer heart desires." He set a leathery hand to her round chin and turned her to face him, so he might look into her eyes as he spoke, so he might begin to take her soul back from Faerie.

But the eyes that met his gaze were not what he had expected. There was no life in them. They were dead, flat, devoid of feeling. Only she glanced wistfully back toward Faerie, wanting her baubles.

Donald knew faerie lore and faerie things, and he knew mortal kin well too. And this thing here was not quite of either.

He sucked in his breath and let her go, as if he suddenly realized he had grasped a snake. He stumbled back from the girl . . . thing . . . whatever it was, wiping his hand on his trousers. It had felt mortal. The iron on his person had not repulsed her. But she had no more depth than a changeling.

Faerie trickery!

Donald turned on his heal, ran to the faerie door. He tore the horseshoe from his belt and hung it from the door, where the cold iron would bar it from shutting. "Ye bring me this soulless thing of glamour!" he screamed at Seoridean. "What is it? Some rotted toadstool ye've enchanted so ye might cheat me again?"

Seoridean glanced confused between Donald and the girl. He did not understand. His fey mind could not comprehend the emptiness Donald instinctively perceived. "This is truly yer Caitlin," he declared at last.

And Donald, who knew faerie folk well, saw truth in the bard. But he shook his head. "No, it canna' be!" He looked back at the dark haired, empty thing, and he knew that, in truth, the essence of Caitlin was not within it. If this was indeed her body, for some reason—he had never before heard of such a thing—the faerie folk had taken away her soul. There was no other explanation.

He had come so close, and yet they had tried to cheat him at the very last. It felt to him then as if he had been dealt many blows. All in an instant, something snapped within him.

"Ye stole her from me, and now ye would cheat me and keep her soul!" he growled and rushed the door, brandishing his axe. He would cut the bard down where he stood.

Seoridean cried out, "Stop!" But it was no good. At the threshold, Donald flung the axe at the bard's head. Seoridean leapt out of the way and the blade whirled past, falling, embedding itself into the earth on the Tylwyth side of the hollow hill. And for a brief moment it seemed time itself stopped, and all nature staggered beneath the impact of what Donald had done. For the Tylwyth realm was at the very heart of enchantment, and no iron had ever entered that place. And now a great hateful wedge of it was burrowed in the hill between the worlds. Lightning flared spasmodically in the Tylwyth realm, flash after ceaseless flash, and the faerie rain became the color of quicksilver, as if the very clouds themselves were bleeding. Seoridean's eyes filled full of pain, and he wrapped his arms around his chest as if struggling to breath. He fell to his knees in the grass, and in the camp beyond the Tylwyth folk screamed and fell as one.

Donald hardly understood the full depth of the damage he had caused, for his action had cut the flow of enchantment between the worlds. Nature itself was unraveling. But all he knew was he had forced open the faerie door, and with the Pact ending they were vulnerable. At last, a mortal could strike the arrogant abductors of mortal children. Indeed, he had made the immortals bleed. And it had only begun. He would press them till he got his daughter back whole, or until he had destroyed them all. "An axe!" he roared to the man closest to him.

But that man stood motionless, stunned by all he had witnessed. He had never imagined this expedition could come to such terrible things. Iron thrust into the Tylwyth world. Assaults upon bards. The Laird's own little ship burned, and the Laird himself murdered. It was too much. Too much. The man shook his head and backed away from Donald.

"Yer beyond quitting now, Coilte," Donald snarled at him. "Yer axe!"

Coilte shook his head, turned to leave. No more.

But then his eyes rolled up in his head, he shuddered, and fell face forward into the grass of the hillside. Donald's hunting knife was buried in his back.

Donald picked up the axe where it had fallen beside Coilte, hefted it. Good, cold steel. The weight of it was satisfying, it felt right in his hands. He stood, turned to face the open door, ordered his men to follow him through.

He would bring iron, and with it he would burn all Faerie. And he would begin with the bard who tried to deceive him. He stepped up to Seoridean, who lay gasping on the earth as if in a seizure, his own faerie life faltering with the shattered enchantment of his world. Donald lifted the axe.

*********

*Sweyn had tracked the young man months after the burning of Cerulean, and he had learned all his habits: where he sold drugs as a middleman for petty street hustlers, where he passed hours with prostitutes, where he drank, and the girlfriends he beat and sometimes spent the nights with. Through it all Sweyn bided his time, planning, waiting for the right moment. And then, one night when Starry Sea lay at anchor not far off in a hidden cove, Sweyn slipped into the city and found him. Sweyn came across him in a dark alley behind a closed bar, half sick from liquor and drugs. The alley was empty and lonely. It smelled of vomit and urine. The pallid red light of an exit sign bled over concrete and bricks. And beneath the light, passed out in a pile of boxes, there he was — Eilwen's murderer.*

*Sweyn nudged him with his boot. Sweyn wanted him to see who brought justice down upon him. Marcus opened his eyes and saw Sweyn's tall form, dark and fierce in the ruddy light. He seemed to recognize in that blurry instant that death had found him out. But he did not react as Sweyn might have expected. He stood instead, wobbly, and mocked Sweyn's suffering, remarked upon Eilwen's lack of grace when she fell into the sea and became tangled in the sail. He laughed over the screams of their passengers as the boat burned, and commented on what fine sport it was to see Cerulean sink. He was impressed, he remarked, by how long it took a boat that size to sink.*

*Sweyn had not been certain till that moment he could go through with it. He was a psychologist. He was a healer. But here was a monster who had no soul. Who did not even want one. He would hurt and kill again and again, so long as he was able. He had no soul. He never would.*

*There was anger, and there were tears, and there was also determination. But mostly there was the deep sickly madness of cold revenge as Sweyn beat him to death, there in the alley, in the bloody light. He pounded him with gloved fists over and over, till the blood flowed, till bones broke, till he was sure there was no life left in the body. And then, for hurt's sake, he kicked the fallen corpse one last time. And then he stumbled away into the night and wondered if now he was the monster. It was a fear that would haunt him ever after.*

*In the darkness he returned to Starry Sea and weighed anchor. Beneath the cold eyes of watchful stars, he raised white sails and turned his vessel into the black, wide sea.*

*He knew, that night, as he made way against opposing waves, that he would never be whole again. In that alley he had left his own soul behind.*

And now Sweyn raced through the forest, galloping toward a clash that could only end in dealing or taking death. He had hoped never to face such a choice again. But from a bard and the memory of a fallen hero he had learned that sometimes even good men must do terrible things. That was all that gave him strength to face this.

The nightmare cleared the forest, and there before him lay the hollow hill. Speeding like a storm wind, he made for it, and saw the door to the hill was wedged open with an iron horseshoe. At the very entrance of it were many men and a single, striking black haired figure, the sight of which made his heart leap to his throat.

Caitlin!

But the heft of the moonstone seed wrapped carefully in homespun, which he clung to in his right hand, reminded him that what he perceived was not his changeling girl.

Donald stood over a red haired man, Seoridean, holding up the blade of an axe. There was murder in the gillie's eyes, and he stood poised to bring the axe down. Sweyn spurred the nightmare forward and she flew like wind furies, like thunder, like the rush of doom. Her dark eyes glowed red with battle fury.

Sweyn drove the mare into the gillie. The impact threw Sweyn from her back. He landed on his back in the thick grass of the hill, somehow still clutching the moonstone safely in his hand. But the wind was knocked from him — he could not breathe. He could not move. His entire body flared in pain. Lying there, motionless, he saw beneath the dark clouds still darker shadows soaring through the air from the east, from the mainland. Some rode the wind on great wings like geese and swans and owls. Some soared on membranes like flying squirrels and bats. Others seemed to run through the atmosphere, as if sprinting across a field. And amidst them a greater thing strode, walking the winds as if they were a stony path, cloaked in billowing dark skins, wrapped in flying skirts of autumn leaves. Grey hair flowed behind the sky-borne figure, but her enchantment burned clear in his mind, the might of a goddess approaching.

Arn'na'sagt'puch was coming, and the old sprites who had lived on the Island before the Ogham wood were with her, ready to retake this most enchanted place.

And he could not move. He could no longer tell if it was from the impact, or from the awe of the sight of her.

Then, from the lightning-lit forest, came another sound, as terrible in its way as the approach of Arn'na'sagt'puch. It was the sound of twigs snapping in rhythm, earth being crushed, great branches scraping. From the forest the Elderman also came, drawn by the scent of the injured Laird.

*********

The sprites in the skies circled overhead, forbidden to touch the Island before the Old Lady of the Wood. But she held back from coming, and also kept her minions at bay. It appeared she was waiting, but for what Sweyn could not tell.

But there was no time to consider it. From beyond the faerie gate he could hear the pained cries of the Tylwyth Teg, and the Elderman was coming up the hill now. There was no time for anything but action.

Sweyn managed to push himself up to his elbow. In the fall his body had taken another great pounding, and even though he had recently been healed by enchantment he was not yet fully recovered. Now every movement caused pain to flare.

Lying on his side, struggling for breath against the pain, he could only watch in horror as the Elderman approached two of the men who had followed Donald, two who had kept watch at the base of the hill against things coming from the wood. He could not even call out a warning to them. Now these unfortunates were caught in the terrible gaze of the horned face emblazoned upon the Elderman's trunk. They never moved as the Elderman simply passed over them, crushing them into the turf beneath the weight of its roots. But their deaths were inconsequential to the Elderman. It only wanted Sweyn, last of the O'Shee line.

Sweyn struggled for his feet, gained his knees, but was bowled over by a wave of nausea. It felt as if his insides were churning on a storm sea. Searing pains and dull, battered muscles and grinding bones protested against any movement.

The Elderman was halfway up the hill now.

Sweyn tried for his feet a second time. He managed to keep his balance, but barely, by sheer desperate force of will. But he could not run, he knew. He could hardly stand.

The Elderman was only yards away then, and he felt his end drawing close, a cold and certain doom. But he did not fear it. Too many he loved waited for him on the other side. But then the nightmare came, racing down the face of the hollow hill. She rose on her two hind legs between the Elderman and Sweyn, kicking and whinnying fiercely. The great tree-thing swept at her with a massive old branch, but she was too swift for it. The nightmare leapt the branch and stood her ground between mad faerie ghost and mortal man.

One of Donald's men, seeing his own village kin laid low by the horror, ran toward it bearing his own axe of iron. He struck at an out flung root and cut it through. It was a useless, valiant gesture. The Elderman merely grasped the screaming man with a hundred other tendrils and pulled him to pieces in the morass of its roots.

The thing was not faerie kin or mortal anymore. It was only the mindless shadow of a murdered lover, and all it knew was it could never, absolutely never be with its love again. And the O'Shees were responsible for it. And driven by that singular knowledge, the shade was all fury and callous strength. It was foolish to stand before it, like defying a force of nature. Yet where the man failed, the nightmare succeeded. At least, she was able to buy Sweyn a few precious moments to make his escape.

But the Laird of Manannan had no intention of escape. He pulled his eyes from the fey battle and looked aside. The bard lay on the ground halfway between the gate, gasping weakly, his face full of pain as if he could not breathe and his heart had failed. Sweyn did not understand what was wrong with him. What could possibly hurt one of the Tylwyth Teg?

And near to the bard stood the raven-haired girl, the sight of whom stole his breath away. Seeing her body alive while knowing she was dead was hard for his mind to grasp, yet there she was, and it was wonderful. Yet she stood beside the suffering bard, impassive, doing nothing. And Sweyn knew for sure then this was not his own Caitlin. This thing was empty inside.

A few feet beside her lay her father. He lay face down in a spreading pool of blood. The hazel haft of his axe lay beneath his chest. Sweyn saw that when the nightmare had hit the old woodsman he had been thrown and landed on the blade of his own axe. It had burrowed into his chest. Now the old woodsman lay dead beside the empty shell of his daughter. All his life Donald had wanted only to regain his true daughter, yet her body was only an empty shell and the real essence of her had been near to him all along, in the body of the changeling, which he spurned. And so Donald, who had once been his friend, died without knowing her. It was a bitter end, the bitterest Sweyn could imagine.

But it was not until that moment that Sweyn saw the most horrible thing of all. For Caitlin O'Shee, who wanted nothing else than to return to her pretty baubles and fine things, her dainty foods and faerie music on the other side of the Tylwyth door, knelt and grasped Seoridean by the arms. She rose and dragged him to the body of her father, only a few feet away, and there she dropped him atop Donald as if they were both nothing more than detritus. It was not until that moment that Sweyn understood why it was the Man-by-the-Sea folk so despised changelings.

Then the empty girl went through the door and, with her mortal hands, pulled the iron axe head from the Tylwyth earth. She went back through the door and deposited it beside the two bodies. The effect of removing the iron from the twilight world was immediate. In that instant the force of the storm lessened, the lightnings coming less frequently, the wind no longer howling like a gale.

But the empty girl did not care for any of that. She was simply making it possible to go back to the Tylwyth world, now that those who brought her here were out of the way. She approached the door and knocked off the iron horseshoe. She meant to shut herself within the door and leave the Island forever to whatever fate befell it. It was not her concern.

Sweyn knew in that moment that he was right about what he must do. He started toward her, unwrapping the moonstone seed as he went.

*********

Coppin emerged from the forest at the foot of the hollow hill, pushing, pulling, and prodding Oak Peg along. She leaned heavily on a staff of wild apple they had taken from a tree along the way. Her breathing came in ragged gasps, for she had taken herself and Coppin through small enchanted gates to leap to this place in order to catch Sweyn on his steed. But it required mighty sorceries which she no longer had the stamina for. Her strength was all but gone.

But she saw the Elderman in front of her now, and released a sad silent groan. How bitter it was that this mindless shadow was all that was left of her noble love in this world. But there was no time for sorrow or tears. The Elderman was less than a stone's throw from the Laird, and only the valiant nightmare stood between it and the Island's last hope. And the nightmare could not long last.

Without pause, she started forward, leaning on the staff and faithful Coppin. A withered hand reached into her satchel, searching out the powder she had not used now in three hundred years. Her mind fixed on the riddle of seeds. That the end and the beginning of things are bound up, and the root and the seed spiral as one. She began to mutter in the oldest Celtic tongue, the language the faeries called their own, weaving a very ancient spell. Nearly forgotten, she had hoped never to need it again, since the ending of the Binding Years.

*********

The soulless girl stepped across the threshold of the Faerie gate, turned to pull shut the door.

Sweyn seized her arm, pulled her out of the twilight, into the wildwood. Her gem-blue eyes turned coldly upon him, another obstacle to vex her.

But he said, "You lost something," and pressed the moonstone seed into her palm. She clasped it in both hands, held it up to see it better, thinking it was a very pretty bauble. Perhaps it would set in a fine jewel. And then the seed melted into her flesh, and she screamed, and she fainted. But her body never touched the earth, for Sweyn caught her up in his arms.

There was the sickly thud of a hard impact on solid flesh and he turned, saw the nightmare knocked aside, staggering at the forest edge. Quicksilver blood bright as moonlight was on her face, and in a gash in her side. The Elderman came for Sweyn then, came for the Laird. He turned to flee through the gate, to carry the damsel in his arms to safety.

But with the iron out of the Tylwyth world, the bard had found his feet again, and he stood before the gate now, heaving, color beginning to return to him. "If ye step through," Seoridean yelled above the storm, "the Pact is forfeit. Arn'na'sagt'puch is here to account for the Laird, and if ye flee that way the Island is lost. In this time the Laird must stay with his land."

Sweyn regarded the bard and knew he was right.

He was the Laird.

He must stay, even if it cost all, as, in the end, it had cost Dylan all.

He would stay, but he was not ready to give up. He started up the hill, carrying Caitlin, trying to get away from the Elderman. But he was bone weary, and painfully injured. He tired quickly.

With regret, Seoridean closed the rowan door, leaving Sweyn to his own fate. But no unseelie thing must enter the innermost realm.

Sweyn made it to the top of the hill, just past the toadstool faerie ring where strange folk had danced the night before. His mouth was dry as old vellum, his throat burned, his legs trembled like aspens beneath him. He was spent, and he fell.

Relentless, the Elderman ascended the hill. Passed over the faerie ring, and there its shadow swept over the doomed Laird.

"Mwdr!," cried a tired, ragged voice, but the voice bore a shadow of beauty that was once unforgettable fair. "Stop, Mwdr! I am here."

Up came Oak Peg, hobbling on the apple staff, half carried by Coppin. A tired, ancient woman she was, ready to fall into dust but for one last task.

Then Coppin let her go, and if faerie folk could cry tears would have streamed down his leathery face. The old woman bent, though the effort of it cost her in pain — but what is a little more pain after so many centuries — and kissed Coppin's tan brow. And then she rose and walked to the wild, senseless tree-thing who had, nevertheless, halted at the sound of his lost love's voice.

She stepped toward the great elder tree, around to where she could see the horned face branded into the body of the trunk, and she touched it gingerly.

Through Sweyn's Sighted eyes he could swear he saw then, just for a fading instant, not the worn Oak Peg, but the fair lithe form of Elidurydd, once a Gwragedd, face to face with a stag of the wood.

Then she embraced the ancient tree, and said the last of the words of the spell, and sprinkled the powder over herself and the trunk. "May we meet on other shores," she pronounced at the last.

A great flame erupted from the hillside, there in the midst of the faerie ring. The smoke of it rose black into the sky and towered like a pillar to hold up the vault of the welkin.

Sweyn saw it. Sweyn would never forget it. Sometimes good men . . . and good women . . . must do black things. It is a kind of doom of heroes.

The flame burned into the night, and into the next day, and into the next evening. Faerie folk came from all over the Island to witness it, and they called the hill after that the Remembering Place, so that they would never forget what Oak Peg did for them. Folk from Man-by-the-Sea also came to witness the wonder, the end of the Elderman, the loss of their oak witch who for untold centuries had guided them and been their strength. They came bearing no iron, yet they came in safety. In this time, not even unseelie sprites would move themselves to harm them. Not with Arn'na'sagt'puch and her host watching from above. And not in the wake of the heroic deeds which had just passed.

On the second evening, the first day of the Celtic new year, the flame ended and all that was left of it was a pile of soft, cool grey ash. Sweyn and Caitlin, with her soul returned to her own right body, approached the ashes. It was dark, the sky still covered in the clouds summoned by Arn'na'sagt'puch, but the mortal folk carried torches, and in their swimming light they saw two hard things, one an acorn, one the small dark nut of an elder. The seeds rested atop the ash as if sleeping in a nest. Sweyn and Caitlin stooped, looked at them closely.

"Seeds of faerie souls," she whispered to him. "Seeds like those that brought the Ogham wood to the Island, and faerie folk within them. But Oak Peg was mortal kin. How can this be?"

Coppin stood beside them, his eyes deep and ancient and full of sadness. Low voiced, he said, "The geas of Elidurydd had been woven into the skein of her horned love since before they conceived the plan to save the Westernmost Tuath, since the Old World was green and she was a wee mortal girl who had never yet known Faerie. She gave her last to bind the husk he left in the green world, and so bound the last of her life to Mwdr. And in this great enchantment, she has kept the promise of which the Gwragedd sing to this day. She has gone to him—a mortal soul into the Dreaming West. I never thought to see such a wonder."

The bright Gwragedd were not there at the hollow hill. They could not wander far from their sparkling brooks and little streams. But Seoridean the bard had come from the Tylwyth realm. He plucked his harp, evoking scintillating bells and chimes of crystal, weaving them into melody as only faerie memory can hold. And he began the brook ladies' song, the Lay of Elidurydd's Promise:

*My love has passed the time we shared,*
*And I outlast the fading day,*
*And yet still falls the honey mead*
*In wooded halls of gathered dreams.*

*The honey mead of forgetfulness*
*To blur the need of a forlorn heart,*
*Locked in the pain of cold love's web,*
*Tied to the skein of memory.*

*I lost the sight of the great horned lord,*
*When he took flight of my stately stream,*
*He once was a strong great horned stag,*
*But fell to a throng with arrows of iron.*

*I lost the vale where my elder tree grew,*
*I lost the dale where I drank elder wine,*
*I lost the shard that cut the cluster of my fruit,*
*I lost my lord to iron.*

*Now in the West my lover calls,*
*He keeps the best of whitened shores,*
*And there my lord holds out strong arms,*
*Upon my word I will come.*
*Upon my word I will come.*

As he sang, Sweyn gently lifted the seeds from the pile of ash. With his other hand he made a small indent in the earth and buried the seeds within, then covered the tiny scar over.

"May they remember us in their dreams," he said. And he rose then, and before all faerie folk and mortal folk assembled there, he declared himself the rightful O'Shee and Laird of the Island of Manannan. And to the keeping of the enchanted forest and the aid of the folk of Man-by-the-Sea he would devote all his days, he and the Lady Caitlin.

In that moment, assured the Pact was kept, the Old Lady departed, as she wished. It had never been her desire to take the Island from the fey refugees from the rising moon.

In days to follow two great trees would spring from the earth of the hollow hill, a towering oak and a broad elder. They would grow high and wide in the midst of the faerie ring, and in their growth they would wrap round and round, entwining like cords of rope, clinging each to the other as a scion grafts to a trunk, till they could not be told apart. And when they had reached their full height faeries returned to that hill to hold their midnight revels, and keep their dances, and tell their tales and recite their poetry. In this way they kept the trees in good company.

But in this very moment, Sweyn and Caitlin were weary, and Sweyn had much healing of heart and body to do. He had come squarely faced with old nightmares, and pains of lost love. The nightmares he had vanquished. To the ghost of the love he had said goodbye. But he was drained to his core. He needed something, something he had not known in so many years he could not say what it was.

But Caitlin knew.

Caitlin took the tired Laird's hand in her own and led him down the hillside. He had hardly slept in many days and he was so spent and battle-worn he could not have kept his feet but for her help. At the hill's foundation, Tylwyth folk laid green cloaks on their shoulders to comfort them, and the faithful sable nightmare cantered to them from the line of shadowed wood. She extended one foreleg and knelt with the other, bowing her noble head low to accept them. Caitlin helped Sweyn over her back, then mounted the steed herself. The nightmare rose then and turned once, full round, then faced the towering trees. The cloud cover began to break with the departing of Arn'na'sagt'puch and her eldritch host. The first stars showed above, and shafts of autumn moonlight speared through like hope, lighting the enchanted forest in dreaming hues of silver and gold. The nightmare carried the couple into the hoary wood, back to Dundubh Cottage, back to home.

## ABOUT THE AUTHOR

Cliff Seruntine is best known for *The Lore of the Bard* (2003), a study of the ancient Celtic storytellers and enchanters. He has also been published multiple times in Llewellyn's *Witches' Calendar*—a global bestseller—and in the online magazine, Witchvox. Cliff is a psychologist in private practice and also a folklorist and practitioner of deep ecology.

Cliff, his wife, Daphne, and their two daughters reside on an old Scots farmstead in the misty wooded glens of the Nova Scotia highlands, ancestral Canadian home of the Gaels. There they keep alive old skills such as horse driving and cheesemaking and teach classes on how to live green while living well. In his free time, Cliff may often be found wandering the wild highland woods, for it is in the deep green places he finds his inspiration.

You can find out more about the author and his work, by visiting:
www.oghamwood.com

You are also welcome to write to him:
Cliff Seruntine
c/o BM Avalonia
Lonon
WC1N 3XX
United Kimgdom

Or through the publishers' website www.avaloniabooks.co.uk

Lightning Source UK Ltd.
Milton Keynes UK
UKOW052126061211

183261UK00003B/123/P